# China Running Dog

A novel

**Mark Kitto**

*For Tim & Karen*
*with best wishes*
*Mark*

A Plum Rain Press book

'In the West, a dog is a man's best friend; but in China, dogs are abject creatures. In Chinese, no idiomatic expression is more demeaning than the term "running dogs".'

CHEN YUAN-TSUNG,
Author, survivor and former
member of the Party elite

For Lucie

## Praise for *China Running Dog*

'Mark Kitto – linguist, actor, explorer, playwright, formerly the creator and editor of a magazine in China (sadly stolen from him by the authorities once he had achieved success) – has drawn on this rich experience to write a hilarious, racy but very dark cautionary tale based on his many years living in China. An upper-class Englishman comes to the swinging Shanghai of 2000 and is hired by a Chinese company to create an English-style club. Money washes in behind, as does the nightlife, as does the corruption – and then the Communist Party takes an interest... This is a magnificent story, and a must-read for anybody who wishes to see how a totalitarian society works.' – *Adam Williams, author of The Emperor's Bones*

### *China Cuckoo*

'A genuinely fascinating insight into China, written with humour and nerve.' – *Daily Telegraph*

'Evocative and lyrical.' – *Irish Times*

### *That's China*

'A racy, amusing read, and behind the humour, the hubris and the adventurism, the adrenaline of Kitto's tale is a cautionary message.' – *Chris Taylor, author of Harvest Moon.*

'A colourful account,' – *Irish Times*

### *Chinese Boxing*

'A good place to start if you want to understand China,' – *Cindy Yu, The Spectator*

'Beguiling, fascinating.' – *Libby Purves, BBC*

'Stimulating and original, I learned lots.' – *Jonathan Freedland, Guardian and Radio 4*

Published by Plum Rain Press
Address: 2 F., No. 8, Ln. 63, Siwei Rd., Housheng Vil., Pingtung City,
Pingtung County 900010, Taiwan (R.O.C.)
Tel: +88673451456
Publication Date: March 2025
First Edition

www.plumrainpress.com

Cover illustration by Nick Bonner
Cover design by Jonathan Stroulger

ISBN 978-626-99173-2-7 (paperback)

The moral right of the author has been asserted.

This is a work of fiction. Names, characters, places, and incidents are the products of the author's imagination or are used fictitiously. Any resemblance to actual persons, living or dead, events, or locales is entirely coincidental.

Set in 11 pt Linux Libertine

# Contents

# A Word from the Narrator

THIS story is about two mates, buddies. We met and didn't like each other. Then we did. Then we misunderstood each other and fought like Greek Gods. We were naked too, come to think of it.

And, like those ancient Greeks again, the story ends in tragedy. But we learnt something, and one of us came out all right. Pretty obvious who.

And the place. That's like a myth too: China, Shanghai. Everyone's talking about China. You did the other day, didn't you.

So, just after it happened, I wrote this story about him and me and Shanghai and those crazy days. Then last week a journalist came up to me and asked me about him, my mate, 'cos he got caught up in a Chinese political corruption scandal and it's been in the papers.

His name is getting bandied about again.

I told that reporter: 'No comment. Read this.'

John D. Trent,
Trent Limousines Ltd, Basildon, Essex
17 September, 2005

# 1

## WELCOME TO THE PARTY

THERE's a word for a prostitute that's poetic, polite and perfect for the whore I'm about to describe.

Courtesan.

You have to think before you say it out loud. How much stress do you place on the 'e'? Swallow it and it might sound like you know about high-class tarts or you're a toff; in which case, you probably *do* know about high-class tarts. Stretch it too long and you'll give the impression you're a bit rough yourself, that you prefer your hookers flat on their back and no time-wasting chitchat.

The courtesan I'm talking about (I put the same stress on each syllable) was the best. Famous down the ages, and still hard at it.

What made this one different from your common whore was how she created the illusion of True Love. Capital T. Capital L. She didn't sell sex. She sold infatuation, emotional and physical. She made you feel loved like you never thought possible.

She ruined lives, bled men dry, beggared them... all the old clichés. She took their money and murdered their morals. There's a new one.

'She' is not a woman by the way.

She's a city. Shanghai.

The metaphor isn't new. Shanghai was the 'Whore of the Orient'. She was also the 'Paris of the East', which is pretty much the same thing in my London-biased opinion.

The time I'm talking about, late nineties, the brothel was hanging out its lanterns. Madame shook the dust from her feather boa, wrapped up her chins and took her place at the front desk. She pulled out a black book, opened its musty pages and ran her finger down a list of American, British and other foreign-Johnny companies who'd made and lost fortunes in a long-gone China. They were the inner circle, her old regulars. She called them one by one.

'I'm back in business darlings,' she said, 'and you can be the first.'

Before they could whisper a sweet nothing she'd hung up and was calling complete strangers, people with no right to know, people like me, a young Brit down in Guangzhou near Hong Kong, teaching English.

We came running, China veterans and virgins, fell over ourselves to make love to the born-again beauty. After a fifty-year hiatus, the moneymaking and debauchery kicked off. Mammon met Sodom in Gomorrah; thousands of white slaves working long days and shagging through short nights.

I fell for the re-born Whore of the Orient all right, head over heels. And she abused me, and I stayed long beyond what was good for me and I begged for more until I wised up and headed home.

I like to think I survived intact, compared to some. I carry a few scars, reminders of how not to go about things, lessons learned.

One that cuts both ways is this story about a friend who reckoned he could win over the heartless bitch, turn the tables on her.

Did he succeed?

You wouldn't think so.

But at one point I did, and so did many other people.

His name was Felix Fawcett-Smith.

Everyone from that time in Shanghai has a 'When I met Felix' story. Most embellish it with a wisdom-after-the-event along the lines of, '... course I could see from the beginning he was heading for disaster. He had that look about him...' and so on.

Bollocks. We fell for him the same way we fell for Shanghai. I'll give you my meeting-Felix story straight.

It was early 2000, just after the turn of the millennium, a dot com launch party at the MushRoom, a Honkie-owned – sorry, Hong Kong – bar and club in a 1930s villa, the latest 'in' place. Meet-and-greet girls dolled up like intergalactic air hostesses in short white plastic skirts and thigh-high boots took our names at the reception desk and handed out glasses of champagne. A young American-born Chinese (ABC) made a speech in bad Mandarin. White guys and more ABCs in V-neck pullovers dished out name cards and job offers.

I was one of the rent-a-mob who, in return for free booze, impersonated the golden future of Shanghai to the foreign backers and investors who'd rolled into town to throw their cash down the toilet.

'Pleased to meet you... can't fail... see you later speculator...'

That was us, bursting with energy and success and bullshit, exactly what they wanted.

Important to note we were foreign. That made the venture capitalists and their mates feel like they were out in front but not alone. And when they got home they'd boast they'd discovered China for the first time since Marco Polo.

I remember the cunning greed in their eyes, like they knew something we didn't, although we were telling them what's what. They listened with patronizing politeness. They couldn't wait to get stuck in, show us how it should be done: the making of a China fortune.

We loved it, the showing off and getting drunk for free. Any joker wanted to make it appear like he was in with the movers and shakers and throw drinks down our necks, who were we to say no?

So, there I was, about to do my China Hand act when someone moved from the bar and I spotted him just along from me, the proverbial penguin at a beach party.

He was in a suit, charcoal with stripes, and a pink-checked shirt with extra-long sleeves and double cuffs, fastened by a pair of those silk knot things like tiny turbans. His tie was plain blue silk. It was late January and cold. So you could justify a suit for warmth, but not at a dot com party. I forget what I was wearing. Probably my leather jacket.

I put him in his early twenties, based on his apple-red chubby cheeks and smooth complexion. His wispy blond hair was already receding, gave him that older-than-his-years thing you see with young city boys, the fair-haired ones. He was fighting back the fringe he'd grown long across his forehead. It kept flopping into his eyes. He wasn't tall. I'd say about five-eight, and chubby round the middle as well as the cheeks.

He reminded me of the blokes I used to walk past at six o'clock in the evening on my way out of Burger King, stood on the pavements outside the pubs by Liverpool Street Station. Half were Essex boys like me, done good (not like me), the other half posh public school.

This one was scanning the crowd, turning his head like he was at Wimbledon. Every few seconds he pushed his hair back or took a swig from his beer. I overheard him ask for another, with a toneless Chinese that had the barman blank him and reply in English.

As if the get-up hadn't been a giveaway.

He was a new boy.

He was turning round with the fresh beer when our eyes met. I stepped forward.

'Nice suit,' I said.

'Thanks.'

He curled his mouth into an 'I'm about to ask the obvious question but pretend it just occurred to me' grin, but before he could get the words out, I said, 'Be careful you look after it. Weather here ruins clothes. Get mothballs and when the plum rains start; dry clean it, stuff the mothballs in the pockets, shrink-wrap it and hang it in a sealed cupboard in an air-conditioned room.' He looked at me. 'I mean it,' I said. 'It'll grow mildew in places your biology teacher never heard of.'

'Er, thanks,' he said. He brushed his hair back and came out with *the* question. 'So,' pause, 'How long have you been in Shanghai?'

Here we go.

'Coming up for a couple of years. And you just arrived 'cos I haven't seen you around and...' I held up a finger. '... and you're not on a business trip because there'd be a bloke from your office with you, or you wouldn't be here in the first place.'

He was impressed.

My mate Joe popped up beside him.

'I see you two have met,' he said in fluent New York.

'Ah,' Pin Stripes said like he was at the Members' Bar, 'there you are Joe. I was wondering what happened to you. You know, er?' He angled his beer bottle at me.

'Johnny. Johnny Trent.' I held out my hand.

His fingers were fleshy and firm, wet from the beer bottle, like washed grapes.

'Felix Fawcett-Smith. Nice to meet you.'

'Everyone knows Johnny.' Joe hit me on the arm and I tried not to wince. He was a punchy bugger and I'm not built to withstand physical abuse. 'How's it going buddy?'

Joe Karstein was All American, from buzz cut to pale brown chinos via grey round neck sweater over white T-shirt. He had that face you see in U.S. TV shows; behind the bar, at the wheel of a taxi; high forehead, clear brown eyes, strong nose, straight mouth and permanent five o'clock shadow. You don't come much more American than that. Only thing that made Joe stand out was that he was tall as a barstool. Well, it didn't exactly make him stand out.

'All right Joe,' I said.

The alphabet soup had gone for dinner. Our job was done, but the free bar hadn't closed. Payback time. Joe handed round a pack of cigarettes. I passed him a beer and we got chatting.

I asked Felix what he was doing in town. He told me he was an estate agent. I told him he better switch to 'real estate', the American way.

He'd been sent to China by a British company called Smyth and Corrigan. I knew the boss and a couple of Aussies there. I was running my own small recruitment business and they were clients. Felix was living in Kingsville Apartments on Anhui Road. He said it was okay for a start but he wanted to move into a concession house, a smaller version of the one we were standing in, on a leafy Shanghai side street, but the apartment had been arranged by the company. Joe said he'd see if he could find a place. Joe was always keen to help. He'd be in it for himself too. I was tempted to say something but if Felix was an estate agent he'd be more than capable of renting a flat.

Joe had news about his event company. He'd found a partner, which meant a local was going to put their name on it, for a fee, so the company became legal, then sit back and let Joe get on with it. As he explained to Felix, this meant he could issue the tax receipts that were the bane of our lives, us small-time Shanghai entrepreneurs. We bought them on the black market.

Felix was losing track.

'Enough already, Joe,' I said. Transatlantic was our Cockney. 'Can we get another beer?' I waggled my empty bottle at him.

I looked about for a waitress, having put my hand on Felix's arm to stop him shouting at the barman in his crap Chinese, and spotted Joe's girlfriend. So did Felix. He and Ivy hadn't met. That was obvious.

She was walking towards us, staring out of curiosity at Felix, not me and Joe. Felix brushed his fringe back. His tongue touched his top lip.

At the last moment, when she was right behind Joe, Ivy dropped her stare from Felix onto Joe's head and planted a kiss. I kept my eye on Felix. His cheeks flushed bright crimson. When I shouted at a waitress he jumped.

Ivy looked Felix straight in the eye when Joe introduced her. She'd enjoyed that.

I helped Felix out by passing him a beer while Ivy spoke to Joe. Felix regained his composure, although he couldn't stop glancing at Ivy. It was hard not to. Ivy was tall, slim and fine-boned and liked to show her figure off with close fitting sweaters and slender knee length skirts. She was a trader for a state-owned exporter of light fittings. I never worked out what she saw in Joe, who was a shambles, but he knew she was good for him. She grounded him in the British sense, not the American.

Felix cottoned on. I was amazed how fast he switched from embarrassed, caught-in-the-act peeping Tom to perfect gent. He was all wit and charm and had Joe and Ivy laughing at a story about him being a Shanghai newbie. Smart bloke in social situations. I know these public-school boys – with the double-barrelled name he had to be one – have a knack for small talk but this was the first time I'd witnessed it up close. I was impressed. I couldn't have done that: have a girl and her boyfriend laugh along with me when only a few minutes ago I'd been mentally undressing her and she'd rumbled me.

Then someone else arrived and Felix went into overdrive.

Anita Zhang wasn't a classy beauty like Ivy. She was shorter and rounder for starters. Where Ivy glided, Anita bounced. Standing still she was always on the move, hopping from foot to foot. Out on the town she wore low cut tops and push-up bras that turned her breasts into upturned bowls of bean curd in danger of wobbling over the sides. It was hard not to put a hand out.

But for all her energy, bouncing breasts and raw sex appeal, Anita didn't do what you thought she would – or many men hoped she would – as in: bounce into bed. She had a long fuse for a sex bomb. I'd known her since I arrived in town. Everyone did. Anita was at every party, half the dinners and almost every chamber of commerce event. She was a fixture. Not a few young men in our crowd found her attractive, not just sexually, including me. There was something innocent yet wise about her. She had our respect. She worked as the personal assistant for the manager of Paradise Island Golf Club. It was out in the suburbs but had an office downtown.

Anita said hi to me and Joe. I was on the point of introducing her to Felix when he did so for himself and let rip with a string of chat-up lines that would shrivel a lounge lizard. I pretended to pay attention to Ivy and Joe.

'You were at the Chivas party? I must've been blind drunk to miss you... Yes, Joe's been showing me Shanghai, but he's obviously hiding the best bits... [if he'd said "tits" that would have been

outrageous but a classic slip of the tongue. He was staring at them.]
Golf? Tennis is more my sport. Social tennis. You play?'

Anita didn't seem to mind the corny conversation or the ogling.
She gave Felix serious answers. When he started asking her about
her job I let my mind wander.

Did I say the party was a dot com? Chances are it was. It might
have been a PR or advertising agency, management consultant, cor-
porate trainer, travel agent or carpet shampoo. Those parties were
much of a muchness. Whoever threw it is probably long gone bust.

Once the bar had run out of free booze the five of us walked a
few blocks to a new place, Big Brother Little Sister, run by a couple of yuppie Shanghainese back from Paris where they'd studied
fashion. There's a gangster and moll connotation to the name. We
called it Big Brother for short, thinking 1984, not the TV show,
which didn't exist.

It was after midnight and packed. I got stuck on the outside of
our little group, ducking and diving like a bantam so people could
get past us to the bar at the end of the narrow room. Joe and Ivy
were all luvvie duvvie and Felix monopolized Anita. I noticed how
his hand moved when it brushed his hair, slow and deliberate, as
if to emphasize the attention he was giving her, and how his eyes
never left hers, in an unthreatening way. At least he'd stopped
staring at her breasts.

So when the next wave of people came in, I let it carry me to
the bar, where I found a space, got myself a rum and coke and lit
a cigarette.

My excuse for slipping off into my own little world: how the hell
had Joe landed the perfect local partner? I'd been thinking about it.

Her name was Madame Zhou. All of us foreign small-business
people had dealings with her because until recently she'd been
the deputy chief of a district trade bureau, the 'Gongshang'. But
now she'd retired and Joe had the idea to take her on as a business
partner. That was clever. She had the connections to make his life
easier. He'd kept quiet about it too. Why hadn't I thought of that?

I had a local partner for my recruitment company. She was my assistant. We had a proper agreement, between us at least. It wasn't legal but I knew what I was doing. For a pumped-up salary she put her name on my office lease and other official documents. She also arranged the tax receipts, for a fee. It worked for now. I'd be all right.

I was starting to feel better when Felix tapped me on the shoulder.

'Johnny,' he said, 'I'm going to cut the heel. It was good to meet you.' His tie knot was slack and top button undone.

I looked past him for Anita but she'd gone. I was sorry she hadn't said goodbye.

'Hang on,' I said. 'I'll come too.' I finished my drink. We pushed through the crush and out the door. It was cold, made me rub my hands. 'Anhui Road, right?' He nodded. 'On my way. Share a cab?'

'Only if you let me pay.'

'Done.'

There was a line of empty cars so we hopped in the front one and I gave the driver two addresses.

'You speak good Chinese,' Felix said.

'Jesus, don't you start!'

'I'm sorry?'

'That's the standard reply to the first word any foreigner speaks in crap Chinese. Drives me up the wall. Imagine a Chinese bloke getting into a taxi in London, giving an address and the cabbie turning round and saying: "Fuck me, you speak good English for a Chink".' I watched his face for a reaction.

'That's what it's like,' I explained.

Felix looked at me like I needed sympathy. 'But it was me that said it, not the driver.'

'Point. But you being a Brit and knowing London cabbies, you gave me a chance to get it off my chest. Sorry. And for the record: I speak terrible Chinese.'

Now he laughed.

He told me Smyth and Corrigan had arranged language lessons. He was keen to learn.

I said most people said that when they first arrived, and few learnt more than taxi and restaurant Chinese.

We got to Anhui Road and the car pulled up outside Kingsville Apartments.

'Here I am,' Felix said. 'And here's a fifty. That enough?'

'Too much.'

'Nothing smaller.'

'Beers on me next time? Give me your name card.'

'Good idea. Here.' He handed it over. 'Or dinner perhaps, with Joe and Ivy and [infinitesimal yet meaningful pause] Anita?'

'I'll have a word with Joe,' I said. 'We'll make a night of it.'

'You're on,' Felix said, like I was a jockey on his dad's horse.

# 2

## FELIX

FELIX was twenty-three, same as me, when he arrived in Shanghai on an 'expat package'. Health insurance, flights home, serviced apartment, everything was taken care of. There'd have been a matron-type figure in his office who made sure Smyth and Corrigan's boys were legal and, within reason, happy. She'd have arranged Felix's visa and work permit for example. Lucky sod.

Felix had worked for Smyth and Corrigan for a couple of years in Fulham. He got the job through a family friend and admitted he was the least qualified estate agent in London. He left school with one A-level and did a course in land management at a college in Oxford, not the university. Said it was dull as watching grass grow. He dropped out after the first year and went to London to do residential lettings.

His clients were his age, hunting for flats to share in those identical little houses you find over that side of London. Felix gave them the keys, showed them the short cut to the tube station, pointed out Mr. Patel on the corner and they were friends for five minutes. Then they got on with their lives.

If he'd stayed in London, Felix could have got on with his: marriage, kids, semi-detached house south of the river, then a proper one in the home counties, summers in Greece, skiing in the Alps...

If it hadn't been for China.

China.

That's another word. No question how to pronounce it. End of the last century everyone was saying it, especially businessmen. They shouted it across their boardrooms like a call to arms: 'China! To China!'

Smyth and Corrigan went in 1998, bang on time for the financial crisis, which turned out to be a blessing. They picked up business from competitors who'd committed too soon and were re-adjusting. By the time the early birds realized China didn't obey the rules, that it was going to keep booming right through a bust, Smyth and Corrigan was established and needed more staff.

Felix put his name down. He'd spent long enough in London to show he was reliable, short enough to be dispensable. His boss sent the application to the head office and the family friend who got him the job in the first place put him top of the list. He was summoned to meet the man in charge of the China operation, John French. He took Felix and the other acolytes for chopstick practice in Gerrard Street.

Felix recounted to a bar of mates in Shanghai how French had a gem of advice: 'If someone puts something *ghastly* (his italics) on your plate, you must at least put it in your mouth, but that doesn't mean you have to eat it. Watch this.' He (French in London) put his napkin to his mouth as if to wipe it and spat a piece of sweet and sour pork into it, scrunched the cloth up and said. 'Only problem is how to dispose of it. Haven't worked that out yet.'

I knew French, and that's the man he was.

'And never stick your chopsticks upright in your rice. It's like candles on the altar at a funeral. Very bad luck.'

He was close. It's incense sticks.

A few weeks later, Felix was throwing a farewell party in a trendy wine bar and the next morning he was on a China Eastern flight for Shanghai.

He landed at the city's Hongqiao Airport on Thursday the sixth of January, 2000, having flown six thousand miles from junior lettings agent, residential, to section manager, commercial.

The second time I met him was at a British Chamber of Commerce drinks event called 'The Sundowner', about a month after the MushRoom party and soon after we'd gone back to work following the Chinese New Year holiday. It was from this evening, and our conversation, that I admit my responsibility for what came later. It might be partial, but I accept it.

You see, I thought Felix was another young toffee-nosed Brit who'd come to Shanghai for a step-up the career ladder, money in the bank, a couple of pairs of silk pyjamas and home for Christmas.

I did not expect him to take what I said to heart, and so soon. And the last thing I expected was that we would become friends. You could have put us in the same room, side by side, and said: 'You must be mineral and you vegetable'.

It wasn't the leather jacket and pinstripe suit either. I was tall and skinny. Felix was short and chubby. I have mousey brown hair. His I've described. His face glowed with good health. Mine was pasty and pockmarked.

But the parameters – I think that's the word – had been narrowed. I was a young Brit in Shanghai. There weren't many of us and certainly none from Essex, let alone Basildon. Now I think about it, there wasn't a single young Brit in Shanghai who had anything like my background.

So me and Felix had a mutual understanding. We might be from different sides of the tracks but we were both British Rail.

When we met at the MushRoom he'd got my respect, just. And in spite of myself I was impressed how he handled Ivy and, not that I was entirely happy about it, chatted up Anita.

I always thought people like him were supercilious, even if they don't mean to be. It's their nature, like it's mine to be cocky. And here he was paying attention, giving me respect.

And so much of what I said was bullshit.

That's where my responsibility comes in.

The Sundowner was an 'opportunity to network'. It was a noun when I was at school.

Making an appearance was worthwhile. I got an idea who was hiring and firing, dished out my name card, did some out-of-hours marketing; 'networking' if you must.

Felix was on his own: same suit, different shirt and tie.

'My first time,' he said. 'By the way, just to let you know,' he flicked the hair out of his eyes, 'I now possess a dehumidifier.'

'Pleased to hear but you won't need it for a while. Plum rains start in June. How's the job?'

'Busy,' Felix said.

'Any recruitment companies on your books?'

He named a massive American one.

'Oh well, there goes the neighbourhood.' I sighed. 'It's been fun while it lasted. At least there's no shortage of business opportunities here.' I was exaggerating for sympathy.

'You're telling me,' Felix said. 'It's amazing. I had no idea. I'd heard stories about China and Shanghai but nothing can prepare you. Did you know office space in Shanghai doubles every six months?' I smiled. 'A new five-star hotel every month?' I held the smile. 'And they're planning the biggest airport in Asia, out in Pudong?' He said 'Poo Dung'. My cheeks were beginning to ache.

'And don't tell me,' my turn, 'there are more construction cranes in Shanghai than any city in the world.' It was the tired, overused and most likely apocryphal illustration of Shanghai's growth churned out in every article my mum sent me from the newspapers. I'd heard and read it a million times and wanted to shove a large construction crane up the arse of whoever was churning it out yet again.

'That's right!' Felix gripped my arm as I was about to light a cigarette. 'Amazing. I heard that too. What a city! And what a time to be here. I feel so lucky.' He took his hand away and I lit up. 'Sorry,' he said, embarrassed at the physical contact. I gave him a quizzical look through the first puff. He brushed his fringe and leaned in towards me. He had to look up. 'You don't realize what this city means to me. I mean, look at me!' He said it like a little boy showing off to his mum and dad. 'No qualifications, twenty-three years old, and I have four staff. I'm dealing with clients whose rental budgets could buy half a block in Knightsbridge. I'm talking to chief execs of massive corporations, telling them, *me* actually telling *them*, and I have only been here a month, what's what in Shanghai. Guess who I'm showing round on Tuesday?'

'No idea. Mohammed Al Fayed?'

'Very funny. The V.P. of HBO.'

'What, the TV people?'

'No, the advertising agency.'

'But forget about those corporations for a moment,' he said, 'it's you guys who impress me.' He stepped back and raised his glass.

'Me?'

'Yes. You and Joe, people like you.'

I cancelled the crane torture. 'Why us?'

'Because you're doing your thing. Making the most of Shanghai and the opportunity. Riding the wave.' He lowered his glass and tipped it towards me. 'Actually. You're making the wave.'

'Well...'

'No, really,' Felix said. His blue eyes blinked – first time I noticed their colour, how clear and clean they were – like they were taking a photo. 'I have utter respect. Envy. You guys have vision.'

'I wouldn't go that far.'

He stared at me and asked, 'How do you do it?'

'Do what?'

'Become an entrepreneur?'

I looked away, as you do when someone is overdoing the flattery. I made fleeting eye contact with a redhead I'd never seen before. She was talking to an accountant I recognized and looking bored. I sympathized.

I turned back to Felix and took a deep breath, as if to add weight to the pearl I was dragging from the depths of my hard-earned experience.

'Get involved,' I said.

That was it. Two simple words. I had no idea how much trouble they'd cause.

I was about to wave my glass for emphasis when I realized I'd look like the accountant.

'That's all it takes mate.' I was talking Estuary suddenly. 'The opportunities are there. All you have to do is look. Fact you don't need to. Step out your front door and you'll trip over them.'

Felix tilted his head like he wanted me to pour my wisdom into his ear. I half expected him to put a hand to the other one so it wouldn't fall out.

Thinking back to how I described his attitude and his innocent blue eyes, I should really work in a metaphor here about me muddying them, those crystal pools of innocence. Or poisoning them. But I'm not taking that much responsibility. Partial. Like I said.

'I'm serious,' I leaned backwards. 'Look around.'

He turned his head.

'Not here, Shanghai. Office space doubling every six months? Start an office furniture business. New hotel every month? Set up a booking agency, or an English language school for hotel staff. Hang on. Someone did that. It's hardly rocket science. Look what Joe Karstein did. Saw everyone coming to Shanghai, started an event business, does their launch parties.'

'But setting up a business requires cash, and local partners, and there are lots of rules, aren't there?'

'Felix, you'd be amazed how easy it is. I started with a few hundred US. That's all. Honest. Grew my business from the ground up. Kept costs low, staff down. And now,' I puffed up, 'I'm established. Got myself a couple of major clients on retainer. All set.'

'How long did it take?' he asked.

'Just under a year.' Minor exaggeration.

'Impressive.'

Truth is I was fighting like an alley cat. But I wasn't going to let that get in the way of a good story. I'd picked up the habit from the bankers.

I gave Felix a quick rundown of how I'd come to Shanghai in '98 from Guangzhou because everyone said Shanghai was where the action was, how I found a job in recruitment soon after I arrived, although I wasn't on an expat package like him, how my first task had been to find other 'local' expats like myself for Smyth and Corrigan, hence I knew his boss John French, and how I set up on my own after a year.

The 'major clients on retainer' was a stretch. They were single, not plural, and they'd screwed me on a long-term deal because I could never have got going without them. As for the war of attrition with the government bureaus and my dodgy legal arrangement with my assistant; I left that out. Nor did I admit that Felix had seriously put the wind up me with the news of that American company.

'Must have taken guts,' Felix said, 'to leave a job and go your own way, plough your own furrow.'

Plough my own furrow? I'd been out of England too long.

'I promise you,' I said, no exaggeration this time, pure lie, 'it's a piece of cake. My advice?' He gave me an upward nod. 'Get to know how Shanghai works. Learn everything you can from John French, for what it's worth. Hang out with me and Joe and our gang and when you trip over that opportunity: bend down and grab it.' I made the motion. 'And Felix,' I added, looking him hard in those blue eyes, 'the most important thing to realize is that it's barely started. We're here at the beginning. Shanghai isn't even a blank piece of paper. There's no paper, no precedents, no rules. We're never going to have an opportunity like this again. No one is. Never forget that.'

Felix glowed like I'd handed him the Holy Grail, which in a way I had, only it was common sense and blatantly obvious. I liked my bit about there being no paper. That came out of the blue.

'Thanks,' he said.

'Don't mention it.'

He raised his beer to cheers me and glanced past my head. He snapped out of his daydream with a smile of relief, like it had been a struggle to digest all that information.

'There's Anita!' he said, and swept his hair back.

I turned. She was bouncing towards us.

'Hullo Anita, selling golf lessons?' I asked.

'Are you ever going to sign up Johnny, like you keep promising? Hello Felix,' Anita gave him a nice smile. 'How are you?'

Felix reacted like she'd patted him on the bum: surprised, pleased and uncertain how to respond. 'Fine thanks,' he said, and his hand went to his hair.

Anita was in a business suit with a white blouse. Suitably formal, not too much cleavage, but she'd gone heavy on the make-up. Her full lips were bright red and she had on deep blue eyeliner that made her black eyes look mischievous.

A guy whose name I'd forgotten appeared at my elbow. He ran an English language school. I guess he wanted to talk to Anita because he kept glancing at her but he bottled it and asked me something banal.

Felix and Anita got stuck into a tete-a-tete, as if picking up from where they'd left off.

'So, you come to these events often?' That was Felix.

'Yes. My boss likes me to. We're members of the chamber. Useful for making *guanxi*.'

'Ah, the famous *guanxi*. Connections. I hear that you can't do anything in China without them.'

'Yes. Very important.'

'So, do we have *guanxi*?'

Anita was confused. She stopped bouncing. 'Sorry?'

'Now we've met twice, are we *guanxi'd*? I mean, can I ask you for favours? Can you ask me?'

Where was he going with this?

'Um, I'm not sure. Well, yes, I suppose.'

'If I asked you a favour, right here, would you do it for me?'

I missed whatever the bloke beside me was saying. He repeated himself and I raised a hand.

'Which is?'

'Would you have dinner with me?'

I laughed. Language teacher looked perplexed. I was watching Anita. She didn't know whether to smile or frown. She chose the frown. 'You're making fun of me,' she glanced sideways. I wiped the smile off my face.

'No, not at all. I'm serious,' Felix said.

Anita didn't do dates. She did parties. I couldn't imagine her having dinner with a single bloke, a gruesome twosome. It wasn't her style.

She looked at me to see if I was paying attention. In her blue-black eyes there was a demand for respect, plain as day. I tried to express something like an apology with an idiotic grin. Anita gave me the stern face a moment longer and turned back to Felix. 'OK. You have my card. Call me.'

I guess it was a face thing. To say no in front of me would have meant Anita losing it. Or was she into toy-boys? She was two years older than Felix. But they shared a certain physical resemblance in their... let's call it cuddliness. They'd make a good pair.

Felix was the cat that got the cream. He avoided my gaze. I think he was embarrassed.

Anita turned to the bloke who had been wittering in my ear and said, 'Kevin, I got your email.'

So that was his name.

# 3

## ANITA

SHANGHAI in the year 2000. It was nuts.

I was in the right place at the right time and I was becoming somebody. People gave me the nod when I walked into a bar. I was moving up. On a rare phone call home, for my Gran's birthday, I boasted about my turnover to my dad. He's a bus driver, doesn't do big numbers. I translated yuan into pounds. 'That's enough for a new kitchen,' he said.

I wasn't 'making waves' like Felix said I was. I wasn't even riding one. I was hitching a ride on whatever floats, which everyone else was sitting on. If you happened to be in Shanghai and into some sort of commercial activity, you couldn't go wrong.

Felix was having a ball too. He had the serviced apartment on Anhui Road, matron taking care of him in the office, and a job that entailed picking up a foreign executive from his hotel, driving him round a couple of office blocks, giving him lunchtime to decide which of them he wanted to put his China office into, and signing the contract in the afternoon.

He became a party animal. He was popular, particularly with the American guys and Shanghai girls who made up our crowd.

He dressed and behaved like a young English gent. They loved that and he played up to it.

And he and I were becoming mates. I was getting over my pre-conceptions and he was getting over his. It did take me a while, however, to get over his patronizing attempts to 'bring himself down' to my level. He laid it on with a spade; dropping out of college, how his heart was in London despite him being a country boy, how his favourite restaurant was a cafe in Westminter where cabbies ate their bangers and mash. He told me with fake guilty delight that he and his mates once went to a pub in the Isle of Dogs on a Friday lunchtime to watch the strippers.

Felix was fixated on the idea that I was a true Cockney, born by Bow Bells, left school at sixteen to work down the market. Hence the constant search for 'common' ground and wanting to roll around in it like a dog in shit because it thinks it'll make him smell nice.

I'd come across similar attitudes with other upper-class Brits I'd met along the road to Shanghai, but Felix's brand annoyed me because a) it was unnecessary b) it was incorrect and c) I just wanted to be friends.

He got over it.

Something that made me wonder for a bit if we really were becoming friends was how he didn't tell me when he moved on from Smyth and Corrigan. It was like he kept it secret.

We were at an Italian shipping agent's party in a house down a *longtang*, the alleys built by foreigners in the old days for office workers. Those houses are tall and narrow, the floors stacked on top of each other like a doll's house, connected by staircases more like ladders. I got Felix to step out onto a tiny balcony for a cigarette and a quiet chat. It was cold but we both had kept our coats on. *Longtang* houses don't have central heating.

I started by teasing him about Anita. I assumed they'd been out for dinner by then. I think he thought I fancied her myself, or had dated her before he came to town, and that made him uncomfortable. Then again, the discomfort might have been because of the new job, which he really was keeping secret from me.

All the time I was half thinking, half hoping, that he was acting awkward because Anita had said something about me. Because deep down I did fancy her. Not that anything had ever happened between us. Anita and I were 'just good friends'. I've already said she was a couple of years older than me and Felix. I like to think we had a connection, nothing more.

Well, that's what I would have said, back then.

I wanted to tell Felix why she was special.

'Your average Shanghai girl cares for one thing,' I told him, 'security: apartment, car, credit card. Material shit, Felix, that's what they like. Love doesn't count. Shanghai girls come in two sizes: haves and have-nots. Anita isn't one of those. I've never seen her play along or around with the rich Chinese, let alone the foreign execs (security *and* a foreign passport, now you're talking)' Felix looked up at that, suppressed a smile, 'and also because I once witnessed her do something bloody surprising.'

'Which was?'

'It was spring last year. Out at Paradise Island, her golf club. Free food and drink and a day out in the country. Bunch of us turned up with sore heads on a Sunday morning at the Portman for the bus...'

... We'd filled it. So that made us about thirty, all foreign. Charlie Thurrold was there, who you'll meet soon, and Joe Karstein. Anita and Ivy were good friends so it all connected. John French sent an Aussie called Dave to do some 'networking'. Bill Connor, editor of a new expat mag called *Shanghai Scene*, was there plus Fred, a Frenchman forever planning a nightclub and China Tim, American Jack of all trades, a couple of British business consultants... I knew most of the guys by name – there were no women – and everyone by face.

The bus took us out through the city's dusty suburbs past Hongqiao Airport and into the industrial plain where every square inch of land has a factory on it, or a cabbage patch.

It was a clear day. The air was warming above the Yangtze Estuary, sucking up a sweet sea breeze across the coastal mudflats like a drink up a straw. High above the city it blew away the thick winter fug that had sat on us for the past couple of months while down below, nearer ground level, the new-built high-rises split and funnelled the wind, squeezed it so it had to accelerate until it crashed back into itself at the junctions. It twisted into crazy little whirlwinds that tore at awnings and the corrugated metal screens around the building sites and made swirling dragons out of the dirt and dust and litter. You had to watch out or you'd catch something in the eye.

After an hour's drive along a potholed highway past factories and cabbages, we arrived at Paradise Island. It wasn't an island. It was a blob on the end of a causeway with a gate on it, stuck out in a lake. And it wasn't paradise.

Anita hustled us off the bus, handed out facemasks and divided us up among a fleet of golf buggies. The tour began immediately, through a World War One battlefield of mud, craters and tree trunks propped up by tripods of bamboo and wire. The wind was still strong but the gusts were less sudden than downtown. I watched and smiled as the buggy in front got sideswiped by a cloud of sand from a bunker. The shouts of discomfort and outrage carried back to us. We realized why we had the masks and put them on. The uniformed drivers grinned with their eyes – they'd been wearing masks from the start – and tilted their heads.

The tour ended at the driving range. That was grassed at least, but brown as toast because the sprinkler system hadn't been connected. A few of us had a go at whacking a ball. I was tempted, but golf is against my religion. Concrete shells of a dozen or so villas stood to one side in an ugly grey clump.

Fat lunches with unlimited booze are not against my religion. That was next, in the clubhouse, which was finished. First we had to sit through a presentation by Anita's boss, Mr. Wang.

Anita made sure her mates like me and Joe got ourselves a drink from the bar. When I say got ourselves I mean precisely that. Joe had to step in and give a lesson in Bloody Marys. We made them strong.

Mr. Wang spoke enough English to deliver most of his presentation in English and Mandarin Chinese. He had to do the Mandarin for a group of Overseas Chinese who'd joined us after their own tour. He asked for Anita's help once or twice when he got stuck.

Wang listed the stats; total investment (US dollars and yuan), number of government bureaus who'd approved the project, government bureaus that had invested and how much, total length of driveways (took me a moment to remember he was talking golf drives not car ones), square metres of the villas, price on five-year mortgage, price to us if we put our names down. We pretended to be all ears. He got a laugh when he made a joke about how fast he'd driven his BMW to the club from downtown Shanghai to prove the claim that it was 'minutes from the centre of the city'.

Lunch was in a room with panoramic views across the Somme. The food was southeast Asian curries and noodles, seafood rice, that sort of thing. The alcohol, as promised, was free flow. The Chinese red wine wasn't bad either, once you'd had a few glasses. I'd pay for it later.

The Overseas Chinese kept to themselves. On the next table to ours was a Singaporean, judging from his high-pitched accent that made it seem like everything he said was a complaint. He was the boss of a factory in a high-tech industrial park down the road. He came over and handed out his card.

When he sat back down at his table he switched to English to show off. He spoke up to make sure we could hear. He boasted how he'd been the first to sign up at the club, the local government helped him get a special membership rate thanks to his company's investment in the area, his name was down for a villa, and so on. One of our table made a snarky comment, which he didn't register, and we turned to our own gossip. Anita was busy behind the scenes.

Towards the end of the meal the Singaporean guy, who we'd christened Big Dick, was red in the face from the booze and even louder. He started laying into the wait staff. They hadn't been exactly slick. I guess they'd been drafted in from a hotel training school.

Big Dick went off about how he was a key supporter of the club, he'd be on the committee or whatever and see to it that the staff sharpened up. Then he came out with the comment, a classic considering he was ethnic Chinese, 'This country and people are so backward. Really third world. I mean honestly. At my club in Singapore...' And that's when he hit the waitress in the face.

Either he wanted to emphasize his point or he was directing his listeners towards Singapore. He punched his hand up and outwards and copped the girl on the cheek. She was leaning in to pour coffee. No chance to dodge the blow. More like she came to meet it. All eyes from our table were looking that way thanks to the idiotic comment. The coffee pot fell from the waitress's hand, tipped in mid-air and splashed onto Big Dick's leg. He screamed and leapt to his feet, almost falling backwards. The way the girl hunched up it seemed like she was cowering and the guy's hand was raised like he was going to hit her again, deliberately this time, although it's likely he was trying to keep his balance.

Aussie Dave was there in a flash. He grabbed Big Dick's arm and pulled him away with an 'Easy mate'. The Singaporean let Dave tug him to and fro like he was a doll, went puce in the face and pointed at his trousers.

Mr. Wang was there in another flash. He apologized to the Singaporean's table and bawled out the poor girl. She had her hand to her cheek and tears in her eyes. From his voice and the direction of Wang's finger, she was about to be fired on the spot.

Anita stepped up.

She looked five years older and ten years more determined. No trace of the party girl. She brushed past Mr. Wang, put her arm around the girl, whispered into her ear, and led her away. She gave the steaming lobster of a Singaporean a look that said, plain to see, 'Another word and I'll cut your dick off,' and to Mr. Wang an eyelash flutter and a smile, 'If you do anything to her, you'll pay too.'

Mr. Wang stared after Anita. The Singaporean didn't know where to look.

We wanted to cheer but that would have meant major loss of face for the Singaporean and Mr. Wang and repercussions for Anita.

As I said to Felix out on the balcony, 'You're thinking: so what? What's so special about Anita doing a thing like that, the natural thing? Anyone with a speck of decency would have done it. It's only natural.

'But for Anita to do that, outside of her personal interest, was not decent or considerate, let alone natural.

'It was stupid. More to the point: a Shanghainese girl who works for a well-connected boss who helped get her parents a new apartment when the family home in downtown Shanghai was demolished, as I happen to know is the case, does not perform embarrassing acts of disloyalty in front of a crowd of people who are going to make her boss a wealthy man. That took guts and a big heart. And she got away with it.'

So Mr. Wang wasn't such a bad bloke either.

That was the side to Anita I adored and Felix wouldn't have known, not because he couldn't see it but because he wouldn't understand how special it was.

A few weeks after that party, when the weather was warming up for spring, the whole lot of us got together to help Joe Karstein. The city's Tourism Bureau had organised a carnival street parade as pre-publicity for a festival coming up in the summer. They asked Joe to bring along a few friends.

He knew the woman who called him well enough. 'In other words, you want foreign monkeys to fill the camera shots and make the event look international,' he claimed he said. She gave Joe permission to bring Chinese girlfriends. She said it would be 'like Rio... in Brazil'.

Joe told us to meet at his apartment and we'd walk over from there. He had a penthouse in the heart of the old 'Chinese' city of Shanghai, a few blocks south of Huaihai Road, on the top floor of a disused factory.

I have no idea how he found the place. Joe had a knack for that sort of thing, bargain deals for cool places to live or work. I doubt he had a proper contract for it. And he definitely didn't have permission to build the glass extension across the roof. But who didn't love slipping along those smelly side streets, dodging slimy puddles, oil thick gutters and rubbish carts, the stretched-out flabby legs of old men sprawled on bamboo chairs, shirts rolled up over their white lardy stomachs, lobbing green mortar bombs of phlegm from their gap-toothed faces, the cackling women in flowery pyjamas and hair-curlers holding Pekingese dogs to their bra-less boobs? Those streets were raw Shanghai, real Shanghai. You stepped through an entranceway into a service lift and the attendant on her high wooden stool lowered her newspaper and without looking up (she could smell a foreigner) pressed the fat knob for the top floor, number four, and up we went to Joe's vast den, sleek and modern, leather and glass.

That was pretty cool.

On the night of the tourism gig there was a steady drizzle.

We huddled under umbrellas as we walked to the venue. I held one for Anita. The thought flashed through my mind that I might have to pretend she was my girlfriend for the benefit of the Tourism Bureau. That was a nice one. Anita studied the pavement as if her life depended on it. The streets were poorly lit, the pavement was uneven and some of the slabs were loose. If you stood on those ones they'd tilt like a swimming float and squirt shitty water right up your leg.

When we stepped into the road to get round a pile of rubbish Anita stumbled and grabbed my arm. She didn't let go for a long stretch, leaned on me as we walked along the centre of the wet black tarmac. There was no traffic because the streets had been blocked off.

We were halfway there and had barely said a word to each other. I broke the silence.

'So. How's it going with Felix?'

Anita turned to me with a sudden movement, looked me in the eye.

'Why didn't you come out last night? We were at Manhattan.' It was a new bar that had eclipsed Brother and Sister. 'Felix showed me a cocktail. It's called a Moscow Mole. Do you know it? I got a bit drunk. There were a lot of people. I thought you might be there Johnny.' She pulled on my arm. She hadn't let go. 'Joe and Ivy were.'

'Yes. I know. He called me. Sorry. I was going to come but I fell asleep.'

I'd leaned against her when she gave me that tug, well, more like a lingering bounce than a lean. Her perfume wafted up my nose. It was flowery, not sweet. Young and innocent. Kind of thing a teenager would wear. I have no idea what it's called but I'd recognise it again. In the wet air it hung under our umbrella. I took a couple of long sniffs.

Anita was talking about waiting to see if I'd turn up at Manhattan, leaving with Felix. By the time I picked up the thread I heard her say what a nice apartment he had. She took her hand off my arm.

'I went home.' She said the three words with a flat tone of voice, like when you comment on the weather to someone standing outside in it; matter-of-fact, stating the obvious, self-conscious. I didn't get it.

We walked on in silence, which she broke.

'Johnny, do you mind if I ask you a question?'

'Go ahead.'

'What do you think of Felix?'

'That's an interesting one.' I wanted to take her arm again, to enhance the confidentiality, make a connection. But when I looked at her face I saw, even in the bad light, that she had on her earnest face.

'Well,' I said, leaning away to make her more comfortable, 'I have to admit he's the first of his type I've ever got along with, so it's hard to...'

'Type?'

'Anita,' I slowed my pace, 'You know we have a class system in the UK?'

The way the words came out, obscured by the background noise of the pedestrians trooping along beside us, I wondered if she heard 'caste' not 'class'.

'Yes, of course.'

'Well, me and Felix come from opposite ends as it were. I'm common as muck and he was born with a silver spoon in his mouth.'

'A spoon in his mouth?'

'It's a way of saying to be born rich, into privilege, well-off, a proper gentleman.'

'Is Felix a gentleman? And you're not? I thought every English-man is a gentleman.'

'Depends what you mean by gentleman,' I said. 'We like to think we're decent, polite and that, which is what a gentleman is supposed to be, but then you have your *real* gentlemen, who get their suits made by a tailor, go to expensive schools, do things like shooting and fishing at the weekends. That's the sort of gentleman Felix is.'

'And you are not?'

'Couldn't be further from it. But to answer your question: nor-mally I wouldn't hang out with someone like Felix. I'd avoid him. But since we've been thrown together by Shanghai, I've been pleasantly surprised. He's a nice bloke. He's gone some way to changing my view. Ironic that something I'm glad to have left behind in England is our class system, and here I am making friends with a true blue example of it.'

The point was lost on Anita. Maybe it was the colour. She ignored it. 'So you think he is a nice person.'

'Nothing wrong with him I can see,' I said. 'Why, has he done anything to make you wonder?' I turned to her. 'Is there a specific reason why you're asking Anita? It's like you want a reference.'

'No. Nothing,' she said. 'It is interesting to hear what you say, about him being a real gentleman.' She looked me back, in the eye. 'I think you are one too Johnny, only not a rich one.'

I didn't want to be called a gentleman by Anita. I wanted her to like the real me. Trouble was, there was stuff to the real me that I'd prefer she never knew. Stuff I preferred no one knew.

I'm not talking class, humble origins compared to Felix and that. I'm comfortable with where I come from. Basildon is as fine a commuter-belt conurbation as any in the Home Counties. Nor am I talking about embarrassing family.

From the vantage point of age and a little maturity, I suppose there wasn't much of a 'real me' at that point. I think the best word to describe myself when I arrived in Shanghai is 'dislocated'. I was several thousand miles from home, in a country where I didn't speak the language, trying to set up and run my own business with no experience, no qualifications, and no financial backing.

But I'm talking about a deeper sense of dislocation.

A young man goes through the passage of growing up with a few signposts to guide him along the way. School and parents are the obvious ones. There's your first boss, senior colleagues, older friends. Maybe a father figure in there, an uncle or a wise old man, or woman, who keeps an eye on you, takes an interest.

Apart from a brief spell working for my previous boss, who wasn't a bad bloke and taught me a couple of tricks of the trade, I'd managed to avoid running into signposts since I'd left school at sixteen, apart from a brief spell during which it had been nothing but signposts and directions and screaming banshees of authority and 'do this' and 'do that'.

I'll come to it.

I was in a void, impossible to tell if I was falling or floating. That was the beauty and curse of millennial Shanghai: a rare, verging on unique, instance of a time and place where anything goes, like a black hole or wherever it was the Big Bang went off, a brand new world created out of nothing. And we were the tiny particles, the atoms that were going to grow into humans, animals and reptiles, and populate it, and fight over it.

That's a stretch but it works when you consider we were nothing when we arrived. We evolved in less than years, months even. It was evolution at the speed of sound. In about a year I'd gone from a nobody to a modestly successful businessman, respected by my peers, though the bar was hardly high.

And we were so innocent. But innocence isn't much use in a void where no one has decided what's right or wrong. And when the void, the vacuum, is sucking everything in with such force, good and bad, and there's no way or telling which is which – because we're so innocent and lacking in guidance – it's going to get corrupted pretty fast. Like the big bang idea, or when the baddie gets thrown out the spaceship: you step outside in that lot and you get pulled in so many directions you explode.

Then along comes Felix and he's so together. He's had the preparation in his expensive school, he's got the family behind him, the smart suits, and a proper job.

When a young man like that wants to join in the chaos where we're all running around like headless chickens, he's going to have an advantage on idiots like me. Here was someone I could look up to.

It seemed crazy that I had been the one giving him advice. I'd been putting on an act. At that Sundowner I'd been egging him on. I wanted company. Every day I could be crushed by competitors, government bureaus, grown-up life. It'd be good to have someone beside me.

I wondered later if Anita's questions about Felix were to do with his new job. They could have been. Or was she asking on a personal level, which is just as likely.

If I could have come up with a polite (gentlemanly?) way to ask, I would have, but I was racking my brains when Joe shouted from behind, 'Turn right!' and we bunched up and turned a corner.

Huaihai Road was wet and shiny under spotlights and crowded with multi-coloured rain capes. I heard a marching band warming up down the road.

The VIP stand was the only one with a roof over it. We filed up the steps on one side, past Joe who'd stopped to talk to a middle-aged woman who was clocking us out of the corner of her eye. She must have been from the Tourism Bureau; counting monkeys. The first guy in our party did the decent thing of walking to the end of the row so later arrivals wouldn't have to fight past our fat foreign knees. Joe broke away from the tourism woman and strode to a spot on the road below us. He shouted up at us to move back into the centre, then skipped up the steps and took the seat next to me.

A car with flashing hazard lights and a number plate with lots of zeros pulled up in front of the stand. The mayor got out and was ushered to his seat right in front of us, in the centre of the stand. He was short and his hair was combed over to cover a bald patch. He wore a plain dark suit and glasses. A starburst of cameras went off as he sat down. TV crews swung their lenses back and forth, at us above him and below where there was a mob of black-suited junior government officials and a scattering of more foreigners.

The rain started coming down in sheets, sparkling like a bead curtain in the spotlights. We were okay thanks to the canvas roof but drips worked their way through. One was falling on Anita, who'd sat on my other side. She moved away.

I've never been to Rio and doubt I ever will. But now I can say I've seen a samba dancer samba dance down a street in a jewel-studded bikini and feather headdress, in the pouring rain. There were three of them, real Brazilians. Behind them came a troop of girls in funky dance costumes. They had their eyes glued on the Brazilians, copied their every move, one spin or sashay behind. The music was provided by a marching band of Latino drummers and whistle-blowers, also genuine so far as I could tell although they may have been drafted in from the South American barbecue restaurants that had sprung up across town. A parade of nations followed with local performers in costume making up the numbers as they had for the vanguard.

'Ironic, isn't it?' I said to Joe.

'What is?'

'That we get fucked around by government bureaus under the control of this man right here,' I held my hand above the comb over, 'yet here we are playing monkeys for his benefit, making him look good on TV. I mean, doesn't it strike you as gutless? We let these guys screw us around from dawn till dusk while we try to do an honest day's work, and when they ask us to do them a favour we come crawling?'

'It's a game,' Joe said. 'So long as we play along, we'll be okay. Get used to it. Let them have their fun, think they're in charge,' he nodded at the mayor's head, 'that they can do what they like with us. I'm gonna keep building my business and when the time's right I'll sell it to the next sucker and head off to Thailand. Buy myself a beach.'

Six cheerleaders were making a pyramid.

'You're shameless,' I said.

'China business is China business,' he replied. He was watching the cheerleaders cartwheel down the street. I thought how dirty their hands must be.

That innocence I was talking about, it was sad.

Felix was innocent all right. That's another thing I liked about him.

The tourism bureau gig would have been a good – and pretty much the last – opportunity for me to have a chat with him before he started losing it, the innocence. But he was over in Pudong choosing his new accommodation. By the next time I saw him he'd started the job. Besides, as he was on the point of showing us, he could look after himself, and teach us a trick or two.

# 4

# THE GODFATHER

IT was Charlie Thurrold who gave me the news about Felix's move. I bumped into him in the Backstreet, an American sports bar, on a quiet Tuesday.

I always imagined Charlie was in his early sixties. Later I found out he was only fifty-four. He worked at the British Consulate in the commercial section, the down and dirty end of diplomacy, escorting delegations of muck and brass businessmen from the Midlands through the larger, muckier midlands of China in search of factories to make their widgets, or factories that needed small British widgets to make big Chinese ones. He briefed his charges on banquet etiquette, the difference between karaoke and KTV, and how to tell when a bribe is not a bribe but an 'administration fee'. The British widget-makers hung on his every word. The locals accepted him as a necessary evil. Charlie Thurrold was a true China Hand, and knew a lot about widgets. He'd seen more of China than Marco Polo, knew more than us youngsters ever would. He was a godfather to the younger Brits. We asked for his advice and he gave it freely. Trouble was we rarely saw him. He travelled so much and kept his private life private.

It was easy to spot Charlie. He had a bald patch as clean-edged as a Japanese samurai's, only his was natural and his remaining hair was grey and curly. It was shining like a beacon because he was sitting under a wall-mounted spotlight at the far end of the bar, reading a newspaper. The light cast shadows under his bushy eyebrows, made him even more remote and menacing. He had a glass of beer and was smoking a roll-up. I went to say hello. I assumed from his jacket and tie that he'd come from a meeting. I asked him how it had gone.

'Oh, more promises of mutual co-operation for mutual benefit and mutual development with some deputy mayor or other.' Charlie had the growl of a lifetime smoker and drinker.

'No boozy dinner?'

'Couldn't face it. Told them I had to take care of a delegation.' He looked at his beer. 'Must stay off the hard alcohol before six o'clock.'

It was half five.

'Know how you feel,' I said.

My pint arrived.

'So,' Charlie looked up and the light bathed his craggy, careworn face. 'What do you think of Felix's move?'

'What move?' I expected him to tell me Joe had found Felix a place to live in an old villa.

Charlie stared down his nose through his reading glasses, 'The silly bugger has left Smyth and Corrigan.'

'What?'

'You didn't know?' Charlie raised an eyebrow. 'I thought you were friends. He's gone to work for SLIC. Started yesterday.' He said it as a word: slick. 'Not only that. He's gone to live in Pudong too.'

'Blimey, I had no idea.' Charlie looked at me like I'd admitted an embarrassing secret. 'What's the name of the company again?'

'Shanghai Land Investment Corporation. Maybe it's "Company". Government backed. The man in charge, Zhou Jianguo, has *guanxi* right to the top. I'm concerned young Felix is off to be a trophy bag carrier.'

I was surprised and disappointed. Surprised because Felix had made a move so fast and I hadn't heard about it, not from him, and disappointed he'd gone to a Chinese company, not jumped in the whirlpool with me. I was genuinely concerned on his behalf too, which was a new and confusing sensation.

'Having a foreigner working for you is like a fashion accessory for those types,' Charlie said. 'Felix is going to get an interesting experience, eye-opening. I hope he's ready.'

I took a swig of beer and ran through what I'd said to Felix at the Sundowner two months before. Was there something he might have misinterpreted? No. I'd never suggested working for a Chinese company. I was certain.

'A Chinese company,' I said out loud. 'Why on earth would he want to work for the Chinese? He can't even speak the language. And what do you mean "eye-opening", Charlie? They dodgy or what?'

'Bent as a butcher's hook, as I believe the expression goes in that cradle of the English language, sunny Essex.' Charlie did a good parody of a pompous ass. He could be all things to all men, a useful skill in his job. 'You show me a Chinese property tycoon who isn't up to his armpits in dirty money,' he said, 'and I'll show you a virgin in that barber's over the road.' He jerked his chin at a fifty-yuan blowjob joint opposite the Backstreet.

I turned back to Charlie. 'It means homosexual, Charlie, to be that bent.'

'How times change.' He smiled. 'But I'm serious about Felix's new boss.' He coughed and his whole body jerked like he'd stepped under a cold shower. 'I have to deal with those goons on a daily basis and they don't play by normal rules. They make them and break them and a lot of people get hurt in the process, from the poor geriatrics getting evicted from the homes they've lived in all their lives to the migrant workers who build the new apartment towers and die when they fall off the scaffolding. They get away with murder. Literally.' He picked up his tobacco and paper and concentrated on a fresh roll-up.

'I must admit,' he said, 'sometimes I miss the China when everyone wore Mao suits and used food coupons, and "Socialism with Chinese Characteristics" meant something, had a purpose, even if it was Animal Farm with pandas. Back when I studied the language, I thought this place was going to change for the better, that people like me could help it along.'

I'd never seen anyone in a Mao suit.

Charlie stuck the fresh roll-up on his lip and reached for his lighter.

'You know what I saw,' he said out of the corner of his mouth, 'at the end of Huaihai Road when they blocked it off for pedestrians last Christmas, in big letters over a sodding great inflatable castle with a Santa Claus sitting on it?' Charlie puffed on the cigarette and squinted. He pulled a shred of tobacco from his lower lip.

'What?'

'Satan's Grotto.' He flicked the tobacco off his finger. 'If ever there was a classic misspelling, mistranslation, or whatever, that was it. Says it all. Gone to hell.'

'But you're still here,' I said. It was unusual to hear Charlie Thurrold talk like this. He was normally so cheerful and wise, a bit of a rock.

'For the pension,' he said.

I ordered two more beers.

'So what about Felix?' I asked.

'Keep an eye on him, will you?' He sounded concerned. 'He's a nice boy. Shame if he gets burnt.' He dropped a tiny bombshell. 'I knew his parents in Hong Kong. We keep in touch.'

'What? You knew Felix too?' I did my best to keep my voice even.

'No, before he was born, which was back in England. But I did see a bit of him when he was a lad.'

'What were his parents doing in Hong Kong?'

'His father was in the army. Staff job in HMS *Tamar.*' He smiled, more like his cheery self. 'It always amused us how the military headquarters in Hong Kong was in a ship that was a building.'

'Isn't that where the handover parade was?'

Charlie glanced at me. 'We'll make a China Hand of you yet, Johnny Boy.'

So, there was a connection between Charlie Thurrold and Felix Fawcett-Smith. For a split second I wondered if he could be Felix's actual Godfather. That'd be ironic. I was dying to know more but you couldn't push Charlie. I'd tried it once, wanted him to dish the dirt. I had been firmly put back in my box, although Charlie was polite about it.

I was trying to come up with a casual question about the Charlie Felix connection when we were interrupted by a Backstreet regular asking if I wanted a game of pool. I told him maybe later. Charlie turned to the television screens over the bar. One was showing ice hockey, the other American football, both with no volume. 'Hotel California' was playing on the sound system.

Charlie turned back to me. 'I had a word with him, twice. A strong one the second time. You could say we had a tiff. But he was determined to go through with it. So I didn't try to stop him. Well, not that hard.' He looked down at his hand, rotated it and flexed his fingers, as if Felix had only just escaped from his grip. He smiled to himself, his eyes on the back of his hand. I wondered if that was ironic despair at losing the 'tiff' with Felix, or amusement at something he or Felix had said or done.

He sighed and carried on. 'The first time it came up, when we spoke civilly about it. He kept saying how he had to get involved. Those were his precise words: "get involved". Repeated them over and over.'

I smiled. Charlie noticed.

'You put that in his head did you?' He shook his.

'I suppose you also gave him the line about modern Shanghai being different from old Shanghai. That it's going to be a Chinese city this time round, not foreign like the old days, so he's going to "get involved" – there you go again – with the Chinese property industry, get on the inside.'

That wasn't me but it made sense, sort of.

I shrugged, 'You must agree Charlie, about Shanghai being Chinese.'

'I don't dispute it in the slightest. It's that Felix is crossing over so soon. He's only been here what? Four months?'

'Probably does seem short for someone who's been here since the Opium Wars.' I gave Charlie a cheeky grin.

He didn't mind being teased, I think. It came with the cuddly Godfather status.

'I know what you mean about bag carrier and that,' I said. 'But wasn't there a Brit in Hong Kong who did well in a big local company? Famous wasn't he?'

'You mean Tom Fletcher. Nice chap, but constantly at the beck and call of his boss. More like a senior white slave than a top executive.'

'Could be different in Shanghai,' I said, 'if this place does become the international city it says it will.'

I was playing devil's advocate, siding with Felix. Or thanks to Charlie's comments about the good old days this had become a young versus old thing, and I was with the young ones. Thurrold knew I was playing around. He was a canny old cuddly bugger. He let me dig myself deeper.

'Maybe,' I said, 'instead of the standard situation of a foreigner coming here, breaking into the market with difficulty, trying to do his own thing, spending a fortune and getting screwed,' – Charlie knew more of those stories than I'd ever forget – 'maybe Felix will be an example of how a foreigner can turn the tables, be invited in, so to speak, paid up front, no loss to him. Hell, maybe he'll earn himself a stake in the company, what's it called?'

'SLIC.'

'Yeah, Slick. Appropriate. Fancy that: a foreigner with a real stake in a dodgy local firm as opposed to a dodgy stake in a real foreign one.' I had no idea how prophetic that was. Felix would get more than a stake. I was wrong about the safety. And it was all dodgy.

Thurrold hummed. 'I have my doubts, but we can always wait and see.'

Wait and see.

There's the older generation for you.
'What's for afters, Mum?'
'Wait and see.'
Rice pudding.

China watchers know the name of Felix's new boss, Zhou Jianguo. It hit the headlines in 2004 with the words 'Property', 'Corruption', and 'Party' in close proximity. *The Daily Mail* stacked them up: 'Corrupt Shanghai Property Tycoon Shows Party How to Have a Good Time' and the subhead 'Sex, Drugs and Secret Deals in China's Showpiece City' for good measure.

*The Economic Journal* did a piece on it, mostly about the deals, not so much the sex and drugs, and early this year the American think mag, *Chronicle*, published an in-depth article about Zhou and Shanghai. The title was 'Sin City' (the film of the comic had just been released) and a few months later when *Chronicle*'s research assistant, a Chinese national, was jailed for 'passing on state secrets' the media circus rolled around yet again.

Zhou has gone down as a classic example of the spoilt brat Party Princeling. To be precise, he was more of a dukeling. His family weren't *that* senior. At the time of his downfall every report on him mentioned his dead revolutionary hero father, well-connected mother, privileged upbringing in a special compound for the cadres and so on.

Zhou studied architecture in Shanghai and graduated in 1982. I doubt he could design a garden shed. He'd have spent his student days obtaining introductions, arranging favours, making friends. Networking. There you go. When he graduated he was given a job with a state construction company in Shanghai.

You didn't work in those jobs. You sat in your office and drank tea and read the papers or you went out to eat and drink in restaurants, with the right people. It was politics, not work.

Politics got him the top job at SLIC too, as an indirect result of the 1989 Tian'anmen massacre.

Time to meet the man himself.

It was April 2000. The setting was a windowless anteroom outside Zhou's private office in the tallest building in Pudong, the World Trade Tower. Shanghai Land Investment Corp (it was 'corporation', not 'company') was in the Pudong Wealth Tower, a short walk away.

The room was furnished with big square armchairs along two sides, antimacassars on the headrests, tables with heavy glass tops over white lace doilies, ashtrays, tea-cups: old school, Mao meets Nixon. You might remember the black and white photos of Americans in square-cut suits with white hankies in their top pockets, sitting side by side with square Chinese in box-like Mao suits, looking like they've got chopsticks up their arses.

It was people like that who'd given Zhou his job and this is where they came to see him, to inspect his progress, which is why he had the room furnished to make them feel at home. There were photos of them with Zhou on the bookshelves, their faces grim, staring at the camera like it had said a rude word.

It was James Li, Zhou's right-hand man, who brought Felix over. He'd already met him thanks to Anita. The two of them had a long chat and on the spot James decided Felix was the foreigner for SLIC. This was the moment when he presented him to Zhou for approval.

Two men, a young, short, chubby foreigner and a middle-aged lanky Chinese – Li was unusually tall – both in suits, were standing in awkward silence when Zhou appeared from a door beside the bookshelves like he'd come out of the lavatory. He was wearing a brown bomber jacket zipped up to below the collar, dark trousers and plain black slip-ons. According to Joe Karstein, those jackets were the height of fashion for the politically connected. Jiang Zemin, the President in the '90s, started it. It was a modern take on the Mao suit, had that utilitarian, everyman plain effect Commies love. But the zip made it modern, allowed a daring dash of individuality, depending how low it was open to. Felix said it made Zhou look like a bovver boy and added, for my benefit, 'Not that I have anything against bovver boys, Johnny.' Typical.

'Nice to meet you,' Zhou said in English.

Having met him myself I'll slip in my own description.

I'd put Zhou at five foot six. His hair was closed-cropped and flecked with grey. His lips were so thin they made his mouth, between his round cheeks, look like a hyphen between two noughts. His eyes were brown and brown eyes can't be 'piercing' like blue ones. But Zhou's were penetrating. They darted about and when they fixed on you it was like you'd been shot, right through, light shining from the holes in your back like those shooting range targets in an American cop movie.

If you had a little experience with these people, the minute you met Zhou, or studied him from a safe distance, you'd realize he was no puppet on a string. He had intelligence and drive, the will to make shit happen, to things and people.

I must clarify, that's what he looked like when I met him. No one has seen him for a while. He's disappeared off the face of the planet, maybe because he's changed. So don't take my word for it.

After the greeting Zhou switched to Chinese. Li was also there to translate. 'Please sit. Drink tea.' He waved at the chairs. As he sat down, Zhou rolled backwards so his feet left the ground. It would have been a playful move if it wasn't for the complete lack of humour. He stared as Felix twisted his body and crossed his legs to face him.

James Li took an armchair at right angles to them.

'Drink tea,' Zhou repeated, looking at the floor by Felix's feet. He picked up a covered cup from the table, tilted the lid and slurped like a drain.

Felix picked up his cup and lifted the lid. There was a dense mass of tea leaves on the surface of the hot water. He put his lips to the rim, tilted it, and tried to suck the liquid through the soggy mess, without the sound effects.

Zhou kept his eyes on him, up and down the suit. It was the chalk stripes.

Despite his attempts to make a mesh out of his teeth, Felix's mouth was full of tea leaves. He pushed them around so they bunched up and when Zhou turned to speak to Li, whipped up his hand in a hollow fist and pushed the leaves into it with his tongue. Zhou turned back to him as he was thrusting the hand into his jacket pocket. He tried to flick the leaves off but they stuck to his fingers like fresh bogeys.

'Mr. Zhou wants to know where you purchased your suit,' James Li said.

Zhou's eyes darted to the pocket.

'London,' Felix said, smiling and blushing. He stilled his hand.

'How much?' Zhou didn't turn to Li when he spoke. He left his eyes on Felix.

'I'm afraid I can't remember. I've had it a while.'

'One thousand dollars?' Zhou was staring at the pocket.

'Gosh, no, not that much,' Felix said.

'May I?' Zhou held out his hand. Felix looked puzzled.

James spoke up. 'Mr. Zhou would like to feel the material.'

The closest piece of suit to Zhou was the sleeve of the arm attached to the hand coated in soggy tea snot in his pocket. Felix grimaced. 'Of course.'

He gave a desperate flick, pulled out his hand and held it over the table. A swollen green tea leaf was stuck on his thumbnail, fat and wet like a baby slug. He let out a feeble laugh. Mr. Zhou ignored it, and the tea leaf. He pinched the cuff of the suit and pursed his lips. 'Good wool.' He let it drop.

Felix retrieved his hand as if he'd held it too close to a fire, first with a sudden jerk and – to show he could take the pain – slowly returned it to inside the arm of his chair. He rubbed the tea leaf onto it.

Zhou picked up a red packet of cigarettes from the table and lit one without offering. 'You like China?' He sat back.

'Yes, very much.'

'Is it better than your country?'

'I am sorry?'

'Which is better: China or America?'

'Er, sorry. I'm not American.'

Zhou spoke to Li in a dialect Felix didn't recognize. Felix checked his hand.

'Ah!' Zhou turned back. He was smiling like he'd opened the Christmas present he always wanted. 'England! Beckham!'

Li could only repeat the transliteration of the name, 'Bay Cam Who'. Felix said the syllables to himself three times before he realized what they meant.

'Beckham!' he shouted.

Zhou and Li looked confused.

'*Bay Cam Who*. Beckham.' Felix explained back and they laughed and chorused, '*Bay Cam Who!*'

'Manchester United,' Zhou added. '*Ying ge lan*. World Cup. Do you like Chinese food?' His eyes locked on Felix.

'Er. Yes.'

'I do not like Western food. Too heavy.' Zhou left his eyes on Felix, while Li translated, in a way that Felix said felt like Zhou was wondering what he tasted like.

James Li brought the chitchat to an end, 'Zhou Zong.' He used a respectful suffix for 'boss' and spoke in Shanghainese. Felix recognized it now. He couldn't understand a word. 'This foreigner has been working for a year with Smyth and Corrigan,' Felix caught the Chinese name of his company. He smiled at Zhou, who wasn't paying attention to him. 'He has done big deals, with big clients. He is presentable.'

Zhou looked at Felix and away again. Felix smiled at the back of Zhou's head. 'I've had a conversation with him,' Li carried on. 'He has shown me he has the right thinking. He is willing to learn Chinese.'

'Not necessary,' Zhou said.

'I can arrange an office near mine, in the Wealth Tower, an assistant, put him on projects where he can help...' Zhou grunted... 'there's the joint venture for example.'

Zhou showed interest. He stubbed out his cigarette like he was squashing an insect. 'Ah. Okay. Good idea. When the time is right. How much?'

'20,000. No need for social benefits. We'll chuck in a few extras.'

'Such as?'

'I was thinking give him a villa in Evergreen.'

'Good.'

'There is one thing that I might have to trouble you with Zhou Zong,' the pitch of Li's voice changed. Felix noticed. He'd been watching over Zhou's shoulder and imagined Li was going to pass on his request for a flight home once a year. He'd mentioned to Li how important that was.

'What's that?'

'We have to get him a visa.'

'Who does that?'

'Entry and Exit.'

'Get Miss Wang to call Police Chief Zhang.'

'I can say you said so? Chief Zhang might want, well...?'

'All right. But get the foreigner in first, see if he's any use.' Zhou turned and smiled with his mouth, not his eyes. 'He seems all right to me. Nice suit. English gentleman.' Felix understood the 'English' but not the 'gentleman'. 'He'll do. I'm busy. Are we finished?'

Li motioned at Felix.

Zhou rose from his chair. He had one more thing to say. Felix and Li waited. The three of them were standing close. Zhou angled his head to Li. 'Any drama, any problem, you deal with it. The foreigner is your responsibility.'

'Certainly.'

Li said to Felix, in English, 'Mr. Zhou is pleased to meet you. He looks forward to you working for us.' The corners of Zhou's mouth twitched. 'You have a job.'

Felix beamed at Zhou, who stuck out his hand. Felix shook it.

'Welcome,' Zhou said in Mandarin.

'Thank you.'

'Now,' said Li, 'Mr. Zhou has business to attend to. I will see you out.'

Felix hadn't understood a word of what was said between Li and Zhou in Shanghainese, and there were no other witnesses, but working backwards from what comes later, that was the gist.

Whether Felix was set up from the start, if it was Zhou's idea as well as Li's, if they were acting on a whim, a punt, who knows? At this stage Felix was set up to be set up. He was put into a position where he could be useful, like a hotel on a cheap square in Monopoly. It was small change for Zhou to pay that salary and the villa cost nothing.

The next day James Li's secretary called to tell Felix he was expected on Monday if couldn't leave Smyth and Corrigan immediately and start tomorrow, which would be better. Felix was on the point of asking about a contract when Amy, her English name, hung up. It was a Wednesday morning.

By the end of the week he was sorted. He hadn't signed a contract but Amy had written up a job offer in Chinese and couriered it to the Smyth and Corrigan office. Felix slipped out for lunch with Anita who took him through it.

The basics were there: salary, payment date (fifth of the month in arrears), thirteenth month's salary as a guaranteed bonus, Chinese national holidays (plus one week extra), accommodation (furnished). There was no indication that he was getting a whole villa. He was losing the health insurance Smyth and Corrigan had paid for but that didn't bother him. What did was the absence of the annual return flight to the UK.

Anita called Amy.

Once she'd hung up she said: 'Amy says Mr. Li cannot put that in the offer because it's never been done before. His personnel department will refuse. He's sorry, but you're not to worry. He'll make sure you're sent to England on a business trip once a year.'

Felix signed and faxed the offer back to Amy in the afternoon. He went into John French's office and announced his resignation with awkward apologies.

On the Friday evening, Felix went to choose his new accommodation. He was expecting another service apartment like the one from Smyth and Corrigan. He also assumed it would be in Puxi, the west bank of the Huangpu River and 'old' Shanghai. He was none too pleased to be told to get himself out to 'Evergreen Life Villa and Apartment Complex' on the far side of Pudong, east of the 'Pu', the new zone the city government claimed would soon become the financial centre of the Far East. In 2000 it was a building site.

The journey took an hour-and-a-half in a taxi. He cheered up when he realized he was getting a whole villa. He might be moving to the arse end of nowhere, but a villa is a villa.

Before he moved he had to pick up a box of stuff his mother had sent to Charlie Thurrold at the Consulate. On the Saturday before he started at SLIC, Felix dropped by Charlie's serviced flat. This was the second time, as Charlie mentioned in the Backstreet Bar, that the two of them spoke about Felix leaving Smyth and Corrigan.

It was the 'tiff'.

I think it was Charlie's fault. He started by suggesting a celebratory drink. He made a couple of strong gin and tonics. It was barely eleven o'clock in the morning and Felix was keen to get going.

When he described it to me, Felix did a good impression of Charlie's growly voice, although he could only keep it up for a few sentences before he slipped back into his own.

'Here's to you, and wishing you luck.' Charlie had started off. Well and good. 'Not only are you going to work for a Chinese property developer with a certain reputation, you're also leaving us for Pudong, symbol of modern China... and everything that's wrong with it.' He rounded off his 'toast' with: 'So you've gone local.'

'Is that your way of wishing me well, Charlie?' Felix says he replied. 'I told you: I'm committed. This is the start of my proper China career.'

'Yes, "getting involved". I remember. But Felix, indulge me. I'm concerned that once you cross that river I won't see you again.' He was using the Huangpu as a metaphor for the move to SLIC as much as the physical crossing to live in Pudong. 'You'll be lost forever amongst a herd of white elephants, trampled beneath their feet as they march across the paddy fields towards the sea, where one day, like giant lemmings, they'll slide off a mud bank and drown.'

'He actually said that,' Felix told me. 'It was like a speech.'

Our own conversation took place when he'd been at SLIC for a few weeks. I can't remember where it was. Felix was laying to rest the rumour that the 'tiff' had turned into an actual fist fight between him and Charlie Thurrold.

He told me how Charlie really had made a speech, about how the Party hated Shanghai and was using it as a honey trap to bring in foreign investment, and foreigners with skills (that wouldn't be me) and how Pudong was a symbol of modern China getting its own back on the old, weak China that had let foreign vagabonds (that *would* be me, or people like me in the old days) take advantage of the country, which was symbolized by old Shanghai and the Bund, the photogenial waterfront copied from Liverpool in the 1920s.

'He's got this wacky theory that Pudong is only full of those new office towers so it can overshadow the Bund, especially in the early morning, when the sun's in the east and the bankers are at their desks reading newspapers. I think he might be losing it.'

Felix admitted he was a bit tipsy after two of Charlie's gins, when they came to the proper argument.

'He finished off with Pudong: yet more tower blocks, white elephants, whatever. You know the Jinmao Tower?'

Of course I did. It was the showpiece of the new city in Pudong. It was almost finished, right up to the eighty-eighth floor.

'You know it's supposed to represent the pen Deng Xiaoping used to sign a document that let China do business with the West, "opened the door"?'

'Yeah,' I said. 'Heard that too.'

'Well, Charlie came out with this,' – he put on a Charlie growl – '"It's a load of bollocks. The Jinmao Tower is Deng's middle finger making a gesture foreigners understand only too well, on behalf of the Chinese Communist Party. And it's directed at Shanghai's foreign history, and you lot who think you can repeat it. That's Deng saying, loud and clear, 'Fuck you,' to all of you."'

'That's when it got feisty,' Felix said. 'I'd had enough of gin and Charlie. I stood up. I wanted to go.

'"Well, fuck it, Charlie. And to be honest, fuck you too." That's what I said. He'd also had a dig at Mr. Zhou, said something about him being a crook. So I told him to mind his own fucking business, and that I'd rather work for a crook who gets stuff done than sit around listening to a crusty old diplomat give a stupid lecture about Chinese modern history, which we're living, making, today.'

I patted him on the arm. 'Don't worry, mate. Charlie Thurrold is getting on. You're right. He's from another era. Doesn't see things the way we do.'

Felix hadn't finished.

'That's when he came at me, holding his hand out. I thought he was going to take my glass from me so I pushed it at him, a bit hard, and I think he thought I was going to hit him, or he was drunk and he fumbled, but that's when we had our "fight" as everyone's calling it. I snatched my hand back, he gripped it, we kind of went back and forwards, and I suppose we were kind of struggling. Neither of us said anything. And he pushed my hand, the one with the glass in it, into a vase on a wooden stand by the door, and it fell off, but not before my hand got cut, so the glass must have broken too.

'He shouted at me and staggered backwards. I think he was shocked by the physical contact. He was red in the face and puffed up.

'As for my hand, well, there was blood pouring onto the floor. Charlie stepped forward, to help, but I was so mad at him. I brushed him off, which could perhaps have been interpreted as a shove, or a blow, if that's what Charlie told you, and it did make a mess with the blood splatting on the wall. I wrapped it up, my hand that is, in my handkerchief and told him I'd get my stuff and be off. And that was that. Haven't seen him since, and to be honest don't want to.'

Felix paused. He'd done a good job of putting his side of the story. The word on the street was he'd got out of line and Charlie had knocked some sense into him.

'So that rubbish about Charlie and me rolling on the floor, or having a fight in the Consulate itself, is just that, a load of rubbish.

Did you hear the rumour that the ambassador had to break it up?'
he laughed. 'The ambassador lives in Beijing for Christ's sake. I
wonder who started that one.'

'You know how it is,' I said. 'Doesn't take much.'

I did my best to make Felix feel better. Not that I needed to. As
he said, he hadn't seen Charlie Thurrold and he was ensconced in
his new job, and villa, in Pudong. What the hell did it matter what
Thurrold thought.

I said something along those lines, and rounded off with, 'Mate,
I've known Charlie for years. Well, since I got here. We all know
him. He's an old fart who sits on a barstool and pontificates. He's
living in the past. He talks about history. You and me, mate, we're
making it.'

He smiled. He was hearing his own words back at him and he
liked that. He didn't give it the old 'that's what I said' whinge.
That gets my respect. I can't keep quiet like that when someone
pinches my ideas.

# 5

## MOVING ON

On the Monday after his house-moving, Charlie-tiff weekend, Felix reported for work at Shanghai Land Investment Corporation.

For the next two months he did nothing.

Nada. Nichts. 什么都没有作.

Monday to Friday he caught the shuttle bus to downtown Pudong. The only other passenger was a middle-aged woman, the cook for Evergreen's security guards. She was from the countryside and shouted like it. Felix called her 'Auntie' and she called him 'Mister Foreigner'. She got off at the wet market.

He arrived at the Pudong Wealth Tower at nine o'clock or thereabouts, depending on roadworks. His office, a large space with empty cubicles, was on the eighteenth floor. He switched on his desktop computer with the Chinese language operating system he'd worked out by guesswork. Once it was running he could switch it to English. Then he made coffee at the filter machine James Li had purchased for him. James insisted his secretary Amy learn to use it but Felix preferred to make his own. That didn't stop Amy coming to stand right beside him, almost touching, watching, without a word.

Back at his desk Felix smoked a cigarette with the coffee. He sent emails to friends in the UK and his drinking buddies in Shanghai.

Between ten and ten-thirty he walked down the hall to James Li's corner office to see if there was anything he could do. Four mornings out of five James was in a meeting, on a phone conference, or out. So Felix chatted to Amy, who although she couldn't translate job offers did speak a little English. Their conversations went one way or the other depending on James Li. If he was in, Amy stared at her computer screen while Felix made inane comments and she replied in monosyllables. If James was out, it was Amy who asked the questions, about English grammar and the British royal family.

The one in five mornings when James Li was available he invited Felix in, gave him a seat and put on a pantomime of thinking long and hard for a task for him.

Li was Shanghainese but had lived most of his life in Guangzhou in southern China, where I'd done my English teaching. I presume his parents' 'work unit' was based there. They were military, or academics. Li was one of the many exiled Shanghainese who returned in the early nineties. He was roughly the same age as Zhou. His parents had maintained their *guanxi,* who helped him get a job at SLIC when it was set up. He started off as a vice president in charge of a desk and not much else. By 2000 he basically ran the company.

James Li 'monetized'. That he was good at it was a major bonus for Zhou because many of the projects that came SLIC's way from the municipal government were hardly odds-on winners. Zhou had to take the losers too. That was the deal.

For example; SLIC was 'invited' by the Tourism Bureau to rebuild a Buddhist temple from the ground up. There was no money in it for SLIC but it wouldn't break their bank. Temples are cheap and easy: a couple of big sheds one behind the other for big fat Buddha statues and you're done. Once Zhou had spoken to some people, James Li had the Bureau cut SLIC a share of ticket sales, plus the rights to the advertising on the back of the tickets *and* he secured the rights to the retail space connected to the temple complex, which he made sure there was plenty of when SLIC's architects drew up the plans. The resulting profit was 'off the books', although a chunk of it went to the people Zhou had a word with.

Today James Li is a major player in Vancouver property. He knew SLIC would pass its sell-by date. Clean as a whistle too. No extradition fight like there will be for Zhou if they find him.

Li treated Felix as a pleasant distraction. Their meetings began with a list of questions picked from a large hat.

A yachting marina for example.

Were there marinas in London? Who regulated the water: the navy or the police? Did London taxi drivers speak foreign languages? How much did a student need for living expenses? Where was the best area to buy an apartment in London?

James paid attention to Felix's hesitant answers, took notes, was grateful, and he'd snap his fingers and mention a new project on the books for SLIC, as if he wanted to reward Felix with the promise of an interesting job.

The projects were always a long way in the future. One did involve a marina.

After that little rigmarole, James would give Felix a task that had been sitting on his desk. He might ask him to research property investment opportunities in the UK or the States. He'd have Felix 'dechinglify' (turn Chinese English into English English) low-priority business correspondence or proofread property brochures.

He was told to compile a list of UK magazines that covered, if only in the ads, expensive, high-end properties, and have them sent over. Felix had his old mates collect the regular estate agency listings mags and subscribed direct to *Country Life*, *House and Garden*, and a few posh regional magazines from the home counties – with titles like *Berkshire Life* and so on – that had sections of smart houses for sale, with glossy photos. James Li was emphatic about the photos.

Some days James invited Felix to join him for lunch after the chat. If it was the two of them, the Q & A might pick up where it had left off, Li trying to second guess what SLIC's government friends wanted to know next. If a client or government contact was there, Felix handed over his name card and James acted as an interpreter for a few minutes of small talk. Occasionally the client spoke enough English for a stilted conversation and asked the same random questions.

James had done Felix a favour with the name card.

At Smyth and Corrigan, Felix's Chinese name had been '*Shi Mi Si*', (pronounced *shi mee ce*) a transliteration of 'Smith'. James Li kept the 'Shi' since it's an actual Chinese surname and chose a new forename, Li-zhi. The characters on their own mean strength and wisdom yet they also make a pun on the word 'determined'. Felix liked it.

'So, what's it like working for a Chinese boss?' I asked Felix in the Backstreet one night. 'Must be different. You sit around drinking tea all day, reading the papers? Lunch box on the desk and a two-hour kip straight after?'

He gave me the rundown of his working day, like I just described it.

'Well, I hope you're going find a future in it,' I said when he'd finished. 'Doesn't sound like they've given you much of a portfolio, or whatever you real estate people call it. Charlie Thurrold might have had a point about the fashion accessory.'

Felix twitched. He'd told me his side of the story but he'd never mentioned 'fashion accessory'. I'd got that straight from Charlie.

'Let's leave Uncle Charlie out of it,' he said.

'Hang on. Uncle?'

Felix's fingers went to the top button on his shirt, like he'd revealed more than he meant to. 'Slip of the tongue,' he said, staring at me straight in the face. 'Charlie knew my parents in Hong Kong. He was a family friend.'

'He told me,' I said.

Felix was staring at me as if he was challenging me.

'Sorry.'

His face relaxed. He almost smiled. 'I suppose you could say he was like a Godfather,' he said. 'I used to call him "uncle" when I was little. He was my mother's friend. They met when she did secretarial stuff in the bit of the foreign office he was working in. It was a common job for army wives, back in the day.'

'How ironic,' I said.

'What is?'

'That I always thought of Charlie Thurrold as a godfather figure for us young Brits in Shanghai, and you rock up and he really is your godfather.' He'd referred to Charlie in the past tense. I didn't comment.

'Not officially,' Felix said, his voice sharp.

'No wonder you got into a strop with him.' It was time to make a joke of it. 'You need to know someone pretty well before you smash their flat up.'

'I told you, Johnny. It was an accident. And I didn't smash anything. He did.'

We were both silent for a moment. I wanted to say the right thing, on behalf of Charlie. It had to be done. No jokes. 'Well, I hope you can patch things up with him. It's a small world here. Best to get along.' And that was all I could do. Pretty pathetic. But I'd prompted Felix. He spoke evenly, like he held the moral high ground.

'I'll get along with Charlie when he apologizes and agrees that SLIC isn't a bunch of corrupt, party-backed goons.' He paused. 'OK, I admit the clients aren't the same as I was dealing with at Smyth and Corrigan. They're Chinese. But they're commercial companies, banks and things, traders, stockbrokers and so on. As for Mr. Zhou: so what if he dresses like a bovver boy if that's the way an executive is expected to dress in Shanghai, like you'd wear a suit in the City. SLIC is a tight ship, professional.' He brushed his fringe. 'Besides,' he said, as if he was about to give me the final, overwhelming point to his argument, 'I couldn't turn them down after everything Anita did.'

'What you mean? How she helped you go through the contract?'

'More than that,' he said. 'She set the whole thing up.'

'Anita got you the job?' I sounded as surprised as I was.

'I never told you, did I? To be honest, it happened so soon after that chat, you remember, at the Sundowner after Chinese New

Year. I must confess I was a bit embarrassed I wasn't following your advice, about opportunities to do your own thing. You and your bending down to pick one up. That was a good one.' He smiled for a split second and spoke seriously. 'Sorry, but I asked Anita not to tell you.' It didn't sound like an apology, more like a confident excuse.

'That's all right, Felix,' I said. 'I'm not going to start a fight over it.'

'I haven't got anything to smash yet anyway,' he said. 'My villa is like an empty warehouse.' He laughed and so did I. We clinked our beer glasses, took a swig, and then he turned serious again.

'Anita's boss, Mr. Wang, is a friend of Mr. Li.' He wanted to get this straight, 'the guy I just told you about. They were having dinner. Anita was there. Mr. Li said he and Mr. Zhou were thinking of getting a foreigner to work for SLIC. She mentioned my name and it went from there. It was quick. I told you about the interview.'

'Well, with your villa and your workload, you haven't started off too bad for a bag carrier.'

'Thanks Johnny. I appreciate that.' He didn't seem to mind my repeating the Thurrold dig this time. Perhaps he missed it, or Thurrold hadn't made it to Felix, just to me.

# 6

## DOCTOR FELIX

Aᴄᴛᴇʀ Felix's housewarming party, which is another whole story, our gang went for dinner at our favourite hideaway, a down-and-dirty Hunan restaurant in a pair of joined-up lane houses in the French Concession. It must have been late September, maybe early October.

A young American called Mike Bennett joined us. He'd arrived in Shanghai six months beforehand with a company called Highway Hotels, abbreviated to Hi Ho. They'd gone into a joint venture with SLIC and been taken to the cleaners. Mike had stuck around, come over to our side. No hard feelings. He had the clean-cut preppie look like Joe only he was six feet tall and built like an American footballer. I think he played for both teams too. At Felix's housewarming I'd spotted him disappearing upstairs with a young Croatian photographer.

The day before, Felix had been to dinner with his boss, Zhou Jianguo, at his actual house.

We ordered beers and lit cigarettes.

'The place is quite something,' Felix said. 'It's on Zhejiang Road. I always wondered what was behind those walls with wicker fences on top. If the others are like Mr. Zhou's, that street must be Shanghai's equivalent of Millionaire's Row in Hampstead.'

'Or the Hamptons,' Joe said, blowing smoke across the table, 'but without the gardens.' Bennett pulled a face. He was a rabid anti-smoker.

'And I say tomato,' I said.

Joe looked at me like I was to be pitied. 'What?'

Felix smiled.

'The house must have belonged to someone who was bloody rich in the old days. And it does have a garden,' he said to Joe. He turned to me. 'Tomato garden that is.'

We smirked.

Ivy raised her hand. Her voice was impatient. 'You do know Felix, that Mr. Zhou is the son of a revolutionary hero?'

'No, I didn't,' Felix said. He looked her straight in the eye.

'Zhou Jianguo's father, Zhou Lishen, "Comrade Lishen", was a county leader in the early days.' Ivy assumed we knew she meant the early days of Communist China. Her words were clipped and precise. 'Under his leadership his county produced record harvests, year after year. It became a model. Chairman Mao made an inspection tour. There's a famous picture. It was used in the newspapers and on posters.'

'You mean the guy with the red face and Mao and the crops going for miles?' Joe said, 'that gets used for food and restaurant adverts?'

'Yes. Well done.' Ivy sounded more like his mother than girlfriend. 'Comrade Lishen was promoted to be in charge of the provincial food bureau and then the ministry in Beijing. When he arrived in the capital, he refused a special villa in the leaders' compound and stayed in a very small house. He is famous for his simple living standard. He never forgot he was a peasant.'

'How come his son gets to live in such a nice place?' Bennett asked.

Ivy twitched. 'He did good deeds, helped many places increase food production.' She paused. 'There is a sad end to the story. Comrade Lishen died in the Cultural Revolution. It was the most famous thing he did and the reason he was made a Revolutionary Martyr. My parents gave me the picture book. I still have it.'

'How?' Joe asked.

'The Gang of Four sent him to a labour camp – it was a false accusation – and in the camp he struggled for the benefit of the peasants, did more good deeds. He died when he tried to rescue a pregnant woman in a snowstorm. He froze to death. It was in northwest China, Gansu.'

'Ah, New Zealand,' I said.

Everyone stared at me like I was an idiot.

'I beg your pardon?' Felix said.

A dumpy waitress in a flowery jacket and matching headscarf put the dishes on the table. The vegetables came first.

'I'm serious. It's a Cultural Revolution joke,' I said, without realising how stupid that sounded. I peered round the waitress. I hoped Joe might know the story and back me up. Seemed he didn't. Anita listened like she hadn't heard it too.

'New Zealand is *Xin Xilan* in Chinese. 'New' comes from the *xin* in Xinjiang Province, the 'Zea' sounds like *Xi* in *Xizang*, Tibet, and *Lan* is from Lanzhou, capital of Gansu. All of them are desolate, arse-ends of nowhere populated by sheep, although that similarity to New Zealand would probably have been unknown to the poor sod who came up with the joke.' I looked at the blank faces. 'They're also home to most of China's labour camps, hence: "I'm off to New Zealand" was the dark way of telling your mates you'd been sent to a camp. You have to admire the humour. It's almost British.' I sat back and waited for Ivy to give me acknowledgement. I got none.

'Dark indeed,' Felix said. Anita smiled at me.

'But how cool is that,' Joe said, going back to Zhou Lishen, 'to have a comic written about your dad? That's awesome.'

'It's not funny,' Ivy said, giving him daggers. 'You must never make jokes about Comrade Lishen. What do you know about... about... ' She looked like she was going to cry.

There was a painful silence for a couple of seconds. I clicked. It helps to have a twisted sense of humour.

'Ivy,' I said, 'he means a picture book comic, not a comic as in funny ha-ha.'

She put her fingers to her cheek, sniffed, and gave me no thanks. 'Well, I hope you understand why Zhou Jianguo lives where he does,' she said. 'His family made a great sacrifice.'

A couple more waitresses clumped up the wooden stairs and bustled into the room. One held the dishes on a tray and the other transferred them to the table.

We admired the food: dry-fried French beans with garlic and ham, salt-fried chilli prawns, spicy pork ribs, a basket of chicken bits and red chillies – like chicken in the basket, where the basket is a volcano – crispy little fish with bay leaves you can eat whole, and one non-spicy bean curd dish with mushrooms. The chilli smell filled the room like mild tear gas.

'Let's eat,' someone said, as you do in China, like saying grace.

Felix described Zhou Jianguo's house. It was a classic foreign-built mansion from the old days, set in a modest garden with a cedar tree in the lawn, a sweeping drive and stone-columned portico by the front door. Felix guessed it must have at least four floors. Being in the French Concession the architecture was continental, a sort of mini *chateau*. He said it reminded him of the ones the Germans always get for their headquarters in war movies.

The furniture and fittings were original, 1920s art deco, inherited from the long-gone owners. There was a drinks cabinet with glass doors full of books, four or five deep leather armchairs, heavy round tables, a blocked-up fireplace with a cushion-topped brass bench in front, panelling on the walls.

'You can't not imagine, in a place like that, standing with your back to what would have been a roaring fire,' Felix said, 'the people that went before, who made their fortunes here. People like us, just a different era. Think of the parties and dinners, the men in black tie, the cocktails, fancy dress balls. Don't you think? You've seen *Empire of the Sun*?' He didn't ask anyone in particular. 'Or films set in British India?'

I had trouble picturing Joe in a stiff white collar and black bow tie. He'd look like a mobster. Then again, most of the rich people in Shanghai in those days *were* mobsters. Anita was a touch plump for a 1920s backless dress but there'd have been women built like her so they must have got away with it. The image of her, a string of pearls and a cigarette holder had me thinking: schoolgirl with belt-fed peashooter.

As for Ivy, she'd have fitted right in. Her slim figure and icy aloofness were perfect. Mike Bennett would have made the ideal matinee idol companion for her, fresh from filming the sequel to *Lost Horizon*.

After the *art nouveau*, Zhou's dining room had horrified Felix. The parquet floor had been replaced with white tiles, the walls white-washed and the table was a modern, shiny black square with gold edging. A frosted white-light chandelier hung over it. 'It was like a hospital corridor. I expected the cook to appear in surgical robes and a mask.' He waited for the laugh. 'The atmosphere was grim. James Li was there, my immediate boss, with his wife – I think she was his wife – Mr. Zhou of course, a couple of youngish men who didn't say a word all evening, and Mr. Zhou's son, mid-teens. They were drinking tea, waiting for me.' He turned to Anita. 'I wish you'd been there.'

Anita laughed.

'How was the food?' I asked.

'My God it was terrible. Zhou's chef cooked the steaks to death and served them up with soggy veg and rice. The gravy was like soy sauce and treacle. Honestly. Pudding was bread and butter pudding, with custard. The lumps in the custard would have sunk the Titanic.'

'Trying to impress, make you feel at home,' Joe said.

'I think it was a test for Zhou's son. I was asked my opinion of how he used a knife and fork. Tricky to answer, considering he was holding them like a three-year-old. Mr. Zhou had his own food cut up, like you would for a three-year-old in fact, and was using chopsticks.' He heard the patronising tone in his voice, caught Ivy's eye, coughed. 'They asked me about the son's English. Got him to talk to me, like it was an aural exam. I didn't know what to say.' He shrugged. 'So I asked him what he wanted to study at university. Tony, that's his English name, can't remember his Chinese one...'

'Zhou Tielong,' Ivy said.

'Thanks. He said he wanted to study business and Mr. Zhou told me he'll be going to the UK for the sixth form, to Eton would you believe it. Zhou wants me to put a word in.' Felix took a minute to explain that Eton was the best public 'which means private' school in the UK. 'You have any Old Etonian friends who can help, Johnny?'

'Very funny.'

'And how was Tielong's English?' Joe asked.

'It was a struggle. His grammar is basic and vocabulary primitive. I suppose that's the polite way of putting it.'

'But I bet he can write a perfect essay with the words he does know,' I said. 'That's how they're taught. I get beautiful emails from candidates who can barely speak a word face-to-face.'

'He'll be screwed when he goes to this Eton place, won't he?' Joe said.

'That's okay. All new boys get screwed there,' I said, and turned to Felix 'They have fags, don't they?' I watched Mike and Joe out of the corner of my eye. It was another 'tomato'.

'I'm sure you don't have to be a fag when you go straight into the sixth form.' Felix was dead serious. He hadn't picked up on my joke, which made it funnier. Joe and Mike were confused. Joe was a bit disgusted. I loved winding him up.

'He'll be all right,' I said. 'He'll be looked after by the other Chinese kids. They're under the same pressure from their parents, as if those institutions weren't cruel enough in the first place.' I took pity on our American friends. 'And fags by the way are junior boys who do domestic shit for senior ones. I'm not sure the system still exists to be honest.'

'So,' Joe said like he wanted to change the subject, 'you were invited to dinner to test young Zhou's English and check his table manners.'

'Well, actually...' Felix's fruity cheeks ripened.

I put down my chopsticks. 'That's rich, Joe,' I said, 'coming from a bloke who for a fee impersonates a foreign manager for Chinese companies trying to attract local investors.'

'The fee ain't so large, Johnny. Goddamn foreign students are ruining the market. The dirty cheap bastards must be sharing the same suit.'

Felix got himself together. 'The fact is, Joe, once I'd given young Tony his table manners and English test he went off to do his homework and Mr. Zhou and James Li gave me a brief on my new role for SLIC. That's what the dinner was for.'

Felix pushed his chair back and stood up, buttoned up his jacket, pulled out a silver name card case, took out some cards and shuffled them, put a few back and hesitated. He was wondering which of us was the most senior, deserved the most 'face'. He stretched across the table with both hands towards Ivy and said in perfect Chinese, 'Please allow me to introduce myself,' which no Chinese businessman would ever say. Ivy accepted the card with both hands and let out a polite gasp when she read it, the standard response.

Felix gave a card each to me, Joe, and Mike, Chinese side up. I flipped it over. 'Dr. Felix Fawcett-Smith, Director of Marketing, Royal Buckingham Park'. The name and job title were in a plain black typeface, the 'Royal Buckingham Park' in a flowing script in gold, raised off the stiff card.

'Doctor? What the fuck?' I said without thinking. Joe suppressed a snort, either at me or the card. Anita gave us her stern face.

'It was James Li's idea,' Felix said. 'He thinks it makes a good impression, scientific plus professional. I must say I was cagey but why not? You can have a doctorate in marketing, can't you? I mean, it is an academic subject, right?' He ran his fingers through his hair.

'I'm sure you can Felix, but you haven't even got a GCSE in marketing, let alone a degree. Was it on that course you didn't finish?' Felix darted a look at Anita to see if she'd noticed the negative.

'Hey, come on. Who needs qualifications?' Joe said. 'Johnny, go easy on the guy. What harm is there in a little reinvention? Aren't we all doing it?'

He had a point.

Anita took Felix's side. 'It's very important to have a title. Especially when Felix meets clients on behalf of Mr. Zhou. Once there were many foreign experts in China. The people Mr. Zhou deals with remember those days. It is a good, how do you say, illusion?'

'I think "allusion" is what you mean Anita,' I said. And why worry that the foreign experts were Soviet rocket scientists?

'So what's this Buckingham Park?' I said.

'Aha,' Felix said like he was about to do a magic trick. He'd stayed on his feet. 'Royal Buckingham Park' – he drew out the Royal – 'is going to be the most exclusive country club and luxury villa complex in China.' He punched his hands out, palms towards us, exactly like a magician come to think of it. 'Think Cowes meets St. Andrew's on the polo lawns in Windsor.' As he said the names he held each one, metaphorically, in a cupped hand, and brought them into the middle with Windsor. 'All together, down the road in Jiangsu Province.' With a movement that involved his whole body, like he was doing *tai chi*, he swept Cowes, St. Andrews and Windsor into a bundle and pushed them into Jiangsu, to his left.

Before anyone asked about cattle playing golf on a polo pitch, he ran off a list on his fingers: 'First ever yachting marina in Shanghai area, first ever fly-casting ponds, stables and dressage ring, polo pitch, clay pigeon range, beach, on the shore of the lake, which,' he added as an aside, *sotto voce*, 'is actually a river.'

Here was someone harping on about the 'good old days' in Shanghai, when that stuff existed – they even went hunting with dogs and horses – and he was boasting that he's going to make it happen for the 'first time ever'?

Felix was counting fingers: 'Most luxurious villas, ever, with underground parking, a club with the biggest wine cellar, cigar bar, swimming pools, indoor and outdoor tennis, squash courts, you name it we'll have it,' he puffed up, 'and it's my job to market it.'

'What about golf?' Mike asked, dead straight.

'Of course. How could I forget.' Felix winced.

'And who are you going to market it to?' I asked.

'Wait 'til you hear this.' He held his hands out, first fingers raised. 'We're not going for the expats or the Overseas Chinese. Royal Buckingham Park is for the local market, the new rich, the business pioneers, people like that chap who sells computers, you know...'

'The cheap computers?'

'Li Weiming,' Ivy said.

'That's right. Li, and people like him.' Felix unbuttoned his jacket and stuck his hands in his trouser pockets. 'And here's the real trick: we're billing Royal Buckingham Park as the kind of place an English gentleman would live. They love that, like Zhou sending his son to Eton. I'm working on a catchphrase. You know how they love them too, something like "Hunting Shooting Fishing", H.S.F. How about that? Something that captures the essence of traditional British life.'

'For some,' I said.

'Johnny, think outside your Basildon box for a moment, will you? The new wealthy in China love class.'

'Quite true old chap,' I said, putting on the voice. 'No one enjoys a little horsey hanky panky after tea and sandwiches more than a Wenzhou factory boss who's made his fortune in cigarette lighters.' I reverted to my usual voice. 'Sorry Felix mate, they don't have a clue.'

'Johnny,' Felix sat down, picked up his beer and took a long swig, reached for his cigarettes. 'That's the whole point. We're selling an idea, a dream. That's what they want.'

'An illusion,' Anita said. 'Felix is right.' She looked round the table. Ivy wanted to be the new rich herself. Joe was neutral. Mike nodded. 'Modern rich Chinese want to be foreign. They don't want to be Chinese, because there are no good things in China, no Chinese style.'

'I think what you mean is no expensive things made in China, with a quality that enhances status,' Joe said.

'Apart from karaoke nights and concubines,' I said.

'Yes,' said Anita. I don't think she heard me. 'As a Chinese I feel ashamed that we have nothing of our own to inspire to, to be aspired by. It's embarrassing we boast of thousands of years of history and culture and we have nothing left.'

'You mean how the Red Guards destroyed it?' Felix said.

'No. Not that. That's what you foreigners think. The Red Guards were a moment in history.'

'A flash in the wok,' I said. Joe moaned. 'Sorry.'

'I mean we don't have anything to be proud of, except how "big" we are,' Anita said, 'How big China is. Haven't you noticed that everything our government boasts about in China is the "biggest in the world"? Or the longest? Sometimes the fastest? If it is the first, it is only because it is the first of its size, not the actual first. We don't invent or create things anymore.'

'Well,' said Felix, trying to get back centre stage, 'We'll change that soon enough. Royal Buckingham Park will teach the new Chinese how to appreciate fine things in life, what quality is: style and class, and you can develop your own again. You'll see. People say things are better in the West but we had slaves two hundred years ago, and women didn't get to vote 'til much later.'

'Your point being?' I asked.

'That these things take time.' He looked at us for support and got none. His fingers did the nervous hair thing. 'That's what someone said.' It was more of a mutter.

I took it the someone was Charlie Thurrold.

After the dinner, when it was me, Felix, and a waitress who was clearing up, I remembered something.

'Hey Felix,' I said. 'I've got a new name card too. Nothing as grand as yours. I've moved across the hall and got a website. You might be needing recruits one day for your project. Here.' I pulled a card out of my own holder, a leather slide-in one, and presented it with both hands. Funny how you got used to doing that.

Felix pulled out his silver case. One side was for his cards and one for other peoples', but the card on the top of his side wasn't the one he'd given out a while ago. It caught my eye because this one didn't say 'Dr.' etc. It said 'Director'.

'Director? You been promoted while we were having dinner?'

Felix was confused. I pointed at the name card.

'Oh, er, yes. Very funny. I mean actually... It's real too. Sorry.' I'd caught him out. 'That's for Hong Kong.'

'Well, give us one. Come on.'

'You don't need it,' he said.

With a flick of my wrist I snatched the case. He made a half-hearted effort to take it back but I twisted my body away. 'Hello. What's this? "Buckingham Consulting, Suite 2, Regal Business Tower, 43 Henderson Avenue, Wan Chai"? And you're a director, Felix? You set up your own little sideline have you, you sneaky China business exec? I'm impressed.'

'If you must know, it's not mine, although I am the major share-holder.' He pushed his fringe up and held out his hand for the card-holder. I gave it back. 'It was James Li's idea. It's a way to pay me a portion of my salary offshore, in pounds or dollars. Very simple and quite clever. Also reduces my tax. The company bills SLIC for consultancy work, which since it's a Hong Kong entity they can pay in foreign currency, and I get to pay myself a dividend or a profit share. It's controlled by James. He's another director, as is Mr. Zhou.'

'Well, I never. You are getting the hang of things aren't you.'

'There's an added bonus that I have to go to Hong Kong every few months, to chair board meetings, would you believe it?' he laughed.

'Nothing to be ashamed of,' I said. 'Wish I had a Hong Kong company. Drives me crazy trying to smuggle cash out of China, on the rare occasions I have any.'

'Maybe I could help.'

'That's kind, Felix. Thanks for the thought.'

'But please don't tell anyone, especially not Charlie Thurrold.' He sounded worried.

'Hey, Felix. Why don't you and me go for a quiet beer? Julu Lu. A bar where no one knows us. One for the road.'

It was the mention of Charlie that made me suggest it. I don't mean Charlie made me think of beer. It was how Felix still hadn't patched things up with him, seemed to be drifting apart. In case you haven't noticed, I was fond of Charlie. I cared about him, and he cared about Felix. I wanted to help.

Julu Lu was round the corner. Not a usual haunt of mine. Too many sad fat expat factory managers wanting cheap female company. It reminded me of Bangkok trannie bars, not that I frequented those either.

We walked along the street and picked one at random. As we approached the bar, two country girls came up to us. 'You wanna good time?'

'No.'

'You buy me drink?'

'No.'

'You homosexy?'

That was a new one.

'Yes.'

'You want a boy?'

'For fuck's sake.' And in Chinese I said, 'leave us alone, okay?'

'Sorry.'

They walked off and we got ourselves two big glasses of cheap Shanghai Beer. Felix took a swig and grimaced. It tastes like piss. 'What are we here for, Johnny?'

'Where, this shitty bar? Shanghai? China? Earth, the universe, the infinite?'

'I mean Shanghai. And I'm serious. Is it the money? Is it for thrills? Is it the lure of the mystical East? The sex?' He glanced along the bar. One of the girls noticed and made as if to come over.

'Don't say that in here, mate,' I said.

Felix waved the girl back to her seat. I kept an eye on her to make sure she stayed away. 'If it helps, let me tell you why I'm here. How about that?' I said.

'You sure you want to spill your secrets?'

'You sure you want to hear? Some might apply to you. But don't worry, I'll save a few for afters.'

He waited a second, 'Go on then.'

I pulled out a cigarette and lit it.

'It's very simple,' I said. I took a deep drag and exhaled over the bar. 'I'm running away.'

First time I said that straight. Came out in a rush with the smoke, like I was worried I'd stop halfway. I carried on before I could think twice.

'What from?'

I pictured my Gran's seventieth birthday party, the fussing aunties and uncles, bickering mum and dad, cheese cubes on toothpicks.

'I think a good word for it is "smallness", the plain pettiness of life back home. Appropriate to run away to the biggest country in the world. The place I come from must be one of the smallest by comparison. Tiny. And we – or rather they do, the people there – live whole lives like that: everyone in everyone's face, friends or enemies because of something that happened on a playground...'

Boy, had I got in everyone's faces at the party. I'd been reluctant to go and my mum and dad trying to force me made it worse. We had one hell of a fight. Gran stepped in and told me not to worry, if I'd rather not be there that was fine by her. What fun would there be for a young lad like me, she'd said, sitting with a bunch of miserable old buggers talking about the Blitz and the good old days in the East End. That shamed me into making an appearance, and when we went down the pub afterwards I'd had a right old time. The miserable old buggers told hilarious stories about Gran when she was my age during the War. That they got me drunk made them funnier. There was yet another row when I got home and woke my parents up when I puked.

That had been the beginning of my 'adult' relationship with Gran. She lived on her own in a tiny ground floor flat. I used to drop in after school, to share my problems, or escape them.

When my troublesome teens got way out of hand there wasn't much even Gran could do. I didn't see much of her – didn't see much of anyone – and when it became obvious I was never going to live it down, Gran was the one who encouraged me to go away.

She wrote to me once a month, a couple of pages at a time, in her tiny sloping handwritten biro. She told me about the birds that came to her feeder, the price of bread and milk, a bit of family gossip, and always rounded off with something optimistic to say about me and China. The letters often included a newspaper cutting. The China news was all positive in those days, so Gran credited me with having the brains to see it coming and get out there. Either she'd forgotten that she'd pushed me to go or she was determined not to take the credit. She joked that one day I'd fly home in a private jet.

'...Baked beans and shepherd's pie, fish and chips on Fridays. Rice fucking pudding. Talk about a small life. Course you can get away to London or join the army. A mate did that.'

'Really? Which regiment?'

'No idea, Felix,' I said, forcing a smile to cover the break in my flow, 'but I'll find out if you like. As I was saying.'

'Of course, do go on.'

'Like I was saying – and Felix?' he looked up. 'Let me finish, will you?'

'Sorry.'

'Like I said, you can get away, but you always come back, on the evening train.' I took a long last drag. 'Not me.' I stubbed the cigarette out. 'You know what my dad is? Bus driver. Couple more years and he gets retirement, pension, cardy and slippers time. He used to talk about setting up a taxi business. Never got round to it. All talk. My mum sits at home. Sister lives at home too. Works in a laundry. Christ knows what I'd be doing if I'd stayed in Basildon. Last job I had, my only one in England, was working in Burger King near Liverpool Street Station. I used to pretend I was commuting to a proper job in the city, like a few of my mates did. Pathetic. My dad had me meet his boss once, to chat about a career as a bus driver. A "career"? I was a nipper. Actually considered it. I was young enough to look up to my dad back then. Course there was no hope after I lost my licence. Good thing too. That was drink, just over the limit. I didn't do drugs myself, although my mates did. There was loads of that about. Remember when ecstasy first appeared?'

Why did I always bring this up?

Felix nodded. His eyes were glazed but he was listening.

'That schoolboy who died from a dodgy pill? Steve Turner? All over the papers?'

There you go, Steve.

A nod and shake. 'Oh yes. Big story.' He seemed to wake up.

'He was at my school. Two years below me.' I made myself conjure up the images like so many sticks to beat myself with: the police, uniforms and plain clothes, interviews in the station, lino splattered with grey chewing gum, social service busybodies, journalists knocking on front doors, one after the other down our street, mum drawing the curtains and putting a finger to her lips. And that place I went.

Enough. I do those flashbacks in small doses.

Bye Steve.

Felix was watching and waiting.

'Let's say I was there when it happened.' Felix cocked his head, didn't say anything. 'His brother was a mate of mine. Was.' I left it vague. Felix didn't ask but the raised eyebrows said he'd taken it on board.

'So there you have it,' I said. 'The petty world of drudgery and recreational drugs I'm running from.' I took a drink and lit another cigarette. 'You won't have been to Essex, Felix?'

'I did actually. Went to Colchester once. A friend of my father's was something to do with the army there.'

'Your dad was an officer, wasn't he?'

He showed no surprise that I knew.

'Yes, that's right, a colonel. But you know what, Johnny?'

'What?'

'He started in the ranks.'

Here he went again, Felix trying to bring himself down to my level. Why did he always do this?

'Come to think of it, if I'm running away from something, like you, that's probably it,' Felix was lucid, 'the pressure to join the army. Live up to expectations. I've got an older brother. Alex. He's a captain in the Paras, went to Sandhurst. He's in a special group called the Route Finders. He was in Kosovo last year. He's the golden boy. My Dad writes letters, doesn't do email. Half of them is about how well Alex is doing: another promotion, mention in despatches.' He smiled. 'D'you know why I've got this double-bar-relled name? It's because my dad thought it sounded better than plain Smith. That's what he was to begin with. Private Smith. Then he became an officer. It was when we were in Hong Kong. He was quartermaster of something, maybe the whole army there, when we became Fawcett-Smiths. Just in time for my brother to have it on his birth certificate. Hey presto, in one generation we're officers and gentlemen, like a character in Evelyn Waugh. You read any of his books?' I shook my head. I'd never heard of an author called War. 'Apart from me that is. I might behave like a gentleman, Johnny.' He giggled for some reason. 'I mean: Johnny, I might behave like a gentleman. But to my father's eternal regret I'm no officer. I think he's given up on me.'

So the coming-down-to-my-level act might be genuine after all. I still didn't believe it. He couldn't fool me. He was upper class, even if it was only one generation. As always when he did his humble act, the laboured modesty and posh accent gave the lie to it.

I didn't argue.

'So you came here to prove something?'

'If you insist,' he said. 'I prefer to say I'm here for the adventure, the opportunity.'

'Except you didn't know that when you put your name down.'

'Granted.'

'And now? Your parents paying attention?'

'Oh, my mother's proud of me all right. Always was. She helped me get the job with Smyth and Corrigan.'

'And helped get you out here, indirectly? Or was that Charlie Thurrold?'

His head snapped up. I was getting near a line. He looked at me for a moment and said, 'I think they had an affair, my mother and Charlie.'

'Get on with you.'

'I've thought about it a lot.'

'If that's the case, have you thought that coming to live and work in the same city as Thurrold might not only make your father pay attention, but put his back right up.' This was getting Freudian. 'You ever thought: maybe you're taking revenge on your father? Winding him up?'

That was the line.

Felix sat up. He was uncomfortable. He pretended it was physical, the hard bar seat. He rubbed his lower back and glanced at his watch. 'Let's go, my backside is killing me.'

Touché, Mr. Smith. You're not running away. You're looking for a fight.

He was still putting on an act, still the gent, but he was human too.

That's when I properly started to like him.

# 7

## TALLY HO

Anita was right about the lack of Chinese style. Take suburban architecture, a window into a country's soul.

The outskirts of turn-of-the-century Chinese cities were more like back lots for spaghetti westerns, or East European soap operas, rather than somewhere a Chinese family could call home. Shanghai had 'Thames Town', with its infamous copy of an actual British fish and chip shop – who sued, as you might remember – and 'Little Holland' complete with a windmill. There was also a Bauhaus 'German Town' built with primary colour building blocks, like a child's toy, which had half a dozen inhabitants.

God forbid someone built a Chinese town in China.

Felix was spot on with the acronyms too. CBDs (Central Business Districts) were popping up in every downtown precinct and IFCs (International Finance Centres) beside every SOHO (Small Office Home Office) block. Those were the sensible ones. Less likely to live up to their promises were the 'New Heavens on Earth', (XTD, based on the Pinyin initials, with a similar ring to venereal disease) the VVIPs (add as many Vs as you like) and the '3G Residence'. That had nothing to do with mobile phone signals. It stood for Green, Golf and Glamour.

So Felix coming up with 'HSF' wasn't a bad effort. 'H.S.F. Lifestyle' to give it its full title. To this day it's splattered across property ads in glossy magazines, airport billboards and hoardings round construction sites of yet more identikit suburbs.

To add to the irony, on the rare occasions HSF was spelt out, thanks to the original production person at SLIC thinking hunting and shooting were the same thing, or they asked an American to help, it's 'Horses, Shooting and Fishing'.

The result gave birth to an urban legend and a short-lived nickname: 'Foxy Felix'.

Zhou Jianguo had been wining, dining and 'entertaining' the provincial officials whose bureaus would be involved in the Royal Buckingham Park project. Zhou didn't need to ask favours, let alone request approval, even with senior people in charge of provinces. His *guanxi* went over their heads. But he still had to be nice to them. The 'face' he dished out with the dinners and gifts was a matter of form.

In November SLIC hosted a prelaunch event for Royal Buckingham Park at Zhou's mate and Anita's boss Mr. Wang's Paradise Island, to thank in public the people they had 'entertained' in private and put them in the same room so they could see who else had been co-opted. The Provincial Party Secretary was the guest of honour.

The choice of venue was clever. Paradise Island was inside the Shanghai municipality, hence Zhou's home turf and somewhere he could play the host, but far enough from downtown to make a show of him coming out to meet and greet, give more face to the Jiangsu people. The province was a few more miles down the road.

In a final touch the party was billed as a sales event. The guests were to be offered an exclusive discount on a number of units that they could trade like futures or bonds. Felix described how he was asked to help draft the terms for the deeds, or contracts, to make them more 'international', but he had to give up because there were so many special conditions for special clients, by which he meant government officials. The deals would be very 'Chinese' he said.

Joe had put Felix and Anita in touch with a new catering company that claimed to do high-end western style party food, set up by an ABC called Andy. Joe wanted to check out how good he was. Felix also asked me to go along, said it would 'be good to have another English gentleman' there.

He asked me to wear a jacket and tie.

I bought myself a silk tie and wrapped it round the over-sized neck of a knock-off Paul Smith shirt. For a jacket I wore a green moleskin one, way too big across the shoulders, although the sleeves were long enough for my lanky arms. I can't remember the trousers but they weren't jeans. The last thing I looked like was an English gent. More like a former Soviet bloc, mid-European businessman, fresh out of the gulag.

Joe borrowed Ivy's VW. It was a damp and windless day, unusual for late autumn. Quite warm. I asked Joe if he'd arranged any entertainment. He told me to expect a surprise.

'Let me guess,' I said. 'Fashion show?'

'Not this time. Felix is going to impress. He not only organised the entertainment. He's part of it.'

'Oh Christ,' I said. 'Extracts from Shakespeare? Morris dancing?'

It was stuffy in the car. I wound down the window and loosened my tie. I told myself to remember to do it up when we got to Paradise Island.

'You Brits find the weirdest stuff funny. But it does involve animals, I can tell you that.' Joe smiled at me sideways. 'Live ones. Light me a cigarette, Johnny, if we're doing windows not air con.' I obliged and lit one for myself.

Above the entrance to Paradise Island there was a red banner with white script strung between two sycamore trees, and more along the driveway. Doubtless they were 'Welcoming the Leaders' and 'Congratulating Shanghai Land Investment Corporation on the Successful launch of Royal Buckingham Park' and so on. One had HSF in amongst the characters.

'See how they've written Buckingham?' Joe said. '*Baijinhan.* "White gold" for *bai jin*, which can also be platinum, and the *han* is the "Han" from Han Chinese.'

'Fascinating.'

The car park was full of BMWs, Audis and Mercedes, black with tinted windows. A yellow Porsche and red Ferrari stood out like disco dancers at a mafia funeral.

We drove round the back to the delivery area and parked beside a horsebox.

That's when I might have guessed what was in store, but sometimes you don't register the out-of-place because it is exactly that: out-of-place. When you've just seen a Ferrari and a Porsche in the car park of an exclusive golf club in a socialist country you are permitted to miss the odd things out, like a sodding great horsebox. We can't all be Sherlock Holmes.

Joe and I went in through the back. A security guard made a half-hearted attempt to stop us. We ignored him and walked down a corridor past a staff canteen where government drivers were drinking tea out of Nescafé jars, smoking like their lives depended on it and playing cards. They were cackling like a bunch of pissed-off hens. That was serious politicking going on. They'd pass most of the gossip to their bosses, except for a few juicy morsels they'd keep for their own benefit, or their share portfolios.

Joe swung open a service door and we stepped into the main reception room. We went from one world to another, cheap linoleum to thick carpet, cigarette fug to scented air conditioning, raucous din to the awkward silence of a scattered gathering of government officials standing around like so many chopsticks at a finger buffet.

It really was a finger buffet.

It was Felix's idea to start with a morning drinks party thing. He'd sold it to James Li as the upper class British way for people to get better acquainted. I'm sure he'd been to hundreds himself; waiters topping up glasses and handing round plates of bite-sized biscuits with anchovies and caviar and the like.

But Chinese government officials don't stand around and chat in public spaces, let alone eat with their fingers. When they want to get to know each other they sit at a table in a private room to eat and drink properly.

They were talking, passing cigarettes, ashing on the carpet. But the men – there were no women – were standing in ones and twos, in their badly-cut suits and bomber jackets, clutching man-bags like travelling salesmen waiting for the bathroom in a Clacton-on-Sea bed and breakfast. A model of Royal Buckingham Park in a glass case made a useful focal point. They circled it with silent, dutiful curiosity, like it was the open coffin of someone they didn't know. Paradise Island staff stood around the walls, stepping forward to proffer their trays of nibbles. No one ate a thing.

Joe and I copped stares as we made towards the bar in the room at the far end. Someone said that Paradise Island was so posh it had foreign staff. We pretended not to hear.

The young barman gave us a warm welcome, like he recognized us, and blew my mind with an excellent Bloody Mary. He was the guy Joe had taught a year ago, and he'd remembered.

'Christ,' I said, 'strong.'

Joe grinned. 'Good teacher. Good pupil.'

Anita bounced up to us with a stack of brochures in her arms. She said a quick hi to me and asked Joe to go speak to Andy, the boss of the catering company. She bounced away. Joe went with her.

I went back into the main room and joined the general awkwardness. I moved towards the model of Royal Buckingham Park, trying to find a gap in the silent circle. I'd met more than enough government officials and can't say they were my favourite people. It's a good thing this lot were from Jiangsu or I might have bumped into one or two 'good friends', as they liked to call me once they'd bullied my staff and me and negotiated another 'service fee'.

I was nearly there when a man in a sharp suit – too sharp to be government – strode up and held out his hand towards me. Behind him I saw two men enter the room, surrounded by flunkeys. One must have been Zhou Jianguo, the other the Provincial Party

Secretary. Zhou was the shorter one. This was my first sighting and I gave you my description earlier. Short, round face, punchy. Only thing to add is that in a crowd, accompanied by a senior Party official, he walked with an air of complete authority. I'm tempted to say it was like he was the kingpin gangster, with his humble senior government slave who's been bribed and blackmailed into submission, but that'd be too much of a cliché, and wrong. He wasn't a thug. But it was obvious who was in charge. The Party Secretary didn't look like a pushover either. He was tall and wore a smart, well-cut suit, and a snazzy tie. He was a step behind Zhou, however.

The man with his hand out was coming straight at me as if it was his job to stop me getting too close to the top guys. He was heading me off, blocking me.

He was tall and as slick as his suit, with a long face, high forehead, and hair gelled straight back but with enough of a sideswipe for a razor-thin parting on the right, i.e., wrong, side. His cheeks were pockmarked and his eyes deep in his bony head. I guessed he was in his mid-forties. We shook hands while he studied me and said in good English, with a very mild accent, 'Where are you from?' His voice was high-pitched.

'East Wind Consulting. Let me give you my card...'

'I mean which country?'

'Oh. Sorry. England.'

'Ah, an English gentleman.' He sounded approving. 'You will see another one soon.' That'd be Felix.

He asked, out of the blue: 'Is it true that in England you have peasants?'

I wanted to say he was talking to one, but his intense stare did not indicate he had a deep well of ironic humour to draw upon.

'Not exactly,' I said, trying to sound as serious as he did. 'We have farmers. Perhaps that's who you mean.'

'Who works on the land if you don't have peasants?'

I thought for a second. 'Junior farmers, who haven't qualified yet.'

'I read that when you go hunting in England you have peasants, or junior farmers as you call them, who go into the fields and walk towards you 'pushing' the animals so you can shoot at them.'

I am not your HSF Englishman. The closest I ever came to hunting foxes or shooting pheasants would be popping starlings off a mate's garden fence with his air rifle.

Mr. Hundred-And-One-Questions was waiting for an answer. His lanky frame swayed towards me from the feet, all the way up, like the leaning Pagoda of Pisa.

'Yes, I think you're right there,' I said. 'But they get paid for it.'

'Do they ever get shot, by mistake? How much does that cost?'

How did I answer that? I was tempted to take the piss. Couple of sacks of rice? Sorry, I mean potatoes.

Joe saved me. He grabbed my arm from behind and without saying anything to James Li, who I later found out I'd been talking to, dragged me to the window. 'You gotta see this.'

I tried to give Li an apology for abandoning him. He stared after me and gave me a nod that said, 'We'll continue later.' He re-joined the group around Zhou and the Party Secretary that was moving towards the panoramic window. Joe led me into the bar. 'We can see fine in here, and get another drink.' Some of the crowd followed us. I'd missed the announcement if there'd been one.

We looked out across a stretch of sloping lawn, over flowerbeds, a concrete lane and beyond that a golf green with a flag. The entire course beyond it was shrouded in a peasouper, a solid wall of grey smog from the local factories. Having been round it a year ago, I knew there were dips and rises and bunkers and stubby sycamores that must have sprouted their tops by now, but we couldn't see them. The *Titanic* could have sailed past and we'd never have seen that either.

But someone had sharp eyes. A voice next door said something. A murmur grew as the crowd picked it up. Joe dug me in the ribs.

'Here they come.'

'Who?'

'Watch. Listen.'

I strained my eyes and ears and thought I saw movement in the mist. The ground in the distance, at the very limit of my vision, was rising and falling like a wave, as if the lake was flooding the golf course. I heard the faint but sharp blast of a car horn. Someone must have wanted to leave and was blocked in. The wave split. A gap appeared as it drew closer. Another gap. It was more like a flock of sheep. Again the car horn, but this time it screeched and went up a few notes. A sheep stood up on its hind legs and waved arms. There were people out there, behind the flock, driving it towards us.

The squeaky car horn went off again. Once or twice it came together, whole round notes strung together in perfect pitch. A screech shattered it. It wasn't a car. It was a bugle.

The splodge that became a flock of sheep was beginning to take on individual shapes. One broke away and charged towards the clubhouse. It grew larger and darker as it bounded up to the flag on the green. It wasn't a sheep. It was an Alsatian dog. It put its nose down, cocked its leg and pissed on the flagpole.

They were everywhere, at least thirty of them, barking, leaping, pissing, chasing each other. One came up to the window, bared its teeth and went for it with that ferocious bark that sometimes means 'come and play' and other times signals a desire to commit grievous bodily harm to anything with two legs. The official beside me gripped his man-bag to his chest and squeaked with fear. He backed away from the window.

'Look!' Joe put his arm round my shoulders and turned me. 'There he is. Remind you of good old England?'

I looked where he shoved me and there he was, trying to hold a position on the concrete road: Felix, in a red jacket and riding hat, on a big black horse.

I'd been transfixed by the dogs so I hadn't noticed him get close, and he'd stopped blowing the bugle, which was slung from his neck on a piece of blue string. He was trying to coil up a long whip while keeping one hand on the reins. It kept slipping from his grip and he had to start again. Other than that he looked comfortable in the saddle, born to it, although he was beetroot red in the face, I presumed from the bugling.

There was applause and laughter coming from the officials in the next room. Felix looked to one side, into the wings as it were, nodded, turned back to the window and raised his hat above his head. The whip hung from it like a ponytail on an old fancy dress Chinese skullcap. The applause increased. The horse was working to his own stage directions. Predictable as you please his tail went up and out plopped a stream of turds. The applause and laughter went off the scale. They loved it.

Joe said, 'Quite a performance hey?'

'Gobsmacked. Unbelievable mate. I am literally lost for words. It's like a Tom Sharpe novel, or a *Carry On* film.'

The dog handlers, who were uniformed policemen, ran to and fro in a vain attempt to round up the dogs and get them together on the lawn between Felix and us. A young photographer I recognized from the party circuit appeared outside the window, camera squished to his nose, pointing it at Felix. He ignored the dogs. I respected his courage. Anita stood beside him and signalled to the people in the next room. She stared, pulled a face and shrugged. Someone she wanted to go outside for a photo call wasn't keen. I can't blame them. It was chaos as dogs, policemen and Felix on his horse milled about, barking, blowing whistles, shitting. Felix turned full circle three or four times as the dogs spooked the horse, although it moved more like a dopey dinosaur than a frisky stallion. Its head went down and swung from side to side, jerking him on the reins like an upside-down puppet until Felix got control back. When its arse swung towards the green he pulled back hard, jabbed his heels and got it to walk in a slow circle and stop at a safe distance. He'd obviously been briefed to minimize the damage, which explained the brown cloth sacks that had been tied around the hooves.

I have to say Felix looked like a proper huntsman. He reminded me of the pictures on the walls of the country pubs I used to go to on the back of a mate's 125 motorbike along those winding Essex lanes. You know the ones, with the jolly red-jacketed gent with bushy whiskers up on his stallion, drinking port outside the inn or blowing his hunting horn.

Once he'd got the horse settled Felix sat up in the saddle and waited. Anita gave a thumbs-up at the window of the next room, spoke to the photographer and a few seconds later they appeared inside and strode up to the VIP group. I moved over to the double doors to get a better view. The photographer asked Zhou and the Party Secretary to stand with their backs against the window. Zhou grinned and obliged, and the Party Secretary joined them with less enthusiasm. He kept looking over his shoulder at the glass, checking it was strong enough to stop a horse. Felix had ridden up onto the lawn so he was right outside the window. The photographer moved into a position where he could line him up behind Zhou and the Secretary. It wouldn't work if he used a flash, which he did. Even I knew that. He took half a dozen shots.

Job done, the photographer waved at Felix and bowed to Zhou and the Party Secretary. He and Anita conferred and looked left and right. A floor to ceiling, wall-to-wall photograph like a mural painting suited their purpose.

The main subject of the picture was a sparse thicket of silver tree trunks with brown and golden leaves that stretched away from the viewer into a murky golden distance. A track ran from the middle of the base, right by the frame, up and away to the right.

Anita asked people to move away from the picture and directed Felix, who had walked into the room, to stand in front of it where the track started.

A photo session began in earnest. The officials lined up to be snapped beside Felix, singly and in pairs. They held up their fingers in the V for victory salute or kept their hands folded across their crotches, gripping their man-bags. One or two put their arms round Felix. He winced but stayed still, his mouth fixed in a broad grin, his teeth sparkling white between his ruddy cheeks.

The fringe had been plastered across his forehead by the riding hat. It stayed there. Seeing him up close, I noticed he was wearing his cowboy boots and had tucked the white trousers into them. That spoiled the authentic English gent effect, and the jacket was baggy.

The officials formed an orderly queue. Off to one side, Zhou Jianguo cracked a joke with the Party Secretary. His eyes were alive with an impish, mischievous pride.

When Felix finished his photo shoot he joined me and Joe.

Joe whistled the tune from *The Good, the Bad and the Ugly*.

'How did I look out there?' Felix said.

'Fantastic,' Joe said.

Felix turned to me. 'You smarten up all right don't you, Johnny. Except...' he made a motion as if he was strangling himself.

'Huh?'

'Your tie.'

'Oh blimey.' I'd forgotten to do it up. 'Why didn't you tell me, Joe?'

Joe stared at me as if I'd spoken Swahili.

'Alsatians aren't pack dogs, are they?' Felix said. I passed him a beer.

'You were great on the horse, Felix,' I said. 'I guess you could ride before you could walk.'

'Johnny, let me tell you a secret,' Felix nodded at Joe to include him, 'I've hardly ever ridden a horse in my life. A few pony treks in Devon, that's it.'

'Come off it.'

'It's true.'

'But you were so at ease up on the nag. Totally in control.'

'Johnny, nothing is left to chance round here.' Anita was coming towards us. He put his head between me and Joe and whispered. 'The "nag" was sedated.'

'Jesus Christ,' Joe and I said, together, but only the first word from him.

'How's the cowboy?' Anita said. 'You were amazing.'

The bar had emptied. As had the big room next door. The audience had scarpered

If I was supposed to have been acting the part of an English gentleman, I'd hardly earned my fee.

Anita suggested we went to the staff canteen. There was plenty of leftover finger food she said.

The room was a mess. Sunflower seed shells and disposable chopsticks were scattered on the floor, sheets of newspaper covered the seats and tables and the air was sweet with the smell of Chinese cigarette smoke. I took off my tie. Andy, the catering guy, was sorting through the vast amount of leftover food. There were dozens of plates; mini pastrami sandwiches, sashimi salmon rolls, asparagus and bacon wraps, none of which had been touched.

Joe went to fetch cold Qingdao beers from his acolyte at the bar and we got stuck in. It was the first time I'd eaten pastrami in Shanghai. Andy was onto a sure thing with his catering service, once he found the people who'd eat his stuff. Anita said she was on a diet.

'You and your horse will go down in Shanghai legend Felix,' I said, in between mouthfuls. I was going to add something on the lines of a 'first time ever', to please him, but Joe spoke up while I was chewing salmon.

'Already has,' he said. 'I had a call from Bill Connor. Couldn't help telling him. It'll be front page news.'

'I think not.' Felix had unbuttoned his red jacket. The riding hat was on the seat beside him. 'I did ask Bill to cover this, but he told me he doesn't do property promotions, and to be honest, his expat-wife readership isn't our market either,' he paused, 'unless of course they divorce their bar-girl shagging husbands and get themselves a nice vice mayor.' That was an odd suggestion. Anita looked surprised. Felix was oblivious. He swigged his beer and carried on, 'I think my little show went rather well, I mean, I didn't fall off, did I? And isn't it the aim of marketing, to fix a product in the mind's eye of your potential customer?' He must have been doing his reading. 'I guess they'll remember today. They've got the photos too. God, it made my mouth ache, all that smiling.'

'It would've been good if the weather had been nicer,' I said.

'True,' he said. 'Real shame, isn't it.'

I had to ask. 'Felix, just a thought, but why did you go for the hunting, or rather the "horses", bit? Why not shooting or fishing,

I mean, we are beside a lake? Or why not do those too? I'm sure your man Zhou could get guns if he wanted.'

'Johnny, sitting on a drugged-out horse is easy. Can you imagine me putting on a display of marksmanship, hooking a fish out of a pond on the golf course, while those goons watched?'

'Yes, I can. Come on, Felix, it could have been brilliant, you with a shotgun under one arm and fishing rod in the other. You must be a dab hand at that stuff.'

'Johnny, I told you. Remember? I'm no officer and gentleman, no "gentleman Johnny". I'm your ordinary, middle class public schoolboy who came out here to get away from things in the UK and make a mark, if I possibly can.'

'Come off it Felix,' I heard myself say. 'You can't fool me. You're a black sheep, a dark horse.' I tried to think of a way to say how the darkness would stand out against the light, in a nice way, but buggered if I could.

# 8

## BATH TIME

Royal Buckingham Park was never built. No horses cantered across polo pitches, no gin palaces moored up for tea and cucumber sandwiches, no nouveau Chinese got to pretend he was an English gentleman living the 'HSF lifestyle'.

The acronym is the only bit of the project that lasts to this day. Respect to Felix.

The site is a riverside container port, crowded with trucks, cranes and portacabins. Couldn't be further removed from a fancy villa complex.

It wasn't the local government who put a stop to Zhou's plans. They were on side and would've been just as happy if he'd built it. The reason Royal Buckingham Park never happened is not so simple. I'll come to it.

But while it was on, it was on, and all systems go for Dr. Felix Fawcett-Smith, Director of Marketing. The next six months, from the end of 2000 into early 2001, was the peak of his China career and he lived it to the max.

I banged on about us being rent-a-crowd. Felix took it to the next level. He was rent-an-endorsement. His presence at your event implied you'd mastered the black art of the Sino-foreign commercial, cultural, social crossover. He opened doors. It took a while for him to realize the power he possessed, but Felix could have your China venture blessed by everyone from local government officials to the leaders of the international business community.

He got involved. And he was a foreigner backed by a vast state-supported corporation that went right to the top.

That trick to marketing he mentioned, about fixing the product in the customer's mind? By late 2000 SLIC and Royal Buckingham Park were super-glued to it. There wasn't a luxury brand, from watches to handbags to cars and booze, whose Shanghai launch wasn't co-sponsored by SLIC, with Royal Buckingham Park as the side-show's centrepiece. It was HSF all the way. Felix hooked up with the high-end British lot when they made their China market entry; cars, raincoats, whisky, whatever.

He got them coverage in the domestic media, which is not difficult when you do it the traditional way, by handing over packets of cash. The brands were pleased as punch when they saw the pictures lifted straight from their brochures and verbatim text from their handouts in the *Shanghai Daily*.

And in among those pictures was Felix; up on a podium, arm-in-arm with a pair of beauties, holding a bottle of whisky or a pair of patent leather shoes. The caption always included the words 'Royal Buckingham Park, HSF Lifestyle'.

In a self-perpetuating cycle he became the darling of the foreign journos trooping through Shanghai in search of the next big China cliché. They loved it that he was a foreigner who moved in elevated local circles. He introduced them to movers and shakers they could christen the 'new wave' of something or other that was 'going to change China'. The hacks churned out stories about how sophisticated, modern, sexy Shanghai was, and rounded up with the tried, tested and tired-out punchline the editors loved: 'Mao would be turning in his grave.'

Mao isn't in a grave.

Felix was called up by respected international broadsheets with 'Times' in their titles and asked for soundbites about China investment, China property and the economy. The BBC had him in their Shanghai studio talking down the line to Radio 4. Hong Kong TV shadowed him for a couple of days for a documentary.

A profile of him in an Italian newspaper was picked up by *Cankao Xiaoxi*, 'Reference News'. They translated it word for word from the Italian and pretended it was theirs. That impressed Zhou Jianguo. Party leaders read *Cankao Xiaoxi* every morning over their rice porridge and the article included a couple of sentences that described Zhou as forward-thinking.

How he fitted it in I have no idea, but Felix also found time to learn Chinese. He had a knack for languages. He said it surprised him as much as the rest of us. I was envious. My Chinese has always been basic and I never got the hang of tones. He picked them up as easily as you or I hummed a Robbie Williams tune.

His language teacher was James Li's secretary, Amy, whose defences he'd broken down thanks to the coffee-making.

That had been their first language exchange. Coffee for Chinese.

'Why does the coffee perk you later? Why can't it perk you now? What is "to perk?"'

It was a favourite joke of his. He claims she really said it.

Amy was a good teacher and Felix a good pupil.

He picked up the Shanghai dialect, not from Amy because she was an out-of-towner, but from hanging out with the SLIC drivers and other menials. He was that good.

One time around then we were having a boys' dinner: me, him, Joe and Bill Connor, in a smart new Hunan place, nothing like our hideaway dive, and the next table were talking about us. They were being sarky. We could tell from the looks, which were snide as you get, and how they switched to Shanghainese for the racist stuff. It happened all the time. I hate it but ignore it. I make an effort *not* to understand.

So, we were ignoring them until Felix twitched like someone had put a thousand volts through him. He stood up, stepped over and said something sharp in Shanghainese. I could tell it landed from the tone of his voice and because two of the men were pissed off. One put a hand up. He smiled and appeared to apologize, in Shanghainese again. Felix nodded. The men laughed.

'What were they saying?' I asked.

'Doesn't matter,' said Felix. 'They were only joking. Let's not worry about it.'

He hadn't blushed. No hand to the hair either. Cool as a cucumber. He'd picked up the inscrutability with the language, learning to act Chinese.

He wasn't going native, like some people do who make a song and dance, thrust it in your face, including in their own homes. Felix only laid it on when it suited, and in Chinese company, in his Chinese world. Like when Li and Zhou paraded him in front of their government mates.

'See how we have tamed and taught him,' they said, although they were polite because they knew Felix's language level.

The mates weren't so subtle or sensitive. For them it was natural to ask Zhou or Li, in front of Felix, 'So where did you find this *laowai*? How much does he cost? Can he use chopsticks?'

Felix accepted their business cards with two hands, admired the characters of their names and read them out. The trick is to give the impression you appreciate the layers of meaning and poetry to them even if you haven't got a clue. He did the gentle elbow grab with the handshake to propel the most important guest towards the seat at the 'top' of the round table. He forced cigarettes on men – never ladies – even if they didn't smoke and accepted them in return when he already had one lit, did the finger tap on the table when tea gets poured. He smiled as they complimented him on how he used chopsticks and tried to get him drunk with toasts of fifty per cent *baijiu*.

An hour or so later he'd be smiling as the guests staggered from the room for a tactical vomit in the bogs. Felix was good at the drinking.

Thanks to that public schoolboy confidence and charm, the innocence that seemed innate and eternal, he could pull off the act like he was only trying to please. And Zhou was very pleased.

Note I say 'seemed' innocent.

Around this time Felix also started doing what any half-decently paid Chinese executive or official does to unwind.

Prostitution is in your face in Shanghai, from fifty-buck back-street hand-job shops to the high-class hookers hunting business-men in international hotel bars. Then there are the karaoke clubs that go from dumpy peasants in triple layers of laddered tights to debutantes in ball gowns and tiaras. There are streetwalkers and student semi-pros.

Check into a mid-range hotel room in Shanghai – any city matter of fact – and on the bedside table you'll find condoms, disposable panties, and a flyer with the phone number for 'massage service'. Don't worry, they call you. Stay in an international branded hotel and you might not find the sex aids and panties in the mini-bar but the phone will still ring.

But the place for pure pleasure, a good massage and anything from excruciating titillation to all manner of deviant perversion, is the bath house, advertised as 'sauna and massage'.

It took me a while to work out what was what. The 'full service', also known as a 'whole dragon' i.e. from head to tail, is pretty obvi-ous, not so the 'extra hour' which you were asked if you wanted before you'd started, or the 'the double' which could mean double time or two girls. Some places use medical terms, like 'prostate treatment'. You can guess where her tongue goes.

Some of the bath houses are straight, as in nothing kinky. They're few and far between and you never know when the girl might take a shine to you, or you say the wrong thing – or the right thing, depending – and her hand has slipped past the waistband of your pyjama trousers and she's giving you a 'happy ending'.

There was a place not far from my flat that was clean and tidy, the sauna always ready, where the girls gave a good massage and offered a few extras. No dragons, just enough to make a man happy for a few moments of pleasant agony. Nice girls too. I got to know a couple: a young single mum and a student putting herself through college. I like to think I helped them out. I also never saw foreigners there, which added to its appeal.

Felix opened my eyes to a whole new class of Shanghai bath house.

One night after a boozy dinner and drinks at a party, he took me, Mike Bennett and Joe to his regular one. It was the first time I went in a group. I preferred my lonesome. I don't believe in sharing or shouting about those experiences.

Until now that is.

It was obvious the place was part of the SLIC empire. The guy on the desk called him Shi *Laoban*, his name suffixed by 'Boss'. The reception was glitzy but not over the top, almost cosy. The changing rooms were well set up, roomy but not stupid big, and the young men who opened locker doors and handed us towels were quiet and courteous.

We stripped naked and put on plastic slippers.

'Jesus Christ,' Joe said as we walked into the showers. He was staring at Mike's crotch. 'What happened to the rest of the mule?'

I consider it bad form to examine a mate's meat and veg, but accidentally-on-purpose my gaze swept up and down Mike. Joe was right to wonder. Mike's cock was massive. Pendulous. Porn star. I won't go into detail. I only glanced.

'OK. So I have a big dick,' he said. 'I got used to it. You'll get used to it.'

'I fucking hope not,' I said.

'I fuck most things, Johnny, but I like them to have flesh on them. Don't worry your ass,' he grinned.

The rest of Mike was impressive too. His chest was hard as rock and the line below it, across his mid-rift, was like it was painted on by a marker pen. His shoulders were rounded like the brown gourds you see in the Shanghai wet markets. He was a classic beefed-up American.

Felix was as chubby in the flesh as he was in his clothes, pale but not too flabby. He had youth on his side. Joe was well-proportioned but pint-sized, and me, well, Mike gave you the idea. Mum always got flak for underfeeding me.

So there we were, four naked white guys of mixed shapes and sizes, sitting on tiny white towels on a wooden bench in a large sauna with a picture window. A young Chinese guy with tattoos was watching a TV that was behind another glass window at one end. Long-haired men and women in fancy silk robes were flying through the tops of bamboo forests, skipping over water and slashing at each other with poles and swords. The volume was off but the regular sharp slapping a masseur was giving one of tattoo guy's mates outside on a massage table made a good soundtrack.

'I had a meeting here,' Felix said, his eyes on the screen, 'with associates of Mr. Zhou's. From out of town. Military. One spoke perfect English and kept staring at my crotch while he was talking to me. Christ. Turned into quite a night.' He smiled. 'It's good. You'll see.'

'Hot chicks?' Joe asked, to the point.

'From the north,' Felix said. 'Tall and beautiful.'

We went out to the warm pool. The TV-watching tattoo guy and his friends had gone upstairs, apart from the one having the massage. He was lying face down on a table in the corner while an old man scraped his back with a pair of loofah mittens. When I walked past I noticed the sweat running down the creases in the flabby muscles on the old man's arms.

Except for Mike we ordered cold beers and stuck cigarettes in our wet lips. Steam rose from the water. We lay back and blew smoke through it. The heat pumped the alcohol through my bloodstream. We'd been drinking all evening. When I went to my local place I'd always be sober.

I was in the habit of using the cell-like solitude in the sauna to go over my problems. There was always something to think about. Recently it had been Gran again. She'd been in hospital for a hip she broke when she took a tumble, and when she'd come out she hadn't got back to her old self. Mum said she was letting things slip. Not like her to do that. I wouldn't be home for Christmas to see her. That's the kind of thing I sweated.

It made a nice change to be in a sauna with mates, talking bollocks.

'You know how people say stuff about China and the Chinese,' Felix was saying in a lazy voice, his face tilted up at the wet blue ceiling. It had clouds painted on it. 'How they're corrupt, no one builds for the future because the Party might nick it. How their family life is fucked up, everyone's out for what he can get, massive waste, and on and on?' He waved his bottle of beer. 'Yet when you think about it, they do have some things right, don't they? I mean, look at this. Where else in the world is it so easy, and so cheap, to take a nice hot soak and have a beautiful girl minister to your every physical desire?

'Immediate self-gratification, soon as you have the wherewithal. Get drunk as a lord. Smoke like a trooper. Live it up. Who gives a damn? It's all in the here and now.' He stubbed out his cigarette in an ashtray by his head and patted his stomach where it broke the surface of the water. Droplets flew out from under his palm. His hair was plastered across his forehead like a bad comb over. 'I tell you,' he said. 'I could get used to it.'

Mike was silent, staring into space, sipping his Diet Coke. Joe was grinning.

'Sounds like you've got it worked out, Felix,' I said. 'Remember though, everything has its price.'

'Yes, but when it's paid in advance, when you've made your money; you spend it.'

'Felix, I don't want to sound like a killjoy, but you can have too much of a good thing. Like drugs. Everything in moderation, as my dad says, makes it all the more pleasurable, keeps you happy ever after.'

'Kept him a bus driver too, didn't it.'

That was below the belt. I sat up and water splashed over Mike. Felix was sheepish. 'Sorry. Slipped out.'

'I should hope so.'

'Your dad drives buses?' Joe asked. 'Mine drives trucks. Nice. Anyone want a joint by the way? I've got one in my jeans.'

Joe pulled himself out of the pool, put on a pair of plastic slippers and flapped across the tiles to the changing room. I lay back, my head on a wet towel.

'Thinking long term, Felix,' I said, staring at the ceiling, 'and more modest gratification – how's it going with Anita?'

I'd lost interest in what went on between them. I asked the question out of mild spite, a desire to get him back for the bus driver jibe. You don't mention girlfriends in those places. No matter how immoral or debauched you are. Everyone feels the guilt, if only a twinge, and doesn't like to be reminded.

'She's a nice girl all right. Nice body too.' The question hadn't made him uncomfortable in the slightest. I might have been misinformed. Not everyone gets the guilt.

I'm also wrong to say I'd lost interest in Anita.

I caught a whiff of wacky baccy. Joe had lit up his joint and was sitting at the table where the Chinese had been smoking.

'You know what?' Felix said. 'Anita is not as randy as she seems to be, or behaves. Plays hard to get too. Bloody hell does she put me through hoops. Drinks and dinners, taxis back to her place, me begging to come up for a coffee, promising I won't overstay my welcome, conniving my way into bed 'just to sleep'. She's a tough one. But she's a sweet person. Wants me to meet her parents.'

I realised with that certainty you get when you're drunk that Felix hadn't slept with Anita, in the biblical sense. I put my hand behind my head and propped it up. His expression betrayed no trace of the implied lie. He was red in the face with the beer and heat.

'Hence,' he carried on, raising an eyebrow at me, 'I've become rather fond of this place. So much simpler.' He put on the voice of a ringmaster in a circus. 'Step right up and come inside gentlemen! Let your prick take its pick!'

'Felix,' I wanted to antagonise him for that dig about my dad. 'Don't tell me you get free run of this place on your "company account".'

'I pay sometimes.' He made it sound like a genuine sadness.

'There's plenty of girls out there. No need to become a habitual whoremonger. This is Shanghai in the noughties. If you're not serious about Anita...'

'I *am* serious about Anita.' He said it fast, with a touch of resentment. 'She did me a massive favour. If it wasn't for her I wouldn't be working at SLIC, living this life. I owe her big time.'

So dating her, or trying to, was returning a favour?

'What's the plan?' I asked. 'You going to marry her so she gets a British passport, consider you've returned the favour, then drop her? Jesus mate. You don't have to do that.'

'Johnny,' he sat forward. 'While I will always appreciate you sharing your knowledge with a new boy like I was, when it comes to my personal life I'll do things my way, thanks. And if Anita wants to be my virgin bride one day once I've finished fucking about, that's her business too. We clear on that?'

'What's clear is that you're being a bit of a cunt, Felix. No offence.'

I'd sat forward too. We were facing each other across a few feet of water. A glint appeared in his eye, sharp and brutal. He held my gaze, swigged his beer and put it down behind him.

I hadn't meant offence. It was like him making that jab about my dad. Like he said himself, it just slipped out.

But Felix didn't see it that way. And I didn't correct myself like he had.

'You're jealous aren't you, Johnny?' he said. 'You wanted Anita and I turned up and she fell for me. You're not trying to protect her as a friend, you're plain jealous, a jealous cunt, that I get to snog her and...'

And I launched myself.

An honest man admits the only time he gets truly angry is when he's angry with himself. Righteous anger, real deep, swells up like a tsunami. And I was angry with myself about Anita. Felix had reminded me. Then there was the joke about my dad, and under that the shame about my gran. The heat, the alcohol, him getting cocky. It was too much.

In that split second, as I threw myself at his lardy naked body, I realised I had no idea what I was going to do once I made contact. I couldn't punch him. That'd be too severe. And I couldn't wrestle him, not naked. I decided to grab him by the back of the neck, give him a sharp bollocking and duck him.

I reached out and grabbed hard, dug my bony fingers into the hollow of flesh above his collar bone and shouted, inches from his face, 'No, *you're* the jealous cunt.'

Bollocking complete. Now for the next bit.

I moved my hands up his neck and Felix stared at me in confusion. His arms were flailing, stretching downwards for the tiled floor of the pool. It was thigh deep. His eyes darted past my right ear and I felt a rubber truncheon slap my buttocks. Strong hands pulled me backwards. I fell onto Mike. They were his hands of course. Maybe he tripped me. He went down too. I slid off him, my head went under, and I put my hand out to push myself up. It landed on the truncheon, which was, of course, his monster cock.

'Fucking hell, Mike!' I shouted as I came up.

He laughed.

'Keep that fucking thing away from me!' I threw myself to the other side of the pool. I turned and sat in the water and looked at Felix. I wanted to laugh with Mike who was cracking up at my reaction, but not yet. Felix and I had to decide whether we'd been play fighting or real fighting.

I'd been angry, no question, and I'd wanted a serious fight, or at least serious words with the arrogant stuck-up prick, but the fury subsided as fast as it had come on. The shock of grabbing a man by his penis had knocked it out of me. Deep in my brain an argument was raging: 'Am I gay? Is this what it takes? What did it feel like, touching a man's cock? Did you like it? Shit. Stop thinking like that.' It distracted me from my anger at Felix, or myself.

Felix was coming out of fight or flight mode too. His face had gone pale and he was watching me.

Joe giggled. He was standing above us with a tiny towel in front of his crotch. 'Here Felix, take a drag of this. Then kiss and make up.' He giggled again.

Felix put his hand up for the joint and took a toke. He didn't pass it to me or Mike but gave it straight back to Joe. He knew Mike and I didn't smoke weed.

Mike propped himself against the side of the pool, his bum on the side, cock dangling in the water like a sea slug. He was watching me and Felix, who seemed to be waiting. I stuck my hand out. He took it. We shook and I pulled him to his feet. Christ he was heavy.

'Cunt.'

'Jealous cunt.'

'Sorry.'

'Sorry.'

We sloshed out of the pool and went over to a cubby hole where pyjama shorts and tops were stacked on wooden shelves. A young man handed us towels and asked us to turn around. We dried our fronts, he did our backs. He caught sight of Mike's cock and stopped and stared. Mike ignored him.

The boy ushered us to the door, bumped into the doorpost because he was suffering from his recent experience of American 'shock and awe' (it was the time of the second Gulf War) and shouted up the stairs. 'Four honoured guests coming up!' As we climbed the stairs I heard him say under his breath the equivalent of 'Holy shit'.

A woman in a sensible white blouse and black skirt greeted us at the top of the stairs. She was deferential to Felix, who asked a quick question that I caught.

'Number 15?'

The woman nodded and he tried to distract us, 'The *mama-san* will set things up. Let's take a suite. I'm sure there's one available.' He spoke to the *mama-san* who called a boy over and had us taken up another flight of stairs.

We tried to give the impression we knew what we were doing, but not too well, not like regular brothel creepers. That we said nothing said it all.

Felix spoiled the restraint by asking Mike, who he assumed, as I did, was the innocent among us. 'Been to one of these places before Mike?'

'Kind of.' He gave me that sly smile and slapped me on the back. I bounced off the wall.

The suite had a sitting room with sofas, flat screen TV, and an automatic shuffle mahjong table in the corner. I wandered into the bedroom: floor to ceiling mirror across from the bed, another on the ceiling, pole in the corner of the room, exercise ball up by the mirror, TV, nice curtains, clean carpet, no stale smoke. Classy.

Felix told us to sit down. A waiter brought in a bottle of Bourbon, a bowl of ice cubes and four glasses. He knelt to pour. Mike asked for Coke. There was a soft knock at the door. Joe shouted to come in. *Mama-san* stepped inside, said a few words of encouragement and the girls filed in and stood up along the wall.

They were gorgeous, each one a stunner, wearing patterned silk *qipaos* slit to the waist. Every dress was slightly different in colour and cut. Some had low fronts, others high collars. The girls' legs, what we could see of them from the side, were like thin slices of pale, sweet peaches. Their faces were similar: high noses, eggshell delicate pointy chins, dark hair of course, done up in buns. I'd say the uniformity was deliberate, either to meet the ideal of the boss-man or *madame* or else a clever way to ensure no girl became a favourite and was taken away to become a mistress.

They were confident too, looked us in the eye, one by one.

It was heaven enough to admire the line-up. Anticipation is always the best bit and this was unbearable. Not only would making a decision mean the evening's delights were about to begin, which means they would also have to end, but making a decision to choose one of the beauties meant I couldn't have the other seven.

'You may choose two if you like,' the *mama-san* said, looking at me.

Mike gave us that sly grin and chose two. He for one knew what he was doing, the cheeky bastard. Felix turned to us on the sofa and said, 'In for a penny…' With number 15 that meant three.

'All right,' I said.

If one day you pass a sad old man on a wet night, huddled under a Basildon bus stop, when all around him is cold wet misery yet on his face there's a beautiful sunshine smile? That'll be me thinking back to that night. No way am I sharing it.

# 9

# HIGH LIFE

A FTER our set-to in the sauna Felix and I went through a cooling off period. I didn't see him for a long while. Joe told me he wore a polo neck to hide the marks from my knuckles. Good thing it was autumn.

I was sorry we'd had a fight. I wanted to apologize and to hear him say something clever and posh, brush it off as a 'minor *contretemps*' and me admit I'd overstepped the mark. I wanted to joke over a beer in the Backstreet. I wanted him to tell me he hadn't slept with Anita.

It didn't help that after our scrap I'd enjoyed the attention of two of the most gorgeous hookers – true courtesans – I had the pleasure of being molested by and Felix picked up the tab. He won the moral high ground there. I wanted to pay him back. Not with hookers. Invite him to dinner, drinks, whatever, so it didn't seem like I was a sponger, put us back on the level.

That's what it amounted to: to be back on the level. Going with Felix to that place had put us there. A low level, but what does that matter? To get naked with a bloke breaks the barriers, doesn't it? I mean, in those public schools the showers are open and they share baths when they're little. That's how they build the camaraderie, the sense of belonging. I've heard stories about how they sit round biscuits and jerk each other off too but I'm sure that's exaggerated. It was different, if still sexual, to go shag a hooker in the next-door bedroom. That could have been a good bonding session.

Normally after a fight you become better mates, but it has to be quick. Me and Felix should have gone and got smashed and laughed it off. But he had to get back to Pudong. We missed the chance. The resentment festered, mine for what he said about my dad and Anita, his for me telling him what he should do with himself and Anita.

He had a point. What right did I have? I've mentioned the freedom, the lack of supervision in Shanghai. Why should I care or feel entitled to put Felix on the spot? I wouldn't take it from anyone – well, maybe Charlie Thurrold but he's an exception – so why should Felix from me? I've said how he was charging ahead, way faster and deeper into China business than me and Joe for example. He was the leader now.

Felix was busy with Royal Buckingham Park too. His social life took off. Now that Zhou had shown off his pet foreigner to his high and mighty buddies, Felix was passed down to their sons and daughters to play with, young kids who drive sports cars with tinted windows and number plates of eights and run companies that trade *guanxi*.

Benny Wu was a perfect example. His family were old school. His grandfather had been a provincial propaganda chief for Mao, back in the day, and his dad was a famous sculptor and chairman of various official art institutions. His studio produced nearly every piece of public sculpture in Shanghai.

Where the Wu family made its serious money was the culture business. No Shanghai exhibition or art event went ahead without Wu senior's approval, which cost money.

The money and his family connections set young Benny up with a high tech software business. He was no rocket scientist but he employed smart people and like all those tech companies, he was always round the corner from getting listed on some stock exchange or other. The company eventually made it onto the Hong Kong one. Benny trousered another Wu fortune and went to live in California.

When Felix met Benny he'd recently got back from Harvard or Yale and spoke perfect American English. He drove a Porsche, lived in a villa like Zhou's but with modern retro style, and never missed a party. He was always well-groomed, dressed smartly but not in the flashy top international brands. His hair was brushed, hands manicured, and while he liked a drink he never overdid it. He had an open, welcoming face that made you like him the moment you met him. His features were almost Western, like a mixed-blood Chinese, although he wasn't; square jaw, straight and larger than average nose, bushy eyebrows and clear round brown eyes. He could have been an actor, or a pop star if he hadn't been so rich to start with.

Benny introduced Felix to KTV and nightclubs and parties in the presidential suites of top international hotels. His gang treated Felix as a mascot. They liked the way he acted Chinese; the drinking games, speaking Chinese and Shanghainese dialect. His language got even better. They used him as a sounding board for their business ideas, assumed he understood stock markets, venture capital and share options. Felix dodged the questions and helped them choose wines and cigars, listened to them talk about cars, and discussed the pros and cons of property markets in the UK, US and Australia.

There were pretty girls. Some had privileged backgrounds, others were hangers-on. Felix said he could never work out if any were in a relationship. Everyone called each other brother or sister or 'little cousin'. Or 'little secretary', which means short-term, well-rewarded girlfriend. He made a pass at one of those by mistake and was surprised when the 'boyfriend' didn't get upset. He'd suggested Felix wait for a week or so and she'd be all his, but Felix should be aware that her apartment rental was a couple of thousand a month, US.

Anita didn't mix with those people. She wasn't rich, she wasn't beautiful in the right way, and her parents weren't powerful. I think she was happy to stay away. She made excuses and Felix stopped asking her to come along.

From the day I met him, and he met her, Felix had been consistent in his pursuit of Anita. In his world you weren't allowed to make a pass at a girl and not see it through, especially if it was made in public. And I think there was a genuine chivalry to him. To give up would be admitting he'd been making fun of Anita, trying out chat-up lines, as if he had been hoping to take her home. Proper young gentlemen don't do one-night stands. And Anita was worth waiting for. Felix knew, not just from me, how special she was. That would have set off his competitive streak, the will to win he picked up on the playing fields of Waterloo or wherever it was.

Yet all the time he was playing the gentleman suitor, whenever he had the urge, off he went to that bath house. South Seas it was called, I remember. He had a point about how practical it was. It was counter-intuitive fidelity. So long as he didn't get into an actual relationship he could claim he was waiting for Anita, and the physical stuff didn't matter.

It was another example of how he was going native, the amoral hypocrisy. If you don't get caught, it isn't a crime. Likewise the separate lives. He had at least three on the go: one with Benny and his gang, a quieter one with Anita, and one with us in the Backstreet. Maybe there was another I didn't know about.

There was actually. Benny Wu told me when he caught me and Thurrold getting Felix's stuff from his villa, the night before we got him out of jail.

It began in a KTV club on a night out with Benny and co. I'm going to tell it like a real story. I know those places and how these things happen, and I knew Felix by then too. I'd witnessed his 'Stairway to Heaven' act. So that description is spot on.

Her name was Maggie Yu and she was a live one, barely out of her teens. Her dad was a general in the People's Liberation Army. He ran a cigarette smuggling operation for Shanghai and the surrounding provinces. He must have been very senior and a sharp operator to get himself that 'command'. There was massive money in it.

When Maggie was born in 1982 her dad had been a proper soldier. He gave her the name because of Margaret Thatcher. He had been impressed by the way the British Prime Minister handled the Falklands War. It's unusual for Chinese parents to give children their English names. Normally the children choose them for themselves, later in life. Maggie's Chinese name was Yu Liming. Like her general father, she liked to be obeyed. I wouldn't be surprised if her dad had her scream orders at his troops for fun, or practice. And I bet he made them salute her.

First time Felix met Maggie was her twentieth birthday. Benny told him to keep the evening free but didn't call till Felix had eaten his dinner in front of a couple of VCDs. It was eleven o'clock.

'We're at the Golden Phoenix KTV, waiting for you.' He made it sound like they couldn't start without him.

Felix put on his party blazer and headed out the door. The club was in Pudong so he didn't have the hassle of crossing the river.

He was at the Golden Phoenix by half past. He found the party in a large suite.

The birthday girl screamed with delight when Felix was shown in, like he was a surprise present. She made him sit beside her.

They were drinking straight Absolut, Chivas Regal mixed with green tea and bottles of Budweiser. Maggie made Felix down a large whisky and green tea for a party fine and when he picked up a Budweiser to wash away the strange taste she made him down that in one too.

There were approximately twenty people. Felix recognised half of them. Friends came and cheers'd him and, as he knew would happen, they told a waitress to interrupt the songs programmed into the karaoke machine. A girl sitting on a puff stool in the middle of the room, cooing a love song at no-one, gave up the microphone. Maggie complained when they took Felix from beside her. She didn't know what was coming.

Felix downed another whisky and green tea and picked up a microphone. He flicked the cable to one side so he wouldn't step on it, pushed his hair back, and stood in front of Maggie. She had the place of honour in the centre of the sofa.

Everyone sat back to enjoy the show.

The intro to 'Stairway to Heaven' began. Felix swayed on his feet, looked up at the ceiling for inspiration. He started to sing, softly, like the original. He can hold a tune and has a good voice. He can even twist it into a good impression of Jimmy Page. He went from one girl to another and looked her in the eye, if she was paying attention, every time the word 'she' came up. Maggie fidgeted as she waited. She was skipped once but she got a 'dear lady'. She clapped her hands and squealed. One of the boys who was half paying attention sang along with the 'makes me wonder', except he said 'wander'. No one noticed how Felix changed 'I look to the west' to 'east'.

Behind him a green dot bounced along the words at the base of the wall-mounted screen. The backing video was a collage of sweeping shots of a boating lake with lilies and pagodas. Girls with sun umbrellas sat back while young men in short-sleeved shirts smiled and rowed.

Since he'd started doing the song as a regular party piece Felix had learnt the words, almost. There were a couple of places he was unsure. He snatched glances at the screen by tucking his head down and pushing his hair back with his free hand, made it seem a deliberate move. His voice didn't falter. He was good. Someone shouted 'Yeah,' as the drums came in. The people playing a drinking game stopped to listen. Felix had captured his audience. He had the gift.

At the line, 'your stairway lies on the whispering wind,' he handed the mike to a friend who knew the routine, pretended to pick up a guitar – nice touch – and hung it from his neck. He pumped his forearm and flicked his wrist for the famous chords that kick off the solo. The volume went up. Whoever had the remote control was onto it. One of the guys started head-banging. Felix's fringe fell over his face.

For the guitar solo he went mad but not stupid mad. He squeezed his eyes tight shut, his left hand shot up and down the invisible neck of the guitar and he held his right hand close to his round tummy and strummed like he was taking incredible care to get it just right.

His head rocked from side to side. Drops of sweat broke out on his forehead. He signalled the guy with the microphone to move closer.

'And as we wind on down the road!' he screamed, bent double to get his mouth to the mike, strumming. The whole room stared at him, impossible to tell if in wonder, delight or horror. 'There walks a lady we all know!' He threw away his guitar – he really did, pretended to throw it away that is, another a nice touch – grabbed the mike and dropped to his knees. He screwed his face into rock star agony and belted out the last lines of the song. His blazer became a leather jacket, the shirt his bare chest. He clenched his fist against it. With the final 'roll' he swayed on his knees, as if he would roll away, which would suit his stocky little ball-like figure but if you were into his act you never thought that at the time, got to his feet and gave it the ultimate, long drawn out 'heaven', straight into Maggie's eyes.

She loved it.

Before his audience could decide how to react, a cheesy Cantopop love song started. The girl who wanted to sing it stepped up to Felix, said a polite 'Thank you,' and took the mike from him. She sat down on the puff stool and waited for the bouncing ball. Felix was panting. Benny stepped over and clapped him on the back. Half the boys and one or two girls showed appreciation, although that might have been because he knew the words rather than for his performance, which, like I say, was brilliant.

I've seen him do it a few times. For eight minutes a short, chubby, balding posh git becomes a rock god. I wish I had a party trick like that and the nerve to pull it off.

Of course, the girl who appreciated it most was Maggie. It must have been the final 'buying a stairway to heaven', the way Felix focused on her, that gave her ideas.

She slipped out the room without drawing attention to herself, like she was going to the toilet. Two minutes later, when she came back, she sidled up to Felix, put her arm through his and whispered, 'Come sing. For me.'

She led him out in plain view. No one said a thing but a few eyes followed them, including Benny's.

Maggie led Felix along a dark corridor with mirrors on the walls. The doors to the rooms had round windows. Through them Felix glimpsed young people out for good clean sing-along fun, or middle-aged men flanked by pretty girls in sensible but sexy dresses squashing their tight bodies up against them, pretending there wasn't enough room on the sofa. It's 'the three accompaniments', *san pei*. They sing, they drink, and you can guess number three.

Fresh-faced boy waiters in gold waistcoats and silver bow ties passed by with trays of bottles and glasses and fruit platters which they handed to pretty waitresses waiting outside the doors. Felix couldn't resist slowing his pace as he passed an open one. The room was empty and looked as if a proverbial bomb had hit it: bottles on the floor and the sofas, ice buckets of upturned bottles on the table, watermelon skin scattered like confetti. A small denim jacket was scrunched up on the floor.

It's the noise in those places that hits you hardest. The narrow corridors channel it, churn it into a cacophony. You hear grown men wailing out of tune like babies into microphones set to maximum echo. They howl, they plead and promise their everlasting love and their friends and pretty companions for the evening applaud, laugh and scream encouragement. Then you turn a corner and catch a voice as sweet as an angel's, one of the KTV girls or a young woman with a sing-along fun lot, who can hit the high notes and gives you butterflies, but only for a fleeting moment until the door shuts and you're blasted by another howl of anguish.

Maggie turned down a corridor and walked to the door at the very end. It was number 13. Lucky for some. A boy waiter opened it.

Number 13 was small. There was a sofa that could sit four people. A bottle of brandy and a bucket of ice were on the glass table. Maggie had the boy pour for them because she didn't want to wait for the waitress. The boy knelt at their feet. The KTV machine had been programmed, started and paused. The boy pressed a button and the video began. Japanese girls with big breasts in small bikinis were throwing a ball on a sunny beach. The music was a Taiwanese love song Felix recognised.

Maggie was taller than Felix and looked and acted like a tomboy although her figure had enough curves in the right places. Her hair was cut short, she had a button nose, and her beady eyes were set wide above her freckled cheeks, unusual for a Chinese girl. She was in low-cut, skin-tight jeans and a high-cropped collarless T-shirt that rode up front and back, showing off her tight tummy.

She dismissed the waiter. 'Drink,' she said to Felix.

Felix tried to keep his eyes off the screen. The Japanese girls had slipped into white dresses for a tropical downpour.

'Happy birthday,' he said, and clinked her glass.

'Thank you.' Maggie took a large sip and the glass touched the bridge of her small nose. She smacked her lips. 'You like Shanghai?'

'Yes,' he said.

'You have a girlfriend?'

'Er, yes. You could say. In a way.'

Maggie was silent. Her small round eyes became flat black arrow slits. 'You want another one?'

Felix looked at his half empty glass. 'OK.' He held it out.

Maggie reached for the bottle. She sighed as she poured. They toasted each other. There was a long silence. Finally she said: 'I meant another girlfriend.' She gave him a smile meant to be coquettish. It came over stiff and formal.

Felix coughed, ran his hand through his hair, and smiled back. 'I'm not sure I could cope. I'm very busy.' He tried to sound apologetic. He also tried not to look at Maggie's tummy. 'With work.'

'I can help that you are not so busy,' she said. 'Mr. Zhou is my father's brother.' She used the respectful 'boss' suffix, and the term 'brother' for that generation means much more than the casual one Benny's friends used.

Felix was used to his new friends' attempts to impress him by telling him how well they or their dads and uncles, and mothers and so on, knew his boss and how much they knew about his job, what he was doing at Royal Buckingham Park. To begin with it had annoyed him but they were only showing off.

For fun he'd tried to play the trick back on Benny with gossip about Benny's dad he'd picked up from James Li. Benny had given him a hard stare, like he was putting the evil eye on him, ignored the question and later, when Felix thought the *faux pas* had been forgotten, made Felix pay for dinner.

Maggie put her hand on Felix's knee. She held her glass of brandy against her cheek and leaned towards him. Her eyes were round and open again. They stared into his, without blinking. Felix didn't move. He thought she was going to kiss him.

She gave a start like she'd just remembered something. She slid her hand into her tight pocket and pulled out a strip of chewing gum, unwrapped it, and handed it over. 'Eat this.'

Her mobile rang. It was on the table. She ignored it.

Felix did as he was told. He put the gum in his mouth, moistened it and chewed. Maggie waited, picked up her mobile which had stopped, either to see who had called or check the time, how long Felix had been chewing. She put the phone down and picked up a large glass ashtray. She held it under Felix's mouth, 'Enough.'

Felix spat the gum out and she kissed him on the lips, holding the ashtray in her hand at arm's length like she could hit him over the head with it if he went too far. Her arm weakened and it dropped to the table with a glass-on-glass bang that startled him, made him back off. She leaned over to him across the sofa, pushed at him with her hard body. Her tongue was sharp. It stabbed and probed, invaded his mouth. (Yes, I appreciate this is stretching my imagination.)

Maggie sat back. She put a finger in her mouth, as if to make up for his tongue not making it. Her phone rang and she ignored it. Felix swept his eyes over her bare tummy, felt the stirrings, reached for his brandy, drained it in a long slug. On the KTV screen a girl in a see-through dress was riding a bicycle through paddy fields. The song sounded the same as the previous one.

'My first foreigner,' Maggie said.

'My pleasure.' Felix reached for his cigarettes.

'Not smelly as I expected.' Felix paused in lighting his cigarette, thought for a moment, and carried on. He took a deep drag.

'So, do you want to be my boyfriend?'

'Maggie, I told you, I have a girlfriend.'

'But you can be my boyfriend when you're not with her. She won't mind.'

'Don't you have a boyfriend?' Felix asked back.

'No.' She paused. 'My father wants me to marry a rich American Chinese so he can retire to America. Or Canada.'

'But he's a general. Would he be allowed to?' Felix had been briefed about Maggie by Benny. That was another thing those types loved to talk about: powerful parents.

'My father is a businessman. He does business with America and Canada too. He has taken me on trips. He also does property business with Zhou *Laoban*.' She paused. 'You know about Zhou *Laoban*'s father?'

Felix nodded.

'Well, if it hadn't been for my grandfather, they would never have made him a martyr, after what he did. That took a lot of trouble.' Maggie's voice was dead serious, conspiratorial.

Felix guessed there were a few hoops a dead person had to get through before he was designated a Revolutionary Martyr. 'Really?'

'Quite.' She assumed he knew the full story. 'So you could say that without my family, which means me, you wouldn't have your job and nice life so, in a way, you owe me a favour.' This was a new angle on the 'we know what you're doing' conversation. 'You know what that means?' Maggie tried the coquettish smile, and this time it came over more relaxed, enticing. 'You have to do what I say...' She leaned towards him, eyes greedy, mouth open.

Felix expected Maggie to shove her hand down his trousers, or up his shirt. He checked to see if the door was locked. There was no way of telling. On the spur of the moment, he decided he would be happy to be Maggie's boyfriend for a few hours. No harm surely? She was attractive; young, fresh, and a virgin, at least with a foreigner. The brandy, on top of the earlier mix, was having an effect. Then there was that broad belt of drum-tight flesh he'd been trying not to stare at. Maggie bent forward to put her glass on the table. Felix couldn't resist a hungry glance down her back at the top of her G-string where it appeared out of her jeans, framing the peachy tight tops of her buttocks. He put out his hand, touched her lower back, careful not to go too low, and ran a finger up and down her spine.

She sat up, hitting his chin with the back of her head, and whispered, 'Not here. You take me home.'

The door swung open. Felix snatched his hand away and sat up. He expected the waiter but it was Benny Wu. His hand went straight to his fringe. Benny ignored him. 'Xiao Yu. Come. Now.'

Maggie said something under her breath in Shanghainese and to Felix, in Mandarin, 'Let's go.'

Felix thought she meant together, to wherever he was going to jump into bed with her.

Benny frogmarched Maggie, ahead of Felix, back to the party room. He opened the door and shoved her through it. There was a roar of welcome. He motioned to Felix to stay outside. He shut the door and took Felix by the elbow towards a service counter by the lifts. A 'three accompaniments' girl was asking the *mama-san* which room she should go to. When she saw Benny and Felix coming towards her, the *mama-san* told her to wait. She asked Benny if he needed anything, tilting her head at the girl as she did so. He ignored her and took Felix to stand over to one side.

'Xiao Yu is not very well, not all there, in the head.' Benny spoke with an American accent but British vocab. 'She gets into trouble, and her father has to take her away for a while.' Benny put his arm round Felix and pulled him towards him. Their foreheads were touching. 'So don't listen to her, okay? Her father might blame you.' Felix couldn't tell if Benny was warning or threatening him. 'And you wouldn't like that.'

I made Benny Wu sound like a spoilt brat when I introduced him. To be fair he was a well-rounded guy. He'd been to the best schools in China before he went to university in the States, and thanks to his father's culture business he came into contact with free-thinking people from China and abroad. He had an open mind, could talk to you about China and its problems without getting upset.

'Don't worry, Benny,' Felix said. 'You saved me from a tricky situation.' He sort of meant it. Benny smiled. Felix added, to set the seal on it, 'I must say, she'll be a catch, young Maggie.' He spotted Benny's cheeks tightening. 'I mean, one day.'

Benny squeezed the back of Felix's neck with his hand. His grip was firm.

'Don't think about it.'

Felix assumed he meant 'don't mention it'. He was wrong. But Benny smiled with so much warmth Felix can be forgiven for the mistake.

'Let's go back and have a drink,' Benny said. 'You owe me a party fine.'

Felix didn't talk to Maggie again that night. I said at the beginning, before I set off on my little fantasy description – and events bear me out, I promise – that I was going to tell you about Felix's other life, or one that I knew about. It was with Maggie Yu, and he kept it well hidden. After that first meeting and flirtation they became proper secret lovers. None of this came out till the very end, so I won't go into it ahead of time, but I do wonder what was in it for him, apart from the sex. Maybe that's all. He certainly gave Maggie what she wanted.

# 10

## FAVOURS

AT the end of Chinese New Year in 2001, Anita called me and asked to meet up. She'd got back from a tour group holiday in Thailand with her parents. It was her first time abroad, first time she used her first-ever passport. I guessed she wanted to tell me about it, but she said she had an important question and I was the only person who could answer it.

It was the final days of the traditional Lunar holiday. Migrant workers with beaten-down faces and faded Mao jackets were flooding back into the city for another 340-day shift, necks grimy from days and nights on trains that stank of sweat and garlic or long-distance 'sleeper' buses streaked with vomit speed stripes. They carried brand-new bedding and heavy-duty bags stuffed with specialties from their home provinces: lychees, oranges and pomegranates from the south, tea and cigarettes from the southwest, grapes, raisins and watermelons from the west, dried mushrooms and bamboo shoots from the hilly central provinces, fish and spices from the flat ones. When they got to their converted shipping container or dusty corner of a half-finished tower block, there'd be nights of feasting and boasts: 'Now *this* is the best in China.'

The men brought wives and children and spare cash they'd spend on better accommodation, like an abandoned retail space with a metal shutter for a front door, and fees for illegal schools for unregistered city residents, or a television.

Way on the other side of town and the wealth gap, the other migrant workers returned with no less dread. But if they were worn out from the journey that's because Tommy's Gameboy ran out of battery on the plane from Chicago and husband Dan, HR manager for a joint venture that made brake pedals, said he needed to sleep because he had an important meeting first thing back in the office. So mum had helped Tommy skip through the in-flight movies when she wasn't comforting his screaming baby sister whose ears were popping because of the cabin pressure.

Then again, they'd had worse trips and, after coping with two pairs of aging grandparents as well as the kids since Christmas, mum was going to find the maid waiting to take it all off her hands.

Migrant workers and foreign executives. Every year they returned for the job they couldn't get back home.

When Anita called I was out on the streets, searching for a new pirate VCD store. It was a cold, clear day that gave a drag on a cigarette an extra kick. Anita was impatient so I agreed to meet at a Japanese-run French bar and restaurant in a villa down an alley. I arrived first. Anita bounced in soon afterwards.

Her face was tanned, and she had a couple of dreadlocks with tiny turquoise beads in her fringe, as you do on your first ever overseas holiday. She was in a long brown winter coat and Ugg boots. She looked like a happy Eskimo.

We ordered coffee and sat on a bench in the window.

'So, how was Thailand?'

'Great. I got you a present.' She stuck her hand into her bag and came out with a small package. 'Open it.'

The paper was that eco-friendly brown stuff tied with a piece of straw. Inside was a clay pot of tiger balm.

'Thanks. Just what I always wanted. I like the dreads by the way. Very cool.'

She pulled them with one hand, tilted her face. Her smile was the brightest thing I'd seen all day. 'I'm not sure I can keep them at work. I hope so.' The smile went up by a few suns, 'I had a tattoo as well.' She undid her coat and was about to pull up her sweater.

I put my hand out. 'That's all right, Anita. I believe you. What is it?'

'A butterfly.'

'Nice.' We drank the coffee. 'So what's the urgent question?'

'Oh yes. That. Felix has invited me to a wedding in England.'

For a split second my body ceased to function. My heart stopped. My hand froze on its way to the coffee cup.

'His brother is getting married. Felix has asked me to go with him. And now I have a passport, why not? The wedding is in April. What do you call the holiday, the one like grave sweeping?'

My breathing returned to normal. 'Easter,' I said.

'That's it. Next next month.'

Felix was taking Anita to England. That was major. If I'd wondered since our scrap in the sauna if he was going to give up on her, and I had wondered, and I'd thought a lot about Anita too – here was confirmation he hadn't. He was going to see it through. I didn't know about Maggie Yu.

I did know, however, what happens at those smart weddings. I've seen the movie. I had to accept it. I hoped Felix would do right by her.

I was sure he would. He couldn't have meant it, what he said in the sauna, or rather the way he'd said it, so heartless. He'd been mucking about. Not the done thing to talk about true love. If he was taking her to England that proved he did have feelings for her.

I had another thought. I could make it up to Felix. His taking Anita to England as if he were 'taking' her from me, not like I was a rival but because I was her good friend; it was like me stepping in to give her away at the altar because her dad died.

I was good with that. Finality.

'So?' I said, 'what's the question?'

She gave me her serious face. 'I must take gifts. Can you tell me what is best? For his parents, and the brother and the new wife?

Felix says I don't have to. So I will surprise him. I was thinking to have clothes made, in silk. I went to look at cloth this morning. Perhaps a red dress for the new wife. Do you think she'd like it?'

'I can't say,' I said. 'Sounds a nice idea, but I'm not sure she'd wear it at the wedding. Brides in England – new wives I mean – wear one white dress. They don't do the fashion show you do in China. And besides, how would you get the measurements?'

'That's what I thought you can help with. We have plenty of time.'

'How on earth can I do that, Anita?' My voice cracked. 'I don't know his family, let alone his brother, and certainly not the future Mrs. Fawcett-Smith. Felix hasn't mentioned his brother getting married, or going back for the wedding. But that might be because I haven't seen him.'

'Yes, he told me you had a fight.'

'He did? I'd say an argument. It was ages ago.'

'That's what I mean. He said you had an argument about China, and you got very angry, and Mike broke it up.'

I wanted to say yes, Mike did put a spoke in it. And I wasn't going to tell Anita that she had been the cause of the fight. Felix hadn't. She'd have said.

'Felix also said he likes you. He's sorry you had a fight. You helped him when he came to Shanghai. He appreciated your advice, but he thinks you are not up to date. You are not, um,' she paused, '"moving to the beat". He says you need a break. He thinks you are getting cyclical.'

'What? You mean "stuck in a rut"?' I smiled at the idea of Felix showing concern.

'No, not that. Angry with China.'

'I think you mean "cynical", but "cyclical" works as well, almost better.'

'I like that you always correct me. It shows you care.' Anita gave me a smile that reminded me what good friends we were. We were all friends now.

'Let's talk about England,' I said.

I suggested tea, silk and scroll paintings for presents. Pretty obvious. And I gave Anita an idea how British weddings work, to the best of my knowledge. I was going to tell her to watch *Four Weddings* but decided against it. And I told her to wear a hat. I wondered if Felix would have thought of that.

'How long are you going for?'

'Two weeks. Mr. Wang has given me extra holiday as a reward.'

'For what?'

'Helping Zhou *Laoban*.'

'What, with introducing Felix?'

'That's one thing. Zhou *Laoban* is happy with Felix.'

'So,' I said, wanting to get back to the subject of England. I must have been feeling homesick. 'What you going to do apart from the wedding?'

'I want to go on a tour, to Scotland, and where Shakespeare was born, and other famous places.'

'What? A tour, in a coach, like a bus?'

'Yes. Why not? It was fun in Thailand.'

'You don't go to England with your boyfriend and go on a coach tour. That's ridiculous. Get Felix to take you round, drive you in his dad's Roller or whatever they have in their double garage.'

'What do you mean?' she said, confused.

I guess she didn't know what a Roller was.

'What do you mean "boyfriend"?'

'Felix.'

'Felix? My boyfriend?' She leant away from me. 'He's not my boyfriend.'

I was confused. 'Come on, Anita, he's been chasing you ever since he got here, over a year ago. And you're going to the UK with him and you'll stay at his house, and go to his brother's wedding, and you know what happens, how people feel at weddings and, well...' Anita was laughing at me, straight in my face, so I stopped. She put her hand on my arm, either to comfort me or stop me carrying on.

'But,' I said. As you do.

'But what?'

'But I thought...'

'Thought what?'

'Well, you know...'

'What?'

'Will you stop saying "what" please!' I started laughing myself. 'And you tell me: why?'

'Why what?'

'Why you're going to England with Felix if he's not your boyfriend?'

'Because he asked me. He owes me.'

'What?' I caught myself. 'Shit, I've started too,' we laughed. 'He owes you a favour for you getting him the job?'

'Yes.'

'And don't tell me: you feel obliged to accept?'

'Of course. I can't turn him down.'

'You want to go? With him?'

'Why not?'

'Well...' I stopped myself. What business of mine was it? 'One thing I'll never understand is this thing you people have with favours. I mean, we do it too. Everyone does. But in China the sense of obligation is so much deeper, almost pathological, with the taking as well as the giving, or returning.' I caught myself. 'Sorry. Pathological means really, really deep.' Anita was about to speak. I held my hand up. 'No, don't tell me. You were obliged to help your boss help Zhou, and you're obliged to accept thanks from your boss, who's giving you the two weeks holiday, and from Felix, with the invitation to his brother's wedding. But do you *really* want to go?'

'I guess so,' she said.

'That's it?'

'I always wanted to see England.'

'Anyone could show you England.' I looked at her, looked away, half turned back, stopped. 'I could.'

Now she turned away. I thought I heard a faint sigh but I can't be sure.

'There's another reason I must go,' she said, still looking out of the window. Her voice carried a hint of exasperation.

'What's that?' ¹

'Zhou *Laoban*'s son is also going to England on the same flight. Felix is to help him find a school, and I am to help look after him as well, and his mother.'

'I thought he wasn't going for another couple of years. And that's a lot of people looking after a lot of people who are looking after someone else.' No wonder she sounded exasperated. I would have been.

She turned back to me and put on her serious face again. 'You remember what Ivy told you about Zhou *Laoban* and his family, how special they are?'

'Of course. His father was a revolutionary martyr.'

'Yes, so he went to a special school for special children. For this generation the special schools aren't special enough, so they send their children abroad.'

'Am I picking up a feeling of resentment at this "special" treatment?'

'What do you mean?'

'I mean, are you angry that people like Zhou do this?'

'Not angry. That is too strong. Maybe the wrong word. There is no point in being angry. It is not simple.'

'Simple?'

'You want to know a secret?'

'Sure,' I said. There was no one else in the bar to overhear but she leaned in to me. I turned my head so she could whisper into my ear. I caught a whiff of her perfume. That perfume.

'Zhou *Laoban* did not get his special life and privileges and position and power because of the good things his father did. She drew back so she could observe my reaction, then leaned in again. 'He got them because of a *bad* thing he did.' She drew out the key word.

'I don't get it.'

'The leaders covered up for him.'

'And the bad thing that he did was?'

'Like Ivy said, it is a good story. But the real one is better than hers, or worse: he wasn't saving a woman. Did Ivy say she was pregnant?' She sat back against the wall.

'I can't remember.'

'Some versions say she was. She might have been, or soon after, because Comrade Zhou had raped her. He wasn't rescuing her. He died after he abandoned her in the hut where he did it. He was drunk. He fell down in the snow and didn't get up. They found him days later. He wasn't a prisoner either. He had been released but stayed in the camp as a worker. People did that because it was safer than going home and getting arrested in the next campaign.'

'Wait a minute.' I stopped her. 'How on earth do you know this? And how come no one else does?'

'I can answer both questions with one answer.'

'What?'

'My grandfather was in the same labour camp.'

'Jesus Christ.'

'And the reason no one knows the story should be obvious.'

'Let me guess,' I said and reached for my cigarettes. I lit one and squinted through the smoke. 'Your parents were looked after by Mr. Wang, your boss, when they had to move out of their Shanghai apartment. Right?' She nodded. 'So Mr. Wang was acting on behalf of someone, and that someone was the person who got your grandfather to promise to never speak about Zhou *Laoban's* father.' Anita nodded. 'Was it only your grandfather who knew? Was he the sole witness?'

'You are clever, Johnny.' She put her hand on my arm and let it rest there. It was a light, soft touch, a caress that did not move. 'By the way, I never told you my family used to own the whole house, the one where their apartment was. My grandfather had a factory. It made knives and forks.'

'Aha, so he was rich before forty-nine, which is why he was in a labour camp. What happened to him?'

'He survived the camp. What did you call it, New Zealand?' She gave me a nice smile, a gentle shove, and removed her hand. 'He lived with us at home. He died when I was thirteen.'

'And he told you the story? It seems amazing, the story itself, and even more that you know it. But why keep it to yourself? And why tell me, now? Have you told Felix? Have you ever told Ivy?'

'Of course, not. So many questions. Slow down, Johnny.' She took a sip from a glass of water. 'Maybe you're not so clever after all. I think it's obvious why I don't tell. It's for my parents, and myself. And my grandfather told me because he wanted to tell someone, just one person, like I am telling you. So someone knows, somewhere in the world. I'd never tell Ivy because she wouldn't believe it and if she did she'd think I was embarrassing her. It's not good to embarrass people.'

'But why me?'

'I don't know, I just...' She stopped and looked me straight in the eye with that plaintive, determined expression I remember my sister using on my mum when she came home with her first earrings, in pierced ears.

'Can I have a cigarette?'

Anita never smoked. I held out the packet, she took one and I lit it. She inhaled, her expression softened, and she said, 'I trust you, Johnny. And I felt like telling you. Is that okay?'

'Do your parents ever talk about it?'

'No. They never mention it. He was my father's father and I think my father is too afraid, and ashamed. My parents almost had me adopted by an American family in 1989, when the Tian'anmen Incident happened. They thought it was going to come again, the Cultural Revolution. That might be what killed my grandfather. He couldn't face it.'

'How did he die?'

'At home, in bed, asleep. He did not want to live.'

'Anita, I am amazed.' An idea came to me. 'Zhou's dad's mates didn't murder the poor woman, did they?'

'I would not be surprised if she died by "accident". Maybe in childbirth. As for Zhou *Laoban*, he was looked after. The Party take care of their own, especially the ones who have committed crimes. I read a book about the Italian mafia once. It is like that. You can never leave.'

'You're suggesting that Zhou is a criminal? They all are? Anita, I'm beginning to wonder if you're going to the UK to ask for political asylum.' I was trying to make a nice joke for once.

'What does that mean?'

'That you want to stay there and not come back to China.'

'I love my country,' she said. 'But there are things wrong with it. It will get better. Zhou *Laoban* has been good to me and my family, but I am scared of him. You have to be careful of a man like him. You do not want to make him angry.'

'Are you worried about Felix?'

'No. He is a foreigner. He is their toy, and they like him.'

'You're making me think you're going to the UK with him, and the reason you've been spending so much time with him, is to make up for the fact that you got him the job, not to let him thank you for it! Christ. Tell me straight, Anita. Sorry,' I was sounding aggressive, 'why do you care so much about Felix?'

Anita looked me in the eye and pulled her lips into a smile that made holes in her cheeks. 'Johnny, you don't get it, do you?'

Get what?

I couldn't ask. We were interrupted, after all that time having the bar to ourselves, by a familiar voice.

'Hi guys! Fancy running into you in here. I thought you were in Thailand, Anita.'

It was Bill Connor.

'Mind if I join you?' He was wearing a knock-off puffa jacket and a woolly hat and carrying his trademark bashed-up laptop case.

'You just got back from Everest?' I said. 'Reach the top?'

'Very funny, Johnny. This is my editing outfit. My flat is so fucking cold. Sun never seems to reach it. You know what it's like.' I nodded. I'd been to his garret once. It was dark, dingy and damp.

'I came out to warm up, get the circulation going.' He sat down and took off his glasses to clean them, rubbed his chin. He hadn't shaved for a few days.

'Nice pun,' I said.

'What?' He squinted at me.

'You run a magazine. Doesn't that have a circulation?'

'Christ, Johnny, you're a sad bastard.' He waved at the waitress, called her by her name. He left his coat on. 'How are you, Anita? How was Thailand?'

'Good thank you.'

'We were talking about a wedding,' I said. 'A Fawcett-Smith one.' I left a long pause so he could get the wrong impression. He looked at Anita and me, his eyes open. 'It's Felix's brother,' I said.

'Oh right. You had me there. Why were you talking about that?'

'Anita is going with Felix, off to see our beloved Blighty for the first time. It's at Easter.'

'Lucky you, Anita. Bring us back an Easter egg. How long for?'

'A couple of weeks.'

'I'm sure you'll have a wonderful time, but it won't be warm as Thailand I warn you. Where does Felix live?'

I answered, assuming Anita didn't know. 'Somewhere near Bath. I imagine they've got a nice big house. His dad's a retired colonel. His brother that's getting married is in the army too. Apparently he's quite a war hero.'

'Watch out, Anita,' Bill was warming up. 'All those dashing young officers and gentlemen. They're a bunch of Flashmans to the man. I expect they'll be in their uniforms too.'

'Flashman?' I said. 'You mean like flash git? That's harsh.' I was asking on my own behalf as much as Anita.

'You never read *Tom Brown's Schooldays*, Johnny? Or MacDonald Fraser's books? They're brilliant.'

'Ask me one on sport.'

'Never mind. Like I say, Anita, a British military wedding will be like a royal one in miniature. You'll love it.'

He ordered a hot chocolate, helped himself to my cigarettes, and asked Anita a question about a Taiwanese pop star his magazine was reviewing. She gave him some background info. It took us a while, me and Bill, to work out that the precise translation of the word she used was 'aborigine'. I thought there were only aborigines in Australia.

When he finished his chocolate, Bill put his hat on.

'Talking of Felix,' he said, to us both. 'You going on this model shoot thing, for the brochure for that luxury club? He told me he needed white faces, asked me if I knew any models. As if I could afford models for the magazine! Ha. That'll be the day.' We shook our heads. 'I think the idea is to go to a sports club or hotel, and get people to muck about for a weekend, for free, but there'll be a photographer there. You need a dinner jacket too.'

'That'll be why he didn't call me,' I said. I was watching Anita out of the corner of my eye. She didn't know what Bill was talking about either. Odd Felix hadn't mentioned it to her. 'So not Paradise Island again?' I looked at her.

She shook her head.

'When is it?' I asked Bill.

'A weekend next month I think.'

'Oh, I see.' Anita sounded disappointed, but not much.

Bill noticed. He assumed, as I had until a moment ago, that Anita and Felix were together. 'I guess he has so much going on he forgot to tell you, Anita. If I go, I'll see you there. Like I say, might be fun. Well, see you around.'

Anita and I sat in silence. I was trying to think of a way to restart our conversation. I was hungry and thirsty. I wanted to eat. I wanted a beer. I wanted Anita to come back to my apartment, to be with her more. To see what happened, what was going on in her head.

She was staring at the door Bill had walked out of. I took a slow-exposure mental photo of her profile; the round forehead, one brown eye under long lashes, the button nose, lips in their pout, firm round chin. That innocent, open face didn't match up with the grim story she'd told me.

I remembered Charlie Thurrold told me once how the cleverest trick of the Cultural Revolution had been the way the people behind it made everyone guilty of something, no matter how small. Hence the collective amnesia and refusal to talk about it, why no one does, even in private. Its reach was like the Second World War for my Gran's generation, when everyone knew a family that was affected, that lost someone. No one was untouched.

The way Anita talked about giving and accepting favours and the inter-connectedness of it all, it was as if the Cultural Revolution had never ended, or set the pattern for the future. Or maybe China had always been like that, involving everyone in everyone else's lives, so no one dared break the mould. Conformity and complicity keeps the masses on track.

She reached for her bag. 'I should be going,' she said.

'Already?'

'We're going to dinner with relatives. It's still New Year.'

'Oh, yes. It's the fifteenth today, isn't it?'

'That's right. Lots of family stuff.'

'Family.'

We stood up. I paid the bill. I walked with her to the door, along the alley up to the main road. It was mid-afternoon. The sun was bright.

If I'd been a gentleman, I'd have taken her arm in mine. But I'm not. I stuck my hands in my pockets, hunched my shoulders, and walked beside her. We didn't speak, at least not until we got to the street. She gave me a glance, just the one, but it reminded me of the time when we walked to the tourism thing. There was something in it. Regret, hope, blame? Again, I'm no gent and I'm certainly no master of the art of silent communication. I smiled at her. 'Getting a taxi?'

'Yes.'

One pulled up beside us. I was going to carry on walking and thinking. I opened the door. She liked to sit in the front.

'See you.'

Anita wrapped her long coat over her knees, put the furry carrier bag on top, and spoke to the driver. She didn't look up or wave as they pulled off.

# 11

## MODEL WORKERS

WHEN I cleared out my office in Shanghai one thing I kept, which had been sitting at the bottom of a pile on the windowsill, was Felix's *magnus opus*, his brochure for Royal Buckingham Park.

It's massive, like a coffee table book. The cover is gold and the titles, in English and Chinese, are in white, which makes them hard to read. Open it up and the untutored eye can tell the layout is a cake and arse party. I believe the expression is 'designed by a committee that never met'.

I can't read it but I'd say there's way too much information, presented in dense blocks of text interspersed with English abbreviations for square metres and dollars, and '<' and '>' thingies. It looks like a science essay, and much of the text is printed over photographs so you can't make it out. English phrases in quotation marks are scattered throughout, at the tops and bottoms of pages, down their sides.

'Where an English gentleman, from Shakespeare to Sherlock Holmes, might make his home and castle,' was one. Note the conditional tense. It got a whole page near the front.

'Be the Lord of your Manor, live like a King!' was on several.

'Live the H.S.F. Lifestyle!' was all over but not explained.

Topping it off for hyperbole, across a double-page spread of a golf course: 'Sail into a land of wealth and comfort to live with pleasure and exclusivity.'

There was one page in English, which they can't have let Felix do a de-chinglifying job on. It has a squiggly signature underneath, alongside 'Zhou Jianguo, Chief Executive' and a headshot of the man himself, wearing a collar and tie. He looks quite the businessman. I guess he or his secretary, or whoever sent the brochure to the printer, wouldn't let anyone make changes because it came from the boss. It's the introduction to the whole brochure and starts off: 'Royal Buckingham Park Luxury Leisure Club and Residences is a project designated by the Central Committee of the Cabinet Council as a number one first grade project for the opening up and developing of the top class property market of new millennium China and takes as its model The Five Forwards with architecture, planning, verdure environment...'

There's masses of photographs, hundreds of them, including a hunt meeting lifted from a *Visit Britain* brochure. There's also the changing of the guard at Buckingham Palace.

There's the photo of Felix on his horse at the launch party, taken through the window. He looks like a Horseman of the Apocalypse thanks to the reflection of the flash on the glass. He looms over the heads of Zhou and the Party Secretary, whose grin makes him a gargoyle. Then there are countless pages of Felix with the officials in front of the painting. His posture and his chubby smile are the same in every one, like a waxwork.

In the back of the brochure are boxed advertisements of big houses and a list of their specs like you see in the window of an estate agent. The houses were real ones in the UK, with big doors, several chimneys and leaded windows. Whoever selected them did a good job of choosing ones that were similar yet different. When I first saw them, I had an idea. I went through them and I was right. They had the same number of front windows. That's how they'd been selected and cut for scanning, from the pages of those magazines Felix got sent out.

The backgrounds of each shot had been cropped and replaced by a computer-generated image of green fields and trees. Skies were deep blue or warm orange and sails puffed in the distance, seabirds fluttered. The same car, a Rolls or Bentley, I can't tell, had been photo-shopped onto the ones with drives.

My favourite part of the whole brochure is us lot at the 'model shoot'. We're all there apart from the girls, like an alumni album or 'yearbook' as the Americans call it.

I was invited after all. I ran into Felix at one of his co-sponsoring events, where thanks to the usual river of free booze he and I got roaring drunk and got back on those tracks I talked about, put the sauna scrap behind us. I wished him all the best with Anita in the UK.

'Give her one for me, old chap,' I said, or something equally crass along those lines. I regretted it. But that's a minor glitch in an otherwise perfect kiss-and-make-up session.

Felix organized the photo shoot at the International Finance Plaza Hotel, across the road from SLIC's head office. He had the run of the place, or most of it. Not that the hotel turned guests away. Despite its prime position in the heart of Pudong's 'CBD', the Plaza was doing little business for a business hotel. It was old and tired after barely a year. The glass doors along the corridor of the ground floor's mini-mall (the hotel's one, not the cavernous one next door) were padlocked, the taps were broken in the gents and the staff at the reception desk couldn't be more disinterested if they tried. There was a general air of apathy.

'How on earth are you going to create a British-style luxury villa complex in this place?' I asked Felix, catching myself before I said 'dump'. I was nervous of upsetting our recent rapprochement.

'Not a problem,' he said. 'We're mostly doing interior shots, and it's the people that count more than the background, but I think you'll be impressed with what I've done with this dump.' He paused. 'You done any modelling, Johnny?'

'No. Only time anyone asked was for an underwear catalogue. I turned them down for obvious reasons.'

Felix snickered. 'Nor have I. But Mike will be here to show us the ropes, and I have a good photographer. He'll make you look fabulous, Johnny, the full-on gentleman at leisure.'

I have to admit the idea of dressing for a slap-up dinner in a suit and tie appealed to me, and having it recorded for posterity. It would be play-acting. I'd always wanted to have a go at drama. My one chance had been the after-school youth club, but I'd been far too shy. My parents never took me to the theatre other than the panto at Christmas. For us, live entertainment was a singsong round the piano in the pub. The oldies sang songs and one or two granddads shuffled their feet like tap dancers in lead shoes. They looked sharp. Made a good show.

I'd always regretted I couldn't sing or play an instrument, or do a turn, a little act, like Felix's 'Stairway to Heaven'. Since I'd been in Shanghai I'd acquired a taste for old movies, the ones where they really act, and do a bit of a song and dance too. It started off when I couldn't find any new releases in my usual pirate store. I'd picked up North by Northwest with Cary Grant. I knew the clip from when the crop-dusting plane tries to flatten him at the crossroads and I'd always wondered what happened either side of it. When I watched the whole movie I was gripped. I loved it, and Cary Grant, how smooth and sophisticated he was.

It's been my favourite movie ever since, and Cary Grant my hero. He was the classic example of the boy from nowhere who made good. His name wasn't even Cary Grant. He started out as Archie Leach, truant Bristol schoolboy, thrown out at fourteen. I had something in common with him there, plus the going overseas. I read a magazine article about him once and they had a great quote. 'I pretended to be somebody I wanted to be and I finally became that person. Or he became me. Or we met at some point.'

How's that, first for an honest admission, and second, an example of how you can become someone else, if you try hard enough, or meet the right person halfway there?

Felix was asking me a question. He had to repeat it: 'You did bring a dinner jacket, didn't you?'

'Jacket? Yes, I brought it, and a tie.' It was the green gulag one.

'I mean dinner jacket as in black tie, bow tie.' He had to explain.

'Oh,' I said, 'no, I haven't got one.'

'Damn.' He gave his fringe a flick. 'I'm afraid you need it. You can't be in the dinner set without it.' He rubbed his forehead.

I'd mucked up his arrangements. 'Sorry.'

'Hang on a sec, I know what.'

'What?'

'You can be a waiter. Yes, that'd be brilliant. You won't mind will you?' He was pleased with his idea. 'There are a few smart jackets with brass buttons that'll fit you. I tried them on the local staff this morning and the sleeves are way too long. That'd be perfect: a foreign waiter, like a butler.'

'Felix,' I said, 'you serious?'

'Come on, it'll be for a couple of shots, Johnny. You don't have to serve us.'

'But, well, I was kind of hoping...'

'It's for fun. And it's not like I'm asking you to do an underwear advert.'

I thought how actors like Cary Grant and Errol Flynn started in Hollywood, as extras. 'All right.'

We sat in the lobby and asked a waitress to bring a couple of cold beers, which she said they didn't have, so we said we'd have warm ones.

'Here's the plan,' Felix said. 'We've got a dozen people turning up. The main thing is the dinner in a private room. But before that we've got tea. And this afternoon we're going to play tennis. There's a court on the fifth floor. I know it's a bit cold but they only need to pose for a couple of shots. After that we've got the run of the health club, sauna, everything. No one else will be allowed in.'

'And someone will be photographing us?'

Felix raised his beer at me and smirked as if to signal there'd be plenty of booze to help get rid of any inhibitions. 'It'll be perfectly natural. That's the whole point. And there'll be no one taking pictures of your fine athletic frame in the sauna either, because it's bust. I'm thinking Mike Bennett. He's bringing a Swedish chick called Elke. Haven't met her yet but she's Swedish so...'

'I hope he doesn't drop his towel,' I said, going for the laugh.

'It'll be very tame,' he said. 'Maybe you can be in the background for the tennis, like a spectator.'

'You're getting your money's worth, aren't you?'

'Wait until you see what we've got for dinner,' Felix said.

'Who else is coming?'

'Apart from Mike and Elke?'

'No locals?'

'No. Can't. I explained to Anita and Ivy. They might come along later. My friend Benny might too.' He paused. 'There'll be Elke with Mike, Bill Connor, French Fred, Joe's bringing a couple of Russian girls who've done some modelling and, to add authority and character, I've got Charlie Thurrold.'

'Charlie?' This was a surprise. 'You patched it up at last? That's great news.'

Felix gave the hair a confident flick. 'He saw sense in the end.'

'In what? To forgive you for smashing up his apartment?'

'No, not that, don't be silly. My going to work for Mr. Zhou. I knew he'd come round.'

I hadn't seen Charlie for ages. This was a double bonus, that I'd see him again and with Felix too.

'You could say that inviting him is a kind of kiss-and-make-up dinner for him and me too.'

I couldn't work out if he was making a connection to me and him or him and Charlie. Whatever. Felix was in an expansive mood.

'And I must say I do appreciate you agreeing to play the part of a waiter,' he said. 'Let me slip you a few extra cigars. They're Cuban. You smoke cigars?'

'Now and again,' I said.

I didn't. I was thinking.

'Felix,' I said, 'if I'm a waiter for the dinner, how can I be a spectator for the tennis and a tea drinker as well? When you go to your parties in country houses you play tennis with the servants? And out of interest, how are the photos of us here going to match up with the reality of Royal Buckingham Park, miles away out there?' I waved towards the revolving door.

'Johnny, my dear Johnny,' we'd been given a couple more warm beers, 'let me explain the concept of marketing with Chinese characteristics.' He smiled and pushed his hair back. 'Funny, isn't it, how everyone talks about "market economy with Chinese characteristics" when what they *should* be calling it is market*ing* with Chinese characteristics.' He stressed the 'ing'. 'I should get a real doctorate for this.'

'I'm all ears.'

'It's back to front. Simple as that. In the West the product comes first, then you market it.' I nodded. 'In China you start with the marketing. You create the image of what you want to sell in the way you think the buyer's going to like it, or you borrow the image, a picture of a house for example, you get the buyer's commitment and then, once you've done the deal, you create your product to match it, brick for brick, in the case of a house.' He threw his arms over the back of the sofa. 'Genius, isn't it? Can't go wrong. What we're doing here today: taking pictures of a dinner party in a beautifully decorated dining room – wait and see what I've done – I tell you the exact same room will exist in Buckingham Park.'

'So long as I don't have to be a waiter in it,' I said.

'Good point.' He was mock serious. 'We'll have to find someone who looks like you,' he laughed. 'Come on, I'll give you a sneak peek.' He took me over to the lift.

In the presidential suite Felix had created an old-world British dining room, not that I'm an expert, but it seemed authentic to me. It was like a movie set. He told me he'd changed the curtains, and the furniture was borrowed from an antique dealer. It was the real thing from old Shanghai: dark wood and leather, proper *art nouveau*. Even I could tell it was genuine. Silver jugs and bits and bobs and candlesticks were stood on the dining table and the dressers. In pride of place on the wall, opposite the centre of the table, he'd hung a painting similar to the one he'd stood under at the Paradise Golf Club for the one-on-one photos. It might have been a direct, smaller copy, come to think of it.

That evening, when the room was full of men in black jackets and bow ties, girls in pretty dresses and pearl necklaces, and me in my white jacket with brass buttons, which did fit, we were transported to genteel, upper-class, country-house England, like one of those TV series whose names I can't remember. The only thing that didn't match but didn't matter since we were doing this for photos, was the babel of foreign languages, and in my case, a distinctly non-genteel English accent. We had Russian, French and American round the table.

The photographer and his female assistant were unobtrusive. The only photographers I'd met before had worked for Bill Connor, usually for nothing, to get published. This pair was professional. In the afternoon they bossed us about but didn't waste our time. I was on the sidelines for the tennis and, of course, nowhere to be seen in the sauna shots. Mike Bennett wanted his Swedish companion to do those, but she went coy on him. I thought Swedes were uninhibited. It made me wonder whether she might have a boyfriend in town, or back in Sweden, and the chance of him seeing the photos put her off.

One of the Russian girls was persuaded to wrap herself in a towel and stare at Bennett like they were a loving couple. The result is clean and wholesome, and Mike looks like Mr. Universe, as usual. I do wonder, from the angle of his knees, his towel and the smile on the girl's face, if he wasn't winking his Jap's eye at her.

The tennis pictures are Mike and the same Russian girl shaking hands over the net. Action shots were impossible because of the tower blocks in the background, and it was bloody freezing. In the 'teatime' set I'm holding up a newspaper, so there was no need for the jacket after all.

And I'm the waiter at the dinner table. I think I make a good one. I see myself as a young, skinny Pete Postlethwaite. They had me standing stiff and watchful against the wall, head up, nose in the air, holding a silver tray with nothing on it, which at the time I thought was silly but the photographer insisted. It works well.

The photo spread, which takes up five pages of the brochure, is nothing like those ultra-cool, top model ones you get in magazines like *Wallpaper* or *iD*, but we look good. The page designer hazed the pictures over to give them a similar mood, or make up for the inconsistent lighting. It was my one and only photo shoot and I'm happy with it. It was also the first time I wore make-up. Thurrold, who came for the dinner, refused point blank. He was perfect as he was, old and wise with his white hair and deep-set eyes. His jacket collar, the silk bit, was worn through at the edges, and his bow tie, which he'd tied himself, was crooked, but he looks like a proper old gent on the page.

'Good to see you, Charlie,' I said when he appeared. 'I wouldn't have expected you to come along for a do like this.' I shook his hand. 'You staying over too?'

He squinted at me through his glasses. 'I've got a good bed at home thank you, and a good book. And I spend far too much time in hotels.'

'So, you're here just for dinner?'

'I found the idea amusing. You youngsters get pulled off the street to model underpants so I thought why not try it. It's not like being an extra in a porn movie is it, and it is fully clothed?' He squinted again with a smile. 'Isn't it?'

'I wouldn't know about porn movies, Charlie, but I did have a fling with a girl from Hong Kong who knew someone in the industry. We were offered a chance to do precisely that, in the Hyatt of all places. A party scene in the bar. To my eternal regret I turned them down. It would have been an eye-opener and amusing to say I appeared in a porn movie, but it meant staying up all night.'

'I thought you were asked to be an extra.' Charlie was sharp as ever.

'Very funny.' I got to the point, 'I hear you patched it up with Felix. That's great news.'

'Yes, it is, I suppose. It's also a good example of the things people will do for a visa.'

'What? A UK visa? He doesn't need a visa.'

'Not for him. It's for a girl he wants to take to his brother's wedding.'

So that was it. For a fleeting moment I thought it bad of Felix not to tell me the whole story, but who didn't have an agenda when they called on friends in Shanghai. It's how the world worked.

'I heard. You going too?'

'No, too busy. But I spoke to his mother about it. She had to write the official invitation letter for the girl. She's keen to meet her. English name is Anita?' He looked round the room as if he might find her.

'That's right. She's not here.'

'Oh. I imagine you know her?'

'Yes, fairly well.' I didn't want to say more.

'Anyway,' he said, 'if helping out Felix for a visa means we can let bygones be bygones, all well and good.'

'So you're not angry anymore with him for going to work for Zhou? Or what happened in your apartment...'

'We had an argument. That's that. It's ancient history. As for Zhou Jianguo and SLIC and this,' his head made a circle. 'So far he doesn't seem to have been too bad a boss. And I have to admit this Buckingham Park malarkey, if it happens, will be good news for us. Anything that helps promote British brands is useful.'

So Charlie Thurrold had a vested interest in making it up to Felix as well.

'Of course,' he said, 'the trip for SLIC is the real reason he's going to his brother's wedding. They're not close, him and Alex. I doubt Felix would have gone off his own bat. I hear from their mother that Alex has been promoted. He's passed a staff exam, set to be a highflyer one day. He'll end up more senior than their father was.'

I wondered if his brother getting a promotion would rile Felix, when he found out, if he hadn't heard already. That resentment must have been dealt with by now. Felix was making his way, had something to show for himself. He'd be going home with a feather in his cap.

Charlie had been looking over my shoulder most of the time we'd been talking. Felix was bustling about, organizing. He nodded at Charlie when he came close, gave him a sheepish grin. I sensed Felix was bugging Charlie. And he wasn't practising his usual discretion, which was odd. I wondered if it had been a good idea to get him along. I also wondered if they'd seen each other to make their peace or it had been done over the phone. The way they were eyeing each other, wary, like two dogs, made me think the latter was more likely.

'Let me get you a drink, Charlie,' I said. 'I am a waiter after all, at least for a few more minutes.'

'Yes, he's put you in your place there, hasn't he?' Charlie said, with the mildest hint of a sneer. 'I'll have a large whisky if it's not too much trouble. Thanks.'

I went to fetch it, glancing back at Thurrold.

'Put me in my place'?

Charlie stayed on his own at the end of the room, made no move to mingle. Felix was making a seating plan and encouraging his 'guests' to pose for the photographer.

I poured a quadruple whisky, topped it up with water – he didn't like ice – and took it to Charlie.

'Here, this will help,' I said, feeling cheeky, back on the side of the young generation versus his old China hand one.

Felix announced dinner was ready and to sit down, apart from me. The photographer's assistant came over, handed me the silver tray, and pushed me along the wall. Everyone took their places. There was a place left for me at the end, beside Bill Connor, opposite Mike and his Swedish girlfriend Elke, who was gorgeous. She was blonde, medium height, and had startling blue eyes and a very pretty face.

The first course was cold soup. Felix had been clever because the idea was to take the dinner photographs at the beginning, get them out of the way. Hot soup wouldn't have lasted while everyone posed. They were patient while the photographer ducked and dived round the table. He tried to get me in the background of most of the shots. I stood stiff as a board and did my best to keep a straight face.

'Thanks Johnny, you can knock off,' Felix said.

I undid my brass buttons and sat down next to Bill. I had to ask a real waiter to bring me a glass of wine and my soup. It was tomato and herbs and green things, mashed up, watery, and with cream in the middle. Felix had got a Spanish chef in.

The drink was flowing. Felix had given instructions that a few bottles should be left on the table for the photos. We kept emptying them and asking for more.

I was having a good time with Mike and Bill. Charlie Thurrold was on the other side of Bill from me, opposite Felix. I wasn't listening to their conversation, but from what I could see of Felix, they were being civil to each other. Felix did the thing of toasting someone every time he drank from his wine glass. I know I said he didn't act Chinese in Western company as some twits did, but there are one or two habits that become just that, habit, and you can't stop them, or it takes time and another environment to grow out of them.

That meant Felix was drinking hard. I also had a suspicion that on his way to and from the kitchen before dinner he'd been diverting to the nearest polished surface and cut himself a line or two. He had that eager eye you get with people on coke at a party, darting to and fro in search of the next opportunity to make a joke, for a conversation to jump into like a kid making a bomb in a swimming pool. The more he drank the more he talked to everyone and no one in particular, leaning forward to shout down to Mike or the other way to Joe, who was at the far end beyond the other Russian girl. His comments were becoming caustic. I overheard him say to Joe, for example, that he needed to come up with better ideas for party locations, that he was getting clichéd, boring. To Mike, opposite me, he said that when he opened his own hotel, which Mike had announced was his intention, he should promote it as an eco-friendly, 'green' one. That's where the money was, even if you only pretended to be eco-friendly. You didn't have to prove it to the customers. Royal Buckingham Park, for example, was going to say it practised recycling and eco-sustainability, and all that 'tosh' as he put it, where the only thing being recycled would be trash which, as everyone knew, was collected and re-used in the countryside, 'by some beggar or other.'

I didn't hear what Charlie Thurrold said at that point, because he spoke quietly and directly to Felix, leaning across the table, so it was like his soft words bounced off it and up Felix's nose, which is where they went, right up it.

Felix had bent forwards to listen. He sat up and glowered. His hand went to his hair and gripped it, like he was going to pull it out. His face went red.

'Is that what you think, Uncle Charlie?' The sarcasm of the 'uncle' was plain to hear. 'Hey, everybody, listen to this.' Everyone except the Russian girls stopped and listened. Well, they stopped, but they didn't listen. 'My old family friend here says that I should be more discreet, that I should curb my enthusiasm.'

'Felix, there's no need,' Charlie said, keeping his voice down, trying to bring Felix down with him. He had the opposite effect. Felix spoke louder.

'Yes, there is a need,' he declared. He sat bolt upright and put his clenched fists on the table, arms out straight.

'I want to make a statement, loud and clear. This city, Shanghai, these people, the Shanghainese,' he raised a stiff arm as if he was going to point a finger at Charlie but it carried on up and over his head and found a waiter who was standing behind him. He probably wasn't Shanghainese, but that didn't matter. Felix glanced up, grabbed the waiter's arm and held it. He shook it. The poor guy hadn't a clue what was going on. The memory of that Singaporean big cheese out at Anita's golf club flashed through my mind. The waiter bent down as if to take an order. Felix turned and stared him in the face, as if he was surprised to find an actual person on the end of the arm he'd grabbed. He pushed him away and turned back to the table.

'They're the future of this amazing country, and this city, which is going to lead the world one day.' He didn't clarify if it was the country or the city that was going to be the world leader. 'Never in modern history has anyone made so much progress in so little time. It's nothing short of a fucking miracle. And we,' he swept his eyes around the table, stopping to give Charlie Thurrold a hard stare, 'are incredibly lucky to be a part of it, to be on the inside.'

Everyone was paying attention. Felix must have snorted a serious amount of coke. He was full of himself, bursting with confidence. In the right place, at the right time, what he was saying would have made a good speech. But this wasn't the time. He was the host of a small party of friends and acquaintances who were here to do him a favour, and in return have a fun evening, and good food and drink.

'I don't know about you guys,' he said, his voice loud, 'but I'm no passenger, I didn't come here to freeload and run off with my winnings.' He kept twisting up and down the table but always came back to Thurrold, as if he was willing us to spot the traitor in our midst. 'I'm committed to this country. I want to be a part of it, and I *am* part of it. Involved.' He avoided my eye. 'I'm the only person here who works for a Chinese company. I don't study them like I'm making a bloody nature programme,' another sharp look at Thurrold, 'and complain about them.' He put on a whine. '"Oh, I do wish they wouldn't spit on the street", "All they care about is money", "It was so much nicer in the good old days".' It reminded me of the fight in the sauna. It was his voice, the sarcasm. It would have wound me up again if it was directed at me, but Charlie stayed silent. I couldn't see his face and didn't want to crane my neck to do so. He was obscured by Bill Connor. I pictured him trying to be objective, scientifically interested to see what his 'Godson' was turning into, keeping calm.

'"Good old days," my arse. The good old days haven't begun in China. We're starting them. And they're going to get better. Hey Joe!' he shouted.

'Er, yeah?' Joe strung the word out.

'When you want to sell your business to the next sucker in line, like you said you will, and piss off to your beach in Thailand, you sell it to me, all right. I'll have it.' He swung back to me. 'Same goes for you, Johnny Trent. And dear old Uncle Charlie,' his tone was sharp as a knife. I flinched. 'Accept it. China is never going to be what you wanted it to be. It's a dog-eat-dog modern capitalist country and it's doing it better than anyone else. So, my dear old dog of a family friend, wannabe God dad... dog dad,' he laughed at his stupid wordplay, 'why don't you retire to your cottage by the sea and let it be. Go on. Give it up. And you can tell my family I've found what I'm looking for. They can come and visit me in my mansion. How about that?'

Charlie Thurrold didn't respond. He didn't even pretend he was 'above' responding. He stood up and looked along the table, as Felix had been doing, but not into anyone's face. He skimmed our heads.

'I think I'll be off. Good night everyone,' and he left the room.

You could have heard the ash drop off the cigar Felix was in the process of re-lighting. His fingers were shaking ever so slightly. We sat in silence for a long minute. I watched Elke across the table. She was wearing a 1920s-style black silk dress and looked like an actress in a silent movie who's been told something shocking, like the butler had run off with her dad. The Russian girls whispered to each other.

During the course of Felix's rant, the photographer had snapped a few shots. That was ballsy. One is in the brochure. It looks like a perfect after dinner speech at the point where Felix has made a bad joke at Charlie's expense. Charlie's mouth is open, his eyes burning with indignation although it looks like attention in the picture. So he was upset.

It was the photographer who broke the silence. He asked if we could go into the sitting room for the last shots, then he'd go home.

'Come on, everybody,' Felix said, 'Let the man do his thing and we can get wasted.' None of us acknowledged him as we left the table. Awkward wasn't the half of it.

There was a grand piano in the sitting room. One of the Russian girls went straight over to it, opened the lid, sat down and started playing. It was a brilliant idea. What a girl. Everyone welcomed the distraction.

She was good. Later she told us she'd studied at a conservatory. Her name was Tatiana. We listened and enjoyed.

The one person who wasn't into the music was Felix. He lolled in an armchair, bow tie undone, without his jacket. He had on a pair of red velvet braces with shiny brass clasps. He'd flung his legs over the arm of the chair and his socks were red too. He was like a dog that's seen off a rival. If he'd had a tail it would have been thumping the leather cushion. He swung his head from side to side, smirking at us in turn, but no one seemed to notice apart from me. I gave him a sheepish grin, which gave him an idea, spurred him to his feet. He left the room and came back after a couple of minutes looking smugger. More coke I guess.

When Tatiana finished and we were applauding her – Felix with so much enthusiasm it was sarcastic – the double doors to the suite swung open and Benny Wu stuck his head in. He raised a hand in greeting and his trendy friends piled in behind him, all but on top of each other. They huddled on the piece of marble floor that demarcated the entrance lobby and stared at us, a bunch of foreigners in white shirts and bow ties, applauding a pretty girl in a silk dress at the piano. We must have been like a 'tableau' (I looked that up) of how we would have been a hundred years ago, when they did do 'tableau' for entertainment. We stared back at the young and beautiful new Chinese generation, with their perfect teeth and smart clothes, who smelt of money so crisp you'd cut your nose on it, gawped across the divide of time and race, culture, costume, and music, thanks to Tatiana.

Felix threw his arms above his head and let out a howl of delight.

# 12

## SERVICE

Benny Wu acknowledged Felix, stepped onto the carpet and walked straight to the piano. 'Tatiana, I didn't know you played.' He air-kissed her Western style, both sides. She smiled, said something I didn't catch – maybe it was in Russian – and shut the piano.

Felix swung his legs off the arm of the chair. 'Come in guys,' he said, 'Let's drink.' He hauled himself to his feet.

There were half a dozen or so. The girls were in jeans and sweaters, apart from a leggy one in a white miniskirt, and the boys in polo necks or white shirts and the close-fitting cotton jackets that were the fashion in Hong Kong.

Benny, who was wearing a classic blue blazer over a green polo shirt, went to shake Felix's hand. 'I thought we'd come by. You did say.' He spoke in English. 'Where's the bar? Any service?' He swivelled on his toes and his gaze landed on me. I was slouching on an upright chair by the wall, where I'd sat through the piano recital. I'd lit a cigarette and was holding the ashtray on my lap. Benny's eyes went skyward when they saw a foreign waiter, in an unbuttoned jacket over a Madness T-shirt, smoking on the job. I smiled in a way intended to express, politely: 'Wrong guy.' One of his eyebrows entered the stratosphere. I pushed my smile up to match and nodded without speaking.

He didn't get it. He glowered at me like he was trying to turn me into a waiter on the spot. I heaved myself to my feet and walked away. Felix could explain.

Bennett and Elke sat on a sofa, watching and waiting. They were keen to leave for their room but didn't want to show it. Joe recognized a couple of the girls and got them drinks. He called for the hotel staff to get the KTV mike and screen up and running. Bottles of Chivas and green tea appeared on the table. A pretty Chinese girl put her arm round Tatiana and selected the songs. They started singing, the Chinese girl first. A waiter appeared with buckets of ice. Everyone except Mike and Elke was smoking. That could be their excuse. I'd started on the monster cigar Felix had given me. The girls made calls on their mobiles.

'Johnny,' Felix called to me, 'come meet Maggie.' He was referring to the girl in the miniskirt.

Felix's description from the KTV night was spot on, right down to the freckles. Like Benny, she clocked the scruffy off-duty waiter and ignored me once Felix had introduced us. She kept looking round the room, at the door, and at Felix. She was pretty in a tight-fit tomboy way. I noticed, which Felix hadn't, that she'd had her eyelids 'done' to make her eyes rounder. I was about to make an excuse to leave her to it when another batch of girls arrived, including two more Russians. They had a screaming fit when they saw Tatiana and Sasha. In the noise and distraction, Maggie slipped off to speak to a new arrival, giving Felix a lingering 'come hither when you get the chance'.

I put my arm round Felix and walked him to the panoramic window. It overlooked a stretch of Pudong and across the Huangpu River to the Bund, which at that time of night was a picture-postcard strip of neon. Beams from spotlights by the pedestrian boardwalk along the river stabbed the sky like glow sticks. They swept along the tops of the old foreign buildings; the Shanghai Bank, the Peace Hotel, the AIA building, symbols of an annoying foreign past, and picked out the giant red flags fluttering on their roofs. They'd turn the lights off at midnight. Below us, downriver beyond an empty block, a building site was working under arc lamps. A line of churning concrete mixers was queuing to pour. We could hear their engines.

'How about that,' Felix said. He meant the whole lot, new and old. 'Amazing, the history, the life, the energy.' He pressed his forehead against the glass.

I'd seen that view many times and it always thrilled me, but my mind was on other things. I was preparing myself.

The way Felix had treated Charlie tonight; it was wrong and I had to say something.

He was drinking in the view.

'Felix, far be it for me to interfere in your personal affairs but since I have an interest: mind if I ask why you had to be so fucking horrible to Charlie in there?'

He pulled his head back and pushed his lips into a wide grin, put his forearm against the glass and laid his forehead on it. 'Are you going to give me a lecture on how to behave? That'd be good.' The glass in front of his mouth clouded over. He wiped it with his sleeve.

'No, well, I just mean to ask why, that's all.'

'You're right.' He turned his head towards me. 'It isn't any of your business. But because you're you, my chirpy chippy friend, I'll tell you.' He turned towards me. His eyes were glazed like they were behind a sheen of ice, yet intense and focussed, burning through it.

'He deserved it,' he said.

'Why? From what I saw all he did was try to cement the peace after making it up to you over that argument, your infamous "tiff"?'

'Oh, he tried to make it up to me but it goes on, the way he interferes, sticks his nose into my life.'

'But you hadn't seen him,' I said, not sure if it was the case.

'He hasn't been doing it in person, you twit. He does it through my mum, which is worse. It's harder to tell her to shut up. I told you we're close. Well, we won't be much longer if Charlie keeps at it.'

'If your mum's passing it on how come she didn't get a mention just now?'

'Not the done thing to talk about one's mum in public, my dear chap.' He laid on the posh accent. 'But every time I hear from her,' he reverted to his normal voice, 'on the phone, in letters or emails – she's just learnt how to do them – I get Charlie, second hand. "Charlie says this", "Charlie says that", his voice did the whine.

'"Charlie says working for SLIC is a dead end." "Charlie says doing marketing is a side track." "Charlie says you should be doing deals." And now? "Wonderful you're coming to Alex's wedding, but Charlie says it's because you're acting as an *au pair* for a Chinese schoolboy."

'Well, sod it. This "Buckingham Park malarkey" as he calls it, it's the real thing. Once I've proved my worth I'll show the old fart. Am I not the director of a company in Hong Kong?'

'Which you asked me not to tell him.'

'And please don't. Last thing I need.'

'But you will one day, right, and he'll be impressed, as he will by Buckingham Park, because it's your handiwork and because it's "British"? He was telling me about that, and brands and image and that.'

Felix was staring at the Bund, lost in his thoughts. Or so it seemed until I noticed he wasn't looking at the view. He was eyeballing his own reflection, hard, straight in the face, like I do when I'm drunk and have thrown up and I look up from the sink into the bathroom mirror and hate myself.

'Isn't the whole point of being in a place like this that we do what we want, how we want, whenever we want?

'Who the hell are they to tell us what we should be doing, the Old China Hands?

'They know about Mao and Deng and the Cultural Revolution, but they've no idea about what's going on because it never happened before. Well, maybe it did, in the old days in Shanghai, but it was people like you and me, Johnny,' he slapped me on the shoulder, 'the young adventurers, with no experience, no China education and, to be honest, no idea. They should bloody well be listening to us, or watching, not the other way round. It's like they want us to be Confucian. There's irony for you. Here we are in a country whose traditional religion or code of conduct, call it what you will, is based on Rule Number One which is: "Do what you're told by your elders and betters and shut up." Confucius says... Confucius says what? "Man having wank in biscuit tin fucking crackers." That's what Confucius said.' He giggled.

He turned and pointed at Benny, who had his back to us. 'You think he's a Confucian? You think Shanghai's going anywhere, or people like him are, by doing what they're told by their parents?'

It occurred to me that people like Benny didn't get anywhere without their parents' cash and connections.

'It's all about the parents, the fucking parents. And Charlie Thurrold's just as bad, if not worse, because he thinks he knows so much and pretends he cares. At least my mum doesn't, except for what she's told by bloody Charlie. "Charlie says..."' he did the whine again. It was getting on my tits. 'Why is it always us listening to them?' Felix repeated himself. 'Why can't they ever listen to us? Have they forgotten the young geniuses like Napoleon, Mozart, even Mao Zedong come to think of it? I'm not suggesting I'm a genius mind you.'

'It wouldn't suit you,' is what I wanted to say. Didn't have the chance. Felix was on a roll.

'But we have brains, don't we? We're not stupid. And there's so many of us; Joe, Fred, Mike, and Benny and his lot, even you, Johnny.' He paused, as if he wanted me to agree, but he was off again.

'It's like sport, that's what it is, being in Shanghai. Sport is for the young, we race ahead, break records. It's about being fit and fast and taking risks, pushing it. Old fuckers don't do that. They can't. This is a young city. It's about being young.'

'Don't sportsmen have coaches?'

'Coaches? What?' He stared at me like I was mad, eyes wide. 'Oh, you mean those coaches. I thought you were getting metaphisolophical on me, Johnny, and were going to tell me we need to catch the bus.' He laughed out loud. 'Yes, sportsmen have coaches but it's them who do it. And what's the point of being young if we don't make mistakes, our own mistakes, not that I think we are mind you. Fact is I think we're the smartest lot of our generation, just by being here.' He gesticulated at the window. 'And we're setting an example, showing the way. Showing the world what can be done in China, showing the Chinese too.'

This was beginning to sound like self-justification. Felix didn't need to give me that. What I wanted to know was why he'd had a go at Charlie again and he'd told me. I was sorry they couldn't be friends, yet. Even if Charlie's intentions were good, it was wrong to interfere. I imagined how I'd feel if my lot kept on my back, or they came out and tried to persuade me to go home. I'd be pretty pissed off.

Now it was me staring through the window at the Bund and the river.

'Johnny,' he said, putting his hand on my arm and gripping it. With his chubby fingers it felt tight. 'We've got to throw it off, this idea that we should be filial, dutiful, attentive and all that bullshit. You and me. And these guys. We have to go for it. Make the difference. Do our thing, *the* thing. Fuck the *old* fuckers, the *Old* China Hands. What do hands do? They pick noses and masturbate, that's what. Wankers. We don't want to be China Hands, do we. We want to be into China body and soul.'

'Yeah,' I said. 'You're right.'

We smiled and turned back to the party.

Mike Bennett was getting to his feet. He waved at Felix and shouted that he and Elke were off.

Felix waved back and shouted, 'See you tomorrow, Mike, breakfast downstairs.'

'Come on,' he said. 'Let's get a drink. I've sobered up. Can't have that. Come and meet Benny. I might have to do my karaoke show to get things going.'

Things were going fine. The girls were singing. The boys were lounging, watching, smoking. Joe Karstein and Bill Connor were swapping stories about government bureau raids. Maggie re-acquired Felix and pulled him over to the songbook. He pretended to protest. A Chinese guy and I got chatting. He was one of those Internet start-up people, planning to change the world in the next five minutes. When I gave him my card he got excited, said he'd heard of me from Felix and always wanted to meet.

'Why?' I asked.

He was working with investors on an online recruitment project. 'Do you want to co-operate?'

'How?'

'Simple,' he said, 'you give me your data and I put it online.'

'And where's my benefit?' I was two in and already bored of asking the obvious questions. How the hell did these people impress investors?

Felix started singing. He was warming up with 'Hotel California'. His voice hit the notes pitch perfect and he put feeling into it too. He was good.

'You get a commission,' my new acquaintance said. He studied my blank face, 'and increased business.'

'Very nice, except I'd be giving you my business first.' I might not have put it like that.

'But you don't understand,' he said.

I went to get a drink.

That was the night I got to know Benny Wu, once he'd realized I wasn't a waiter. He struck me as a decent bloke. He was well-educated and wanted you to know it but he wasn't arrogant about it. His conversation was serious. I can't remember what we talked about but it was more sensible than a stupid Internet start-up proposal, although it was to do with business. While we talked, his eyes kept tabs on what people were doing, especially Felix and Maggie. Benny was the leader of the pack. He didn't look like a boss kind of guy though, despite the more mature clothes. His wide-eyed face was friendly in the American way, that 'Hi, my name's Chuck,' kind of openness. Maybe it had rubbed off on him when he was studying over there.

By two in the morning I was ready for bed. The piano was dusted with white powder, two of the Russian girls, Sasha and another whose name I didn't know, were giving a soft-core lesbian show on the sofa, and Felix was playing the generous host. He'd done 'Stairway to Heaven' and it had gone down a storm.

I'd had my fun and a skinful. I was tired. Besides, these people weren't my type: too rich, too beautiful, too unattainable, and I don't go near Russian girls. They have big ex-boyfriends, who have lots more big friends, one of whom is sure to let you know he served in Spetsnaz, and they drink vodka for breakfast. As for the boys like Benny and co., you had to be careful with them too. Let them treat you too often and the demands for favours begin, or you start having to pay your way and they break your bank like a disposable chopstick. Best to stay on the edge of their orbit, don't get sucked in.

Joe and Bill were going to crash out. I said I'd come with them. Felix was playing drinking games with Benny and this time it was Maggie watching out of the corner of her eye. Judging from the colour of Benny's face, Felix was winning. Benny was losing gracefully, laughing.

Me, Joe and Bill were in rooms on the same floor. We got in the lift together.

'Enjoy the party?' Bill asked Joe.

'Yeah, not bad. Intimate. At least to start with. Food was good.' It had been. Probably the best food ever served in the Financial Plaza. 'Think we could have done without Felix's speech. Jeez, he was nasty to Charlie Thurrold.'

'I agree,' Bill said.

I told them I'd had words with Felix.

'They're family?' Joe said. 'No shit?'

'Yes shit. Charlie's like his Godfather.'

'Well, that explains things,' Bill said. 'Not sure I'd like the person supposed to be taking care of my spiritual and moral guidance looking over my shoulder while I live it up in Shanghai. Christ. Think about it. What a curse. No wonder Felix goes off at him now and again.'

'Now and again? More like a regular basis, when they're on speaking terms at least,' I said, 'which is rare enough.'

We reached our floor and the doors opened. We walked along the sterile corridor to our rooms.

'Night both,' I slapped the key card against the metal lump beneath the door handle, waited for the beep and click, and let myself in. I was more tired than drunk. I tugged off my shoes, glanced through the glass wall of the bathroom at the bathtub and thought how nice to have a hot bath but I'd probably fall asleep and drown. I threw my waiter's jacket onto the floor in a corner and lay down on the bed for a minute, preparing my mind and body for the effort of undressing. It was soft. I kicked off my shoes and pushed myself up, propped my head on the pillow. The room was classy, with nice lights and furnishings, big flat screen TV, underused, brand new. I realised I hadn't seen a single person like a normal paying guest all the time I'd been in the hotel. The place must have been bleeding money.

I was woken by the phone. I can't have been asleep for more than a few minutes. I answered, assuming it was Felix summoning me back for more fun and games and drinking.

A woman, impossible to tell her age, said in English, 'You want massagie? I come your room. Special service.'

'Don't want,' I said, 'thank you.'

Why was I so polite? I slammed the phone down to make up for it.

I've never worked out how those girls know. They always call after ten minutes. The reception desk tips them off I suppose, but it also happens when you've bypassed it, like I had. It must be the security guards, watching the close circuit TV, the same guards who charge the girls a fee to look the other way when they come in by the service entrance.

I started thinking of Anita and that conversation we'd had a few weeks ago, and the fact that she was going to England not because she was Felix's girlfriend but because she felt obliged to take the opportunity. It had also cheered me up, without my realizing it, to see Felix getting fresh with that girl Maggie. It was the first time I'd seen him chatting a girl up as seriously as when I introduced him to Anita. Had he given up?

I might have a chance. The thought of Anita made me feel virtuous, and lonely. It was a nice room. Seemed a shame to waste it.

The phone rang. I picked it up. Another woman's voice, in English.

'No, I do not want a massage, please leave me alone, I want to sleep.' I spoke in Chinese. I was tempted to add that I didn't want a blowjob either. I pulled the phone away from my ear and heard a faint voice.

'Is that you, Johnny? Johnny? Is that you?'

What the fuck? They spoke English and they knew my name?

I put the phone back to my head the way you would a pistol when you're about to shoot yourself.

'It's me, Kath.'

Kath is my sister.

I sat bolt upright.

'Jesus Christ, Kath. How the hell did you get this number? What's up? What is it?' I felt the dread.

She choked, although it might have been a cough, getting her head together. 'Mum's been trying to call you for ages, Johnny. Why didn't you answer your mobile? She had to go to the hospital. It's Gran. It's bad.' She stopped to let me ask the obvious question. These conversations are mapped out like film scripts.

'How bad?'

'Prepare yourself.' She let out a sob. 'She died Johnny.'

I stayed silent. I put a hand to my head.

'About three hours ago. Mum was there. It was quick.'

My cheeks went tight. A football inflated in my throat. The tears were going to come any second.

'Why didn't you answer your fucking phone?'

Why do sisters always start with an inquisition?

'What happened?' I asked. Silent tears were flowing down my cheeks. I held my hair tight in my spare hand, pulled it so it hurt. It helped.

'She was old and weak. She wasn't taking care of herself, and she wouldn't let Mum do what should be done. They had a few flaming rows. But she seemed okay enough, then,' another sob, 'yesterday she had a stroke, a bad one. I don't know all this medical stuff but she was left for too long. It damaged her heart or brain. Mum found her when she went round before work and called the ambulance, and they put her in intensive care but she,' she was crying properly, 'she didn't want to bother, she didn't fight or nothing. Just went away. She gave up. Had enough.'

'Oh fucking hell, oh fucking fucking hell.'

I said it a few more times. My head was full of bad stuff. Bad stuff that was my fault. There was guilt, sorrow, self-loathing, regret, and lots more guilt. And more.

'Kath, I'm so fucking sorry.'

'There's nothing anyone could do,' her voice went quiet, 'even if you'd been here.'

I wasn't going to explain what I was sorry about, how I'd avoided coming home for Christmas, the last get-together I could have had with my Gran. How sorry I was that I'd taken myself off to this shithole called Shanghai and pretended to everyone, including Gran, that it was one fabulous adventure that could only end in fantastic financial success. How much I missed them, how sorry I felt for myself, how I wished I'd never left home, what a lie I was living. And now I'd have to go home, no matter what. No excuses this time. I couldn't not be at the funeral. I'd have to see them. I'd have to let them make me feel like they loved me. And for that I wasn't sorry. I was glad, because I'd wanted to go home for a break for a long time. I could never bring myself to make the effort. But at the funeral I'd meet the well-meaning friends and relatives and Mum and Dad would have told them how exciting a life I was leading in China and they'd want to hear about it and the lies would start and next thing I'd be believing myself again.

'When Mum gets back can you ask her to call me, Kath? It's,' I looked at my watch, 'three o'clock in the morning here. I'd better book a flight. Do you know when the funeral will be?'

'Best you come straight home, Johnny.'

'Yeah. I will. Soon as I can.' I was wondering how long I could be away from my business, what had to be done before I left. Kath and I spoke about her looking after Mum and we hung up.

The tears kept coming. Self-obsessed misery. I got up off the bed and undressed. The room was well heated. In my Y-fronts I went to the mini bar and opened the fridge. It was empty apart from a few cans of soft drinks and two cans of Qingdao beer. It hadn't been turned on. I cracked a can of Qingdao and sat back on the bed, cross-legged.

I drank the beer, forced myself. I raised it towards the ceiling. 'God bless you Gran,' and finished it in two long swigs. I got the other one from the fridge. I lit a cigarette and inhaled so hard it came back out with a monster burp from the beer. I smiled a wet smile at what Gran used to say. 'That'll be the gasworks.'

I slept late in the morning. It took a few seconds after waking up for the sadness to catch up with me. I wasn't dehydrated or hung over, which was a surprise, but the emotional drainage made me feel bad enough, worse even. I went down in the lift to the Western restaurant for breakfast. I was just in time to catch it before it shut at ten o'clock. I meant to stuff my face, drink bad coffee and slip away, get back home and go for a long walk through the concession area, ending up at a travel agent.

Felix was there, on his own, bright-eyed and bushy tailed. He was smiling like a Cheshire cat. There's a reason for a smile like that in the morning.

'Morning, compadre,' he said, 'How goes it?'

'Pretty fucking awful,' I said.

He giggled. 'I think I'm still drunk. You should try a bloody Mary. Joe's been at the staff. He left by the way. Wow, what a night. Shame you guys went up so early. We went crazy. Trashed the place. I'm going to be in trouble, and for something else too.' His eyes shone with mischief, the grin widened.

'Oh yeah? What for? Throw a sofa out the window?'

The smile split Felix's face in half. He leaned forward across the table. 'I shagged Maggie.'

I raised my eyebrows. 'Uhuh. So?'

He was disappointed by my reaction. He wanted to brag like he'd scored the deciding goal in the final minute. 'Christ what a sex maniac she is. It was unbelievable. We were at it all night. She popped me a pill before we started, so maybe I'm high, not drunk. Fuck.' He drank his coffee and sat back, ran both his hands through his hair. 'There was plenty of hot totty last night. Unlike you to pass it up.' He stopped. Maybe noticed the redness in my eyes. But it wasn't that. 'Shit you do look like death. Maybe you did drink too much.' He was joking around.

'Funny you should mention death,' I said. 'I got a call last night, from my sister.' I felt my cheeks tighten. I gripped my chin and squeezed. I let out a breath. 'My grandmother died.' I held it together.

'Oh Christ,' Felix was quick to change his mood. He sat back as if it had been a blow to him too. 'I'm so sorry to hear that. How awful. You were close? Was it expected?'

'Yes and no. She was a great woman. And no it wasn't expected. Very sudden. Fatal stroke by the sounds of it.'

'I hope by that it was painless. Was she old? I mean, a good innings?'

'Just turned eighty.'

'Full life?' I think it was a question.

'If you call surviving the Blitz, moving from the East End to Basildon and working in a Marconi factory on and off when you weren't bringing up five kids, I suppose so, yes, a full life. She was a good woman, very special.' I filled up at the word 'special'. 'The funeral will be quite something.'

'When is it?'

'I spoke to my mum at five o'clock this morning. It isn't fixed yet, but probably next weekend, or the week after. I'd better get back by Friday, bloody hell. I could use one of those free flights you get yourself.' It helped to talk about practicalities.

'Sorry we can't put you in a suitcase.' Felix pretended to be thinking how he could help me out, which he patently couldn't. 'But look on the bright side,' he said. What bright side? 'We're going to be back in the UK at the same time, so we can meet up in London and have a few pints. That'll be cool.'

I did my best to show enthusiasm but my words came out like I'd volunteered to clean a public toilet. 'Yeah, that'd be great.'

'Make sure you give me your UK number,' he said. 'And I'll give you mine.' He got up to go to the buffet and stood by the table, hovering above me; the ignorant, naïve, pompous, Godfather non-fearing, yet for all that well-meaning ass. 'Come on, you need some food in you.

# 13

## HOME

I FLEW home in business class. Economy was full of Chinese students and the airline said I was a 'compassionate case' so they bumped me up. Bill Connor had tipped me off about telling them why I was flying at short notice.

When your gran's died and people do nice things like that you want to cry.

I recognized the bloke beside me from chamber of commerce events. You always knew someone on those flights. Can't remember his name. He ran an exhibition company. He was a member of what I called the 'Pro Pudong Party', who believed Pudong was the future of Shanghai. I disagreed. The first thing I said was Pudong wasn't even in Shanghai. That got him going.

I was keen to talk. It was good to be distracted. He was up for it and quite amusing. He described the enormous conference and exhibition centre and the 'Maglev', a German-built high-speed train that would connect it to the new Pudong Airport. The centre was booked out for a year in advance, and one expo he'd organised there had broken all his previous records. It was a wine one. Most people, me included, thought the Chinese would never take to wine.

I quoted Charlie Thurrold's white elephants at him and said how I'd heard the Maglev was never going to pay for itself.

I told him why I was coming home and he was sympathetic, encouraged me to talk about Gran. He shared his own family history, told me details about his wife and how their marriage was going, which maybe he shouldn't have.

We were matey by the time we landed at Heathrow in the afternoon, and that's when it got tricky. I don't think he noticed. If he did, he was too polite or confused to show it.

We were standing beside the baggage conveyor belt, talked out. We'd reached that point where it was time for a break. Both of us wanted to get home or outside for a cigarette.

There was an additional factor: I couldn't go through customs with him, or in front of him, so I needed to wait for his luggage to arrive and pretend mine hadn't.

This being my first experience of business class I had no idea your bags are supposed to come out first. Note the 'supposed to'. Heathrow could mess it up for me like it always does, couldn't it?

My cheap black shoulder bag was the very first thing to appear. I stared at it, trying to be casual. The guy was right beside me. I avoided eye contact. I could swear he was watching me. The other business class passengers were around us. They picked up their luggage and disappeared, except for my friend of course. For some reason his bag didn't make it with the business class load. My own one came round again, and again.

He started telling me a story about losing his luggage in New York. Mine passed under my nose one more time. I think he saw me glance at it out of the corner of my eye. I brazened it out and we stood in silence until, thank God, a brown leather suit carry case popped out the chute in front of us. He picked it up with obvious relief. The students were pushing and shoving to get their massive shrink-wrapped suitcases and laundry bags.

'Well, nice to see you,' he said. 'Hope your bag turns up. I better run, my sister will be waiting. And I hope you have as good a week as possible, under the circumstances.'

'Thanks, yeah. Good to see you too.'

We shook hands and he left.

I watched him enter the nothing-to-declare corridor, counted to twenty, and walked to meet my bag as it came round. I slung it over my shoulder and approached the wide entrance under the white-on-green arrow, took a deep breath, and set off along the walkway between the polished metal tables.

A man in a white shirt with black and yellow epaulettes stepped forward. They're tipped off by passport control.

'Excuse me, sir, may I ask you to come this way please?'

I didn't respond. What's the point?

I glanced at the big white double doors into the arrivals hall as they swung open and saw the brown leather bag and the back of my friend's head. He was embracing a nice woman. She was smiling straight at me. The doors shut.

The customs officer showed me into an interview room with a table and three plastic chairs. I put the bag on the table and opened it. He went through it, removing the contents: a pair of black shoes, unpolished, a grey jacket borrowed from Bill Connor, a copy of his magazine to show my mum because my picture was in it, T-shirts, jeans, green tea for gifts.

'Looks okay to me,' he said. 'Shall I let you repack, sir?'

'Sure.'

He thanked me for my co-operation.

'Someone will be along in a minute, sir,' he said. 'Do sit down.'

'It's all right.' I threw my stuff back into the bag, along with two hundred duty free Marlboros, and pulled out a plastic chair. It could be half an hour before they came.

This one was quick, ten minutes. I was surprised. He was in plain clothes and he was old. He had grey hair and his face was wrinkled, bags under the eyes. He was a chain-smoking, hard-drinking, old school copper. In my previous experience the 'interviews' were with young policemen in uniforms. I imagined they were sent to Heathrow to practise their technique. This one must have been close to retirement. He sat down opposite me.

'Good afternoon, Mr. Trent. Welcome back to the UK.' I couldn't detect any sarcasm. 'Business or pleasure? Or both?' Now I did detect it, the sarcasm that is. There was a tiny hint. He couldn't help himself. He wanted me to know he'd read my file. It was on the table in front of him. Inside were my potted bio, criminal record, and a list of my 'associates'.

'My gran's funeral.'

'Oh. I'm sorry to hear that. My condolences.' He paused so I could thank him. I didn't say a word. He cleared his throat with a noise like a truck moving off in low gear and came to the point. 'So, you'll be seeing your old mates, the family.' He made it sound like the mafia. 'You've been keeping in touch? Up to speed on the comings and goings?'

Let me get this straight: I'm not a career criminal. I'm not a criminal at all. To be a criminal you have to mean it. You have to intend to break the law and profit by it. I made a mistake. I was misled. I got mixed up with a bad bunch and one thing led to another and next thing I was selling pills in nightclubs. It was good money but I didn't do it for that. Everyone wants to be your friend when you've got gear on you, including the boys and girls from the sixth form. I could afford to buy them drinks too, but like I say, the money was secondary. It was the popularity.

I was not in Shanghai because I was running from the law like a marked man, nor was I one of those clever bastards they can never pin anything on. I haven't got the wits or the balls. And if I was I wouldn't be swanning through Heathrow like this; unless Gran's funeral was a set-up to get me back home so the law could grab me.

That only happens in movies.

I got caught, didn't I. You don't not get caught when your best mate's little brother dies in hospital because he ate a dodgy pill and everyone thinks it's your fault. No one's going to help you.

The things that did help were my age and the lawyer. He was young too, wanted to make a name for himself. He got me off the manslaughter and dealing charges. I went down for possession and accessory. The guys I bought from did a runner, disappeared.

I wanted to claim the pill wasn't mine but the lawyer had better ideas and I suppose he was right, in the long run. Though I still wonder.

I did ten months in Young Offenders. Mum and dad called it by the old name: Borstal. I prefer the new one. It makes it sound like you were rude to a policeman.

When I came out no one would talk to me. My family too, apart from Gran of course. I gave it a go, did that job at Burger King in London for a bit. My probation officer set that up. But it was impossible to stay at home – I couldn't afford to rent – with the constant sideways glances, the hushed voices in the kitchen when I was watching television, the basic fact that everyone hates you.

So I said, 'Fuck it', and went to Hong Kong.

Talking of being rude to a policeman. I wanted to say 'Fuck you' to this one.

'Officer, I haven't been in touch with the people you call my 'old mates' since what happened, seven years ago. I'm clean, I've been clean from that day, and I will stay clean for the rest of my life.' I meant it.

'Johnny, do you mind if I call you Johnny? ' He put his elbows on the table. I shook my head. 'You understand. We have to do our job. Anyone with a record we see coming home from whatever country. I'm sure you think it's a waste of time. But it has to be done. Merely a formality.'

My arse. He was getting a kick out of it. It was his last chance to be a clever cop before he put his slippers on.

'I can assure you it *is* a waste of time,' I said, keeping my voice extra polite and as flat as possible. 'And if you don't mind me saying, it's a waste of mine too.' I forced a smile and sighed at him, like I was in charge of the interview. 'If you could see the temptation out in Shanghai, how easy it is to score, the smarties you can buy in every club, and witness how I'm totally not into that stuff, you'd never bother with me. 'Fact, you'd give me a medal.'

He sat back, cleared his throat. 'So there's a scene in Shanghai is there? I'm surprised. I thought the Commies wouldn't allow that sort of thing. What are we talking? Pills, E, harder? Crack? Don't tell me they still do opium.'

I can spot a leading question a mile away. I might as well humour him. 'Since you ask, the most popular at the moment is the 'head shaker'. It's E but sometimes it's other pills, like speed. Doesn't matter. It's an image thing. They pretend to be on it. You don't want to stand too close if you're holding a drink.' I hoped he'd get the joke.

'Cheap?'

He didn't get the joke. Give him credit for trying to catch me out. I spoke slowly. 'I have no idea.'

I gave him more on the Shanghai crime scene for the hell of it: the Japanese gangsters, the local mafia, the secret gambling dens. I skipped the fact that the police were in cahoots with most of them. He might have thought I was casting aspersions on his noble profession.

'All right. Interesting. But we're here to talk about what you do in the UK. Not China.'

It was my turn to sit back. 'So let's get on with it shall we?'

He put his hand on his pocket. It must have been where his cigarettes were. He wanted to light up. He frowned and gave me the spiel: should I run into and have a chat with my previous associates who happened to be pushing pills, or engaging in some form of criminal activity, and if the substance – nice pun, I smiled – of that chat might be interesting to the boys in blue, or brown suits in the drug squad, then be a nice lad and call the confidential number I was about to be given. In return I could rest assured my travels would proceed smoothly as in; they wouldn't tell the Chinese I'd lied like a Spartan on my initial visa application about former convictions, and they'd also, being the souls of generosity they were, make sure my passport got renewed without a problem when it was due.

They had the idea, which wasn't a bad one, that a bloke like me who came home once a year at most, when I got together with my mates I'd get a nice summary of the highs and lows of my one time partners-in-crime's activities in my absence which they, the police, could match up with info from other informants. Time and again, and here we were, yet again, I insisted I didn't associate with that crowd anymore, never would. But they kept me on their books, kept their tabs on me.

'Have a nice stay,' were his parting words. He'd forgotten the funeral.

Before I went downstairs to the Piccadilly Line I stepped outside for that cigarette. I half expected the copper to be there too.

It was late when I got to Basildon. Mum and dad had stayed up. My sister was in bed. The moment I walked in the door I had a new sensation, one I'd never experienced when I came home. It was that mood you get when there's been a death in the family. In the course of things it doesn't, or shouldn't, happen that often. Everyone turns nice in a subdued, reverential way, nothing like you get at other family events. It was as if Gran had dropped a blanket of peace on her way up to heaven.

My mum gave me a warm hug. She hadn't done that in ages. She said something nice about me coming home, and I said something grown up about how tough it must have been for her. She'd loved her mum despite the endless fights, and she'd borne the brunt of looking after Gran for little thanks. Gran had never been impressed by my dad, and her constant, unquestioning support for me after my drama had grated too.

Mum made me a cup of tea, sent my dad to bed and listened to my straightforward account of my journey. I didn't mention the interview. I never do. She described Gran the last time she saw her alive and gave me a sketchy description of how she'd found her dead. There was lots more to talk about but it could wait, she said. I had a room of my own, the smallest one, for obvious reasons. I'd hardly used it from the age of nineteen.

'I've put some post on the table for you,' my mum said before I went up. 'And there's a cutting from the newspaper from Uncle Tony. I didn't send it because you were coming home.' I gave her a peck on the cheek and another hug.

Last time I'd been home I'd taken down my teenage posters, centrespreads from football magazines, a couple of foxy ones from the earliest issues of *Loaded*, that sort of thing. The only picture left on the wall was a print of a battleship my dad had given me when I was a youngster and a cheap silk scroll painting my mum had hung up to 'make me feel at home.' A small set of bookshelves held a row of tattered paperbacks and a stack of magazines including those early *Loaded* ones. They were the nearest thing to porn I had. I'd sneaked the real stuff out the house and chucked it in a skip before I left for Hong Kong.

As Mum said, there were letters on my desk, nothing personal, only circulars, like a couple of reminders from a youth club I'd been 'encouraged' to join by my probation officer. Underneath the small pile was a full page from the *Daily Telegraph*, folded into quarters. I opened it up and saw Uncle Tony's scrawl on the top: 'Thought you might be interested.'

Uncle Tony's nickname was 'Tory Tony'. He was as blue as the Chelsea strip. He'd held a minor post in the local government for a while. He loved to talk about his 'time on the council'.

I sank into the soft single bed with its familiar brown bedspread like I was an old dog on its favourite rug. I felt good, safe. I stuck my head in it and sniffed. I was transported back to when I was a young, innocent schoolboy, naughty but not bad, not evil, like this was my refuge, my time capsule. I'd slept in this bed all my life until I left home. I could pretend Steve Turner was alive, that I was going to college, to qualify in something useful and get a decent job. I'd fancied myself as a computer scientist, as they were called back in the day. Maybe they still are. I didn't know what it meant. I dreamt I'd work in a big outfit like a bank or an accounting firm in the city and I'd be the 'go to' nerd for the top managers and I'd create programmes – and websites of course, but they weren't invented. Maybe I'd have caught that first big internet wave and made a fortune.

But that hadn't happened. Nor did the other careers I'd dreamt of, like vet, musician (I'm crap, that was pure fantasy) or profes-sional footballer (kick a ball I can). I turned back over, stared at the white chipboard ceiling and wondered if anyone ever fulfilled their childhood fantasy. I decided the answer was no.

I switched on the bedside light and held up the newspaper page. Uncle Tony's article was a couple of columns halfway down one side.

'So and So Appointed General Secretary of the Party' the title said. There was a line underneath: 'Possibly the first smooth and peaceful transition of power in Communist China.'

It started off with how the Party was handing over to the next generation of leaders in what was, as the title said, the first smooth transition, so far. But the writer noted it had only just started. The man who had been made Secretary wouldn't become President for a few more months and there was a fair bit of wheeling and dealing to be done. What he focussed on was the regional rivalry that might spring up between Shanghai and Beijing. The outgoing President was a Shanghai boy and he'd filled the top positions with his local buddies. The new guy was a Beijinger. They never get on at the best of times, the two cities, but these two had more reasons to be set against each other. It had something to do with what their fathers had done to each other in the Cultural Revolution. Already the first shots had been fired in the 'smooth and peaceful' transition, although they weren't physical. Those battles are fought behind the closed doors of disciplinary committees and the like. Sure enough, a senior Shanghai official had been charged with corruption, related to land he'd sold to a Hong Kong developer. It was a couple of blocks in the heart of the city and he'd screwed the price down for them in return for a cash bribe and an interest in the development project. The Torygraph's writer was an old hand whose name I recognised. He said to stand by for the 'corruption scandal' to spread to more Shanghai officials and property developers. I remembered Charlie Thurrold's words about them being up to their armpits in dodgy commercial stuff.

I yawned, a big one. All of a sudden I was exhausted. I say with jetlag that you've got to hold out to the last minute but when that minute comes, get your head down quick or you'll be up all day and night. I stripped off and climbed under the covers. I was out like a light.

The next few days are a blur of sitting around with relatives and Gran's funeral itself. It was a big do. People who'd known her when she was young, during the Blitz, came out from London. There must have been two hundred in the pub for the knees-up. Gran was a character, pillar of the community, everyone loved her.

There was a fight too, not physical. And like the Chinese government we kept it behind closed doors. There's always one when my family has been together for longer than a day or two. We threw off the peace blanket. It started when Mum went off at Dad for not being nice enough to Gran's old friends. Kath took dad's side, and I was worried that soon as I opened my mouth they'd be off at me about Borstal and buggering off to China, which is what always used to happen until Gran told them to shut up. So Mum got pissed off at me for not supporting her, and got herself into knots because she said how with Gran gone it looked like she was filling her shoes, but when she said that she remembered it was Gran who stuck up for me and she wasn't ready to do that yet. So, she switched tactics and started on Kath, whose new boyfriend had been sick in the pub car park halfway through the wake because he'd been necking the drinks. He looked like a loser to me, but I wasn't going to say so.

I was already beginning to get uncomfortable. The dog-curling-up-in-the-old-basket – I said rug didn't I – feeling was wearing off. I had a couple of days before my flight back to Shanghai, so I made up a lie about going to see a client in London on recruitment business, and said I'd stay with an old mate, Richard, who Mum and Dad knew as Tricky Dicky, his school nickname. They approved of him. He'd traded everything from second-hand textbooks via sports bags to porn mags. He never did illegal stuff either (porn doesn't count). It was harmless and he never screwed anyone, just got them the best deal and took a fair slice for himself. He was well-liked, the closest thing I had to a good influence at a similar age. He'd watched me go astray with a mixture of pity and concern and he was the only person to say a kind word when Steve Turner died: 'Now you know what a tragic stupid cunt you've been.'

Tricky and I kept in touch. He'd called me 'Me Old China'. He'd done well in the City and lived in a penthouse in the Docklands with his girlfriend.

After a good catch-up the first night, Tricky was chill about me going off to see my 'China plates' at the other end of London. His girlfriend had dropped a strong hint that she fancied a night in with a movie.

It had been in my mind when I was making the excuse to Mum and Dad, but the real reason I wanted to go to London was to see Anita. I knew she was there with Felix. I was keen to see him too, or curious. I wanted to observe him on his home turf, the real Felix.

I called him on a London number he'd given me and he suggested a pub in Fulham. He too was staying with a mate while Anita was with Zhou Jianguo's son Tony and his mother in a service apartment in Knightsbridge. When we spoke on the phone, Felix and me, he promised to tell me about Mrs. Zhou and her son and what they'd done at his brother's wedding. I was keen to hear the story. Anita had already done her whirlwind tour of the UK.

It was a Wednesday, early evening. While I walked to the Light Railway from Tricky's house the commuters came at me in waves. They carried jackets on their arms or over their shoulders. It was a late spring day that had started cold and turned warm. At Bank, where I changed from the DLR to the Circle Line, the commuters swirled around me like a Jacuzzi. That's what it felt like, honest. They buffeted me, massaged me, said sorry when they stepped past me. I felt like I was being emotionally and physically caressed.

So when I walked into a Fulham pub full of Henries and Annabels and suits and braces and striped shirts, I gave them some love. I chatted to a young bloke at the bar while I waited for Felix and Anita. Sure enough, he was an estate agent. I mentioned Shanghai and he went wide-eyed and told me he was thinking of applying to come over with his company who were in the process of setting up a China office.

'Come and join the party,' I said, and he got more excited but I spotted Felix and Anita and excused myself.

'How was the funeral?' Felix asked as I handed him a pint. His face was stern. He was keen to get the sombre stuff over with.

'Good send-off, thanks, and a right old knees-up down the pub.'

'Good for you,' he said. He reached up and patted me on the back. I was staring at Anita.

Her clothes were different, nothing like her Shanghai style. She was wearing a white pullover like a Scottish fisherman's, tight blue jeans and calf high boots, and she'd let her hair hang straight. She wasn't wearing make-up. She looked plain, tired, like a washed-out hippy.

She'd greeted me with a hug but it was a hold-away one, not a clincher. She was awkward. I could feel her discomfort, the tension in her arms, heard it in the way she'd agreed to a glass of wine. I gave her the warm smile I'd been dishing out round the bar and she gave me back one of those mouth twitches you do when you don't want to be spoken to.

'And what about the wedding?' I asked them both.

Anita didn't speak. Her face was blank.

'It was a great bash,' Felix said. 'Wasn't it, Anita?' He put his hand on her arm, meaning to include her. What he got was a grimace and a shrug, obviously meant to remove the hand. 'Yes, well,' Felix said. 'It wasn't as bad as I expected.'

He turned back to me, 'Remember I told you how my brother is the favourite of the family, military hero and so on? Well, get this. Even on his wedding day, when he's star of the show, and his bride, of course,' he stopped to push his hair back, 'I was mobbed by people wanting to speak to me, non-stop, about China, congratulate me on making the move, how envious they were and so on. Old and young, let alone Alex's fellow officers. I bet we'll see a few of them out in China one day, when they leave the army. They're worried shitless about what they can do on civvy street. Hey, you run a recruitment business. You could get them all jobs in Shanghai. How about that? Think of the money you'd make.' He raised his hand to high five me. 'China traders, Johnny! That's what we are. They haven't seen our like since Marco fucking Polo.' He leaned in and lowered his voice, 'Wouldn't it be cool if we could get everyone in the pub drinking *baijiu*?'

I felt obliged to say yes.

'Ha, found you Fawcett-Smith!' I swear I heard a donkey speak. It hit me in the back of the head with a brain-piercing shriek. A podgy, red-faced twenty-something with a pullover round his shoulders slapped Felix on the back. With him were two others, one in a waxed jacket with sleeves too short for his lanky arms, the other with the same pullover thing. They radiated good health and heartiness, and shaggy haircuts. Compared to them, I looked and felt like a liberated Second World War Jap POW.

Anita brightened up. She recognized one of them from the wedding. While they brayed at Felix and each other, I wanted to ask her what was up, and why she was giving me the attitude, but Felix was introducing me.

'This is Johnny Trent, a good friend from Shanghai.'

One of the three knew him from Oxford, another had been a colleague at Smyth and Corrigan in London.

'So is it true?' Donkey Voice moved in beside me while the Oxford friend spoke to Felix. The third guy cornered Anita and offered to buy her a drink. 'That Felix is right-hand man to the top Shanghai property Taipan? Isn't that the right word? That he lives in a massive villa, flies around the country in a private jet looking for projects and he's running Shanghai's most exclusive country club since the old days?' Felix caught the tail end and gave me a sly grin and a wink.

'Pretty much,' I said. I wondered where the private jet came from. Not necessarily Felix. My family said the same sort of thing about me.

'Sounds amazing. In fact, the whole place sounds amazing.' He lowered his voice, 'And is it true about the revolution?'

'I beg your pardon?'

'The revolution the magazines are writing about,' he whispered, and stole a glance at Anita, which, bearing in mind what he said next, made me want to throttle him. 'The sexual revolution.' He stressed the 'sexual'. He leant in so I felt his breath on my cheek. 'The Chinese have discovered sex. They're at it like bunnies. You can pick up a girl any time of day or night and she'll, well, you know.' He went coy. He backed off an inch and coloured up the way Felix did.

I knew what he was talking about, and I could take it calmly now he stopped ogling Anita. I'd met the 'journalists' who wrote those articles. They trooped through Shanghai, buttonholing the likes of me, Joe and Bill in bars and asking us to help them find a *mama-san*, a drug dealer, a pimp and a homosexual but a lesbian would be best. I talk about it myself, how free and easy it was in Shanghai, but the idea that Chinese people had all of a sudden discovered sex was ridiculous. How do you get a population of one point three billion if you don't have sex for Christ's sake?

'Don't forget the construction cranes,' I'd say to the journos.

'I suppose you could say it's a good town for a party,' I told Felix's friend. 'But why don't you come and see it for yourself? I'm sure Felix could put you up in his country club, or his villa.'

'I might well come out with my girlfriend next year. Everyone is talking about Shanghai.'

'Bringing your girlfriend defeats the purpose, don't you think?' I said.

'I'm sorry?'

'Never mind.'

When the time came for a round, Felix stepped forward. I went to help him fetch and carry. 'You haven't got your young charge with you,' I said. 'Tony, isn't it? What you done with him?'

'Oh, there's a story.' Felix was trying to catch the eye of a bar girl. He spoke out of the side of his mouth. 'The whole plan was brought forward. Sudden last minute decision. It was organized from the Shanghai end the week before we left. All I had to do was drop him off at a crammer, a tutorial college here in London, and set up his mother in a service apartment. My main job is to find them a flat. Guess what the budget is?' He nudged me with his elbow.

'No idea. Half a million?'

'Come on, we're talking Mr. Zhou here. And Knightsbridge.'

'So?'

'Two million.'

'Christ. You get a commission?'

'Ha, very funny. He's my boss. But apart from that I'm back doing my old job. How ironic is that? Of course, if I was doing my old job, I'd get a commission. On two million. Imagine that! God knows what they'll do when me and Anita go back. Mrs. Zhou doesn't speak a word of English and Tony's is basic, plus he has a habit.' The bar girl spotted him. Felix ordered and turned back to me.

'Drugs? At his age? You got to be kidding.'

He laughed. 'No. Games. Slot machines. The day before the wedding, Anita and I took them over to Weston-Super-Mare to see the sea and we lost him. Christ, what a nightmare. I almost called the police. Anita found him in the over eighteen or whatever age it is side of one of those arcades, where you can play slot machines for money. He was winning too. Bloody hell. No idea how he got in there. He's sixteen.'

'Probably told them his Chinese age, which'd be eighteen the way they count. How did they get on at the wedding by the way?'

'Good point. As for the wedding, Anita helped out, translating and so on. They stayed together in a local hotel, a little country house-type place. I went for dinner one night. Bit tricky with the food but the evening worked out well... very well, in the end.' He gave me a smirk. I would remain unaware of its significance for a long time. He moved on. 'As for the wedding itself, they seemed to enjoy it, especially the church bit. Not suggesting they're Christian, of course, but they do love ritual, don't they? Mrs. Zhou was taking photos every five seconds, and I expected her phone to go off. But it didn't. She's a nice lady. She used to be an academic and she's on a government think tank-type thing, to do with land, as you'd expect. I suppose she's sort of an official. Very sophisticated, apart from one small, or rather, big thing she did...' Felix paid and we picked up the drinks, three each.

'Which was?'

'The *hongbao*, the red envelope. Their wedding present.'

'They gave one of those?'

'Of course.' Felix squeezed up beside me in the crush.

'All right,' I said. 'Go on. Tell me how much.'

Felix spoke into my ear. 'Eight hundred and eighty-eight quid. Cash.'

'Jesus Christ.'

'That improved my family's opinion of China, I can tell you!'

We'd reached the group, which had found space by a big mirror with a mantelpiece. Before we got back into the conversation, Felix had a final word on the Zhous.

'My main worry is that young Tony might find a casino in London. I hope his mother can control him. She doesn't have much else to do.'

'You going to stay on, settle them in?'

'I'll have to. How about you? When you going back?'

'Day after tomorrow. Things to be done.'

'Which airline?'

'China Eastern.'

'Might be the same flight as Anita. That's when she flies.' He glanced at her and turned to his mates. He started talking up Shanghai.

They couldn't get enough. They must have had a fair bit at the wedding. I watched and listened and kept an eye on the guy who was chatting to Anita. She was more like her usual self.

Maybe, now she'd discovered the gentrified English boys, she'd gone off me, the oik from Essex. She was a Shanghai girl, measuring up the material benefits, looking out for the opportunity. On my way over, and a few other times besides, I'd daydreamed how different things might have been if Anita hadn't come to the UK with Felix and the Zhous, but with me. Not for the funeral – another time. Just a trip. What would she have made of my rough lot compared to Felix's? Naturally, I thought she'd have more fun with me, but I had to admit she might not be as impressed by suburban Basildon as I am sure she was by 'H.S.F.' Wiltshire. Watching her laughing with Felix's mate in the pub, it seemed like I was right.

I joined in with Felix and his two friends. He was demonstrating the difference between Shanghai dialect and Mandarin. Next he explained his boss Zhou Jianguo's government connections, how important they were, how nothing could be done in China without *guanxi*. It was obvious he was implying he had the *guanxi* too, thanks to his job. The bloke I'd had a quick chat with when I got to the pub came over and asked if he could join us. He wanted to hear more, like everyone. We were holding court.

Felix laid it on with a trowel, and if you saw how hungry these people were for the good news, you wouldn't mind the exaggeration so much, his endless string of superlatives. He was telling them what they wanted to hear. Making them happy. Like those journos and their editors and the public who read the stories.

It made me wonder why I was the cynic in these conversations. Was I that jaded? What had happened, apart from the usual hassles from bureaus and stuff, to make me that way? As Mike Bennett said to me: if I was so pissed at China, why was I there? I was making money wasn't I? My recruitment business was doing fine.

Quite.

And why was I about to fly back in two days? Why did I whinge about the lack of basic freedoms like I was a politician or United Nations busybody? You live in a place, you abide by the rules. So what if they make them and break them? That's the rules.

For all the grief, I loved it. I've gone on enough about how it was a big con, how Shanghai was a *mama-san* one minute and a seductive courtesan the next, and how racist the Chinese are, but you can love someone despite their faults, can't you?

Can't you?

So I picked on a bloke in the circle and told him, like I had Felix, about the opportunities, the money I was making, the clients flooding through my door. I told them how we worked hard and played harder. I described the restaurants, how they moved the Shanghai Concert Hall a few metres, brick by brick, to make way for a highway, the sophisticated Shanghainese who understood the outside world.

I even mentioned the cranes. Felix hadn't said it.

Once or twice I caught Anita staring at me like she was wondering about something. I grinned at her. It's all right I wanted to say. I'm up for it. I mean it. Tell you on the plane. This time I'm going to crack it.

She gave me a weak smile.

Like an afterthought I remembered the article in the Torygraph, about the government changes in Beijing. When we were back at the bar, him buying another round, I mentioned it to Felix. 'Keep an eye on the papers,' I said. 'You're more likely to read stuff here than in Shanghai. And I hope you have a job when you get back.' I was joking.

'What do you mean?' Felix said. I started to explain the potential ramifications, but he stopped me. 'No way. Not SLIC. We're *guanxi*'d to the very top,' he said.

'But it's the top that's changing.'

'No, it's not. Only the figurehead. The real power is behind the throne, and it stays there. That's where our *guanxi* is. We'll be okay.'

'And it hasn't crossed your mind, like it has mine, to wonder why Zhou sent his wife and son to London? That maybe he's getting them out of the way, somewhere safe?'

Felix's hand went to his hair. He hadn't considered that. After a short pause he said, 'Don't be ridiculous!' and we had to get the drinks back to our audience.

We didn't speak about the subject again in the pub. I barely spoke to Felix again, and exchanged only a few words with Anita, to see if she wanted to meet up the next day before I went back to Basildon in the evening to say goodbye to my folks. But Felix had arranged for a friend of his, a girl doing part-time secretarial work who had time on her hands, to take Anita shopping. So that was that. I'd see her on the plane. We'd confirmed we were on the same flight.

# 14

## LAND GRAB

'So, what did you think of England?'

'It's okay.'

We were a couple of seats apart in economy class. The one in the middle was vacant. On this flight it was business and first that were full of men in suits studying 'Business Mandarin' phrasebooks, and the back was empty. Compared to the way over, economy was like an abandoned classroom. I expected to find an old exercise book under my seat, or a wad of chewing gum. My compassionate upgrade had been one way.

Once we'd taken off, Anita shut her eyes in a blatant display of fake nerves and kept them shut, as if she was asleep.

I flicked through the in-flight magazine and watched her out of the corner of my eye. She was back in her Shanghainese get-up; short skirt, cutaway jacket and tight designer T-shirt, and she'd put her hair back up in its bun. I'd have loved to nuzzle my head into her neck, lean on her shoulder and doze off myself, or pretend to, like she was.

We must have been halfway across Europe when she opened her eyes. She stared at the seat-back in front of her. It was my turn to pretend: that we were having a conversation.

'Which part did you like most?'

'What? Oh.' She didn't turn. 'Edinburgh. Nice shops.'

'You never told me about Felix's brother's wedding. You enjoy it? Good party?'

'It was okay.'

'Lots of handsome young men in uniforms, officers and gentlemen?'

'Yes.'

The Anita I knew would have got out her digital camera and scrolled through dozens of pictures of herself with Felix, with Felix's parents, the brother and the bride, Anita holding her hand up in the V for victory. Then shots from her coach tour, in front of a statue of Shakespeare in Stratford, on that famous street in Edinburgh, standing in front of her bus, with the driver, and so on.

This wasn't that Anita.

'Come on, Anita, what's on your mind? Something up?'

'Nothing. I'm tired. I'm going to go to sleep.'

'All right. You do that. Want me to wake you when they serve food?'

'I'll be okay, thanks. I'm going to the back.' She got up to go find an empty row.

'See you in Shanghai,' I said.

'See you in Shanghai.'


Felix flew back a couple of weeks later in mid May, having found an apartment for the Zhous, a touch over two million. He'd arranged things through his old company. Mrs. Zhou and her son stayed in the service apartment while renovations were done. The boy was beginning to acquire an odd accent from the Arab teenagers he met at tutorial college and whose apartments he visited to play computer games.

In Felix's absence, things had not been developing at Buckingham Park, and if you're a developer, that's a problem.

You might think, as I did, that after the party at Paradise Island and Felix producing the brochure, plus the other sponsorship stuff he organized, SLIC would at least have 'turned the first sod'. They'd done nothing.

The project stalled before it started. I told you it never got built in the end. Here's why.

They hadn't got the rights to the land.

Red herring. Brief but relevant.

In the early 2000s when the Chinese Communist Party made its all but counter-revolutionary concession to common sense and recognized private property as a legal right, they left one item off the agenda: land. All land in China is state-owned, every square inch of it. Urban land is clearly specified as such, while farmland is owned 'collectively'.

When a property developer wants to build a luxury villa complex on farmland, they cannot 'own' it, they can only purchase the right to use it. But that right cannot be purchased from the 'Collective' because collectives are trusted only with farmland. So it first has to be transferred to the state.

But who is the Collective? How do you negotiate with them?

There is actually no 'Collective'. Farmland is claimed by the family whose great granddad jumped on it when the Commies lynched the landlords in 1949. And his descendants rarely act collectively. That allows the state, which is the county government, in this case, to skip the boring business of negotiating a price. They decide what they're willing to pay, based on the 'agricultural value' of the land, and tell the farmers they can take it or leave it. The county government then sells the land-use rights to the developer, valued on what it's worth covered in villas or a golf course, which is a heck of a lot more. County governments love land 'sales'. So much easier than collecting taxes.

If the farmers don't like the price and kick up a fuss, the government orders them to accept it. It's in the collective interest after all.

And if the farmers won't budge? That's *against* the collective interest, which amounts to the state, which equates to civil disobedience. So they kick the shit out of them.

That, in a nutshell, is everything you need to know about land sales in China, except for one extra twist with Royal Buckingham Park.

The total area of the project was 300 hectares. That's approximately 750 football pitches. Massive. It included two neighbouring villages, and neighbouring villages in China tend to despise each other, so that makes two very un-collective collectives. The county government, based in and named after a town called Dongchang, had to keep them both happy, which meant they had to pretend to give each one special treatment, while doing the opposite. But above all the Dongchang government did not want to lose a cent more than necessary in their sweet deal with SLIC. Bonanzas from selling off three hundred hectares do not come along that often. This could set them up for life.

Dongchang set out to find someone who could speak on behalf of the farmers, the voice of the collective, in other words: someone to lean on them.

We'll call them Village A and Village B.

Village A was straightforward. It had a local hero who'd made a fortune in the long distance freight business and multiplied it on the Shanghai stock market. He lived in style in the big city when he wasn't touring the country to shag his mistresses. Back home he'd built a new school, a couple of roads, and employed hundreds of locals.

After a round of boozy banquets and the promise of more jobs driving trucks and running warehouses, Village A agreed to the government price and promised not to make trouble. The local hero received a tidy 'consultancy fee'. He also had to employ a couple of children of the Dongchang government officials in his Shanghai office.

Village A's farmland was set for transfer to the State, way undervalued.

When the self-appointed representatives of Village B, who didn't have an equivalent eminent citizen, were made the same offer, however, even after the boozy banquets and a men-only 'research' trip to the casinos and brothels of Macau, they wanted more. The excuse: their land was on the bank of the Yangtze River. It was a wasteland of reeds and mud, but, they claimed, they were about to develop it as a pearl farm. A few years ago a Shanghai-based cheap jewellery entrepreneur had expressed an interest in renting the wetlands for that purpose. That nothing had come of it didn't prevent Village B's claim it could still be a pearl farm, and there was money in pearls, which they would be losing.

Village B persuaded Village A, against the advice of the local hero, to demand higher compensation.

The Dongchang government refused. The potential pearl farm was a sham. They themselves had introduced the Shanghai entrepreneur, which Village B seemed to have forgotten, and he'd told them it would never work.

There was a stalemate while the government and the villages, who had put aside their traditional enmity, tried to find ways to influence each other. Although things were testy, neither side wanted a fight, yet.

For the Dongchang government, 'influence' meant sending in the tax bureau to catch out a small business – for example, a factory that employed many of the local women and was owned by one of Village B's representatives. They also ordered a clampdown on un-roadworthy farm vehicles, which was pretty much every tractor and small truck, and had the Environmental Protection Bureau ban pesticide and chemical fertiliser within five kilometres of the riverbank. They claimed there was a national clean-up campaign. The farmers used chemicals like footballers use aftershave.

Then Dongchang got in touch with James Li, Felix's immediate boss.

They gave him two options, raise the purchase price or would SLIC like to 'satisfy the villagers' demands' directly? He was given assurances that the local police would be supportive, for a small fee.

Li went for option two.

On his return to his office in Shanghai, the first call Felix received was from a journalist for the *Washington Herald* called Harold Beecher.

Beecher was well known. His name cropped up in our state-of-China debates in the Backstreet like the '66 World Cup does in every pub quiz. I'd seen him at a couple of parties and had a good chat once. He was a nice guy but a nasty journalist. He went for stories like a pit bull, took no prisoners. People said he was a shit-stirrer who hated China. After Shanghai he went to Afghanistan and got blown up by a landmine. He didn't deserve that.

'Felix, are you okay,' Beecher asked, 'to comment about the situation involving your company in Dongchang County, Jiangsu Province?'

'I'm sorry, what do you mean by situation?'

'The stand-off between the villagers and the government over the land for your development. It's called Royal Buckingham Park, right?'

While he'd been in the UK, Felix had been in touch with his office. They wanted every detail about the Zhous' apartment. His regular question back was about the date for the Buckingham Park ground-breaking ceremony. It featured in his marketing plan and he wanted to be there. The office had mixed the good news with the bad. The good news was he wouldn't miss it while he was in England, the bad news was there was a 'small problem'. They'd given him the barest details. Felix didn't know SLIC had been invited to step in or that Li had already sent people to 'help'.

Li was away in Beijing with Zhou Jianguo and his secretary Amy couldn't say when he would be back. Felix was flying blind.

On the phone to Beecher, Felix tried to sound confident. 'Stand-off? You make it sound like the Wild West. We're fine-tuning the deals to transfer the land, that's all.' He laughed to make his next question sound casual. 'May I ask what you've heard, and how you heard?'

'Sure. My assistant's family home is down the road, in Dongchang town. She was there last weekend and everyone was talking.

I sent her back to investigate and she just came back to the office. You prepared to go on the record?'

'Sure.'

'I can quote "fine-tuning"?'

'Er, yes, why not?'

'You consider as "fine-tuning" the arrest of a couple of villagers by the police, on charges as yet unknown?'

Felix sat up and ran his hand through his hair. 'Shit.'

'What was that?'

'Nothing. Harold, maybe I should speak to my colleagues. To be honest with you, I got back from a business trip today.'

'I'm going to Dongchang tomorrow. Want to ride with me? You can see for yourself.'

'Thanks for the offer. What's your number? I'll call you straight back and Harold?'

'Yeah.'

'Can I take what I said back off the record.'

'Ha. Sure thing. By the way, the locals have got Chen Daming on side.'

'Who?'

'He's a "barefoot" lawyer who a few years back fought a big case about forced evictions in Shanghai. Got jailed for it, but he made the government pay.' The 'barefoot' bit means self-taught, and implies that Chen was an activist – for workers' rights and so on – as well a lawyer.

Felix clicked. 'Ah yes, I remember.' What he remembered was James Li speaking about the good old days when a pair of concrete boots, appropriate for a 'barefoot' lawyer he'd joked, and the waters of Suzhou Creek would have sorted out Chen Daming.

'Well, with Chen involved, it might get interesting,' Beecher said. 'According to our sources, he's got a couple of civil lawsuits accepted by the Jiangsu provincial court in Nanjing, one for the land grab and another about a battery factory that the Dongchang government bent the environmental regulations for in return for a nice fee. The pollution is nasty. Oh, and I haven't confirmed this but it seems the police chief of Wuzhou, the municipality that covers Dongchang, could be facing disciplinary action for putting the husband of his mistress in charge of the traffic bureau, among other suspect promotions. I'm not sure if that's Chen's doing too.' Beecher paused to let the juice sink in. 'But I'll let you get on with things. Much appreciate to hear your side when you're ready. I'll be in touch when I get back.'

'Hang on a sec, Harold,' Felix said. 'You're going tomorrow?'

'Sure am.'

'I'll see what I can do.'

Felix went down the hall to Amy's office and called James Li's mobile from her phone. That way he was sure Li would pick up. It was a trick he'd learned early on.

An idea was forming.

James Li was in a meeting. His voice was sharp. 'What is it Xiao Li? I asked not to be disturbed today.'

'Sorry, James, this is Felix.' He heard a sigh. 'Urgent. About Dongchang.'

Felix overheard Li make apologies and a voice say in Mandarin with a slight Beijing accent: 'Do take your call outside. We can wait.'

'What's so urgent?' James asked once he was outside wherever it was.

Felix gave him the basics of the conversation with Beecher.

'Damn,' James said.

'Don't worry. I think I can handle it,' Felix said straight back. 'I mean, I can handle him, the journalist, if I go to Dongchang myself, tomorrow.'

He reminded Li that he knew how to deal with the press, local and foreign, as he'd proved. The profile in the Italian newspaper was a perfect example. He also told Li how PR was part of marketing, which was his job.

He was touching the right nerve. Li hated the foreign media. They didn't accept envelopes of cash and they didn't, like the national media, listen to the State Council Information Office, where Zhou had good *guanxi*.

'OK. You go,' he said. 'Deal with it.'

Felix was happy.

The idea, as he told me and Joe later, was that this was his chance to show his true worth to James Li and Zhou, to make a real contribution. As he saw it, or hoped, the situation in Dongchang might become a genuine crisis, assuming what Beecher said was true about the detentions and the lawyer. He imagined the headline in Beecher's paper: 'Foreign executive of major Chinese corporation crosses cultural divide', or something like that. 'British businessman bridges gulf.' That'd be shorter, but it didn't give much detail. How about 'diffuses dispute'? But he couldn't come up with any more d's.

When Felix was unpacking in his villa, James called back. He'd been distracted when they first spoke. He'd had a word with someone in Dongchang. The situation was in hand. It was only a couple of stubborn farmers. The police could handle them. They could also handle a nosey foreign journalist in the time-honoured fashion: shove him in a taxi and send him home with an escort. No need for Felix to waste his time. He could get on with planning the ground-breaking.

But Felix had been thinking too. In the taxi from the office he'd daydreamed about foreign camera crews surrounding him at the Buckingham Park site, his explaining for the benefit of overseas viewers, and his friends back home, how land rights worked in China, how it took gentle persuasion and patience to satisfy (could he say mollify?) uneducated farmers who thought they had been hard done by, despite the fact they didn't own the land in the Western sense. They'd been squatting on it for fifty odd years (this to be an aside to the camera, as if he didn't want to upset the farmers with the hard truth). How they needed to understand that the long-term benefits of a land transfer would exceed by far the measly income they earned from surplus rice and cash crops. He'd single out a man and ask him, on camera, where his son or daughter was. The reply would be, 'college in the big city'. They all were. Next Felix would ask, 'so what will they do when they graduate? You think they'll want to come back home to be a farmer?' Farmer would be dumb but attentive. 'Of course not, and you don't want that either, do you?' Farmer nods and shakes his head. 'How about you put the education you struggled to pay for to good use, in a management position at the development my company is going to build here, or in the many local businesses that will spring up around our project?' The man's face would light up and Felix turn to the camera and explain, direct to the viewer, 'There you are see. It only takes patience, and reasoning. Of course there are developers who have a reputation for forcing people from their land and homes, but SLIC isn't one of them.'

This would show them, once and for all, he said. He had the speech planned out.

Here was his chance to make his name. I believe the real driver, however, was the lifelong competition with his brother. That supersedes, predates and overrides everything. Felix was doing this to show one single person: the decorated, high-flying army officer who'd made his life a misery. Felix Fawcett-Smith wanted Alex Fawcett-Smith to read the papers (better yet, have an officer in the mess pass it over), see him on TV, hear him on the radio. The rest would follow, starting with his dad, and then us, including Thurrold.

He was still on the phone to James Li.

'Boss Li, if you have the journalist sent away he'll either write up the farmers' side of the story or he'll send his assistant and get the story undercover. It'll come out, but without our side in it. If I go, I can get him to put the company in a good light. You know how the leaders read the foreign papers. You saw what happened when *Cankao Xiaoxi* picked up that story about me last year. It made a good impression in Beijing. You can't deny it.'

Felix was pressing the right buttons. He'd made Li think about the implications of negative coverage. Li and Zhou needed friends in Beijing. Uncle Tony's cutting from the *Telegraph* had been spot on. Zhou and Li were in the capital because they'd been summoned to answer questions about their property dealings, in particular how they acquired land rights from the Shanghai Municipal Government. The new regime was looking for more corrupt officials to make examples of. The Royal Buckingham Park land was not under investigation because it was in Jiangsu Province. They were safe on that score.

What could Li lose? If Felix pulled it off, Li could take the credit. If Felix mucked up, he'd be the foreign scapegoat. Whose idea had it been to employ Felix? Zhou's. SLIC wouldn't be in the firing line. Or would it? Li thought about the people he'd sent to Dongchang to 'help'. They were deniable.

'All right,' Li said. 'But will this reporter accept payment? That makes it easier.'

'Definitely not. I know him well. He's a friend.' Felix stretched the truth. He'd been at the same party where I met Beecher.

There was a moment's silence and a sigh of relief. 'Why didn't you say so?' Li said. 'That's different. If he's a friend of yours, of course you should go. Have Amy arrange a car. I want someone to go with you. He needs to get out there and Felix...'

'Yes.'

'It is best if there is no story.'

'I'll try to make it happen,' Felix said, knowing he wouldn't do anything of the sort, but James would be pleased. 'How are things in Beijing?' he asked out of politeness.

'A few small problems.' Li could stretch the truth as well. 'I'll be back soon.'

# 15

## DOWN TO THE COUNTRY

A CAR horn woke Felix from deep sleep. He'd been drinking whisky late into the night to beat the jetlag.

It was six o'clock. His body told him it was near to midnight. The echo of the horn bounced around the cul-de-sac like a ball bearing in a pinball machine. Fresh blasts burst in before each echo could die away in a never-ending circuit of noise.

He got out of bed and pulled back the curtain. A black Buick was outside his front door, facing towards the narrow road's exit. A man in a dark suit and red tie was leaning on it, smoking a cigarette. Felix didn't recognize him. The man waved and said something under his arm. The horn stopped. Felix opened the window and shouted that he'd be right down. He threw on a short-sleeved shirt and pair of trousers. He pushed open the front door and invited the man in. He explained he needed a cup of coffee.

'No time,' the man said.

Felix was expecting to be in charge today. He hesitated. 'I'll be quick.'

He went to the kitchen to make a cup of instant and lit a cigarette while he waited for the kettle. He took the coffee out to the car in a chipped cup he'd found in the villa. It was expendable.

The man sighed, opened a back door for Felix and got in the front. The driver was running the engine for the air conditioning. Felix didn't recognise him either. He realized he should have brought a jacket. The air conditioning was cold. He didn't dare ask them to wait, and the car was moving. He held the cup of coffee out from his body, over the footwell.

'You know Boss Li?' Felix spoke to the back of the stranger's head in the passenger seat. The man turned.

'Yes. Old friend.' His voice was curt, severe. He had a round face and small eyes. His hair was cut short and spiked with gel. Felix put him in his mid-thirties.

'May I ask your name?'

'You can call me Xiao Zhang,' he used the modest 'young' or 'little' prefix. He grinned.

'Pleased to meet you Lao Zhang,' Felix gave him the 'old' one. The grin broke open to show a row of uneven brown teeth.

'Today we're going to have fun in the countryside. Right?' Zhang said. His breath smelt of garlic. He was a northerner.

'That's right.' Felix leaned across and away to make it easier for Zhang to talk round the back of his seat. He also wanted to distance himself from the garlic breath. 'You often go to the countryside to have fun?' If Zhang was a joker, he'd play along.

'Now and again. I take care of things for Boss Li.'

'What sort of things?'

'Things.' Zhang's grin was stuck on his face. 'We met before,' he said.

'I'm sorry,' Felix said, 'I have forgotten.'

'That's okay. Couple of dinners. One time in the South Sea Bath House.'

'Oh, so we do know each other.' Felix tried to make it sound like a joke. He still couldn't place Zhang's face or connect with his humour.

'Yes. We do.'

'So, how do we handle this 'thing' today?' Felix asked.

'Shouldn't be a problem. Get people to see sense. Preparations have been made. And you're taking care of the foreign reporter, yes?'

'That's right. Shouldn't be a big problem either. I think he could help.'

The grin vanished and Zhang's face darkened. Like an actor, he rearranged his features into an artless blank. The corners of his mouth twitched. He nodded and turned to his front.

The journey took two hours. The new elevated highway through the city was empty and the inter-provincial expressway had a few trucks on it and fewer cars. The driver stuck at a hundred and twenty kilometres per hour in the outside lane. He paid no attention to the other vehicles except the ones ahead of him. He flashed and hooted from a couple of hundred metres, charged their rear bumpers and swerved past on the inside lane. Zhang and the driver chain-smoked. They opened their windows a crack to throw the butts out when they'd finished. Felix tried to counter-act their sickly sweet Yunnan tobacco with his Marlboro Lights. He lit up and opened his back window a crack but the driver used his master control to put it back up and locked it. Felix stubbed his cigarette out in the ashtray and didn't try again. He fell into a doze.

After the exit toll booth, a large truck pulled out of a dusty track right in front of them. The car braked hard and swerved, throwing Felix forward, waking him. They had come to a dead stop on the wrong side of the road. An old man in a Mao cap with a hoe over his shoulder bumped his bicycle onto the dirt to get round them, his washed-out eyes fixed on his front wheel.

The driver leaned across Zhang and screamed in Shanghainese through the passenger window, which was shut, 'Stupid country bastard!'. The truck driver put it into reverse so he could renew his swing out into the road and tried to get past. The car shuddered forward in second gear and swung further onto the wrong hard shoulder of the feeder road. The big truck was on their inside, inching round. Another one was coming at them from the opposite direction. It blared its air horn but slowed to let them crawl back onto the right-hand side, inches in front of the first truck.

'Fuck you too,' the Buick driver said at the second truck. He leant on the horn and the engine found the revs to pick up speed. He clunked it into third and it shuddered. 'Why can't these stupid peasant cunts learn to drive,' he muttered.

They passed a strip of repair shops, rundown restaurants and barber shops and drove out into the open country of rice paddy, orchards and pearl ponds. Through the tinted glass everything was brown, including the scrappy grass along the verge and the leaves in the trees. Felix asked the driver to open his window. This time he obliged. Felix held his hair from his eyes. In the middle distance two rows of pylons ran in step beside each other. The haze and low sky made the cables look like faint brush strokes in a landscape painting. There was a splash of colour below them. It was a hut, roofed and wrapped by a bright red advertising hoarding, looted from beside the highway. The window slid up.

'Ha!' said Zhang. 'We've gone down to the country!' He used the two-character expression from the Cultural Revolution, the one that meant banishment for years, not a day trip. He laughed.

'We've gone down to the country,' Felix repeated.

'To think these peasants are fighting to keep this shithole,' Zhang said. 'Look at it: fields, mud and shit. And Boss Zhou is going to develop it, open it up. They must be mad. And the shacks they live in.' They were passing white tiled houses with chrome cages fixed to every window. 'They think someone's going to rob them. What the fuck have they got to steal?' he laughed.

Despite the poverty and shittiness, Felix said to himself, it's farmland. People have worked and lived on it for generations.

'And Boss Zhou has made them a generous offer too,' Zhang said. 'All the peasants care about is money but it's never enough. Petty-minded cheapskates, that's what they are. This land isn't theirs in the first place. The Party gave it to them. They have no right to it. Give them a house and a job, preferably in Xinjiang out near the border, that's what I say. Fuck the compensation. Greedy bastards.'

Felix wanted to say: 'Wasn't the whole point of the liberation to give the peasants the land? And doesn't taking it back make hypocrites of the Party?'

He dismissed his thoughts in Zhang's language, 'Fuck logic.'

He leaned forward, put his head between the two front seats and offered Zhang a Marlboro. Zhang stared at it for a second and took it.

'So, how long have you worked with Boss Li?' Felix asked.

'Four or five years.'

'And before that?'

'I was a soldier.'

'Really? Which service?'

'Army, Nanjing Military District.'

'Army? My brother is in the army. He's a paratrooper.' Felix hung his hands from imaginary parachute straps. 'Did you ever parachute when you were in the army?

Zhang looked at Felix like he was crazy. 'No, I worked.'

'What sort of work?'

Zhang gave Felix one of his grins and spoke to the driver in a strange dialect, right across Felix's face. Stale cigarette smoke joined the garlic. The driver replied and they laughed. Felix sat back. His mobile rang.

It was Harold Beecher. He'd arrived in Dongchang and the local police had told him he and his assistant should go straight back to Shanghai, 'for his own safety'. They were making his taxi wait. Could Felix help?

This was a good start.

Felix told Beecher he'd call him straight back and spoke to Zhang who said, 'That's normal. Nothing we can do. Tell him to take the day off. It'll save you trouble too.'

Felix reminded him Boss Li had agreed that he, Felix, deal with Beecher on the spot. He wasn't going to give up his day of glory before it was eight in the morning.

'Nothing I can do,' Zhang repeated, with a tiny yet significant alteration.

'Yes, you can,' Felix said. 'You can call the police and tell them to let the journalist stay.'

'I don't know the police, sorry. Don't have their number.'

Felix made his voice sound as if he was sweet-talking a child, 'I can call Boss Li and get him to help. Like I say he did...'

Zhang voice was gentle and insistent too, mimicking Felix. 'I'd help if I could, I really would.'

'I've an idea,' Felix said.

He called Beecher back. As he expected, a policeman was standing beside him. Felix asked him to put him on the phone and held the mobile towards Zhang. 'Here's the police.'

Zhang turned, his eyes hard and cold. He took the phone and shouted into it, staring with annoyance at Felix, straight in the face. He gave the name of a police chief. It sounded like Hu. So he did know someone. He made an effort to sound exasperated but made the request on behalf of Felix, who interjected, 'and Boss Li'.

'There you are,' Zhang said, and passed the phone back. He didn't say another word until they were at the outskirts of Dongchang and they hit a police checkpoint.

The car pulled over. Zhang motioned at a policeman to come round to his side and let his window down.

'You going into Dongchang?' the policeman asked.

'Yes, we've made arrangements with Bureau Chief Hu,' Zhang said. That'd be the policeman Zhang denied he knew.

'Who?'

'Bureau Chief Hu, chief of the Wuzhou Municipal District Public Security.'

'Ah. We're from Nanjing.' The policeman peered into the car and saw Felix. He gave Zhang a 'what the fuck?' face. 'Who's the *laowai*?'

'With me. Don't worry.'

'Wow. Okay, give me a minute. There's a situation in Dongchang, some kind of labour trouble. We've been told to recommend people don't go there today. I'll check with my boss for Chief Hu. If he okays it, you should be fine, but I don't know about the foreigner. Another one sneaked in this morning, right before we got here, and my boss got it in the neck.' He smiled. He sussed that Zhang was on his side.

'This one is all right,' Zhang said, 'and be quick.' The policeman walked away, talking into his radio.

Felix sat back in the seat. He didn't want more police to see him and wonder.

A large patch of ground had been cleared and flattened for a factory and a brand-new access road ran down its middle. Three dark blue coaches were parked up on it and opposite them police vans with metal grills over the windows and surveillance cameras and the roofs.

Felix made a quick calculation: forty seats to a coach, a hundred and twenty police.

The officer came back to Zhang's window. He frowned at Felix again.

'All okay,' he said to Zhang. 'I hope you know what you're doing.'

'See you later,' Zhang said.

The police officer saluted.

Dongchang township had begun as a collection of buildings around a T-junction where a major road from the south met the old trunk road that ran along the Yangtze River from Shanghai to Nanjing. As the road grew busier and the buildings spread, the junction moved southwards, away from the river, block by block, until the brand-new highway Felix had driven down bypassed it for good. In the meantime, the place had prospered enough to become a proper town of about twenty thousand people. There were several hotels, a few half-decent-looking restaurants, a large, covered wet market and a couple of supermarkets. The shifting T-junctions left a series of crossroads in their wake, each with a hotel on it. The further south, the newer the hotel. Note I don't say 'nicer'.

Felix wanted to find Harold Beecher, make sure he was happy, relatively speaking, and ask him to wait while he went to see the men in detention. Zhang had the car pull up at the middle hotel.

Half a dozen local police were in the lobby. One ran to the door with his hand up and thrust it at Felix's face. 'Foreigners can't come in here!' he shouted. Felix ducked and spoke to Zhang. The policeman stared at him, his hand in mid-air, like he was on traffic duty. 'He speaks Chinese,' he said, his mouth gaping.

Zhang asked who was in charge and a fat policeman, smoking and clipping his fingernails in a oversized pleather armchair, heaved himself to his feet. His tunic buttons were undone, cap on the back of his head. There was no mention of the phone conversation, but he was probably the man Zhang had spoken to. He was polite. 'What do you want?'

'I've come to find my colleagues,' Zhang said, giving no detail about who they were or who they worked for. 'And this *laowai* here will deal with the reporter for you.' He slipped in a snort of derision. 'Bureau Chief Hu will be coming over from Wuzhou. Perhaps you can arrange lunch for us in a decent restaurant, if there is one.'

As he was speaking, the policeman did up his buttons and pulled his cap forward. He stood up and sucked in his belly. He'd realized who Zhang was. Felix was impressed, against his better judgement. 'You,' the policeman shouted, 'pour tea. You, call the Peninsula and book a private room. You, er, you,' he muttered, 'go upstairs and tell Xiao Xu to tell the *laowai* there's someone to see him.' And finally, to a man by the door, 'You take Mr. Zhang to that place.'

He turned to Felix, 'Mister American, please sit down. Drink tea. You can go and see your friend in a minute.'

'He can't come down?'

The policeman froze. He couldn't think of an answer. 'Later,' he said, and he took Zhang to the door and stepped outside with him.

A policeman indicated Felix should sit in the big chair vacated by their boss. Another thrust a cigarette at him. He sat and slurped the tea, fighting the leaves. The junior policemen stared at him. No one spoke. The man who'd been sent upstairs returned. 'They're ready,' he said to Felix, 'Please come with me.' Felix put down his tea.

The stairwell and corridors were carpeted in green felt on bare concrete. The smell was like a wet compost heap in a garden shed. The grey paint on the walls of the corridor was blistered and cracked up to knee height.

A door was open and a policeman, presumably called Xu, sat on a chair beside it. Beecher was standing by the window, looking out onto the street. The room was standard for a small-town cheap hotel: twin beds, TV on a low cabinet, mini-bar fridge, switched off and empty, and, although the door to it was shut so he couldn't see inside; Felix guessed a tiled bathroom with a small bath and a sink with a marble surround cluttered by disposable toothbrushes, combs, tiny tubes of toothpaste and a plastic rack of condoms and disposable knickers. On the bedside cabinet, which was also a control panel for the lights and TV, was the usual advertisement for massage.

Beecher's assistant was sitting on one of the twin beds, talking into her mobile.

'Hi Harold,' Felix said, and waited for him to turn around so he could be sure they'd met. 'How are you doing?'

Harold Beecher was in his forties, with a goatee and glasses. His hair was grey and thin and long enough to be swept back from his forehead. The face was familiar. Felix was relieved.

'We've met before, haven't we?' Felix said as if he wasn't asking.

'I guess so. Good of you to come.' They shook hands. Beecher's speech was tight and clipped. 'This is Xiao Huang,' he indicated the girl on the bed, 'my assistant who picked up the story.' She smiled at Felix. She was petite, with ponytails, like in a Cultural Revolution poster.

'This happen often?' Felix asked, nodding at the doorway.

'All the time. Don't worry. If it hadn't been for you speaking to whoever, we'd have been kicked out. Thanks for that. You got *guanxi.*'

'I suppose so.' Felix was speaking to a veteran. He was careful to sound casual.

'What else can they do for us?' Beecher said. 'Get an interview with the two guys who've been detained? The head of the local government? Police chief? We've already spoken to people, locals who are involved.' He nodded at Xiao Huang, who smiled, and tapped a finger against the mobile by her ear.

Felix appreciated that Beecher was joking, at least about the government head and police chief. He smiled and moved into the room to stand beside the television. Xiao Huang closed her phone and shifted up the bed. Harold rested his backside on the windowsill. Policeman Xu, outside on his chair, leaned back towards the open doorway. His English was the best in the station but didn't amount to much. He couldn't understand a word.

'Well,' Felix said, feeling important. 'I think, as no doubt you do, that it's obviously wrong, the police detaining these people. I know one should negotiate from a position of strength,' he wanted to make a joke too, 'but I think we're taking things too far by locking them up.' He forced a laugh.

Beecher didn't find that one funny. 'I'll say.'

Felix coughed, pushed his hair back and carried on. 'So, well, I'll see if I can get them out, or failing that at least make sure they're being well treated. Whatever the case, my aim is for me, in person, to get a clear idea of their demands so we can see what we can do to satisfy them, monetarily speaking, but perhaps there are other things too.'

'Such as?' Beecher said. 'Only curious.'

'Oh, maybe a contribution to the community, jobs, build a school...'

'I think you'll find that's been taken care of.'

'Ah, well...'

'And Felix,' Beecher spoke kindly, 'I don't think you have a hope in hell of getting them out of police detention. 'Fact I'd be surprised if they let you see them.'

That stumped Felix, and he must have shown it.

'Tell you what,' Beecher stepped from the windowsill into the room, hands in his pockets, arched his back.

'Here's what you can do that might be more realistic,' he said. 'It'll also give me a nice angle about you trying to help.' Felix ran his hand through his hair. Had Beecher seen through him? 'It's all right. It's very simple. I only want to know what charges they are being held under, what their demands are – like you do – and I'd love it if you could get me quotes from the police chief or the most senior man you can find, first about what they are going to do with these people, and second, a bonus but it would be worth trying, is what they think of, or are thinking of doing about, what Chen Daming is up to, the stuff I mentioned on the phone. If he has riled them, it would be great to get a dismissive quote, an official or police officer saying they were going to "break his legs" or something. That'd be nice.' He corrected himself. 'I don't mean actually break his legs. I mean the quote.'

Felix took that as a cue. 'Or throw him in Suzhou Creek with a pair of concrete boots on.'

'Yeah, you get me.' Beecher smiled. 'Not that I am going after the sensational angle of course,' he smiled.

Felix regretted the concrete boots. He'd exposed himself. 'But seriously,' he said. 'Can you wait until I've reported to my boss and found out how we are going to handle this? I could get a statement or a press release. Might take a few days.'

'Sure, I'm not going to file this tonight. I might make a feature out of it. We've got time,' Beecher continued in his kind voice, 'unless, of course, something dramatic happens.'

'I doubt that very much,' Felix said.

'You reckon I could speak to your boss too, get a quote? I assume you mean Mr. Zhou Jianguo? You could give me his number.'

Miss Huang smiled.

'I don't mean Mr. Zhou,' Felix said. 'I meant my immediate boss. I'm sure he'd be happy to say something. His name is Li.'

'All right. Thanks.' Beecher looked at Felix as if he was trying to work out whose side he was on. 'I have to ask you, Felix,' Beecher said. 'But do you *really* think you can get in to see these people? Sorry, but I've been in these situations a heck of a lot of times, and well...'

Felix put his hand up. This is what he was here for. 'Harold, this is the new, international face of state-backed companies, or one of them,' he pointed to himself by touching the tip of his nose, Chinese style, and grinned. 'I'll get you a statement that'll show how things have changed, or are changing... can change. No hiding the facts, state secrets and all that bullshit. What we have here is a land transfer dispute, a claim for compensation, pure and simple. SLIC is a business. We'll deal with the problem as any business would, by negotiating with the interested parties and coming to an agreement.'

'Can I quote that?'

Exactly what Felix wanted. 'Of course. The whole idea today is to give you a quote.' Beecher looked at Xiao Huang, so did Felix.

She nodded at her boss. 'Why not?'

'OK. We'll sit it out here,' Beecher said. 'Be good if you could get us something to eat. Or ask if we can get out for a walk.' Another nod from Xiao Huang. 'I've been detained in nicer hotel rooms.'

'Of course,' Felix said. 'I think a lunch is being arranged for all of us.'

'That'll be the day.'

'Just you wait.' Felix said, and, 'I'll be off then.'

He was in the doorway when Beecher said to his back, 'By the way, there's a rumour the farmers are coming to town this afternoon, to demonstrate in front of the local government offices. Only a rumour mind.'

Felix turned. His short speech had restored his confidence. 'Right, well, I'll see if we can nip that in the bud too. See you later. Or I'll give you a call.' And he strode past Policeman Xu down the smelly corridor.

Xiao Huang raised her eyebrows to Harold Beecher. Beecher shrugged.

It was not yet ten o'clock in the morning, but if Felix didn't hurry the police would suggest they stopped for lunch, that he could see the detainees in the afternoon, and with lunch they'd force alcohol on him, and his day would be gone. So, when a policeman downstairs told him to sit down and drink more tea and a car would be along soon, Felix announced he'd find his own way, if the policeman would tell him where the station was.

'Drink tea,' the policeman repeated.

'No thanks, I must be going.' Felix walked towards the door.

The flustered policeman leapt to his feet and followed him.

Felix stood still and looked along the street, his back to the door and the policeman. 'Which way?'

The policeman didn't point. He'd been told to keep the foreigners in the hotel. He hadn't expected one of them would be so determined, and apparently on his side too, let alone speak Chinese. He nodded up the street to the right. Felix caught the gesture out of the corner of his eye. He thanked him and set off.

The town was going about its business. People were walking home from the wet market with blue plastic bags of vegetables. A family noodle shop with bright orange chairs and dirty Formica tables was cleaning up before the lunch rush. Granny sat in the light by the doorway, hand stuffing dumplings with bent brown thumbs. As he passed the brightly painted wall of a kindergarten Felix heard dance music and children's laughter and a woman shouting the numbers one to four over and over into a megaphone. A cluster of middle-aged men stood chatting and smoking beside a row of minivan taxis. A supermarket's windows were blocked by stacks of cardboard boxes on the pavement. A flattened one served as a doormat. A coin-operated rocking horse that was a monkey on all fours stood beside it. A little boy with a split in the seat of his trousers was patting its nose while his grandmother stood by. Most of the shops were hardware stores or builders' merchants selling window glass, PVC piping, doors, the chrome window cages Zhang had remarked on.

Felix heard the usual chorus of '*laowai!*', caught the dumb stares, and forced himself to smile at a bobbing gaggle of children who danced around him and screamed at his face, 'Hallo!'

The police station was a white-tiled building near the town's original T-junction. A civilian security guard stepped out of the gatehouse to stop him but Felix waved a hand, 'My colleague is inside waiting for me.' The guard let him pass.

In the station car park, a group of officers in uniform and civilians in dark clothes were standing around black cars, smoking. One of the uniformed men glanced at Felix and made to move towards him but a man in a black jacket caught him by the arm. The policeman stared. Several of the cars had People's Armed Police number plates. They start with the initials WJ for *Wu Jing*.

Inside the station was a large open space and a corridor to each side. Felix had hoped for a reception desk. He looked down one corridor and saw an office with an open door. Apart from the characters for 'office', he couldn't read the sign that stuck out from the wall above it. A middle-aged woman with short hair was sitting at a desk.

She looked up in surprise when Felix spoke. 'Hello, I'm here to find my colleague, Mr. Zhang. From Shanghai Land Investment Corporation,' he gave the abbreviation, *Shangtou*. 'He came here earlier to see the two people who have been detained with regard to the land issue.'

The woman stared as if he'd asked directions to the toilet. And he was speaking Chinese.

'Not here,' she murmured.

'What? He must be. This is where they have been detained, isn't it?'

'No one here,' the woman said, slurring her words like a northerner but speaking with increasing authority. 'You've come to the wrong place.'

So she did know what he was talking about. 'Could you please tell me where to go? Or where you think they might be, if you were to guess, where they have been taken? Perhaps I should call my *Shangtou,*' he stressed the name, 'colleague Mr. Zhang myself and you can speak to him.'

The woman didn't move her eyes from Felix. Her mouth hung half open. She waited, as if for someone to tell her it was okay to tell this Chinese-speaking foreigner where to find Zhang and the two detainees. But there was no one who could approve or disapprove. She made a decision. Her voice went quiet, as if to prevent anyone overhearing, and her northern slur turned fuzzier. '*Shangtou's* matter is next door, in the KTV.'

'Ah, thanks. Left or right.'

'Left.'

Felix went back out onto the street.

The KTV was on the far side of the police car park where the men were standing. It was the smartest building Felix saw in Dong-chang, which isn't saying much. It was painted bright red, the window frames white. Blue mirror glass in them reflected the tangled wires between the telegraph poles that jutted at angles from the pavement. He entered a red and gold lobby dominated by a statue of a gilt Buddha in a wall recess, behind a cluster of fresh incense sticks and a bowl of fruit.

Two men in bomber jackets were sitting in the lobby. They looked like soldiers. Their hair was cut so short it was all but shaven. They were younger than Felix. One stood up and said, 'Mr. Shi? We're expecting you. Please follow me.' He pushed the button for the lift.

Felix gave his fantasy one last run-through, like an actor preparing to go on stage: reassure the two farmers he spoke on behalf of SLIC with a direct line to the top; find out what charges they were being held under and see if he could get their release; if not, make sure they were well treated and find out what they wanted; get it on paper, and have them chop it, or sign it; ask them to tell their legal 'consultant', Mr. Chen, to negotiate with SLIC direct; promise to go back to Shanghai and present their side, see where SLIC could give ground a little (the man in the lift looked at Felix with surprise when Felix smiled to himself)... what else was there?

The lift pinged and the doors slid open at the top floor.

Felix's mind rushed through the last part, for today at least: give Beecher a quick rundown on what he'd found; show confidence the matter could be resolved; remind him to wait for the press release or official statement; Beecher to slap him on the back and get in a taxi with Miss Huang and no police escort and go back to Shanghai.

Job done.

The young man was leading Felix along a corridor of private KTV rooms. They came to a floor-to-ceiling mirror at the end. The man pushed its edge and it clicked and swung open. It was the hidden entrance to the inner sanctum. Felix was entering a full-on brothel, most likely operated by the police. The corridor continued as before.

The man stopped outside a door on the left. Felix heard raised voices, clapping. The young soldier opened it and waved him inside.

Behind the door was a small vestibule. On one side through yet another doorway was a room divided by a glass wall. A reclining sofa chair and television beneath a row of clothes hooks was on one side and behind the glass a large, padded bed, waterproofed. Above it hung a showerhead. Plastic slippers lay on the meshed non-slip floor beside its aluminium legs. This is where punters got their body scrubs. The sight of the red bed and the wet soapy smell gave Felix a tiny butterfly-in-the-balls thrill. He was about to be shown into a bedroom with floor to ceiling mirrors and soft red lighting. He couldn't help the sense of anticipation.

# 16

## KTV

'FIRST thing that hit me wasn't the heat. You know how they keep those places really warm. Nor the stink of sweat and cigarette smoke. Want to know what it was?'

Felix turned from Joe Karstein to me. He was sitting on the sofa in my apartment. Joe and I were across from him; Joe in my other comfy chair, me on a wooden one I'd put in front of the TV, like we were a debriefing team in a special agent movie. We were all smoking.

'It was a bloody tooth. Actual blood. Actual tooth. Square on the chest. Jesus Christ. I couldn't see how much blood because of the soft red light. It was pretty dark too. I expected there to be a speck or two. When I went outside, later, it was a fucking great splodge and it had dried so I couldn't get it off.

'Zhang was bringing back his fist the very moment I went in. He was so focused he didn't notice me. I watched him, seemed like slow motion. He took a real swing, way out from the side, fist like a sledgehammer. The guy's face exploded, like this.'

Felix put his right hand to his right cheek in a loosely clenched fist, stretched out his left one, also in a fist but tighter, and punched himself in the head. His right hand flew from his cheek and opened out, its spreading fingers were the flying blood and teeth. He keeled over, spat out a sound like Thomas the Tank Engine's last gasp, and collapsed across the sofa, blood and tooth hand over the armrest, mouth gaping, tongue hanging.

He waited for us to be impressed and sat up. 'If I didn't feel the blood, I felt the tooth all right. It was like a little bullet, or piece of cork, and I knew for sure it was a tooth because I saw the guy's mouth, with a hole in it where the tooth – teeth rather – had been.'

'A punch like that's called a haymaker,' I said.

'Why's that?'

'No idea.'

Joe had brought ready-rolled joints. He and Felix had shared a fat one while Felix went through the build-up to the KTV room. The joint hadn't calmed Felix down. As he told his story he'd jumped backwards and forwards and repeated himself. Sometimes he stopped for long breaks, as if he'd blanked. I guessed he'd snorted something before coming over and it was combining with the pot. He'd start again, animated as a cat on a hot tin roof, and we'd get a little play-acting like the haymaker. He'd begun with the phone calls to Li in Beijing and his own plan for Dongchang. He'd even given us the speech for the cameras that never got filmed. He had to share it with someone. That had been a performance. I was sorry it never got seen in public.

'I'm amazed the man's head didn't come off,' he said. 'Christ. The two prisoners – yes, they were prisoners, forget 'detainees' – weren't tied to the chairs or anything, like in the movies. They sat there, in the middle of the room, taking it, or at least the one who was being hit did. The other one was pleading, not with Zhang but with his buddy. I couldn't catch what he said but it sounded like he was trying to persuade him to give in. Zhang said, to the guy he'd hit, and this I did get, word-for-word. "I'm getting bored of you." He had a cigarette in his teeth. He was a classic psycho with his baby face and short hair.

'The local man was a tough one. He didn't put his hand up to his mouth, which was dribbling blood onto his shirt – I could see it despite the dark and the red light because there was so much of it and it was shiny and his shirt was white. "So," Zhang said, "I think I'll have a go on your friend. You wouldn't want him to get hurt too?"

'The other guy started screaming his head off, begging for mercy, put his arms over his head like Manuel in *Fawlty Towers*. "Please Meester Fawlty!"'

Felix did an impression.

'You know *Fawlty Towers* Joe?' I asked.

Joe shook his head.

'Never mind.'

Felix lowered his hands. 'There were two more men in there, leaning against a double bed. It was upended by the window. To stop the noise I guess. The doors had been closed behind me. This guy's begging his friend to give in, from under his arms he's holding up.' Felix slowed down a fraction and took a breath.

'After what seemed like forever, the guy who'd lost his teeth shook his head, really slowly. This part was like a movie, I'm telling you, except normally it's the brave guy who gets the punishment, isn't it? And the coward has to watch. Well, sorry to disappoint you but that's not what happens in real life.' He sat back on the sofa, waiting for me and Joe to show appreciation.

'It was then that Zhang noticed me and spoke to me, like he wanted to draw it out for the guy he was about to hit. "How do you like our negotiating methods, Mr. Shi? Won't be long. Sorry for the mess."

'Sadist. I didn't realise he was talking about the blood on my shirt. I thought he was being sarcastic about the guy with the bloody face. One of his eyes was closing up. Like I say, it was so dark and red in there, the shiny bits stood out: the eyes, the teeth, or rather, the missing teeth, the blood on the guy's shirt, and Zhang's sweaty psycho baby-face.' Felix drifted off for a moment.

'I couldn't say, "Well,"' he put on an upper-class la-di-da voice, '"actually Mr. Zhang no, I don't like your negotiating methods, not one little bit," could I? And I couldn't stop him either. The two other guys were laughing at me. I guess I looked horrified. I was pissed-off at the let-down. I mean: there went my chance of solving the crisis. No way was I going to talk to those men. That sadist Zhang had got me in there to make that clear and get his own back for me putting him on the spot when Beecher called in the car. I had blood on my hands, well, my shirt. That wouldn't be good on camera.'

'So what did you do?' I said.

He brushed his hair back. 'I told Zhang I'd better go and make sure Beecher left town. I wanted to get out of that room.

'"You do that," Zhang said. "Good idea. I'll finish off here." The wimpy guy let out a whimper. His hands were up in front of his face. I guess his eyes were shut. I couldn't see. I turned away just at the moment the poor bastard got hit. Zhang gave him an upper cut to get under the pathetic defence. He howled like an animal.

'A young gun from the lobby was waiting for me outside the room. He asked if I'd finished, as in "had enough?" I said yes, enough, and he laughed out loud. I realised he hadn't asked if I was finished: '*Wan le ma?*' What he'd said was: Had I had fun? '*Hao wan le ma?*" Bloody hell. He thought I'd joined the brotherhood, like I'd been through an initiation ceremony. Zhang caught up with me at the secret door, shaking his hand to loosen it up. He told me to tell Beecher the dispute was settled, both sets of villagers accepted SLIC's offer. I asked him if there'd be a demonstration, like Beecher said. He said it wouldn't happen. Of course, he was giving me the old "say it ain't true". They love that. Zhang is old school. "One last lesson," he said, "Doing him a favour. Then I'll be done."'

'So what *did* you tell Beecher?' Joe asked.

'What could I do? I couldn't grass on my own company. And I didn't fancy being on the receiving end of Zhang's fist either. I'm sure he wouldn't have appreciated reading about his "traditional negotiating technique" in the papers.' He stopped and grinned. 'Come to think of it, he'd be chuffed I expect.' He stared at the coffee table between us.

'So?' I said.

'Let me tell you the best bit,' he perked up, 'I told Harold the bloodstain was from lunch. Chilli sauce.' He laughed. 'I said I'd taken the two "representatives" for a slap-up lunch and we'd hammered out an agreement. "Slap up". "Hammered out".' He put his hand up to his hair and laughed harder. 'How about that? I really said it, without realizing. When I did, realize what I'd said that is, I almost cracked up, right in front of him. I pretended I'd had a few drinks. I deserve an Oscar. Shit.' He stopped as suddenly as he had started, as if he'd realised how ridiculous he sounded. 'Obviously Beecher didn't fall for it. He might have done, if only...' Felix's voice trailed off. He fumbled in his pocket for his cigarettes. They were on the table. 'If only...' he repeated as he saw the packet and picked it up. He took one out and lit it with a shaking hand. 'Oh, fuck it.' He dragged hard on the cigarette and blew the smoke out with a hiss. 'Johnny, you wouldn't have any booze here, would you?'

It was two days since Felix had been in Dongchang. The story appeared in Beecher's paper the day after. He didn't make a feature out of it. It was front page news. The rumours spread like wildfire round the expat bars the same evening. One of the TVs in the Backstreet had been on the BBC, which had got hold of the amateur video taken the late afternoon of the day Felix had been there. We were lucky to catch it. When the BBC went back to the studio, the screen turned to snowflakes. Blocked. The chatter started straight away. Everyone in the bar wondered where Felix was. I said I had no idea. I'd been trying to track him down myself but his mobile was off, there was no answer at his home or office, and Anita said she hadn't seen him since England.

He'd called the next morning from a number I didn't recognise. I saved it, in case. I was at work. He asked if he could see me at my apartment. I ran home and got there about eleven o'clock. Felix was walking into the compound, wearing a wool hat – on a warm spring day, hardly a great disguise – sunglasses, and a raincoat with the collar up. I'd have laughed if he hadn't sounded so earnest when he thanked me for coming. His face was pasty white and when he took the glasses and hat off, I saw bags under his eyes. His hair was plastered to his skull by the hat and the heat. He hadn't slept much.

He told me he'd been in the Financial Plaza Hotel. He was under strict instructions to wait there till his company sorted out the mess. He'd sneaked out thanks to the staff turning a blind eye. He didn't have much time.

He told me all he wanted was to talk. It was my idea to get Joe round. I wanted to call Charlie Thurrold, but he insisted we left him out of it. 'I don't want the old sod telling me "I told you," a hundred times.' That was harsh and I said so. 'Charlie Thurrold can go fuck himself,' Felix said.

Anita was dismissed likewise, without the expletive: 'I haven't seen her since England and I don't think she'll want to see me right now, let alone help out.'

So it was me and Joe.

Felix's attitude went from self-justification, confidence verging on arrogance, to begging for sympathy. He must have been aware that Joe and I knew how his story ended.

One thing he never asked for was help. All he wanted was someone to listen, and cigarettes, joints and alcohol.

I found beers in the fridge, cracked three open and handed them out. Felix took a swig. I offered him another smoke. He thanked me. I'd emptied the ashtray once already. It was half full.

'Come on,' I said, conscious I sounded like a psychiatrist, 'Tell us how it happened. Give us the real story. Get it off your chest.'

'It couldn't get much worse.' Felix sucked the cigarette and bent his head down towards his knees. He started to speak, thinking as he went along.

'So there was a demonstration. Of course there was. Zhang was bullshitting. I knew it but chose to ignore it.' He looked up, 'sometimes I worry we take this "doing things the Chinese way" too far. Why do they do it, ignoring the obvious, lying to your face?' he took another hard drag. We waited.

'Ah, sod it... There was a demonstration. They got together outside the town and wanted to march in and picket the police station, because that's where they thought the two men were. The police in buses I'd seen outside town, the ones from Nanjing, moved to block their way. While the march was approaching and the police lining up, diggers and wreckers moved onto the Buckingham Park site to demolish the first houses, starting with one that belonged to one of the guys in the KTV.

'I was with Zhang in the police station by now. The police chief he'd mentioned, called Hu, from Wuzhou, had turned up. He was pissed off because Zhang, thinking there'd be no demo, had sent his own men – the ones in the KTV and the others I'd seen in the police station car park – back to Shanghai. He needed them, Hu that is, because he couldn't ask the police to disperse the demo. Not their job. To be more precise, he hadn't been paid. The police were there to keep the fight contained.

'So Zhang called his men and told them to come back to where the roadblock had been in the morning. To meet them and brief them he had to get through the police lines, and the demonstrators. He couldn't use the car because it might get flipped by the demonstrators. So he made another call and a sodding great dumper truck pulled up outside the station. He told me to come with him. My job with Beecher was done – he'd left town in a taxi, with his assistant, or so I thought. I think Zhang's idea was to get me out of the way. You ever ridden in those trucks?'

Joe said plenty of times, with his dad.

'Massive, aren't they? Like climbing a rock face to get up there. So I got up first and sat in the middle, between Zhang and the driver, who stank. When we got to the edge of town, it was like a medieval battlefield before the fighting. On one side the police in neat lines: blue uniforms, riot shields, helmets. They were on a road that backed onto a new housing development, like it was their fort. Actually, forget medieval. The police were more like Romans. And on the other side, milling about in the dried-out rice fields, were the barbarians, the savages, the local farmers and villagers with banners and loud hailers, shouting and waving their fists and flags. Some had made headbands out of white cloth, like they were kamikaze pilots.'

'Any idea how many?' Joe asked.

'Oh, at least a few hundred. The police let us through. Zhang had his head out the cab window. He yelled that he'd be back soon with his guys. We drove down the road towards the demonstrators, hooting the horn like you would at a pedestrian crossing in Shanghai. We weren't going to stop. The driver was nervous and Zhang had to egg him on, bloody suffocating me with his bad breath. Well,' he knocked back his beer, 'we were literally up to the row of people in the road itself – they hadn't put up a roadblock – when they went crazy, ape shit, like real savages come to think of it, screams and shouts and panic. They ran in every direction. Our driver guessed he'd scared them out of the way, so he put his foot down. He thought they were running away from him, you see, that he had a clear run. Truth is they were running because they'd got word that the bulldozers were knocking down their villages. And the driver didn't have a clear run either, did he?'

He paused. 'Give me another cigarette, would you?'

I handed one over and held out a lighter. He sucked on it then bunched his hands into fists and put them up to his temples, elbows on his knees, holding the burning cigarette in his knuckles, holding himself together.

Joe and I sat still. Felix was silent for a long few seconds. We couldn't see his face.

'Fuck,' he said to the table. His voice was small, with a tiny tremor. 'We didn't feel a thing. Not a thing. Not even a little bump. That's how solid a human head is. A woman's. They threw stones at the cab to get our attention. Jesus that made a racket. And the screams, real high-pitched banshee ones. The driver saw the body in the wing mirror. He's probably the only one who did. They crowded round so fast. He said something and Zhang went nuts. He shouted at him to drive. I should have got down in my seat, I know.' He raised his face. 'I know.'

He had our sympathy. No question. What he did next, and that there was a picture of him doing it on the front page of an international newspaper, was stupid. But he still had our sympathy.

'You can't help it, can you?' he said.

Joe and I nodded and made the right sounds. Who knows if we wouldn't have done the same? It's a natural impulse.

'Zhang hadn't wound up the window,' Felix said. 'I'm surprised, thinking about it, that no stones came through it. But they'd stopped throwing them. We came to a turn in the road, so I leaned across Zhang and stuck my head out to look back the way we'd come. All I could see was the backs of the people crowding round the body. People were rushing all over the place, some the same way as us, back to their village, others towards the small crowd.'

Felix stopped and sat up straight, like he was ready for the verdict. Head up too. Fringe over one eye. Silent.

'And that,' I said, 'is when Beecher's assistant got the photograph.'

'She got me all right.' The anger came. 'The sneaky little bitch had stayed behind. I assume you've both seen the paper?' He made it sound like he'd prefer we hadn't.

''Fraid so,' I said. 'I had to bribe a girl in a hotel shop to sell me a copy she was supposed to give a guest.'

That issue of the *Washington Herald* sold out in Shanghai in record time. It was a piece of history, our history. We'd be hanging onto it. Mine had been spread over the bar at the Backstreet – once the surface had been checked and wiped. People who hadn't managed to buy one crowded round like it was a naked photo-spread of a famous celeb who'd been in Shanghai and they'd met her.

'You got it here?' Felix asked.

'No, back at the office. You read it?'

'Oh, yes. The hotel got one for me. When the maid brought it up to my room she pointed at the picture and gave me the thumbs up. "You famous!" she said. Jesus Christ.' He allowed himself a smile. 'You see the BBC before it got blocked? At least I got that in the hotel.'

'Hell, yes. Of the fight at the site? Saw it in the Backstreet,' I said. 'That looked mean.'

Nowadays the video would be up on the internet in a flash. This was pre-YouTube. The quality was like an old home movie: dim lighting, unsteady, muffled sound.

The police are off camera. I imagine them watching from the sidelines, protecting property, which would be SLIC's earthmovers and equipment, not the locals' homes. The cameraman stood with his back to them. It would have been a safe spot and explains the shoddy filming because he'd have had to hold the camera low to keep it hidden.

Zhang's men appear out of the gloom from one side. They're dressed in a sort of uniform of army surplus gear and waving metal stakes and wooden clubs. To start with they throw rocks. A couple of loud bangs must have been fireworks. There's shouting and they run at the farmers.

Felix was right about the Middle Ages and Romans thing. It was exactly how you'd imagine a battle in those days, or like you've seen in the movies; a big scrap with everyone hitting everyone else. The farmers white headbands helped us make out the good guys, but they'd also made them obvious targets for the goons.

The clip ends with one of Zhang's mob running right past the camera, very close, shouting his head off. His body blocks the shot and the camera gets dropped, or pointed down, ready to be turned off. In the last second of darkness, you can hear a nasty thwack of metal or wood. I hope it wasn't the cameraman. The film lasts ten seconds.

Harold Beecher must have kicked himself for missing the fight. It happened after he'd already jumped in a car to get back to Shanghai to file his story on Felix and the truck accident, 'British Worker in China Implicated in Violent Death of Protestor at Construction Site'. There were two photos: one was a panoramic shot of the truck and the crowd, and the other, inset in the big one, was a close-up of Felix's face in the truck's open window, blonde fringe floating in the wind above his horrified eyes, staring down the road.

Beecher gave the background of the dispute, including Chen Daming's role, the barefoot lawyer. He also identified the dead woman. She was a young teacher from Dongchang who'd come to see what the fuss was about. Tragic. She might have been from the kindergarten Felix walked past in the morning.

The focus of Beecher's story, however, was Felix. In Dongchang, Felix had fed Beecher a line, and Harold Beecher did not forgive people who fed him lines. He went for them like a pit bull.

Straight after the opening paragraph, which gave a graphic description of the death of the young teacher, he got in the first stab. 'Barely minutes before the tragedy, Mr. Fawcett-Smith said to this newspaper, "What we have here is a land transfer dispute, a claim for compensation, pure and simple. We [Shanghai Land Investment Corporation] will deal with it as any business would, by negotiating with the interested parties and coming to an agreement." Mr. Fawcett-Smith has since been unavailable for comment.'

He mentioned the Hi Ho story too, Mike Bennett's American hotel chain that got ripped off by SLIC, so it got exposure at long last. Beecher could justify digging up that dirt since it was an American paper. '... According to Mr. [someone-or-other], a senior executive at Hi Ho's head office in St. Louis, Mr. Fawcett-Smith played a prominent role – Mr. [someone-or-other] likened it to a 'honey-trap' – in drawing in and gaining the confidence of the company as it entered its ill-fated joint venture with Shanghai Land Investment Corporation in 1999. Mr. Fawcett-Smith organised and accompanied Hi Ho executives on visits to karaoke parlours and nightclubs – those places are often brothels in disguise – and on at least one occasion hosted at his residence an extravagant party where women offered sexual favours. When the relationship and joint venture broke down a year later, Mr. Fawcett-Smith represented his company in its refusal to negotiate a settlement with Hi Ho.'

'That's so unfair!' Felix said when it came up in our debrief. 'I had nothing to do with Hi Ho. I'd hadn't even started at SLIC.'

'You can sue him for libel.'

'Or send Zhang and his boys round.'

'I haven't seen him since I got back,' Felix said. My boss, Mr. Li – who you met, Johnny – is due back from Beijing this afternoon.

I've got to meet him at the hotel, four o'clock. I'm not looking forward to it. I told him I'd turn this into a PR victory, not a disaster.'

'Well, you did disobey the first rule of PR pal, didn't you?' Joe said, smiling.

'Which is?'

'Don't become the story.'

'Joe,' I said. 'I don't think a lesson in PR is going to help.'

'All right, all right,' he said. 'Trying to cheer you up, Felix. So, to be serious, you're under house arrest.'

'I wouldn't call it that,' Felix said. 'I'm avoiding the spotlight for a few days. It's the sensible thing to do.'

'Don't you think you'd be better off somewhere other than the Financial Plaza, somewhere neutral for example, like here with Johnny? Maybe you should get out of China for a while. What about Hong Kong?'

'Are you suggesting SLIC won't take care of this?' Felix sneered. 'They'll take care of me. We've got the *guanxi*. If anyone can get away with murder, it's Mr. Zhou. I've told you how he goes right to the top.'

A socialist sainthood for rape was indeed a good indicator the Zhou family could get away with murder.

'Hang on,' I said, raising my hand. 'First, it wasn't murder. The woman's death was an accident. At worst it was manslaughter, it was an accident and it wasn't Felix's fault.'

'Thanks, Johnny.' He gave me a knowing wink. 'Manslaughter,' he repeated, leaving his eye on me.

'But,' I added, 'just to be sure, I still think you should let Charlie Thurrold see what he can do.'

'No.' There was a flash of annoyance. 'I told you. I don't want him involved.'

Felix had got it off his chest, problem shared and that. He was feeling better.

'I wonder how much the family will want,' he said. 'I bet they'll squeeze us for every cent. And it was an accident, you're right there.'

I wouldn't be surprised if you don't see Beecher's newspaper on sale in Shanghai much longer. Mr. Zhou can take care of that too.'

'That's the spirit. This'll blow over.' I looked at my watch. It was two in the afternoon. 'Hey, you'd better get back to your hotel. You have your phone?'

'Not allowed to use it.'

'OK. Which room?'

'1305.' Felix turned to Joe, 'You got any more of those joints, Joe?'

'Sure.' He put his hand in his pocket.

'Anything stronger?'

'Not wise,' Joe said, 'even if I did. Not when you're in a hotel room on your own, buddy. That's how famous people die. And you're famous at this moment in time.'

'Take it easy, Felix, if I were you,' I added. 'Pot and other stuff ain't good for paranoia, and I have a feeling you're susceptible at the moment.'

'You'd know about the effects, wouldn't you, Johnny.' It wasn't a question.

Joe looked at me.

'What do you mean by that?' I asked. I felt the butterflies in my stomach. I had a premonition.

'Come on, Johnny. I know why you're really in Shanghai,' he said. 'Did you, Joe, know Johnny's big secret?' He didn't give Joe a chance to answer. He looked at me as he spoke. 'Good old anti-drug campaigner Johnny here used to be a dealer. Pills, wasn't it, Johnny.' It wasn't a question.

I was, for a moment, lost for words. What had got into Felix? He'd flipped. He was lashing out like a drug addict or alcoholic in rehab. And how the hell did he know?

Joe was staring at me. I'm not sure who was more surprised, me or him.

'Felix, this is not the time or place,' I said. It was an incredible struggle to keep my voice calm, get it out, like a snake was strangling my throat and the way to survive was let it think it had got me.

A thin smile cut into Felix's chubby cheeks like cheese wire. 'Not the right time and place?' he said. 'I'd say it's the perfect time and place. Haven't I joined your exclusive club? It *was* manslaughter, wasn't it? I think I'm more of an accessory myself.'

'For Christ's sake, Felix! What the hell are you trying to prove?' Joe spoke up. 'We're here to help you for Chrissakes. We're your buddies. What you got to go bringing this shit up for, whatever the fuck it is?'

Felix looked at his watch. 'You're right,' he said. 'I'd better get going. They're always early.'

He'd turned into one ice-cold bastard.

He stood up. His face was as pasty white as it had been when he arrived a few hours ago. He pulled his raincoat round his shoulders, put the hat on, his shades, and reminded Joe about the joints. Joe passed them over and Felix put them in his pocket, mumbled thanks. I turned away. He walked out without another word.

'What the fuck?' Joe said, staring at the door.

I went to open a window. The flat stank of cigarettes. The noise from the street, five storeys below, smacked me in the face. I hadn't noticed it like I usually did during the rare daylight hours I spent at home.

I looked across the street at the opposite tower block. I heard Joe go to the fridge. When I turned round he was staring at me with a mix of curiosity and sympathy. It was my turn.

'You all right?' He passed me a beer.

'Yeah, I'm okay.' I clicked it open. The short hiss sounded like how I felt. The effort of hearing out Felix and getting metaphorically kicked in the guts as thanks, it was almost physical. In fact, it was.

'What was that?' Joe asked.

I stood with my back to the open window. The sound of the traffic, which normally I hated, was reassuring. Life goes on.

'I think Felix is hyper-sensitive,' I said. 'And I mean truly hyper-sensitive. Perhaps it's the pot, no thanks to you,' I cheers'd Joe with my beer to show I wasn't blaming him. 'And he has been through a major trauma. He's in shock. Besides, you know how we sometimes say he's gone too Chinese for his own good?'

'Yuh.'

'Well, the first thing they do when in trouble is blame someone else. Except he is not blaming me, but he is trying to deflect criticism.'

'But is it true, you dealing pills and "man-slaughtering" someone?'

'Mind if I tell you another time? It's a long story.'

'Can you give me the basics, so I'm prepared, if it gets out? You know how people talk. Be nice to be able to stand up for you.'

'Good of you put it that way.' I wanted to light another cigarette but I resisted. Without thinking, not for a split second, about what I was going to say, I started. It was the first time I ever said this in Shanghai, in my adult life come to think of it: straight, no embellishment, no excuses.

'I was involved with a bad bunch at school. We swapped pills, then we traded them, sold them, mostly E but the occasional tab of acid or harder stuff, crystal meth was the worst. Party drugs. Raves. They were big. I was selling E and a teenager, younger brother of a mate of mine, overdid it, physically, not the pills. He dehydrated. Went for a rest, more dehydration. Woke up in a coma. Into hospital, intensive care, didn't come through. Body shut down. His brother blamed me. Might have been my pill. Wasn't definite. I hadn't given it to the kid myself. I was sure of that. Not so sure now of course. I got the rap. Underage, can't go to jail, did ten months in young offenders. Didn't have many mates when I came out. And a criminal record. Two choices: go for it, as in dealing, or get the hell out and start again.'

'Jesus. You kept that one real quiet, buddy.'

'Wouldn't you?'

'And you're gonna let Felix hit you with it like that?'

'I know,' I said. 'He needs a slap. But I can't stop myself feeling responsible.'

'For what?'

'Him. Felix. Young and stupid, granted. And he's pissed me off before. You were there. He's also burnt his boats with Charlie

Thurrold. But there's something about him that makes me want to look after him. It's hard to explain. Maybe I'm trying to make up for something, or, to be accurate, make up for my mate's little brother. Maybe I see Felix as a little brother. I don't have one myself. Only a sister. Then there's the Thurrold connection, and he's been good to me, and that I feel like I pushed Felix into SLIC.'

I didn't tell Joe how I'd surprised myself at liking him to begin with and that had developed into respect and genuine affection. He wouldn't have understood where I was coming from.

'Take it easy on yourself. We're adults,' Joe said.

'Are we? Sometimes I think we're kids in a playground.'

'Well, he sure was behaving like one.' He nodded at the door. 'Why put up with it? And why help him? Let him deal with it.'

'Talking of little brothers and stuff; if I was a psychiatrist I'd say Felix has a thing about father figures or people who try to keep him on the straight and narrow. You should hear what he says about his dad. And now I've joined the enemy because he's come to us for help – he never asked for it, but that's what he was here for – like he would Charlie Thurrold, or his dad, or his older brother. So he has to have a jab. Pre-emptive strike. Attack is the best form of defence.'

'Maybe you *should* be a psychiatrist.'

'I'll take that as a compliment.' I lit a cigarette.

'So what do you think you can do?'

'Me? Not much. But what I will do is patch things up between him and Thurrold, who can definitely help him out. I'm going to go see him and get him on side, even if it means Felix turns on me and, and...'

'... Tells everyone you were a drug dealer who killed your school buddy's brother?'

'Maybe.'

'I've heard worse,' Joe said.

'What, about me?'

'Ha! No, not you. Friends back in the States.' He swigged his beer. 'You better get going.'

# 17

## RUMOURS

CHARLIE Thurrold had two things to tell me. They were actually for Felix. But it was me that got them, and the temper. His face went blotchy red and his nose solid pink.

He was standing behind his desk. He raised his hands to his head every time he said 'idiot', and he was saying idiot a lot. The regular motion made him look like a puppet on a string, and Felix was pulling it. It was three in the afternoon.

'What the hell did he think he was doing? He's an idiot. A complete bloody idiot. Anyone with half a brain cell knows to stay away from a land dispute. And to try to deal with the media at the same time, on the spot, in person? Utter fucking stupidity. Especially when it's that Harold wots'isname. He's a ferret if ever there was one. And to get his face in the papers. Unbelievable.' He gasped and swayed on his feet. 'Idiot.'

Charlie's office was functional. The filing cabinets were gunmetal grey. Directories and file binders with blue spines and white labels were crammed onto bookshelves. There was a row of red and gold banners on one wall, like football club pennants; acknowledgments of the investments Charlie had helped bring to China. The one window, which I could see through because I was standing up as well, overlooked a block of brown–roofed lane houses walled in by new tower blocks, like a rat maze in a research lab.

'You have no idea how bad this is,' Charlie said. 'And now you tell me the idiot,' the hands started moving upwards but stopped at his chest, 'is hiding away and came to your place and you didn't call me? I thought you had some sense Johnny. Why didn't you get me over?' The hands dropped in despair. 'This is official. All kind of a stink's going to start: a British citizen involved, culpable to a degree, in the murder of an innocent bystander, a woman too. Jesus Christ. And you boys think you can hide away till it blows over, or that bloody bent company Felix works for – against my advice from the beginning, but I'll spare you the told-you-so's – is going to step up and take care of him? You bloody believe that?' He stretched his hands out towards me like he wanted to grab me by the shoulders and shake me. The desk was too wide but he had that look in his eyes, and the red face, and for a moment I did think he might launch himself.

'Felix didn't want to call you precisely because he didn't want this to be official. And I agree it'd be a good idea to spare him the told-you-so's.'

'He thinks he can decide?' Charlie shouted, rocking backwards, hands reaching for the ceiling. 'Who is he kidding? Jesus! Who are you kidding, Johnny? This'll make the Belgrade Embassy bombing look like a diplomatic parking ticket. Christ! And as for my thoughts on the matter and how I share them with Felix, I'll deal with him as I see fit.'

I repeated what Joe and I and Felix had discussed as outcomes.

'Oh my God, you lot are naïve. There are two factors going on that affect this in a bad way for Felix.'

'Mind if we sit down, Charlie?'

He grunted and lowered himself into a big leather chair. I pulled up a wooden one with thin grey padding, the square-armed type you find in British institutions like hospitals and police stations. I shifted it to the left so I could see Charlie past the brass stand with a Union Jack and Chinese flag on the desk. An ashtray was beside it. I wanted a cigarette but didn't dare to ask.

'What factors?' My voice sounded feeble, more concerned than I meant it.

'You want a cup of coffee? I forgot to ask. Something stronger?' Charlie said.

'A cup of coffee would be great, thanks.' I glanced at the ashtray again.

He pressed a button on the phone on his desk, asked for two cups and brought his hands together under his chin.

'Factor number one,' Charlie said. 'I hear from Beijing things are not going well for Felix's boss, Mr. Zhou. You know there's a power struggle going on?' I did. 'And you know how these things work.' I nodded. 'Well, Zhou is in the unfortunate position of being a pawn in the current game, and he's going to be "taken". They'll get him on whatever they want. It's unlikely to be the incident out at Dongchang, although they might have used it if it had happened earlier. I expect it'll be tax evasion or bribes.'

'What'll happen to him, and SLIC?'

'Depends,' Charlie said, 'on how big an example they want to make of him, how strong a signal the new guys want to send to the old guys. Maybe prison, maybe sacked. As for SLIC, that's too big to fail. They'll do some housekeeping and put one of their boys in charge I guess.'

'And the housekeeping will sweep out Felix.'

'If only it was so simple. Oh no. He's in more trouble than that.'

'What do you mean? They going to pin murder on him?'

Charlie looked me in the eye. 'Probably. That's part of factor number two'

Fucking hell. I might have said it out loud.

'Johnny, let me give you a recent example: who are the worst intellectual thieves who pinch Hollywood movies? Who makes the most money out of the pirated VCDs, and those new – what are they called – DVDs?'

'The Chinese.'

'More precise? Who's behind most of the IP theft in China?'

I hesitated. 'The government?'

'Correct. Well done. Next, name the most notorious case of pirating that made headlines in the domestic media and the *Shanghai Weekly*? It was last month, April. The culprit was sent to jail for five years.'

'Of course,' I said, 'It was that American guy, Sawyers.'

'Dave Sawyers. That's right. And he was guilty as sin, and so is everyone else but they don't go for them, do they? And how perfect the Americans pushed a case at the WTO on behalf of their film industry, claiming the Chinese are IP thieves. How perfect the Chinese could show one of the worst criminals was American, and how clever and strict they were in catching and punishing him. That made a nice point.

'This isn't public, although it will be soon thanks to Felix, but Her Majesty's Government has had the bright idea to stop carping on about Tibet and human rights and try a new angle with China; they want us to make a point by criticising the state's forced land requisition. It's part of Blair's new "ethical" foreign policy. It's quite neat in that it falls between human rights and commercial malpractice, or combines them. British companies are being "encouraged" not to build or operate factories, or deal with them, if they're built on land taken by force or unfairly. Don't ask me what I think of the idea. It's created a mountain of extra work. It's also impossible to implement. But it sounds good.' He gave me a sarcastic grin. 'Makes it seem like we care. Typical New Labour. The Chinese are mightily pissed off. Too right they rant about us interfering in their internal affairs. And now we, or rather our young friend Felix, have handed them a propaganda prize like Sawyers was for the American IP kerfuffle: a British national engaged in exactly what the British Government is accusing China of.'

'But it's SLIC who are responsible, and they're Chinese,' I said.

'Does that look Chinese to you?' Charlie opened a drawer, pulled out the *Washington Herald* and laid it on the table, Felix face up.

He smacked the cheek in the blown-up headshot with the back of his fingers.

I knew the photo by the pixel but I made a show of leaning over as if to check it was Felix.

'No,' I said. 'It, I mean he, doesn't.'

'So,' Charlie said, 'Felix will be dragged over the coals for this one, and his boss, even if he wanted to, is in no position to help.'

'But if they're going to arrest him why haven't the police done it already?'

'Oh, Johnny Boy,' Charlie sighed. 'You've got so much to learn. It's never a case of right or wrong, breaking the law or not. There are other things to consider. They know Felix wasn't driving the truck and wasn't in charge of it. They'll have spoken to the police in Wuzhou. I guess they're asking the people who are going for Zhou in Beijing if they want to make an example of Felix, or go for the other fellow... what was his name?'

'Zhang.'

'... and if they do want to use this accident to get at Zhou Jianguo. One of them will ask the Propaganda and Foreign Affairs ministries if they want to use Felix as ammunition against our "ethical" foreign policy. If they say yes, the Ministry of Civil Affairs has to be consulted because it'll bring attention to the peasants and the land-grabs and they'll go back to the Propaganda Ministry. You with me?'

'Sort of,' I said.

'That takes time, and that's why they haven't arrested Felix. Besides of which, they know exactly where he is so...'

'So?'

'So we move first. We shift Felix where it won't be easy to get him, where they'll have to create an official incident, like here in the Consulate, or my apartment. And we prepare a case for him.'

That wasn't going to happen if Felix had anything to do with it.

'I don't understand,' I said, 'how Mr. Zhou could lose his influence so fast. Surely he has allies who can help him.'

'It'll be a long time before he's put in his place. He might even get away with it if he can hold his enemies to ransom. He's bound to have dirt on people.' Charlie glanced at his files. 'But that's not his problem, whether he gets sacked or prison. His problem is that he is under investigation. He is tarnished. I expect he'll be under *shuang gui* in Beijing, or he will be when he comes back to Shanghai, if he ever does.'

'*Shuang gui?*'

'The twin rules: no going out to see anyone and no one allowed to come see you. House arrest.'

'Sounds like Felix in his hotel,' I said.

'No. He would never have got to your place.' Charlie thought for a moment. 'And that means we can get him. Right...' Since we had sat down his face had resumed its normal pale, unhealthy pallor. 'I've been in touch with a local lawyer I've dealt with over the years. Trade disputes. He's always been on the other side but we're friends. He has contacts you wouldn't believe. I'll get him round,' he looked at his watch, 'in an hour. Let's say four-thirty. You go fetch Felix for me, sharpish.'

Charlie stopped and stared at me. He registered the look I was giving him, the facial shrug you do when your mate finds out you've finished the curry sauce he was dipping his chips in. 'Is there a problem?' he said.

'Well,' I was wondering how to put it. 'You could say he and I had a tiff, not as bad as yours, in my flat. He went for me, when he was leaving, like he was biting the hand that wants to feed him.'

'Don't let it get to you,' Charlie said. 'Felix has always done that. The more you do for him the less he likes you, or seems to.'

'In my experience, not that I have much,' I was thinking of my sister, who can be a right pain, 'once people like that have gone for you they find it hard to back down. It's as if they've put themselves in a corner and have to stay there.'

'Point. Call me old-fashioned but my way of dealing with it, when you're short of time, is fight fire with fire. Here you go,' he sighed, tapping a fingertip on his lips, then taking it way. 'You tell

Felix that Uncle Charlie doesn't want a repeat of Cowley Road. That's all you have to say.'

'Sounds like a magic word. Mind if I ask why you didn't use it yourself, when you had your own scrap with him?'

'I did. That's why it got out of hand.'

'And what happened on Cowley Road. Where is it anyway?'

'Oxford, when he was at college there, and what happened doesn't matter.' He leaned over the desk towards me. 'Just shut him up and get him here.'

I heard him open a drawer. His hands appeared holding his tobacco pouch and papers. He pulled a paper out of the little green pack, v'd it in his fingers and sprinkled some leaf. So I could have lit up after all.

'Well, go on,' Charlie said. 'Don't hang around. I'll see you with Felix, and the lawyer,' he looked at his watch again, 'in a couple of hours. If the office is shut, don't worry. The security chap is used to me working late and my strange visitors.' He smiled and glanced from under his bushy eyebrows at the newspaper. He flicked a speck of tobacco off the photo. 'Let's get this mess cleaned up.'

I walked out of Charlie's office and along the corridor. A maid was vacuuming. The security guard buzzed me out through the double security door.

It was wet outside. The plum rains were starting early.

While I was in the taxi queue at the hotel beside the Consulate, I called Felix's mobile. It was switched off. I'd forgotten. I dialled enquiries but couldn't work out how to say 'Financial Plaza' in Chinese. The hotel concierge at the front of queue helped – the name had nothing to do with finance or plazas – and I got put through. The number Felix called me on yesterday flashed up. Stupid me.

'Room 1305 please.'

'Guest name?'

'Fawcett-Smith.' I had to spell it out. She thought Smith was the first name. I corrected her. I didn't know how to say 'hyphen'.

'Sorry, sir, but there is no person by that name on our guest list.'

'Try Felix.'

'No, sir.'

'Fucking hell. Sorry. How about SLIC?' And no way could I say Shanghai Land Investment Corporation – or was it company, I'd forgotten. I had a go.

'I am sorry sir, we are not allowed to put you through if you do not have the correct name.'

I wanted to tell her that it hadn't been a problem for the hookers. But she'd hung up.

I got in a taxi and told the driver to go to Pudong.

'You speak good Chinese,' he said into the mirror.

'Oh, fuck off,' I said in English.

'Thank you.'

When I got to the hotel I hurried up to 1305. I hammered on the door, shouted for Felix. No response. I hoped he was asleep, or stoned and drunk, so I hammered harder. Nothing. A cleaner pushed past me with her trolley of soap, towels and toilet paper.

'Check out,' she said.

'Fuck,' I replied. I asked her when, feeling like a bad amateur detective.

'Long time this morning.'

She made it sound like he checked out before he came to my place. Felix would have said so. Someone must have checked out for him. I really was thinking like a detective. So where the hell had he gone?

While I waited for the lift I considered the options. I could go to his office or his home. The office was round the corner, the obvious place to start. I had just enough time to get there before it shut for the day. I had a bright idea. I'd seen him being chummy with the hotel concierge, who was at his desk by the big revolving door in the lobby.

'Excuse me. Did you see Mr. Shi come back today?'

He shook his head and told me he'd seen Mr. Shi leave in the morning.

I set off along the wet, empty pavement.

I tried to remember the name of the street in Oxford Charlie Thurrold had mentioned. Cobley? Cowslip? It wouldn't come back. I could say, 'something in Oxford, on a street,' if I had to. I wondered what had happened. Obviously, Thurrold had got Felix out of trouble. Student drug bust? Couldn't be. Felix said, no reason to disbelieve him, that he hadn't done drugs before coming to Shanghai. He must have crossed the law. Theft? Speeding? Drunk driving, maybe knocking down a pedestrian. What's it called? Reckless driving. I thought I may as well mention it to Felix when I found him, even if he came quietly, perhaps when we were in a taxi on our way to the Consulate. I'd be gentle but it would be a good way to settle the score, put him back in his box after what he had said in my flat in front of Joe.

I'd never been up to the 18th floor of the Pudong Wealth Tower, or into Felix's office. He'd met me in the lobby of the Financial Plaza Hotel the few times I'd seen him for lunch in that part of town.

I was impressed. The wooden panelling and deep carpets reminded me of a smart law firm I'd done some recruiting for. The receptionist told me Felix wasn't in. She hadn't seen him for days. She also stared at me like I was a plumber come to fix the toilet on the wrong day. I must have looked out of place in the jeans and T-shirt I'd worn to my office in the morning. I'd been expecting a quiet day, no meetings.

I remembered the name of James Li's secretary. 'I'll leave a message with Amy,' I said. The receptionist stared at me. She didn't do anything that might have been helpful, like get out a pen and piece of paper, or show me where to find Amy.

There were two corridors, one to the left, the other to the right. I guessed right. 'She's down here, isn't she?' I said and walked off. The receptionist stood up but I ignored her. I had no idea what Amy looked like but I remembered Felix mentioning the coffee machine. Maybe I should be a detective. I sniffed to see if I could smell it. No need. I went round a corner and saw it beside a three-piece sofa suite behind a glass partition, and there, by the glass and at her desk, was a plain girl who had to be Amy.

I pushed open the glass door and addressed her like we were good friends who'd never met. That wasn't a good start. I explained who I was but she kept staring at my scruffy T-shirt, right at the centre of my chest. 'Do you know where Felix is?' I said.

She shook her head.

'You do know what happened? Out at Dongchang?'

She shook her head.

'I think Felix might be in trouble, and we need to help him.'

The words 'we' – I used the one that specifies 'you and me' – and 'trouble' got a reaction. It was small, but it was there. Her eyes left my chest, which had been beginning to feel like it was being drilled. She was thinking about Felix, not me.

'What kind of trouble?' she said.

'Your boss Mr. Li should know.'

At the mention of his name the man himself appeared. I'd forgotten – and didn't think of it – that Felix had told us Li wanted to see him that afternoon, that he'd come back from Beijing already.

'What's going on?' Li's voice was polite and firm, verging on hostile.

'Mr. Li, do you remember me? John Trent. We met at Paradise Island, at the launch for Buckingham Park.' I smiled and held out my hand.

Li's shirtsleeves were rolled up, his collar undone. I saw patches of sweat under his armpits, odd considering the air-conditioning. He was holding a sheaf of papers in his hand.

He stared at me, not like he was trying to remember my name, more like confusion. Through the doorway of his office I noticed his desk was a mess and the safe beside it on the wall, where he'd keep his precious company chops, was open. He moved towards me as if he wanted to block my view.

'I came here,' I said, stepping back, putting my hand down, 'because I'm trying to find Felix and his phone is switched off. You must know the situation.'

Li pulled himself together and measured me up. He was asking himself if he could brush me off or if he had to give me some respect and tell me what was going on.

I must have come across smarter and more confident than I felt because he chose the latter.

'Yes, I am well aware of it. I have come back from an important meeting in Beijing to deal with it.' He gave Amy a stern look. She was staring at her hands in her lap. 'We cannot let the foreign press, or the domestic media for that matter, not that they'd try, speak to Felix. This is in his own best interest. He is taking a break while we deal with the situation.'

'May I ask where?' You don't ask direct questions with people like Li, but it was worth a try.

'He's being taken care of.'

I had one last go. 'Mr. Li, the British Consulate is very keen to contact Felix. He is a British citizen, and he might be in trouble with the law.'

He cut me short. 'Mr?'

'Trent.'

'Mr. Tent. Felix works for us. We will look after him. There is no need for the Consulate. As for the law,' he smiled. 'We are more than capable of dealing with that. Please do not worry.'

As soon as I got down to the lobby I called Charlie Thurrold.

'Bullshit,' he said. 'Li certainly is scared of the law, the national law. He's scared out of his wits. Maybe he did have to come back to sort out the Dongchang mess but more likely he's using it as an excuse to get away from Beijing so he could prepare his own escape from the fallout that's coming Zhou or SLIC's way. And don't forget Dongchang is in Jiangsu Province, so his *guanxi* with Shanghai judges and the authorities won't count for much.' He was jumping around. 'It's how I said: they're waiting to see which way Beijing wants to play it, and in this case 'they' is Li and his gang. I wouldn't put it past them, or this Li fellow in particular, to be thinking: if he can get the credit from Beijing for presenting Felix, if they want him, he might get out of the trouble he's in with Zhou, and maybe replace him as head honcho.' There was a short silence. 'What it boils down to is Felix is missing, probably held against his will, and we've got to find him.'

It was now seven o'clock. I decided to go to the Backstreet, have a beer and pick up the gossip. I told Charlie. He said he had to make some calls to the UK, but he'd be along later.

I was mobbed when I walked into the bar. Everyone wanted to know. Where was Felix? What had happened to him? The 'Dongchang Incident' had sent the rumour mill into overdrive. Was it true Felix was under arrest; that he'd done a runner and been caught in Nanjing; that he'd tried to jump on a flight and been hauled out onto the tarmac? Had he been driving the truck and his famous powerful boss was going to get someone to be the fall guy for him? Someone who was friends with a local journalist said the woman who got squashed was the wife of one of the men being detained and she had been pushed by one of Zhang's gang. He also passed on that the pitched battle between the hoods and the locals had ended in a stand-off but they'd rescued the two men from the KTV place. One was okay but the other, I guess the stubborn one Felix described, was in hospital.

When I got a word in edgeways and said I'd 'been in touch' with Felix they calmed down. 'He's a bit shook up, to say the least. He'll be all right, but right now he's, um, how shall I say: taking it easy, staying away from the limelight. I'm sure his company will take care of him.'

Someone brought the chatter back down to the usual level of Shanghai expat conversation, and self-interest, when he wondered how long the BBC would be blocked. I relaxed.

Charlie Thurrold arrived and pulled me to one side.

'Right, I've spoken to my legal friend, and he's been in touch with a chap called Chen Daming, a lawyer, a "barefoot" one.'

'I've heard of him.'

'Well, Chen's spoken to the family of the woman who got run over.'

'Is it true that she's the wife of one of the men that got detained and beaten up?'

'Where did you hear that?'

'Someone was just saying.' I nodded along the bar. 'Never mind.'

'She was pregnant.'

'Oh God.'

Talking to Charlie was on a totally different level to the wild conversation I'd had with everyone else in the bar. Charlie dealt with hard facts. It's what he did with them that confused me.

'Tragic. Of course, her family will be demanding compensation. What happens is a lawyer like Chen starts to fight the case and in a blink of an eye the government goes round the back, offers a tidy sum and the family accept it. They'll be happy, don't worry. Then the government can get on with making Chen's life hell. Anyway, Chen has tracked down the driver of the truck and had him arrested on suspicion of manslaughter.'

'I thought you said the government makes his life hell. How come they arrest someone for him?'

'Don't ask.'

'What about Felix?'

'Chen knows what happened, and that Felix is innocent. But he warned me Felix's presence pissed off the villagers. They can play the foreigner versus China card. If they choose to do that, along with the other stuff I mentioned about catching a foreigner red-handed doing something that the West – in this case us Brits – complain China doesn't do enough to stop, the land-grabs and so on, the authorities are going to roast him. If they don't, this land dispute will grow into something much bigger. No way can the Party refuse a request from the peasants to right a wrong inflicted by a foreigner when the Party itself plays the nationalism card so hard.'

'Doesn't sound good for Felix,' I said.

'No, it doesn't, but here's where Chen can help. He doesn't want this to turn into an 'evil foreigner versus China' fight either. If the villagers go down that road, the government will crucify Felix, tell the villagers that they've got what they wanted, the good old Party's done its bit for them so, by way of gratitude, they can hand over those pesky acres of farmland they were fussing over, and shut up about a few broken bones and a couple of deaths.'

'There were more?'

'Yes, one more. In the fight that got onto the BBC. A man had his head cracked open.'

'Shit,' I said. 'But do I take it this Chen bloke is willing to help Felix?'

'Precisely. But we need to find him.' He sounded exasperated. 'Oh, and I called his mother.'

'How did she take it?'

'I'm lucky she trusts me to take care of the boy. Otherwise she'd have been on the first plane out.'

I was well and truly confused. Like I said, Charlie had the facts straight. It's what he extrapolated from them that got me.

To my way of thinking, Felix had been in the wrong place at the wrong time, and on the wrong side. He had meant well. He had done no wrong himself, apart from being a witness, and not telling the truth to Harold Beecher, and not stopping – if he could have – the truck driving over a pregnant woman. All he had to do was step forward and explain himself to the police. The British Consulate would help, if it went to court he'd get a lawyer, and it would be cleared up.

But his own company had to abduct him, presumably against his will but not necessarily, and his 'uncle' Charlie was coming up with a conspiracy theory every five minutes, each more complicated than the last. I was losing the plot.

I was also wondering: why was I trying to help, especially after that outburst in my flat. And how the hell did Felix know about Steve Turner?

I slowed down and had a think, at my own pace not Charlie Thurrold's.

Felix had come to my flat. He saw me as a mate. I was pleased. A friend in need and so on. I'd do what I could. On balance and considering his fights with Thurrold weren't my business, he'd been a good friend. And I meant what I said to Joe about him lashing out because he was helpless. You don't need to be a shrink to know that when people do that they don't mean it.

It wasn't dealing with my sister – she's bad but she isn't psycho – that gave me the patience to deal with those attacks. It wasn't helping my mum and dad resolve their endless fights either. I realised – at long last and after her dying – it was Gran. The grief I'd given the family, her family, as in she owned it, the patience she'd made a show of so the others would back off. The patience she'd exhausted on me. What a thankless bastard, running to her in the last resort.

Now I had my chance to stand by someone like she had for me, no matter what a mess they'd made of themselves and what they'd done to me.

Besides all that, Felix was one of us, the Shanghai gang, and we had to stick together. No one understood. All you lot who dropped his name at posh dinner parties, or mine in the pub, or Joe's in the 'diner'. We went out to Shanghai because we wanted you to give us the respect, from a distance, that you'd never given us at home, to our faces. You carry on talking about us, you be envious, admiring, jealous. Go on. Don't hold back, because we'll be back one day and we'll hold it up, right up to your face this time, what we did out there. And you won't understand, but you'll respect it. Because we went and did it. Felix was our flag bearer. He'd tried too hard and he'd mucked up but we... I... wasn't... weren't going to desert him. He had no one else.

And my family would see it in the papers. It was sure to be in the UK ones. The cuttings would be in the post. When I saw them I could tell them the full story, the part I played in it – if that didn't get into the papers too; bloody hell, I was fantasising like Felix – and I'd get the respect.

Of course, I never considered that someone might mention the coincidence: Johnny Trent gets himself involved in another manslaughter.

# 18

## BLACK JAIL

Sorry I had a go at you. I didn't mean it. I was trying to capture the moment. That's what I thought at the time. It isn't now.

It took us a week to track Felix down. He'd vanished, except in the newspapers. He was in them on the Monday, an editorial in the *China Daily*:

'Yet again we suffer the unwelcome, uninvited interference of a foreign country in China's internal affairs, at government level, with the recent instructions from Britain's Foreign Office criticising China's policy of land asset re-allocation, and coincidentally – and ironically – at the local level where a citizen of the very same country, in attempting to interfere with the lawful process of a transfer of land-use rights, exacerbated the situation to such a degree that the lives of two innocent Chinese citizens were lost and tens of thousands of dollars' damage done. That the British citizen in question is based in Shanghai, a city that under the humiliating Unequal Treaties was for a hundred years the centre of foreign rape and plundering of China's resources and domestic markets, adds to the poignancy. The commercial organisations of Shanghai must proceed with care if they are not to repeat the historic mistake of allowing foreign companies and governments to reap the rewards of their own efforts.'

Wednesday's *Shanghai Weekly* was more practical, and disingenuous. It also told us where Felix was, or at least had been at the beginning of the week, and rehashed the story from the week before.

'Felix Fawcett-Smith, a British national resident in Shanghai, who claimed he was acting on behalf of the Shanghai Land Investment Corporation when present last week at the scene of the accidental death of two residents of Wuzhou township in Jiangsu Province, was detained by police on arrival at Pudong International Airport on Tuesday morning. Mr F.F. Smith is being held in custody pending the preparation of charges by the judicial authorities. Witnesses at the scene of the accident, which occurred on 20 May in Dongchang District of Wuzhou Township, say Mr F.F. Smith took control of a vehicle that crushed an innocent bystander to death and fled the scene of the accident, and refused to comply with requests from the local police to appear and explain his conduct. Mr F.F. Smith attempted to leave the country via Hong Kong on Sunday but was apprehended by Hong Kong Police at the request of Shanghai Public Security Bureau and returned on the first flight after necessary procedures had been completed. The British Consulate has been advised and visits have been arranged.

When contacted by this reporter, the Shanghai Land Investment Company, which is directly under the control of the Municipal People's Government of Shanghai, stated it will co-operate completely with the police and authorities in Jiangsu Province and Shanghai in ensuring that justice is done. In the meantime the Corporation's development project in Wuzhou, Jiangsu Province, with a total investment of 30 billion yuan ($400 million) and covering an area of 300 hectares, is proceeding as planned. The development will bring much needed economic benefit to the Yangzte River area. It has the approval and support of national level bureaus.'

'Visits have been arranged? Rubbish,' Charlie said when I called him. 'I haven't had a peep out of them and I've been asking every day. Funny when you think it comes from the *Shanghai Weekly*. First time it ever had any news. Soon as I saw it, I quoted it to the Public Security Bureau, and they deny they're holding Felix. I also called Foreign Affairs. No luck. He might be in a black jail of course.'

'Black jail? I thought those were in Beijing, for locking up peasants who've gone up there to petition the central government.'

'Oh, they have them in Shanghai too, or their equivalent. They have them everywhere.'

'If he's in one of those, how do we find him, let alone get him out?'

'I've been thinking, and I've got an idea. Can you have a word with that girlfriend of his, Anita, isn't it?' Charlie said. 'I'll try my legal friend. Good news on that front too.'

'What's that?'

'Chen Daming, the lawyer I mentioned who wants to help the Dongchang farmers, where the "project" is not "proceeding" as the *Shanghai Weekly* claims, just as the police claim they don't have Felix, so I reckon the whole article can be discounted as baloney... anyway, Chen has got the locals to agree to testify Felix was nothing more than a passenger in the truck. But he has to go public with his first-hand witnessing the beating up of the two reps in return.'

'So he'll get off.'

'That depends. We have to factor in the Beijing angle and how judges do what the Party tells them. Mind you, now an editorial has appeared in the *China Daily*, they might be happier. They've scored a point. Our ambassador was called in by the Ministry. That means he has to make a report to London. With any luck this is the last I'll hear of ethical foreign policy.'

'Charlie, I'll call Anita, who's not his girlfriend by the way, just a friend. I have an idea too.'

When Anita heard the theory that Felix was in a black jail she didn't believe it. She too doubted they existed in Shanghai. And she believed the newspaper, which she hadn't read, if it said the police had Felix.

She agreed to help however, because in China you always agree to help a friend, even if that friend has been a complete bastard.

Anita called Amy, James Li's secretary, and after work we both met her in a teahouse, a funky new one where the seats hung from ropes and the view of the street was blocked by plastic bamboo plants.

Amy was nervous about meeting me since she'd witnessed my frosty reception by James Li. 'You must not tell my boss that I have met you,' was the first thing she said.

We assured her we wouldn't.

'Can you tell us where Felix is?'

'I think so. You will help him?' She looked at Anita with what I guessed was jealousy. It was transparent that she idolized Felix and was upset there was another girl who cared for him.

'Yes, we are his friends.'

'I want to help him,' Amy said. 'Felix is an English gentleman. He brings me presents from Hong Kong.' She was having a dig at Anita. I think Amy was simple, a country girl.

She told us that when Felix got back from the board meeting in Hong Kong she had organized a car to pick him up at the airport.

'Hang on a second,' I said, 'He went to Hong Kong for a board meeting?'

'Yes. It is normal.' Amy didn't read the *Shanghai Weekly*. I let it pass. Must have been a story made up by Li.

Mr. Zhang, Felix's comrade-in-arms in Dongchang, had gone in the car to the airport. Amy couldn't be sure but she guessed, from listening to James Li on the phone, they had taken Felix to a police station in the Wankou District, an industrial suburb of Shanghai, more like a satellite town.

Wait a minute. He'd come back from a board meeting, but the car sent to pick him up had taken him to a police station. So *Shanghai Weekly* had been partly correct?

The Wankou police chief had been calling Li – she knew because she picked up – once a day. She frowned with conviction. 'Yes, that must be it. And Mr. Zhang used to always be there when they met too. So I am sure that is where he is.'

She couldn't give us an address or phone number, which was odd since she was in touch with the place every day. Maybe she was trying to protect herself. Anita said it was all right. It wouldn't be hard to find.

After Amy had gone I asked Anita if we could believe her. With a woman's intuition she'd realized that Amy was jealous of her but at the same time Amy couldn't do anything to help Felix herself and she did want to, so the answer was yes. 'Besides, there's no harm in trying.'

I reported back to Charlie Thurrold. He was pleased. He needed an hour or two the next morning to get some documents from the Public Security Bureau and we'd go out to Wankou, find Felix and bring him back. Since his Security Bureau contact had denied they had Felix, Charlie couldn't call him back and contradict him, but he could get something out of him. One of the documents he was talking about was an official denial the police were holding Felix, which they had to give him if he made a formal Consular request for a visit. Once he'd got that he'd take it to Wankou and present it as evidence that Felix was not in custody and he could leave with us.

I know it sounds mad. I wanted to make a joke: 'What if they say Felix isn't Felix?'

The plan didn't work so it doesn't matter.

But we did get to see him – Felix, that is. It was more thanks to old-style bribes than low-level diplomacy and cunning.

The lawyer Chen Daming came with me and Thurrold on yet another drive through the Shanghai suburbs, another day under a dirty, grey sky, and another taxi driver saying, 'Wow, you speak Chinese,' when we told him where to go.

No, I didn't tell him to fuck off.

I said 'Wankou.'

I sat in the back with Chen, Charlie was in the front. Chen didn't talk much, to start with. I stared out the window at the factories and building sites.

Chen Daming began with the standard questions, 'How long had I been in China?' and so on. He seemed interested. He was a small man in his late thirties, prematurely balding and he wore big glasses with thick lenses. His eyebrows were extra broad but almost hairless, like a pair of spiders had landed on his face. He spoke good English.

Once he'd been polite to me, he explained to Charlie how he'd persuaded the villagers and farmers in Dongchang not to fall for the anti-foreign game. It boiled down to money. Chen told them the compensation for a person killed by a foreigner would be roughly a hundred times less than a fair price for the land. He said this without trace of irony. It was a matter of fact.

We arrived in Wankou at local lunchtime, eleven o'clock. The streets were quiet and a light 'plum' drizzle was floating in the air like that water spray you get at raves. We found the police station no problem. It was down a road to a small factory zone, potholed and broken, and the pavement beside it had slabs missing and piles of rubble alongside it. There was a row of concrete poles for electricity and telephone wires, half on, half off the pavement, with thick guy wires made of heavy, twisted cables that crossed the pavement at head height.

A security guard stopped us driving in so we parked on the side of the road. Chen got out and went into the gatehouse. He took a black plastic bag from the boot of the car. I'd seen him put a few in there when we set off.

While we waited, a stream of young factory workers in blue short-sleeved shirts walked towards us from down the road, at least a hundred of them. A dozen or so stopped off at a hole-in-the-wall noodle shop, up on the left, where they queued to order and sat on pink plastic stools round low folding tables to eat. The pavement around them was black with cooking oil where the shop owner had chucked his slops towards the gutter. The rest of the workers filed past us, chatting among themselves, pushing and nudging, laughing. I wondered how they would spend the rest of the day. In internet bars playing computer games I suppose, a few hours' sleep and back to work in the middle of the night or the early morning.

Chen came out. His face was blank and he didn't have the bag. He pushed through the workers without registering them.

'Well?' I asked as he got back in beside me.

'Not here,' he said, and spoke to the driver in Shanghainese, and to me and Charlie in English. 'Wait a minute.'

We drove down the street towards the noodle shop and pulled up about fifty metres short. Chen peered across me at a cheap guesthouse on the same side of the road. 'Number 58,' he said. 'Five Continents Guesthouse. Here it is.'

'This is where Felix is?' Charlie said, trying to turn to Chen but giving up with the awkward twist of his heavy old body.

'Yes. The police use it as a place to keep people. More comfortable, for the police and the prisoner. Let me go first.'

I heard the boot open and shut. Chen crossed the road with another carrier bag and went inside. He was longer than at the police station. Every three seconds the wipers pushed the water off the windscreen. When Chen came out he looked worried. He crossed the street as if he was afraid of being run over, turning his head both ways. He didn't get into the car. He opened Charlie's door and said, 'We must be quick. Come.'

Charlie and I climbed out and followed Chen across the road. Charlie walked tall like he was the main man and Chen was his local rep, me his personal assistant. He held his jacket closed against the damp, and to protect the papers in his inside pocket.

The guesthouse was cheap and nasty. The lobby was tiny. A wooden sofa with no cushions was beside the wall and the reception 'desk' was a lectern type thing made out of cheap pine that had a hole kicked right through it at knee height. The varnish was flaking like dead skin. Chen Daming spoke to the man behind it and he stepped out to open a solid metal door. It had a chunky lock. Behind the door were some stairs. We went up them.

I waited for the sound of the door closing. After what seemed like an age, as if that man wanted to torment me, it did, with a heavy metallic clang. A shiver went up my spine and into the back of my brain where it played havoc for few seconds. Signals went one way saying 'welcome back' to a nice cosy prison, no responsibility, no worries, 'just do what you're told' and everything will be all right, you can relax, and others going the other way screamed 'Get out! It's a lock-up. Stop. Turn round. Run.' I clenched my fists. I might have bitten my tongue. I hadn't prepared myself for this. It never crossed my mind.

I got a grip, tried to shut down the memory. I noticed Chen Daming had a limp. I hadn't seen that before. Maybe it was only on stairs.

On the first floor there was a small room, like one for the maid in old-school state hotels who opened rooms, delivered flasks of hot water, and kept an eye on comings and goings. Here it was occupied by a man in a private security guard uniform; dark blue trousers, light blue shirt, belt with shoulder strap and a badge like a police one. He came out and led us down the corridor, stopped at a door with no number, and unlocked it.

'Be quick,' he said to Chen.

It was a shitty bedroom like in Dongchang where Felix found Harold Beecher, only shittier. There was no carpet. A hundred times more interesting than the décor was the technicolour character clash that went off the moment we walked in.

Felix was lying on the bed watching TV. He was in a pair of shell-suit tracksuit trousers, red and blue, and a dirty white T-shirt with Chinese characters on it. Besides the clothes it was his face, white, washed out, and his unwashed hair stuck in strands across his forehead that made an impression, and the surprise, then anger, that flashed across it.

'Oh fuck,' he said. 'Here comes the fucking cavalry.'

'Nice to see you too,' Charlie said, 'you took some finding.'

He got straight to it. 'This is Mr. Chen. He's a lawyer, and he's pretty much got you off the potential charges of manslaughter, murder even.' Felix stared at Charlie as if he was speaking a foreign language, or he was drunk.

'You okay mate?' I said. Felix's head lolled at me. He grunted. I went over and pulled the curtains back, which made him put his hand to his face and say again, 'Fuck.'

'Pull yourself together,' Charlie said. 'We're here to get this sorted out. Like I said, Mr. Chen...' He pointed at Chen, who sat down in a chair by the window. He was watching Felix like he was a sick chicken in his backyard.

Felix wasn't listening. 'Good old Uncle Charlie,' he said to no one. 'Can always be relied on to turn up in my hour of need. I thought I made it clear. I don't want your fucking help.' He turned to me. 'You saw didn't you, Johnny. You asked me too. Remember what I said? Can you tell Uncle Charlie for me?'

I shook my head.

'Go on, be a good Johnny boy. You know why Charlie's here. I told you. It's because of my mother. My mum.' He trailed off in a weak voice. 'Mummy.' Felix pulled his legs up and sat cross-legged.

'Felix. Pull yourself together, will you,' Charlie said, sitting down at the foot of the bed, his body side on. 'I'm here to help.'

'Help who? Help what? Help yourself get into my mother's good books, back into her bed, once you've got her darling boy out of trouble yet again?'

'Let's not talk about that,' Charlie said.

Chen Daming was either pretending not to listen or not catching the meaning. I was all ears. I thought I was about to get the story of Cowpat Road.

'Why not?' Felix said. 'What have I got to lose? Johnny here's a friend with his own skeletons to hide,' he turned to me, 'aren't you? Aren't you my friend with a skeleton? You don't just look like one,' he smirked. 'And if this gentleman is a lawyer,' he indicated Chen with his elbow, 'I'm sure he's taken the Hippocratic oath.'

Charlie looked at the floor.

'Come on. Let's have it out, Uncle Charlie!' Felix spoke up. His voice was uncomfortably loud.

'Felix.' Charlie turned towards him.

'What?'

'Don't.' He stretched his hand, palm out like an American Indian chief doing the peace thing. Felix reacted like it was throwing off a force field. He kicked his legs out and pushed himself right up against the bed head. He ended up in a crouch, knees to his chest.

When he spoke, his voice was calmer and meaner. 'Can't you see I've had enough? Can't you see I want to be left alone, by you specifically?' He grinned at me. 'You're all right, Johnny.' He turned back to Charlie, who was looking away from Felix at the wall above the TV. 'Not again. Not like the other times, or that one you never let me forget.' Back to me: 'Guess what. Uncle Charlie here once helped me out of a police cell in Oxford. Proper cell, British one. Didn't have TV.' He nodded at the TV. 'Charlie's always had this thing about rescuing me. Helping me. He thinks my mum will thank him the best way a woman can. They used to be lovers. Didn't you?'

Thurrold took it with a straight face, but it was obvious he was trying not to wince.

'It was before I was born,' Felix said, 'so I can't speak as a witness, but from the way she talked to me about you, it's obvious, and you too, Charlie, that look in your eye...'

'What was it you did to get locked up in Oxford?' I wanted to get him off Charlie and his mum. I was interested but felt like a voyeur who's seen enough. I made the question sound like an idle one, a minor detail, matey talk from one ex-con to another. We were on the level.

'Not telling you. Maybe Charlie will.' He squinted at me. 'Maybe he has. But what I *will* tell you is how he used to fuck my mother in Hong Kong in a cheap hotel or his government apartment while my dad was on parade or up at the border catching illegal immigrants.'

Strands of his blond hair slid down his forehead and over his eyes, which were burning with malice. They darted from side to side. His cheeks had recovered their colour but it wasn't the fruity ripeness, the peachy pink that used to betray his naïvety and innocence. This was a fiery, angry red, like he'd slapped himself.

Charlie looked up at the ceiling. His hands stayed by his side, on the bed, clenched hard. The bald top of his head made him look like a monk saying his prayers. I was worried he was holding himself back and it wouldn't last long, that he'd lose control and this was going to get physical. Or Felix was going to lash his legs out and kick Charlie off the bed. I'd never be able to stop it if they did go off. They were within easy striking distance. But neither made a move. It was like they'd done this before. It was a ritual.

Charlie stayed twisted away, with his back to Felix, right at the foot of the bed. He looked at me. He gave me what I believe is called a 'wan smile'. It was unsettling to see Charlie like that, as if he was powerless to defend himself, resigned to the abuse.

'Yes, you fucked my mother and fucked up my life. You know how. My dad has always wondered if I was his son or not, and that's the real reason he's hated me all his life. Thanks for that.'

I let out a gasp of astonishment. Chen looked at me with wide eyes as if he was about to say 'bless you' because I'd sneezed. Charlie shut his eyes for a few seconds. This couldn't be true. Not in this day and age.

'And my brother too, who thinks he's my half-brother. Nice to have him on my case. And neither of you, neither my dad nor you prepared to have a test. "Not the done thing." Was it you said that? Or was it him? You thought it would go away, be forgotten, swept under the carpet, like it would in the old days.' He stopped and breathed. 'Well, you try living under a fucking carpet your whole life! You try.'

With that Felix put his hands up, pushed his hair out of his eyes and left them there, holding his head, heels of his palms pressed into his eye sockets. 'Fuck, why can't you leave me alone?' he said through his wrists. 'What did I do to deserve this? Why can't you let me live my life the way I want. I chose to go work for SLIC, I chose to come to Shanghai. I chose to go out to Dongchang. I agreed to speak to Harold Beecher. I take responsibility. All right? I agreed to go to Hong Kong.'

'What?' I said. This was a good chance to get to the point. 'You agreed to go to Hong Kong? The paper said you were running away.'

'That's a good one.' He dropped his hands, looked at me with red eyes. 'I go there on a regular basis. Have done for ages. This was the last time. They told me to. No choice. Some nest eggs involved, including mine.'

'Then what the hell are you doing here? Why did you come back if no one arrested you?'

'Is that what they said? Nice. Because it's true in a way.'

'What, that the Hong Kong police...?'

'Police? There were no police.'

'Hang on,' I said. With Charlie sitting in silence, I took charge.

I went and sat on the other chair beside Chen. It brought me closer to Felix's level. 'Felix, can you tell us what you were doing in Hong Kong and how you came back?'

Felix couldn't have appeared more bored if he tried. He swung his head from me to Chen and back. Charlie was staring at the wall. He'd zoned out.

'All right,' Felix said. 'I went to make a last big payout from SLIC for Zhou and Li, and a little one for me. That rhymes, ha.' The laugh was pathetic. 'And now I've done it, under my name, they've also got their case against me. I am the sacrificial lamb, the bait, and I fucking fell for it. Well, to be honest I didn't have a choice. But soon as they had the money – it wasn't them in person, of course – they had a goon escort me back to Shanghai, from right outside the boardroom door. All the way. We had to share a hotel room in Kowloon for a night. Fucking Y-fronts on the washing line above the bath. Yuk. And he picked his nose.'

'You do what for Zhou in Hong Kong?' Chen Daming leant forward and spoke softly, like a doctor. Those were the first words he said.

Felix turned to the small, neat man who was asking a polite and precise question. He smiled.

'Amongst my other duties? Sorry, Mr?'

'Chen.'

'Mr. Chen, amongst the duties I perform for Shanghai Land Investment Corporation, one is to serve as managing director of a company in Hong Kong, of which, it so happens, I'm the major shareholder, the legal representative as you call it on the mainland. I am sure you have heard of similar set-ups,' Felix stopped himself. 'You're a lawyer, aren't you?'

Chen nodded.

'Mr. Zhou Jianguo, our chief executive, has a lot of money. An awful lot of money. It's in yuan, in China, and he would prefer it to be abroad, somewhere safe, like Hong Kong or London.'

Charlie Thurrold put his hands between his knees, clasped his fingers together and was looking down at them. He was concentrating on what Felix said.

Felix swung towards me. 'Hey, Johnny, remember I told you I had to find a flat for Mrs. Zhou? Guess how many they bought in the end?' I shook my head. 'Five! Yes, five fucking flats in Knightsbridge. Close to a total of ten million pounds. Imagine the commission I lost on that. And a lucky bastard in a London estate agency like Smyth and Corrigan would have got it too. There's irony for you. I came here to make my fortune and ended up helping a guy who took over from me make one. Well,' he turned back to Chen. 'The question was how to get the money out and into London property, and I'm sure I don't need to tell you but it went through me, and I did get a commission,' back to me, 'nowhere near what I'd have got in London, but still a commission, so can't complain. Trouble is, this one came with strings attached, as they do with laundering money. You know what they call people like me who do this for people like Mr. Zhou?'

Chen and I were silent. Felix looked from him to me and back. Chen shrugged.

'White gloves.' It was Charlie Thurrold. He put his hand in his pocket and pulled out his tobacco.

'That's right.' Felix's voice remained calm. 'Well done, Charlie. White Gloves. Keep their hands clean.' He held up his own to his face as if he was looking for dirt on them, like Lady Macbeth with the blood. It was the only Shakespeare I did in school.

'Hey, Johnny, got any Marlboros? These cigarettes are shit.' He pointed to a pack on the bedside table. The ashtray was full of butts and ash. I hadn't noticed the stink of stale tobacco. I was used to it in places like this.

We lit up, except for Chen.

'So, in answer to your question, Mr. Chen, I make investments on behalf of my own Hong Kong company, investing its profits, which come to me via SLIC, into things like London property. Oh, I did a shopping mall too, and a golf course. There's another irony, if only my dad knew. Ha ha. It's one he always wanted to play in Berkshire. And it's in my name, sort of. The number four irony only get bigger. Geddit?' He did that with a silly accent: 'numba floor.'

I looked at the overflowing ashtray, the concrete floor, and flicked my ash onto it, under the table with the TV.

'And now that I've served my purpose, and big trouble is about to hit my company and my boss because of this power transfer up in Beijing, once they'd got me to do one last significant transfer, they tied me up with bells and bows on and are set to hand me over to whoever suits their plan to get themselves off the hook.'

I've said Felix was a quick learner. He'd nailed it. Of course, the question is that if he was a quick learner why hadn't he picked up on this. Oh. How could I forget? He'd been living in a large villa, had an open account at the best brothel in town, his face and story in countless magazines, flew round the region, and back and forth to London, in business class, and got to pose like he was a real somebody. That does blur the clear view he might have had of the one-way road to hell and damnation he was speeding along.

'You are not yet "tied up",' Chen said.

'How so?'

'You are only at risk of being held responsible so long as you are the legal representative of the company in Hong Kong.'

'I know that. And for me to cease being the rep I need the signature of the other directors and shareholders, who are Mr. Li, Mr. Zhou and another person called Wang, who could be a woman or a man, who I have never met.'

'There may be a way,' Chen said.

Felix's hand went up to his forehead and pushed his hair back. It was the first time in the hotel room he made the trademark gesture. He was interested.

'You mean you have a way out of this?' Felix waved his arm around the room. I took in the damp marks along the top of the walls, the brown air conditioning unit, the windows, which I noticed were pasted on the outside with a thin film to make the sky blue and the room darker. In the corners it had peeled off and the light outside, for all it being a grey day, was bright and cheerful.

Despite his perking up, there was a tinge of regret in Felix's voice. He would have to accept help from Charlie Thurrold. He stared at the back of Charlie's head. I watched him. His expression went from disgust to annoyed acceptance.

There was silence. Charlie must have guessed what was going through Felix's mind. He turned and opened his mouth to speak. I cringed. Whatever he said was going to sound like 'I told you so.'

# 19

## THE PLAN

CHARLIE Thurrold never got to say anything. The metal door at the foot of the stairs banged open like someone had driven a truck through it. Feet thundered up the stairs. It's a good thing the door to the room was ajar or they'd have kicked it in.

It was Zhang and a couple of heavies. He was how Felix described him: military haircut, baby face, stocky. They stopped in the doorway.

I glanced at Felix. He was smiling at Charlie. He was being rescued from being rescued. 'You see,' he was saying without speaking, 'nothing you can do, Uncle Charlie.' He fell backwards onto the bed. His shell suit trousers cracked with a sound like a flag snapping in the wind.

Zhang spoke to Chen. He ignored me and Charlie. He used Shanghai dialect. Very sharp. Very short.

Chen stood up. 'We must go,' he said. 'We'll see you later, Felix.'

Zhang barked one word in Shanghainese. I understood it. 'Out!'

Felix laughed.

Charlie heaved himself off the bed. He was exhausted by the effort of his self-control. He pulled up to his full height, stood in front of Zhang, and put a hand inside his jacket. Zhang flinched but caught himself. No fat old foreigner could carry a gun in China. Charlie pulled out a folded piece of paper, opened it and held it out. 'Please read this,' he said in Mandarin, and to Felix in English, 'You're coming too.' Felix watched Zhang, who didn't look at the document although he must have clocked the letterhead at the top and chop at the bottom.

'No use,' he said to Charlie. 'Nothing to do with us.' And he snapped off another round of Shanghainese at Chen.

'He says the police have no authority here, and even if they did that paper would be no use.'

'But no one other than the police has the authority to hold some-one,' Charlie said, his voice rising. Zhang pushed the paper back at him, in the chest. Charlie looked at it with surprise.

'But...'

'No buts with Mr. Zhang, Uncle Charlie. Take it from me. You run along. I'll be all right. I told you. Nice to meet you, Mr. Chen. Maybe you can tell me your cunning plan another time. Oh, and Johnny, be a good chap and get those cigarettes, would you? Drop them at the desk downstairs.' Felix stood up as if he was seeing us off from a tea party. He was showing a little paunch. 'Nice of you to come by.'

Chen led out past Zhang. I motioned for Charlie to go before me. I wasn't being polite. I was worried he'd linger with Zhang and argue.

'See you around, mate. I hope you know what you're doing,' I said to Felix. Zhang grinned at me like I was in on the joke. I saw the impish humour. Felix had been spot on about that too. I threw my half-finished pack of cigarettes onto the bed. 'I doubt we'll be allowed back in,' I said. One of Zhang's mates shut the door after us. The other shepherded us along the corridor, down the stairs, through the door, past the reception desk and out the front.

Our taxi had gone, scared off by Zhang and his mates getting out of the well-polished black Shanghai GM Buick with People's Armed Police plates in front of where we'd left it.

The Buick's driver was in the car, engine running, air con on and a crack in the window for his cigarette smoke. The windows were black and the windscreen was tinted. The driver was wearing sunglasses. I wondered if he could see a bloody thing.

We walked past the police station and up to the main road. It wasn't long before a local taxi came by. The driver, a woman, agreed to take us to the city limits of Shanghai proper but she'd have a friend take us into town from there. Her rural licence plate would get her a fine. Chen started to argue but Charlie and I didn't care. We agreed, even if it meant being ripped off.

Charlie got in the back with Chen. I listened to their conversation.

'You see what I mean when I told you how he was a difficult one?' Charlie said.

'He is young. He is stupid. You know what Confucius said.'

'Yes. A young man at twenty and so on. Shakespeare wrote a poem like it too.'

'I think I read it,' Chen said. 'They are similar.'

I was in my early twenties and I found the exchange offensive, even if they meant Felix, though I didn't know what Confucius or Shakespeare said about it.

'What next?' Charlie said.

Chen agreed Zhou was keeping Felix as a bargaining chip for his battles in Beijing. Even if Zhou didn't have a clear idea how he would use Felix, like when he employed him in the first place, he'd come up with one soon and it wouldn't be good for Felix.

Chen said he had a plan, but the details needed work. We had to bear in mind it was pointless getting Felix out if his name was listed as director and main shareholder of the Hong Kong money laundering company. Escaping from a black jail is one thing. Absconding from a Hong Kong company with serious amounts of dirty money on its books is another. Hong Kong has extradition treaties, a financial crime unit, and well-kept records. At the very least Felix would never be able to visit the place. At worst they might come after him, and if he was in the UK, they'd get him.

We faced a simple dilemma. Spring him too soon and Zhou and Li would get him back for the Hong Kong company. Get him off the books of the company – we hadn't got there yet – and they'd lock him up tighter than the Bank of England to be sure he couldn't do a runner.

We had to do both at the same time. Get him out and get him off the books.

Chen said we'd need help. The three of us weren't enough. Ideally, he said, looking embarrassed but trying to make what he said sound like professional legal advice, 'We need pretty women.'

It was going to be a sting.

Chen laid out the basics.

We had to get authority, most likely from Zhang, to let us see Felix. Then we had to persuade Felix to do a runner with us.

I asked if that was where the pretty girl came in. To entice Felix out of his hotel room, like a honey trap in reverse.

No, Chen said. He didn't need girls for that. He didn't think they'd work. Charlie, or a friend of Felix – he looked at me – had to come up with the enticement. I said, 'Let's call it motivation.'

While Felix was being 'extracted' – that's the word he used – someone, he looked at me and I wished he'd stop it, had at the same time or near as damn it, to get the signature of the other three directors of the Hong Kong company to release Felix from his responsibility.

'All three of them?' At once? For fuck's sake. I didn't swear. 'We don't know where one of them is, let alone *who* he or she is, except the name is Wang, the most common in China, and the other two are in Beijing, or were.' Li might have stayed in Shanghai for the moment but it was safe to assume Zhou was still holed up with the Politburo, horse-trading his future.

'You forget,' Chen said, 'the company is registered in Hong Kong. Thanks to you British, there is transparency and a rule of law. Company law too. We can find out who the directors are and trust me, I think we will find that all of them, apart from Felix, will have entrusted their power of attorney to one man, Zhou Jianguo.'

'You sure?'

A glint appeared in Chen's eye. 'As you English say: you wanna bet?'

I humoured him. 'OK. You're on. How much?' I expected him to name a small sum, which to a Chinese gambler would start at around a thousand pounds.

'Five bucks,' Chen said. That's fifty pence.

'Done.' We shook.

'Once we, or I, have established who holds the power of attorney, and it will be Zhou,' he smiled at me, 'we need to present him with the documents at the same time we get Felix.' Again he looked at me.

This time I said it. 'Stop looking at me, please.' I turned back to the windscreen.

A hand touched my shoulder. It was Charlie. 'What's the name of that girl?' he said.

I'd guessed what Chen had in mind for the pretty girls. I wasn't sure I wanted Anita involved, even as a fixer.

'Anita,' I said.

'That's it. Do you think she'd help?'

'Why her? Why can't we hire girls from a brothel or a KTV place?'

'It will be good if we know the person, and better if they are familiar with Felix,' Chen said. 'And we need brains as well as a pretty face. Besides of which, if we pay them, I am afraid they will take the money and run.'

'OK,' I said. 'I'll ask.'

I should have also asked Chen what Anita would have to do. But I didn't. I didn't want to know because it might put me off calling her. I was still confused by the attitude she'd been giving me since that flight back from the UK. Apart from the calls about Felix and our meeting with Amy, I hadn't seen her or been in touch. We'd been cooling off. I don't know from what.

Chen asked me and Charlie to come and see him later, and me to bring Anita. He said he had to make some calls from his office, presumably to Hong Kong, and he couldn't finalise his plan until he'd done that. So no point talking about it.

We got stuck in traffic on a city overpass. It took us an hour and a half to get through. There'd been a minor accident. As we passed the two cars involved, the drivers, both men, were standing under umbrellas, ignoring each other, talking into their phones. I studied the vehicles and couldn't see a scratch.

We dropped off Chen at one of the new metro stations. As he was getting out, I remembered a question I'd been meaning to ask.

'Mr. Chen, what was in those black bags today?'

He laughed. 'Nothing. Just the old fashioned way of getting past security men.'

'Which is?'

'Cartons of cigarettes. They prefer Zhonghua brand. They're expensive.'

'Thanks. I'll remember.'

I got out soon afterwards, close to my office, and walked. I had a couple of things to deal with. It wouldn't take long. Charlie was going to call his contact at the Public Security Bureau and have a go at him about Felix being in what was apparently police-sponsored detention. 'Have fun with that,' I said.

While I was on the street, my mobile rang. I picked up.

'Johnny, that you? Can you hear me?'

It was early evening, the time of day for UK calls.

'Hi Mum, nice to hear you. What's up?'

I'd not thought about what would be going on at home, how mum was adjusting. Her life must have become emptier without Gran around to look after, and fight with.

'I've got news for you. Are you in a place where you can talk? Somewhere to sit down?'

'No, but that's all right, I've got a good signal. What is it?' A couple of cars and a bus had an air horn duel on the road beside me. The noise was deafening. Mum said something about Gran and money, that's all I heard. I had a horrid, guilty feeling they'd found a note in her flat describing how much I'd pinched from her. Maybe she kept a record.

'Sorry,' I shouted, 'I didn't get that. Can you repeat it?' I was nervous. I didn't want this conversation. Not now.

She spaced the words out, 'Gran... has... left... you... some... money,' she said.

'Oh, that's nice.' I was more relieved that I hadn't been rumbled than excited at the prospect of a few quid in the bank.

'It's a lot.'

'That's kind of her,' I said. 'How much?'

'Forty thousand.'

'Jesus Christ! How the heck? I mean, why? Where does it come from? How the hell did Gran save that? Shit, that's amazing.'

'Do you want to sit down now?'

'No. I can't. I'm outside, on the street.'

'There's one more thing.'

'What?'

'It's a condition. You're only allowed to spend it in England. I think she wanted you to buy a house when you come back or something.'

'What else was in her will?'

'Not much. But we didn't expect anything. It's for the best. We know how she loved you. You keep it for a rainy day, or the monsoon, or whatever it is out there. Now you can come home without too much pressure, if you want to, one day.' Another car hooted and I missed a bit, 'because it'd be good to have you around. We do miss you.'

'Thanks Mum, and thanks for the news. I better have a think.'

'You do that. If you want to chat, call me.'

We said goodbye and I hung up. I was gobsmacked, amazed. I had no idea Gran had that much cash. And typical of her to attach the condition. She knew all along, despite her encouraging me to go, that I'd have to come back and it would be hard. I'd been thinking, on the plane, and when I'd been knocking about in London, that the way things stood it was impossible to imagine going home at the moment, just when I was beginning to think I should.

Before I walked into the lift lobby I raised my eyes to the grey sky. The drizzle kissed my face. I couldn't see the top of the building. It was lost in the cloud. I'm not religious and I don't believe in Heaven either. But where else can you look?

'Thanks, Gran.'

I let myself into the office. It was close to knocking off time, about half an hour left, but my two staff had already gone. I sat at my desk and started my computer, logged in, and opened the files I needed to work on for the clients I'd just taken a commission off. Commission as in job, not payment. That always came months later. I was in a position to ask myself if I wanted the work.

I sat back. Put my feet up, hands behind my head.

Forty thousand quid. Jesus effing Christ on a bike. What would I do with it? Put down a deposit on a house, like Mum said? Punt it on the stock market? Give it to Tricky Dicky and let him work his magic? I went through few more ideas and hit on one so hard it made me shout 'Yes!'

I could start a business in England.

I looked around my office. What was there to lose, to miss? What did I have? What had I built?

I had clients. I had two staff. I had an office on a lease and the furniture and computers. I had a fax machine I never used. I glanced across the top of my desk. There was an open box of name cards on it, beside the phone. I took one off the top. 'John Trent, Managing Director, East Wind Human Resources.'

I had a name and a half decent reputation.

I had no creditors, though the office rent was due in a few days, but I had a long list of debtors. I reckoned I was owed at least five thousand pounds in yuan. I had enough in the bank to pay the rent and salaries.

I'd built a business. It wasn't big, but it had lasted almost two years, and it was still going.

Three years before I'd floated into Hong Kong Harbour like a proverbial turd off a passing tanker. I'd done bar work, gone up to Guangzhou for the teaching job, and here I was in Shanghai, twenty-four years old and running my own business. I hadn't mucked it up. Why couldn't I do it back in England?

It was common practice that no foreigner ever bothered to shut down a business in China. You walked away. None of the formality and hassle like Felix had to go through in Hong Kong, or we were about to for him. I'd pay my staff, cancel my lease, give my assistant a little something to thank her for letting me use her name, collect as much as I could from the clients who owed me, and I'd be off home to Blighty and Basildon. Thanks Gran.

Wait: wasn't I forgetting something? Hadn't I left for a reason, like I told Felix? What about the pettiness, the losers in that queue beside the kebab van and – now it's in the open – Steve Turner's family and the stigma?

I turned it on its head: the biggest loser in the kebab queue had been me, the previous me, the idiot teenager who thought he'd give himself a leg-up into the cool world of the big boys and girls by selling pills. The pettiness and the smallness had been me too. I was a nobody. And when I'd come home from Young Offenders I was worse than a nobody.

Now I was a businessman. I'd proved myself. I'd proved it to my family too. Even Tricky Dicky had given me respect.

But Turner's family. How did I face them?

I'd face them. Simple as that. Just do it. That's another thing Shanghai taught me. Stop worrying about what people think and say about you.

What was there to miss about Shanghai? Car horns, construction noise, adults spitting at your feet while their toddlers took a shit in the gutter or the corner of the restaurant, neighbours playing majhong all night, the shouting, smog, heat, damp. Let's not pretend living in Shanghai had been an urban idyll, despite what the *Shanghai Weekly* said. Good things? Cheap food, cheap booze and easy sex. That's about it. I'd refrained from the latter ever since Felix's model shoot, the night Gran died, the night I realized I cared about Anita.

Anita. She was all I could think of.

Right, before I left China I had to put my cards on the table, the ones I'd held to my chest way too long. I'd ask her straight up: do you fancy me, had you ever... might you... for God's sake, can we get over this 'best friends' business?

Other 'best friends', genuine ones, mates, like Joe. What about them? We'd stay in touch. I'm sure of that. Felix?

Shit. Felix. I'd lost track of the time. I took my feet off the desk and looked at my watch. And I had to call Anita.

Chen had said to meet at seven. It was six.

Here you go I said to myself: your last blast can be helping Thurrold and Chen sort out Felix. It doesn't matter how much trouble I get into if I'm leaving straight after. I don't see how I could get into trouble anyway. I hadn't heard Chen's plan yet, mind you.

And I won't see Felix again. He'll go back to the UK where our paths will never cross.

One good deed, one final act in the drama of Felix Fawcett-Smith, the story of how I met him and moved on.

Then move on.

I turned the lights off, locked up and went to meet Chen and Charlie in Charlie's office. In the taxi I called Anita.

'Can you do something for me?'

'For you or Felix?'

'Good question. It's for Felix but I'm the one who's asking, if you know what I mean.'

'What is it this time?'

'I don't know. A nice lawyer said he could use a bright young woman. I guess you need to charm someone.'

'So you found him all right? Was he in detention?'

'Sort of.' I gave her a quick rundown.

'And if I do what you want, he'll get out? What next? Is he going to leave China?'

'I think he'll have to.'

'Never come back?'

'Can't say for sure, but I expect so.'

'I'll help.'

'Thanks. I owe you. We all owe you Anita.'

# 20

## THE BREAK

THREE days after finding Felix, on the fourth of June 2001, I had a new name card. 'Mr. John Trent, British Education Agency (BEA), China Office, Chief Representative'. Chen Daming had them printed and sent over. He'd taken the trouble to put it in Chinese on the reverse. He gave me a new Chinese name because he didn't know my usual one.

I was wearing the gulag jacket and a tie I'd nicked from Felix's bedroom when Charlie and I went to get his stuff.

It was late afternoon and the rain was sheeting it down, hammering the roofs and the tin shacks in the alleyways, drumming on the shop awnings. Long stretches of the streets were flooded. The water was a sinister black mantrap. Under its surface were potholes and open drains and, if you were unlucky, manholes whose covers had popped off. Pedestrians and cyclists in red, yellow and blue ponchos crawled along the streets like beetles with fancy coloured shells. They kept their heads down so the rain ran off their hood brims, stepped with care through the deep bits, or hop-scotched on the bricks shopkeepers had put out for their customers. They pedalled in slow motion to stop the water spinning up their back-sides. Shanghai was sinking.

The road outside my flat was knee-deep. I rolled up my trousers, took off my shoes and socks and held them in one hand. In my other I had one of Joe's golf umbrellas. Finding a taxi was a nightmare. Once I got one, I sank into the soggy back seat, struggled to put my shoes and socks back on and thought to myself: how appropriate. It was like the climactic scene in an old movie. This was how they ended, the wind and rain lashing the boat or the moorland.

I was on my way to the Shanghai district where top leaders lived down dead-end lanes, and in among them their chosen 'few', like Zhou Jianguo.

He wasn't in Beijing. He'd been sent home but was under house arrest, the two-way version. That saved us a lot of hassle. Imagine if I'd had to fly to Beijing. Who'd have paid for the ticket?

And Chen won his five bucks, which I sent back with the courier who delivered the name cards. Zhou had been granted power of attorney by the other directors of the Hong Kong company.

Chen told me on the phone that Zhou was being treated leniently. He had powerful friends and the implementation of the law was as flexible as an Olympic gymnast. Zhou was under *shuang gui* but he got a special one-way version. He wasn't let out, but people could go see him, by prior arrangement.

Thanks to Chen, I was one of them.

I was nervous, of course I was. I was about to meet a powerful, well-connected businessman who while in favour could do what he wanted including get away with murder, and when out of it, favour that is, and under house arrest, carry on almost as normal. He was like a kingpin in Wormwood Scrubs, Mr. Bridger in *The Italian Job*. There'd been a kid like that in Young Offenders. None of the luxury cell, mind you, but you gave him respect, and if you crossed him you suffered.

I had to chat Zhou up and – I didn't think it would work – get him to sign a piece of paper so his pet foreigner could be released from bonded service. They do say that once you've sold your soul like that, like Felix had, you can never leave. How the hell was I going to do it for him?

Chen said I was the best person for the job, and he'd come up with an incentive for Zhou. When he explained it to me I was sceptical to the point of disagreeing with him, but I kept my mouth shut. In the end I didn't use it, so I won't repeat it.

Getting Zhou to agree to meet and his guardians to let me in was the hard part, hence the name card. It was the British Education Agency, which did exist, not Felix, who'd got Zhou's son Tony his place at Eton. Chen Daming had come up with a story that the application lacked one important document with a signature, or 'chop', from his dad. The people guarding Zhou 'understood' and Zhou himself agreed to see me as soon as possible. There was also an understanding that since my visit was on a personal, family matter, we'd be left alone, unsupervised. I found that a comfort. I was nervous enough. I didn't want an audience.

Chen had supplied a fake document from Eton (that tickled my funny bone, me pretending to be a bloke who could get a kid into Eton) and with it a set of real docs from Hong Kong, the ones we needed to release Felix from his responsibility for the company down there. I'd witness Zhou's signature with my real name. No need for an alias. That was a nice touch too.

While I was in with Zhou, Chen and Charlie were to go back to Wankou and spring Felix, which depended on Anita playing her part in downtown Shanghai at about the same time. We each had to do our thing pretty much simultaneously. This was a co-ordinated operation, like a heist in a movie or a sneaky military operation.

I'm going to switch to Charlie and Chen and come back to me later. Their evening was way more dramatic than my walking through the back door of a downtown villa for a chat and cup of tea.

Chen told me how it went when we met up. They succeeded. But it came at a high price.

It wasn't worth it.

Felix wasn't worth it.

Chen and Charlie borrowed a car, did the two-hour drive out to Wankou and got there at about six-thirty. It was already dark thanks to the heavy rain clouds. They parked a hundred metres along the road from the guesthouse, beyond the noodle shop and on the far side from the police station so they wouldn't be noticed. There were no streetlights, which sort of helped although the guesthouse was lit and the entrance to the police station was floodlit by a couple of spotlights on the wall. The noodle restaurant was shut.

Chen had the bright idea to turn the car so it was facing the right way, back up the road past the hotel and the police station. With hindsight it was a mistake, but if they'd parked nearer the main road, they'd have had to walk past the police station to get to the hotel, and that might have attracted attention.

They had to wait for a signal, which was Anita's job. I'll cover that next. She was in Shanghai with a key player in this sordid drama, persuading him to make a call to the Wuzhou Guesthouse.

So Chen and Charlie had time for chitchat. I asked him what they talked about.

He said they did the usual China topics: pollution, food safety, the environment, and Chen told Charlie at length about his daughter's school, and that got them onto the education system in China, which everyone knows is crap. Charlie had a theory that the reason for it being so tough and the kids doing extra lessons and working so hard for tests was so they didn't get a chance to run amok on the streets and upset the Party's precious social stability. Chen said he had a point, but was that a problem back in the UK, children out on the streets, making trouble?

And that got Charlie thinking about Felix and he told Chen: 'Yes, kids can be a problem. Like the one we've got here. But we do all we can. Drop everything, put ourselves out, go way beyond what we should do or they deserve, because we love them.'

That surprised Chen, but not me.

When he realized Charlie was talking about Felix, he asked, 'What if he refuses to come out?'

'I'll make him this time,' Charlie said.

I thought I was going to get the Oxford story but that's when Charlie got the text message and said: 'That's it. The girl says we can go.'

They got out of the car and walked towards the guesthouse, keeping in the road to avoid the obstacle course along the pavement.

Chen was relieved to see the same man as before on the reception desk. He had a carton of cigarettes ready.

The man frowned. 'You've come,' he stated. 'Half an hour.' He came round and unlocked the heavy metal door. 'You know the way.'

He took the cigarettes without a word and stashed them.

Chen hoped they wouldn't need half an hour. He didn't want to hang around and tempt fate.

The security guard in the cubbyhole at the top of the stairs recognised them too. He waved them down the corridor. From a couple of rooms came the sound of television, high volume. They heard the smash, clap and shriek of sword and sorcery soap operas.

Felix's door was unlocked. They knocked and went in. Felix was dressed in jeans and a shirt with a collar, lying on the bed, smoking. He was watching the same programme as the others must have been, because if he watched anything else he'd still hear it. He looked up.

'My knights in shining armour,' he said grinning. 'What? Bored of saving virgins are we? I didn't think there were any in Shanghai.'

'Let's keep it civil, shall we?' Charlie said.

'Hello, Mr. Chen,' Felix looked past Charlie.

'Good evening,' Chen said.

'Felix.' Charlie's voice was firm.

'Yes.' Felix sat up. He was clearheaded. 'What is it this time, Uncle Charlie?'

'There's something I'd like to tell you. It's the reason we've come to see you.'

Felix sighed. He muted the TV but left the picture. He motioned to Charlie to sit on the foot of the bed, as he had before. Charlie walked round and sat in a chair. He leaned back.

'First thing to get straight: Felix, I am not your father. Could you please look at me?' Felix turned. 'There's no question. I want you to forget that idea once and for all. There was no need for a paternity test because I never slept with your mother.' He waited for the information to sink in.

'Carry on,' Felix said, politely, but he turned away.

'On the other hand, yes, I do feel a responsibility, and affection, for you that I agree might imply a connection. Your mother did want me to be your godfather, and although I never was, officially, because she asked me, I've tried to behave like one over the years. I'm sorry that you've taken against it, and me. Fact is your father vetoed me. He and I never got on.' Felix should have liked that. He made no sign of it.

Chen hadn't expected Charlie to make a speech. He looked at his watch. They'd used up five minutes.

'And I'd like to apologize,' Charlie said, 'for the way I've interfered with your life here in Shanghai. It was not my intention, to interfere or upset you. I only, well... I only wanted to help, to look out for you. I was clumsy the way I went about it, Perhaps it's a good thing that I'm not your actual godfather. I'd have been a pretty useless one.'

Charlie didn't stray near the territory of 'but events have proved me right,' 'told you so,' and so on. That's what I'd have done in his place and rounded up with a 'so here we are back in Cobley Road, now get your shit together and let's go and this is the last time I get you out of a mess.'

Respect to Charlie.

'Mr. Chen and I are here not to criticise or blame you. Are we straight on that?'

Felix gave nothing away except for a determination not to react. His face was blank, his eyes fixed but unseeing on the TV screen. Mr. Chen, despairing of a quick exit, picked up the thermos of hot water and made tea.

Charlie waited and Felix spoke. 'So what are you here for?'

Charlie smiled. 'We'll come to that. But first you should know that Mr. Zhou has been sent back from Beijing and is under house arrest in Shanghai.' Felix's eyes flicked from the screen to Charlie's face and back. 'The incident out at Dongchang is not being used against him. It's a side issue. They're going after him for tax evasion and corruption, standard stuff. So that leaves you and that fellow Zhang in the truck with the two deaths in Dongchang to deal with.'

Charlie paused.

'Mr. Chen here,' Felix turned and gave him a cold smile, 'has got the family of the woman who died to agree to a certain, large of course, sum of compensation from the construction company. It'll be paid by SLIC. You won't read about it in the papers, or about yourself for that matter. Their silence has been bought, the family's and the papers. Your charming friend Zhang is off the hook as well. He's a serving member of the People's Armed Police. That's the good news.'

Charlie paused. Felix pursed his lips and nodded but left his gaze on the TV.

Charlie tried again. 'There is bad news, however, I'm afraid. The Buckingham Park project has been cancelled. I'm sorry about that. I know you put your heart and soul into it.' Charlie was being nice to Felix. 'The reason they're giving at the moment – and it may well change to suit their purpose – is "proper procedures" weren't followed in the land transfer process. A few provincial officials will get into trouble but they're not the people they're after. Beijing wants Zhou and his political backers out, and Buckingham Park has given them the entry point to investigate Zhou, Li and SLIC's finances.' He paused and added, superfluous, 'It's because of the leadership change of course.'

Charlie took a sip of tea.

'So, Felix, I honestly, with genuine impartiality, not as a family friend, but as a China acquaintance who happens to have the inside track, and the help of people like Mr. Chen here,' Charlie pointed, as if he was trying to spread the responsibility for what he was about to say, 'and, I might add, the agreement of your friends [he meant me] but I think your employment at SLIC is over. You said so yourself when we last met. And they're only keeping you as a potential trading chip, as you also said, so my point is: why don't you come with Mr. Chen and me?'

Talk about the 'softly softly' approach. Charlie could be a real diplomat. He must have driven Chen mad with impatience. Felix had sat through the whole thing with the same expressionless face.

When Charlie finished Felix stayed like that, silent, staring at the TV screen, for a good while. Chen, who was by now physically agitated – twenty minutes had gone by – was about to intervene when Felix burst into life. He spoke up, loud and clear.

'You mean to tell me you want to get me out of here?'

'Yes,' Charlie said.

'Why the hell didn't you say so sooner, Charlie? What was the point of that? Let's go. For God's sake. You got a piece of paper that will work this time?

'No.'

'What?'

'We got in to see you on the pretence of it being a visit. We told them it was your birthday. Your friend Anita helped set it up.'

'Anita? That's a surprise.' He swung his feet onto the floor. 'So how do we get out? Walk out the front door.'

'In a word, yes. We're going to bluff it. Like the good old days.'

'You have a car outside?' Felix said.

'Down the street.'

'Then what?'

'We go to my place for the night and put you on a plane tomorrow, or soon as we can. It's best that you disappear for a while. I've had a temporary passport issued. I assume you don't have it. Johnny and I packed a bag with some clothes from your villa. They're mostly summer ones. And I remembered your swimming trunks.' Charlie gave Felix a warm grin at that. Felix looked at the ceiling. 'I suggest Thailand or Malaysia and take it easy for a while. It'll be the monsoon of course, but it doesn't rain all the time. And easy to find a cheap place to stay. That's a point, have you got money? I guess you have. I hope you can access it; we can talk details in the car.'

Mr. Chen was on his feet and moving towards the door. He stood in front of the TV as if to stop Felix watching it. But Felix was busy grabbing things off the bedside table and stuffing them in his pockets.

'I must say I have been getting bored,' he said to his knees. 'There's only so many flying immortals you can take,' he nodded at Chen's crotch, which was in front of the TV, 'before you start climbing the walls yourself.'

He walked past Charlie into the bathroom, came out with his wash bag and put it into a Hong Kong airport duty free carrier bag, along with a dog-eared paperback.

'No more luggage?' Charlie asked.

'They gave me the tracksuit. I'd rather not keep it.' Felix nodded at a pile of clothes in the corner, 'and I don't suppose I'll have time for laundry.' He paused. 'Shall we?'

'Wait here first,' Chen said, smiling with relief that they were about to get moving. 'I will go down and get the door open. I'll pretend I've left you both to have a word in private. You leave this door open,' he indicated the door onto the corridor, 'and soon as you hear the one at the bottom of the stairs open – I'll make it bang – you walk out.'

'Just like that?'

'Yes,' Charlie said. 'And let me do the talking, if there is any.'

'You say so, Uncle Charlie. Lead on.'

'When you hear the door,' Chen repeated, and let himself out.

Charlie and Felix stayed inside, close up against each other in the mini-vestibule. They heard Chen's voice echo up the staircase and the metal door bang open.

'Right, let's go,' Charlie said. 'Stay right behind me and don't look at the two security people. Try to make it appear like I am in complete charge.'

He lumbered down the corridor. The guard in the maid's cubby-hole nodded at Charlie, saw Felix, and got to his feet, 'Hey...'

'We're going,' Charlie said.

'But...'

'I said we're going.'

The man stuck his head out of his den. He was short, puny and old, more a night watchman than a prison warder. He wouldn't put up a physical fight. 'You can't go. My boss hasn't said he can go.' It was a plea more than a statement. Charlie pulled Felix past him and sent him down the stairs. The man made as if to step out and confront him. 'Step back,' Charlie said, loud but not a shout. He wanted to obscure the guard's call for help, without raising an alarm. 'Keep going, Felix.'

Charlie blocked the guard but kept his eye on Felix. When Felix was about to exit through the metal door, which was wide open, he said one last time to the old man: 'Stay inside.' He turned and thumped with his heavy steps down the stairs.

Chen had been waiting in the lobby, under the 'watchful gaze' of the man behind the desk. After Chen had given his excuse for coming down first, they hadn't exchanged a word.

Chen said the man must have been a Red Guard back in the day. His age was right, and he had that look of lifelong resentment at being wound up to fever pitch in the Cultural Revolution, let loose but reined back in before he had the chance to satisfy his appetite for destruction, then 'returned' to a society where he'd missed his chance for a decent life. There was a lot of it about in that generation, the resentment. Chen was familiar with it. He knew this guy would be a problem.

Hence he'd positioned himself near the metal door in case he had to stop the man shutting it. There was no need. The man, while watchful, was casual about security, arrogant too.

That changed when Felix appeared. He didn't hesitate like the feeble guard at the top of the stairs. He leapt out from behind the counter and grabbed at Felix's arm.

Felix winced as the sharp fingers sunk into his fleshy arm. He was barely in the lobby. The man held him tight and looked at Chen, furious. 'You stay here,' he shouted.

Thanks to his anger at Chen the man didn't see, though he must have heard, Charlie thundering down the staircase. Using his weight and momentum, Charlie smashed into the man's bony wrist, pushing him and Felix apart. The guard bounced off Charlie into his counter. He yelped as it dug into his ribs. Felix went the other way against the wall. The man recovered himself enough to shout, 'You have no right!' and stepped forwards.

Charlie bellowed and pushed him away. 'Go on Felix, go Chen.'

Felix moved towards the door onto the street. The guard was shouting. He was coming forwards, fury across his face. Foreigners like this had bullied, humiliated and raped his country. They were lower than dogs. The propaganda flooded back and fired him up. This was his chance for revenge. He was going to hurt the old one and grab the young one and hold him and never let go until help came. He shouted for his colleague. He raised his fists at Charlie then changed his mind. He dove back behind his counter, grabbed the phone and dialled.

Charlie also prevaricated. He didn't know whether to stay and block the two guards, stop the man making his call, or up and run like Chen and Felix. His hesitation was fatal.

Chen and Felix were away, running down the street. They were almost at the car when they heard the shouts behind them. Half a dozen, maybe eight, policemen were rushing out of the station and sprinting towards the guesthouse. Some were dressed in trousers and vests, one was in shorts that might have been underwear. They were shrieking like madmen escaping an asylum. They clocked Chen and Felix up ahead and were running after them when Charlie lumbered out of the guesthouse door much nearer to them. He was speed walking, a stumbling trot. He'd run out of puff.

It was Chen's turn to be indecisive. He was a lawyer, a brainy fighter not a physical one. He stopped, turned and stared.

If only Felix had stepped up, shown his mettle, his coolness under fire like his brother's, demonstrated the pluck he'd picked up on those playing fields, the instinctive leadership public schoolboys are supposed to have.

Not a hope. All he cared about was himself and his physical safety. He shouted at Chen to get a move on. Chen stood stock still for a second longer and pulled the car keys out of his pocket.

The police were about to catch the easy prey, Charlie, who'd made a second mistake. He'd dodged off the main roadway and onto the pavement. Perhaps he thought the police would trip up on the obstacles. They kept hurtling down the centre of the tarmac. Charlie was at a disadvantage.

He wasn't going fast enough to have his head ripped off by those nasty cables I mentioned, if he'd hit one, but what he did hit was the patch of oil-covered pavement outside the hole-in-the-wall noodle shop. Chen was at the car, facing back up the street. He saw Charlie go down. He fell hard. Chen said he was sure Charlie wasn't pushed by the police, but soon as they caught up they laid into him. They kicked him, punched him back down as he tried to get up, once. Chen didn't see any batons. A few of the police were running, slower it seemed, towards the car.

Felix got in the passenger seat and shut the door. Chen started the engine and drove at moderate speed and with care. He didn't want to hit the policemen. He swung out onto the far side of the road. He was lucky none of them had the presence of mind, or the courage, to stand in front of the car. They did go for the doors, however, pulling hard on the handles. Chen picked up speed. Two policemen ran alongside, smacking the windows with their hands and screaming at Chen to stop.

He knew he couldn't, and that he couldn't stop for Charlie either. He was confident, in those fleeting, chaotic moments, that Charlie wouldn't come to harm or be threatened with serious charges if he left him. He was a diplomat. He was capable of taking care of himself.

The car drew abreast of the gaggle of cops round Charlie's body. Chen took a quick glance past the hand flailing his window. Charlie wasn't putting up resistance. He wasn't moving at all. A policeman had a knee on his chest. Another one glanced up at Chen as he passed. Their eyes met. Chen said he saw concern. They'd overdone it. But that reassured Chen. They'd look after him. If Charlie had been fighting like a madman, he'd have been more worried. That's how he put it, and it does make sense.

Chen put his foot down and the last policeman took his hand off the door handle and did a tumbling, arm-flailing run like sprinters do when they cross the finish line.

All this short time, Felix sat in the passenger seat staring straight ahead through the windscreen, ignoring the drama. Chen said it was like sitting next to a terracotta warrior. Nice metaphor.

They got him though. Got him out. Charlie would be let go as well. For the moment I'll leave him, like Chen and Felix did.

While that little drama was playing out in Wankou, my taxi was winding its way to the back door of Zhou's villa. It was dark down there too. I think that's deliberate, to make the houses less inviting or interesting to passers-by. But if you look closely you'll see searchlights on the street corners and the tops of the high walls, along with security cameras. If anybody did create a disturbance or seem like a threat he'd be lit up like a Christmas tree with the flick of a couple of switches and recorded from every angle. There were police in sentry boxes at the junctions.

The taxi driver had given me an odd look when I told him the address. I'd considered walking from a block away, but Chen said I was to get out right beside the back entrance of Zhou's place. He gave me a number to call. I was to let it ring twice and hang up, get out and push open a door in the wall. It had a number that I was told not to tell anyone.

The taxi arrived at the crossroads and turned down Zhou's street. I saw the number.

'Stop,' I said. I had my phone prepared. I pressed a button, put it to my ear and let it ring twice. I picked up my laptop case with the papers in it, no laptop, and got out the car. The door opened like magic as I put my hand on it. A tall young man in a white shirt and dark trousers was waiting behind it. He looked like a soldier. We were in a broad car port, open on one side. The lights were on, very bright, and there were a couple of black cars. An old man was polishing one. He stared at me. My escort ignored him. He waved me straight ahead to a door into the house. I tried to walk like a young executive who worked for an upper-crust British education agency, someone used to visiting posh Shanghai villas, usually through the front door. I held myself up straight, swung my arm like the young man did and put a stiff grin on my face. I probably looked like Mr. Bean.

Inside the back door I was hit by a fug of cigarette smoke. They were local cigarettes but quality, sweet yet not too sickly. I guessed they were Chen's 'Zhonghua' brand.

A man sitting at a kitchen table asked me to open my case. He peered into the main compartment, not the side pockets. He didn't pull the papers out. I guess he was checking for a gun. He nodded and handed it back.

We went out into a wood-floored corridor, panelled up to chest height. There was heavy wood furniture along the sides – narrow benches and solid art deco side tables. Above our heads on one side were windows set in stone, small ones with leaded diamond shapes like you get in posh mock Tudor. Our footfalls were cushioned by a soft red carpet that ran down the middle.

I made an effort to keep calm.

My phone beeped in my pocket. I pulled it out. There was a text from Chen.

'We have Felix.'

He didn't mention them not having Charlie Thurrold. He would have thought that superfluous information. The news came at precisely the right time.

My escort knocked on a door and I was shown into a large study. We entered right behind the desk, like from a secret door. Two men were standing on the far side of it. One was another tall young soldier in plain clothes, the other was Mr. Zhou. He seemed happy for a man under house arrest

'You've arrived,' Zhou said in Chinese.

'I've arrived,' I repeated, following the formula.

Zhou told me to sit in a large leather armchair beside a coffee table.

'Xiao Zhang, Xiao Liu,' he said to the two guards, mine and his. 'This is a family matter. I have nothing to hide. All I'm going to do is sign papers and ask about my son. We won't be long. Why not go outside for a cigarette?'

'Thanks boss,' my one said. 'But he is a foreigner. You don't want us to stay, just in case?'

Zhou smiled. 'No,' he said. 'And you'd be bored.'

The two men walked out another door, the main one. Zhou turned and looked down at me in the chair with my case on my lap.

'This whole conversation will be recorded,' Zhou said. 'And since we're going to speak in English... you do want to speak English?... those two wouldn't understand a word. It'll take their colleagues a day or two to translate, and your task will be done.'

Zhou Jianguo's eyes were laughing themselves out of their sockets while he said this. He was having restrained hysterics, like Tommy Cooper fluffing his lines. I was struck dumb. The canny bugger was speaking word-perfect BBC English. No accent or pretension. Straightforward plain English, like a train station announcer.

'Let's get started,' he said, and threw himself down into an armchair across from me. He gave it the feet up in the air move Felix told me about.

# 21

## INSIDE

Mr. Zhou sat up and fired his beady eyes at me. This was the time I mentioned earlier, about me getting up close and personal with him. I said how his eyes had a mischievous glint. It's hard to explain but the way he looked at me made me want to laugh, like I was being tickled, that kind of helpless, guilty laughter, like you've been caught out.

Or maybe what made me giggly was the relief. Here I was in the dragon's lair and I wasn't going to be eaten alive. Zhou was a nice bloke, nothing like I expected.

I got to my feet to hand over my card, Chinese side up, with two hands. Mr. Zhou read it, flipped to the English one and said, 'Nice to meet you, James.'

'Er, actually it's...'

'James.' He said it loud. 'I like the name James. That's how I shall address you.' He handed back my card. 'Keep it.'

The room was more personal than I'd expected, compared to Felix's description of the other parts of the villa. One wall had a big TV screen and shelves full of VCDs and music CDs. A glass cabinet held a collection of bottles – whisky, brandy, Baileys and the like

– and crystal glasses. A computer monitor and an over-sized glass ashtray were on the desk. There was another massive ashtray on the coffee table, and a red packet of Zhonghua.

Mr. Zhou watched me closely while I got organized. I took out the papers and shuffled them so the fake Eton ones were on top, the Hong Kong company underneath, sticking out a bit. My hands were trembling. I moved the ashtray out of the way and laid the papers on the table. I was desperate for a smoke. I sat back, tried to look him in the face, couldn't, looked down, coughed, and was about to start off with a 'Well...'

'It is a shame about Felix,' Zhou said, in English. The way he spoke was precise. It struck me how he didn't compress pronouns and verbs. 'I am sorry that he has been caught up in this,' he waved his arm around at his comfortable confinement, in his own home, and pulled a sad face as if it was a prison cell, or a shitty room in a shitty hotel. 'It is unlucky for him that he is held against his will. That is unnecessary. I do not approve, but...' he sighed as if he had no choice in the matter, which I thought hypocritical, so I interrupted.

'He isn't anymore.'

That wasn't in Chen Daming's script.

Zhou's reaction was the opposite to what I expected. Come to think of it, I should have expected him to know, but he didn't, which made sense in a minute.

'Oh, that is good.' He seemed pleased. 'I hope he will be okay.'

'I am sorry, Mr. Zhou,' I was talking like him already. 'But why do you think it is good that Felix is no longer under your control?'

'My control? That is not the case. He was in my employment, but his recent situation was not under my instruction, nor was Felix under my control when he was in that place.'

'Who, may I ask, gave the instruction? The police? Is it true he was arrested?' I might have to call Chen and tell him to put Felix back, sharpish.

'No, not the police. Li Zhenbing.'

'Li Zhenbing?'

'Perhaps you know him by his English name James, James Li.'

'Oh, of course,' I couldn't help sounding happy at the recognition, though I didn't feel it. It's a habit I'd picked up from Felix.

'You know him?'

'Yes, we have met,' I toned it down. 'At your party for Royal Buckingham Park, and when I was trying to find Felix. He came back from Beijing.'

Zhou was one of those people who made you say more than you meant to. It was those eyes. If they were bullets, when they hit you your secrets came out with the blood.

'Li wants to use Felix,' Zhou said, 'like I did, except he did very well for me.' I assumed he meant the Hong Kong gig, not the marketing. 'Li thinks Felix can land me in trouble. There is a power struggle and I am losing.' He glanced around. 'Li is trying to push me out of our company. He wants control. When the new leadership takes over in Beijing, he wants to be their man. It will not happen. But he has made a good start.'

I'd heard enough confusing conspiracy theories thanks to Charlie Thurrold and I'd made a clear and conscious decision they weren't worth bothering about.

That said, I was curious about Zhou, and this was a unique opportunity. I also feel I owe it to him to get it 'out there' considering what a demon the Western press made of him, no little thanks to the clever Chinese propaganda. And he spoke such excellent English. It'd be a shame to waste it.

'You mean you're under this *shuang gui* thing because of James Li, not because of the change of leadership, or a corruption investigation?'

'They amount to the same thing,' Zhou said. 'It is a question of who is using who to get what they want. That is what it is about: using people. That is the most important thing to remember in China. You must use people like tools, without mercy or consideration. This is why you foreigners will always fail. You are too kind. You believe in doing good, that good actions are rewarded by good actions.' He laughed. 'It is as if you are the Confucians. But to use people you

293

must build a relationship. Everything is personal. I presume you engage in business in Shanghai?'

I said I did, human resources.

'And is it going well?'

I said it was getting along but it wasn't exactly thriving.

'Then you are not using people enough. That is odd considering your business is trading them,' Zhou laughed. His feet rose a couple of inches off the floor.

He had a point. The only time my business had thrived was when I started up and was 'using' the contacts and clients I'd nicked from my previous job.

Zhou stopped laughing as suddenly as he'd started and sat up straight. 'All my life, I have been used,' he said. 'My relationships were forced on me. I didn't develop them. I inherited them. From when I was young, and since my father died, I have been used by the Party. They made me a memorial, a trophy to be displayed as living evidence of their virtue, symbol of the spirit of service to the people. What rubbish. My father was a murderer.'

He spat that last sentence. I didn't know where to look. I think I frowned like I'd been asked what I thought of China joining the World Trade Organisation. I hadn't got a clue what to say.

'But I had to let them use me,' Zhou spared me. 'They took care of me. I see you're surprised I speak English, for example.' I smiled like I'd been caught out. 'My school did that for me. I would have been a fool to turn the opportunities down. You can't turn them down. I swallowed my principles.' He was watching my reaction. 'You are confused, James, but yes, I have principles, and I think much in China is against principles. Is that the way to say it?'

I gave him what I hoped was an agreeable, wise-beyond-my-years, nod. 'I know what you mean.'

'I think the way the government takes land from the peasants, for example, is against principles.'

'But Mr. Zhou,' I had to interrupt, 'That's what your company does, and what got Felix in to trouble. Surely you could have stopped it, or done it better, fairer, with "principle"?'

'Good point. And I have a good answer. First, I am not able to control these activities by "my" company, as you call it, because it is not "my" company. I am paid to make it look that way. And second, I am afraid all property developers must be involved in such affairs, even the ones with principles, even angels, if any companies like that exist. There is no other way, and some of these developments are successful, you must admit.'

I wasn't sure, but I nodded.

'It is the government's fault. They confiscated all property and land in 1949 and since then they have deliberately avoided making clear rules about ownership. So, they make up stories about "public benefit" from golf courses.' His voice went up a few clicks in volume and his head lifted towards the ceiling. It was as if he wanted to be overheard. Either that or he believed in God and this was a 'forgive me but it wasn't me' prayer.

'A broken system built on lies can only fix itself with more lies,' he declared. 'The truth is too painful, too dangerous. Once you apply the truth to one part of the system, the rest will collapse and that is dangerous for everybody, including people who are suffering and fighting the injustice, like in Dongchang.' He lowered his gaze and looked at me. He spoke quietly, like this was between us. 'What can we do? And I wanted to use people too. I needed to use them. I had my own aim, and Felix has helped me.' I assumed he was talking about the money and the Hong Kong company. 'Besides, I had little choice. When you are asked to run a company like SLIC you do not refuse, especially when you have a family.'

'That's why you do it?'

'Of course. And I have achieved my aim. Everyone has been taken care of. My wife and son are in your country. You are English, aren't you? They have more than enough money, they have an apartment.'

'Er,' I couldn't stop myself, and Zhou was being so open, and that way he had of making you speak up, I said, 'Don't you mean apartments, more than one?'

'I beg your pardon?' I'd overstepped the mark. But what the hell? He wasn't going to hurt me.

'Apartments. Plural. You bought several, according to Felix.'

'Ah, yes.' His voice was petulant, in a grown-up way. 'They are not mine. I was instructed to buy them.' He softened. 'You do not believe me? Why should you?'

'I believe you, Mr. Zhou. What I find hard to believe is I am sitting here having this conversation. May I speak frankly?'

'Please.' He was so polite.

'Mr. Zhou, I have heard about you, from Felix and his friend Anita Zhang, do you remember her?'

'Zhang Ruhui, of course.'

'Well, from what I've heard, kind of, so far, I'm surprised to find you so calm and collected in this situation,' I wanted to wave my hand around, but I would have been copying him, 'let alone you getting into it in the first place. We, I mean, me and Miss Zhang, for example, thought you were too high up.'

Zhou smiled. He made a pyramid with his palms and pushed his fingertips into his round chin.

'I told you,' he said. 'I have achieved my aim. My family is safe. They can do what they want with me, and that won't be much, thanks to the curse of my father.'

'Curse?'

'Yes. My father helped build the Party, built the walls of lies. You've heard of the Great Leap Forward?' He used the Chinese name for it first. When he repeated it in English I nodded. 'The starvation? The millions who died? My father was responsible for many deaths and yet I have to bask in his glory, his reputation. Have you any idea how hard that is? To be famous and favoured because your father murdered thousands of innocent people.'

I wanted to say, 'and don't forget the girl in the labour camp', but I had a sudden flash of intuition. What if it wasn't true? Or worse: what if it was true but Zhou had never heard it. He didn't mention it.

'But surely,' I said, 'you believe in China?'

Mr. Zhou sat bolt upright. I'd made him happy. He looked up at the ceiling, mouth open, like he was giving thanks. 'What a perfect question, James,' he said, with emphasis on the wrong name. 'Yes.' He put his hands together, paused, and said. 'Shall we smoke?'

He leaned forward and picked up the packet of Zhonghua. He pulled out a cigarette and half-slung, half-passed it to me. I thought back to Felix's description of his job interview, how he said, like it was significant, that Zhou didn't offer him a cigarette while he smoked himself.

We lit up.

'Do you know what China has become?' Zhou said, jabbing his cigarette towards me like a pointed finger, voice loud, almost shouting. 'China is a country where the people only care about themselves, where the leaders care about themselves more than the country they are supposed to be leading. Those apartments in London? I purchased them on the instructions and behalf of those leaders. I have, with Felix's help, moved money for them, large amounts, into my – their – company, and on to Hong Kong and abroad. You have heard the term "naked official"?' Again he said it in Chinese and I had to ask. 'It means an official who has moved his assets abroad. Those are the leaders I work for, who the country follows. There are hundreds of thousands of them. How can you say you are a leader of a country when all you do is prepare to abandon it? How will a people believe in these leaders, if they ever find out the scale of the betrayal. The Party is no better than an African dictator. They are thieves, common thieves.' He repeated the word at the ceiling.

'A kleptocracy,' I put in, trying to help. He looked at me like I'd burped. He didn't know the word.

'How can I love a country like that? I love the Chinese people, for sure, like you love a stupid friend, but I cannot love my country. I do not feel loyalty. "Love the motherland," they say. "Protect the motherland!" "Without the Party there would be no modern China!" But the Party does not love it!' That last sentence he shouted at the ceiling. There must have been someone upstairs he wanted to catch this. 'They do not protect it. And how ironic that the Party is abandoning China when it says there can be no China without it! In other words: they admit that there will soon be no China.'

He calmed down and spoke quietly to me. 'My son will be safe and have a good life, his own children in a good place. Maybe he will go to America. He wanted to study there because his school friends went. I considered Australia and New Zealand but they are backward, and Chinese students gamble in the casinos. And Felix is English so his connections were with the schools there.'

He stubbed out his cigarette, squinted up at me through the smoke. 'By the way, I know who you are *James*. We thought of offering you the job we gave Felix. Did Miss Zhang tell you?'

Bloody hell. Where would that have led? I stuttered my pathetic answer. 'Oh, really. No. She didn't.'

'But Miss Zhang said you did not have the right connections because you did not go to the right school.' So she did think I was an oik. 'But also that you were too clean, how do I say, too white perhaps, to be a pair of white gloves, to be my running dog.' That's nice. 'Miss Zhang said it was unlikely that you would be willing to be the director of the Hong Kong company.' He paused. 'Is that so?'

How weird that would have been. But I'd never have done it. I was sure of that. Just like I never did the fake foreign expert thing like Joe. 'She's dead right.'

'I am glad to hear,' Zhou said. 'Otherwise I would not be so comfortable talking to you like this. You can be the white container for my black secrets, you can bury them like a dog buries a bone. Only you are a good dog. You are not a running one. How about that?' He smiled at his idea. He was egging me on. I was being used.

We all had our uses.

I'd served mine for the evening and this was payback time.

'Let us get to business,' Zhou said. 'You want me to put my chop on a document, right? Then you can go.'

I sat forward and put my hand on the documents. I was on the point of another feeble mutter.

'Give me the real ones, for Felix. I know there is no problem with my son's entrance to the school,' Zhou spoke softly and grinned. 'It has been nice talking to you, James.' He reached across, took the papers from me and scanned down the pages for the place to sign.

From a small box on the table that I thought contained cigars, he took his personal chop and a flat tin of red ink. He lifted the lid, placed it to one side, and pushed the chop into the red surface. He pressed it onto the papers.

Zhou also chopped the fake papers for the British Education Agency. 'Put the Hong Kong ones in your pocket,' he said, 'and leave these in your case. The people outside might want to see them.'

They didn't. But it was nice of him to think of it.

And I was done. The last act in my Felix story had been completed with remarkable, unexpected ease, and in pleasant circumstances and company too.

Everything was too easy. I knew Felix was out thanks to Chen's text message, and I'd got the documents in my pocket that let him off the hook in Hong Kong. Felix was free to leave China. No one could come after him. Li couldn't pin the money laundering on him, which was the real reason he'd been keeping him.

Even I had worked that out. The bullshit and the fuss in the papers had nothing to do with Dongchang, let alone Britain's ethical foreign policy. It was simple and personal: Li had been told to protect SLIC's masters who'd been using the Hong Kong company to shift their cash. He chose to do it by making Felix a murderer, and he thought he'd get rid of Zhou while he was at it.

As always, it boiled down to money. The power struggle – for SLIC, for China, for everything – was for the cash.

Getting back to that night. Like I say, it seemed too easy.

But it wasn't.

While I was enjoying my cosy chat with Zhou, Charlie Thurrold was nursing his broken ribs in a local police station. Bad, awful, horrible shit had been happening to Anita too.

I have to steel myself. Deep breath.

This is going to hurt. But I have to do it. I have to get it down.

Anita's job was to get Zhang, Li's muscle, to call Felix's main guard, that Red Guard nutter on the desk, and tell him it was okay for Charlie and Chen to see Felix because it was his birthday. No one thought to check his passport, not even us.

Anita invited Zhang to dinner with no prior notice, as you do. She called him that afternoon and booked a private room at a glitzy local joint. Zhang had met Anita at Paradise Island, when he'd been 'on duty' with Li. For her to invite him for dinner was perfectly normal. He expected to be asked a favour to do with security at Paradise Island. He wouldn't have asked over the phone. That would be rude. You wait for the other party to mention it, once you've eaten.

Anita took a friend called Xiao Yu, which sounds like Little Fish, appropriate in the circumstances. I knew her vaguely. She was about the same height as Anita, and lithe in a foxy-fairy way. She had bewitching eyes and wore long fake lashes.

Xiao Yu was the bait. She was a good time girl, not a semi-pro. Let's call her a quarter. She owed Anita for Anita introducing her to her boss, Mr. Wang, who'd rewarded Xiao Yu handsomely for a year of her 'spring'; in other words, for being his young mistress.

Zhang brought a couple of mates.

Anita, being a smart girl, had a cover story, a cock-and-bull about a club member having a labour dispute at his factory and needing help persuading the workers to wait for their wages. By the time they got round to it, they'd had a few drinks and the atmosphere was convivial. Xiao Yu had been flirting with Zhang as directed. The hard man was softening.

Unfortunately, Xiao Yu was a little too good. Zhang was paying so much attention to her that the whole dinner, not only the eating part, was done before Anita could roll out her story and reel in Zhang.

They went on to a KTV club. Zhang's idea. He called some of his mates to join them. That put the numbers in his favour, although he also called in half a dozen of the KTV house girls, so Anita and Xiao Yu weren't on their own either.

I implied Zhang had a soft side. I didn't mean it. He was a thug, through and through. So were his mates. They're ex or serving People's Armed Police and used to getting their way. I wish Anita had been more careful. I also wish Xiao Yu hadn't been such a come-on. The girls were playing with fire.

Zhang's mates were sticking their hands down the tops and up the skirts of the club girls when Anita, who was sitting beside Zhang, with Xiao Yu the other side, said into his ear, 'I just heard from Felix's friend that it's his birthday today. They want to go see him. Can you make a quick call? Then I'll leave you to enjoy the company of my friend.' Zhang smiled and turned and Xiao Yu fluttered her eyelashes.

Zhang was not stupid. Without letting on that he was wise to Anita's game, he agreed to make the call, but he ordered the girls to leave the room except for Xiao Yu and Anita. That upset his mates, who were horny as ships' cats.

'Little sister wants a favour from me,' he said. 'Do you think I should do it? What shall I ask in return? Anything you can think of my brothers? What would you like?'

The Chinese term for lecher is 'colour wolf'.

Anita was in a pack of them and they'd had their tasty little lambs removed from their reach. They scented blood. They were familiar with Zhang's games. They knew what he liked. He liked to earn their loyalty by giving them favours, special treats. The more you enjoyed the favour, the happier Zhang was, and the happier Zhang was, the more generous a boss he was.

'So if I do her this favour,' he said, enunciating the word so it rang some bells, 'I think she should do me one, and I can think of nothing I want more than to see you happy my brothers. How shall I make you happy?'

Xiao Yu had moved away from Zhang. She'd clicked. She'd knew his type. She watched him like a scared cat. Anita was right beside him. Zhang took her arm. She stiffened. He grunted. He put his finger to her cheek and rubbed it up and down, slid it to her nose and brushed its tip. The finger moved from her face in a circular motion and came to rest mid-air, pointing at one of his men, a weasel-face with the standard military buzz cut. The man smiled with his tongue sticking out between his teeth and stepped around the table towards Anita's side of the sofa. If she shied away from him, she'd put herself on Zhang's lap. The man reached down and groped her breast. Anita's arm went up in an automatic defence. Zhang grabbed it from behind. The man leaned in and pushed his sharp nose into her soft neck. He sniffed, hard. The hand stayed on the breast while another touched her leg. She was wearing a business skirt suit. She was the *mama-san* this evening, and Xiao Yu was supposed to be her girl. This was not how it was meant to be.

Weasel Face shoved his hand up her skirt, grabbed her knickers. Anita started to fight.

Zhang, the evil bastard, gripped her from behind, said into her ear, 'Excuse me. I have a phone call to make,' and over his shoulder, 'You,' at another of his guys, 'Take over.'

Xiao Yu backed away, pulled her knees to her chest. Zhang stood up. 'You don't have to worry,' he said. 'Too skinny. Not enough to go round.' He turned to the men. 'Let this one watch.'

The second man he'd called stepped into his space and took hold of Anita, pushed her down onto the sofa. The volume went up on on the KTV machine. The lights went down but not so low that Xiao Yu and Anita couldn't make out the hungry faces. Zhang stepped outside the room to make his phone call. Anita's skirt was above her waist.

# 22

## THE PRICE

I IMAGINED that, about Anita being molested. It happened. I was told. Only that it happened. No details.

The description is my penance. I need to see it in my head, to let the horror screw me up. I'll feel bad about it forever. See how I cut it short? No one wants to know the rest.

I take it for granted that more than one had his way. How Anita sent the SMS I'll never know. I imagine her bent over the table, or on her face on the sofa, getting out her phone, hiding it under her body. She had a message ready or typed it out there and then. It's amazing how some people, especially girls, can tap their phones in the weirdest, most distracting circumstances.

That's sick. Sorry.

It was Ivy who told me. She was explaining why Anita refused to have anything to do with me or Felix, or any foreigner, ever again.

Anita suffered. It's impossible to imagine what she went through, how she's affected.

But she got off lighter than Charlie Thurrold.

The police didn't beat him up too bad. They sat on him, given him a few slaps and stopped when they noticed he wasn't resisting.

He'd gone down hard and a metal hoop in the pavement that held a support cable for a telegraph pole hit him in the guts, round the back. It broke two ribs and burst something important like his kidney or pancreas, one of the bits that flushes your system and in Charlie's case had been working overtime for too long. And he was only fifty-four.

The police got him to his feet. They were nervous because he was a foreigner and the last thing they wanted was to have him drop dead on them. But they were pissed off. The grouchy old guard from the guesthouse came over and spat on him. He bleated how he'd been punched, held his chest to prove it, and said he'd been hit so hard on the head it had incapacitated him. He was giving it the, 'It wasn't my fault, don't blame me,' routine.

The police took Charlie to the station and put him in a chair while they worked out what to do with him. An officer kept him company. Sitting upright made Charlie feel better. He asked the man: how come the police were acting like guards for a 'guesthouse' that was supposed to be independent and besides that, he'd been told by a senior official in Shanghai, who was this man's superior, that Felix was not being held by the police, so why had they come after him?

The officer said they had nothing to do with the guesthouse but if the place called up they could go along as a favour, like good neighbours.

Charlie said the conversation reminded him of a Monty Python sketch called the 'Argument Room'. I said I hadn't heard it. He did an impression of John Cleese giving the punch line: 'Aha, I could be arguing in my spare time.'

He told me this when he was in hospital, a local one with a special floor for foreigners. The doctors were supposed to speak English. It was an excuse to ramp up the fees, which were paid by international health insurance, so everyone was a winner. Charlie was in a private room.

He wanted to laugh at his Monty Python joke but the trouble with his guts made it too painful.

'Christ,' he said. 'Say something miserable.'

I stifled my laughter, not at the joke but his face. He could have won a prize with it.

It wasn't funny though. The abuse was catching up with him; the drinking, the roll-ups, late nights and early mornings, the polluted cities and dirty factories, zero exercise. And he'd gone and run down a street and prat-fallen onto a sharp metal object. Charlie was in a bad way.

There's so much more I should have said, and done, like kick his doctor up the arse, or hijacked a helicopter to fly him to the airport and a plane to Hong Kong, and tracked down Felix, wherever the bastard was hiding, and dragged him by the scruff of his worthless chubby neck into the hospital and made the arrogant shit make his peace, and apologize, and beg forgiveness, and tell the old codger he respected him, loved him.

But I didn't know, so I sat there and tried to make Charlie miserable so he wouldn't laugh.

'Make me a roll-up, would you? There's a good fellow.' He nodded at the bedside table. 'Don't worry. There are places you can still smoke. Thank God for Chinese healthcare.'

I opened the drawer and took out his papers and tobacco. He turned his head to watch.

'What's the latest from the doctors?' I asked.

'Tests and more tests and waiting for results from the other tests. Bloody tiresome. I want to get out of here. I feel fine,' he turned his head back to the ceiling and pulled a face, 'except for the pain.'

'What about painkillers?'

'The only one that could do any good, according to a specialist, is morphine, and the hospital refuses to use it. Guess why: it's brilliant.'

'No idea.'

'Opium. Morphine is opium-based, which brings back bad memories the Party has cultivated so long about the bloody Opium Wars. Bloody hell,' he grimaced, 'makes me want to laugh. We imported opium, started a war over it, screwed China with it, and here I am, a British diplomat in dire need of the stuff and they won't let me have it. Is that, or is it not, poetic justice?'

'Want me to see if I can find some, or something like it. I know people who know people.'

Charlie frowned. 'I'll be all right.' He looked at my hands. 'You call that a cigarette? More like a piece of string. How about you put some tobacco in it?' I handed it over and he held it above his face. 'There's an ashtray on the other side.' Charlie put the roll-up in his lips and pushed himself up the bed onto the pillows. He screwed up his face tight with the pain and a bead of sweat appeared on his forehead. His lips clamped the roll-up so it stood up straight and touched his nose. I worried my handiwork would break in two. It was horrible to watch.

He made it and after a long, thoughtful pause, he grinned. 'That's better.' I put the ashtray on the bed where his right hand would land and pulled out my lighter. He took a long first drag.

I pulled my chair forward on the ashtray side. I wanted to light up myself but didn't want to make the room too smoky and Charlie cough.

'How miserable is this?' I said: 'I think I'm going to throw in the towel, leave China, Shanghai. I've been asking myself more and more: what's it for, is it worth it, the never-ending fights, the constant, "I'll cash in one day" line we keep telling ourselves.' I paused. Charlie gave me a grunt. 'And I can't find a decent answer.'

'And?' he said.

'You've been here so long, Charlie, and you've stuck it. Should I stay and see it through, will it get better? I mean, why are you still here? You're a contradiction. You slag the place off yet you stick it out.'

'God, that is a miserable question,' Charlie said. 'One I've been pondering thanks to this.' He raised a hand to demonstrate his immobility. 'And I'm afraid my conclusion is pretty grim too, though I think it's what you're after.'

'And it is?'

'I made a mistake.' He gave the admission a tiny pause. 'I shouldn't have come here. Not that I have regrets. It's been a good life. I've done something useful. But it's the place that's wrong, gone wrong.'

'You mean there was something good about it once and now there isn't? That's hardly making a mistake. It's them mucking it up.'

He held out the roll-up for me to stub out. I squashed it into the ashtray. It was bone dry where it had touched his lips. 'You really think it's that bad? No hope?'

'Let's do a comparison,' he said. 'You tell me the good things about Nazi Germany, and I'll tell you what's good about modern China?'

'Serious?'

'Come on. Give it a go.'

'All right,' I started at the top, 'Autobahns.'

'Good one. Lots of nice new highways in China.'

'Trains run on time? Low crime rate? Massive public works projects. Gold medals at the Olympics. Booming economy thanks to state control...' I was running out. 'Have I missed anything?'

'Yes, lots. But you've got the good bits. What about the bad ones: the nationalism, the sense of racial superiority encouraged by a one party government, a totalitarian regime, the persecution of religion, homos and gypsies, for which substitute migrant workers, a vast underclass which the government itself created? And the genocide, oh so quiet but very much happening in Tibet, Xinjiang, and then the territorial claims to Taiwan, northeast India, the South China Sea? Instead of *lebensraum* say natural resources...'

'Say what?' *Autobahn* was the only German I knew, thanks to Kraftwerk, the band.

'Living room. Room to expand. The bullying and influence peddling with weaker states who think they need China's patronage, that they're better off with them than without them, like Africa, and Australia for that matter. The propaganda, censorship, repression of free speech and exchange of ideas. Locking up dissidents, twisting the laws and creating new ones, basically a mafia state. The sense of injustice, national indignity. Here's a precise parallel: instead of the humiliation of Versailles you have the "hundred years of shame"'. Charlie's face was going blotchy.

'Now think about the medical experiments, stem cell research that's illegal everywhere else in the world, the organs of executed prisoners given to officials or people who can pay, and the way they call it *zugou* or *woguo*, like the Fatherland and,' he sighed, 'all the fucking Volkswagens.'

I leaned over and patted him on the forearm. I'd never touched him like that before, not even a slap on the back.

'Then who's the Chinese Hitler?' I asked, mock serious.

'There isn't one yet, but there might be. Maybe a general in the army, which does what it wants remember, and doesn't listen to the government, and is running things from behind the scenes. Or the Party can be your Hitler. It believes in its utter infallibility, its right to lead, and it'll stop at nothing to hold on to power. Listen to the speeches. The Party does such a good job I don't think the Chinese need a Hitler.'

'And the Jews?'

'Simple. Anyone who isn't Chinese.'

'And they're going to start a world war? Is that what happens next?'

'Yup.'

'Come off it, Charlie. You don't think that.'

'Why not? It's the only possible result.'

'China's got too much to lose and if the people lose their "economic benefits", they'll depose the Party.'

'Precisely. That's why there'll be a war. Most likely with Taiwan. The Party will start it to prevent the people pulling it down, like the Argies with the Falklands. Or if they leave it to the last minute, when the people are getting upset with them, the Party that is, they'll do what they've always done when the shit hits the fan: blame someone else and they'll have to go to war to prove they're right. Last time China had someone like a Hitler, which was Mao, he wanted to start a nuclear war based on the premise that with the country's massive population, if half got killed there'd be more than enough left to rule the world, or what was left of it.'

'But he didn't, did he,' I said.

'No, he was too busy killing them himself. More than Stalin or Hitler ever did.'

A nurse came in. She put a few pills in a metal dish and a glass of water on the bedside table. She picked up Charlie's hand to measure his pulse, looked at her watch and into Charlie's eyes, checking his pupils.

She was tall and pretty. She said something soft.

Once she'd left, Charlie said, as if he could read my thoughts, 'That help?'

I grinned and turned away. 'She's pretty,' I said. 'You know her name?'

'No. But take her for example, one of the nameless millions of decent people in this country who could, or would, or to be more precise *should*, be standing up for themselves, turn modern China into a decent place.'

'Just like there were decent people in Nazi Germany,' I said. 'And look how effective they were.'

'So I've convinced you.'

'Charlie, I think I've known it for a while. It's taken time for the scales to fall from my eyes, I must admit, to wake up from my China Dream. It's good, painful in way, which is appropriate in a hospital, to hear you say it. Someone like you...'

'The China Dream?'

'Yeah.'

'D'you know the poet Philip Larkin?'

'No.'

'I thought you were a cultured yob. He's the sad bugger who spent his life as a librarian in Hull, writing poems about how miserable life is.'

'Now you mention it, rings a bell.'

'One of his famous poems was about parents. "They fuck you up your mum and dad, they may not mean to but they do." That's how it starts.'

'Nice.'

'I came up with a version for China. Lying here, staring at the ceiling.'

'Is that how it starts?'

'Oh, do shut up. And don't laugh at your jokes. Gives me a pain in the side.'

'So, come on, give us your poem.' That was the moment I felt close to Charlie. The closest ever.

'Right.' Charlie drew a breath, shut his eyes and recited, a pleasant lilt to his gravelly voice:

> It fucks you up, the China Dream
> You don't believe it, but it will.
> With all your dollars, in you stream
> And walk away with nothing. Nil.
>
> But it was fucked up in its turn
> By old style fools with books and drugs
> Who half the time were soppy stern
> And the other half behaved like thugs
>
> Man passes on his dreams to man,
> They fool us like a cheap made fake
> So wise up early, if you can
> And give the China Dream a break.'

'I thought you wanted me to make you miserable,' I said. 'You're doing a perfectly good job.'

'You should read the original,' he said, opening his eyes. 'I'm pleased how I've kept some of the words and phrases or found something close. The second last line in the original is: 'so get out early if you can', which is appropriate but doesn't fit so well. It assumes you're already here.'

'You should get it published.'

'Thanks but I doubt it. No one likes bad news. They want to hear the good stuff.' He looked at the spot on the bed where the ashtray had been. 'Make me another roll-up would you? With some tobacco this time.'

'Sure'.

I bent my head and when I looked up, Charlie was watching me. I might be making this up but I am pretty sure I noticed a hint of a tear in his eye. 'You take care, Johnny,' he said. 'You've given it a good shot. You're young enough to start again. You have an idea where you want to go?' I handed him the roll-up. 'Thanks. That's better.'

'Home,' I said. I held out the lighter.

'To do what?'

'I don't know, start a small business. I've got a few ideas. One thing I've learnt here is how to get on with it. It's given me confidence.'

Charlie exhaled. 'That's better,' he said, referring to the cigarette or me, I'm not sure. 'And talking of confidence, or arrogance, any news of Felix?'

I was surprised he'd waited so long to ask. I guess he didn't care. He'd done his bit and didn't expect thanks. Charlie himself had said he should disappear, so he can't have been expecting Felix to come see him in hospital.

'No sign. I think he took your advice.'

'Contact?'

'None. Did you get in touch with his mother?'

'Not yet. I'll do that when I get out of here.'

'Charlie,' I had to ask. 'Is there any truth in what Felix said, that you're his real father?' I hadn't had the debrief from Chen yet. Besides, although I know what Charlie said when they got Felix, I don't believe it. I think he was saying it to get Felix back on side.

Charlie exhaled. I could see from the way his bushy eyebrows twitched that he was thinking, his eyes roving the bare white ceiling. They stilled, he was staring at a spot above him, projecting an image like an old movie reel. I peeked into them as I leaned forward to move the ashtray to under his hand. He didn't register my face, being so close. He flicked the cigarette without looking. The ash landed on my wrist.

'No,' he said finally. 'No, I'm not.' He smiled at the picture on the ceiling. 'But we did have an affair. [So I'm right to doubt, because I found out from Chen he'd denied that.] I couldn't help it and nor could she. Her husband was a career-obsessed social climber. She was a country girl, no idea what she'd let herself in for, marrying into the army. Her parents ran a pub on Salisbury Plain, in one of those little towns full of off-duty soldiers. She used to help out behind the bar. That's where they met. I think Felix's dad was an instructor at a training base. Hong Kong was a million miles from that. She was lost.'

He smiled. 'She was damn beautiful too. English rose. Red cheeks that flushed the moment you spoke to her. Long brown hair. Deep green eyes. Freckles. To begin with I was more like a big brother, or a young uncle, teaching her the ins and outs of life and society in a big, strange, foreign-yet-British city. Smith, as he was, had recently been commissioned, become an officer, joined the 'mess', another strange place that she was trying to get used to. My God she was innocent.

'She'd just had Felix's older brother Alex, but he was looked after by the amah, as we called the *aiyis*, and I think she had a case of postpartum depression. So she wanted to get to work, lose herself in it, and that's how she turned up in my office one day. I didn't interview her. The army and our admin department had a thing designed for the wives. It worked well. I suppose I made an impression. I was single, experienced, no, not that way, older...'

'What's her name?'

'Oh, of course. It was Judy.' The way Charlie said it in the past tense made her sound like one of many. Perhaps the memory he was enjoying was more about himself. 'Yes, I was older, but not much, single, knew my way round the markets and noodle places where we started going to lunch. Next thing it was after-work drinks. Smith was consumed by regimental life. He was sporty too. Lots of extra activities with the men. You can imagine how it went. I'll never forget the first kiss. It was...' He stopped. 'Sorry, you don't want to hear this tripe.'

'No, Charlie, it's all right.' I was interested to hear about Felix's family like this, from Charlie. I found it satisfying, in a mildly sadistic way.

'We were on a junk, round in Tai Tam Bay. It was a mixed party of all sorts: diplomats, civil servants, service people, wives and girl-friends. I went down below to get changed for a swim and Judy was coming out of the cabin. We'd had a bit to drink. She put her arms round my neck and gave me a sweet, girlish kiss, that's all it was, and thanked me for making her life so much fun. Women, eh? They have no idea what power they possess. I was smitten. She responded. It lasted a couple of years and we parted as good friends. Still are. Her husband might have suspected. It never came up. She never said anything to indicate he did. I don't think he cared either way.'

'And still,' I wanted to get this straight, 'there's absolutely no way you could have been Felix's father?'

Charlie snorted. He pursed his lips and his eyes came down from the ceiling. I'd asked one too many times. I'd also diverted him from his trip down memory lane, pulled him up at a red light. He held the roll-up in front of his face. It had gone out. There were a couple of drags left.

'Do the honours,' he held it towards me.

'You sure you want my germs?'

'I'm in a bloody hospital.'

I took the sliver of paper and tobacco from him, pinched it in my lips, tipped my head back and squinted as I tried to light it.

'Don't smoke it all yourself.'

I passed it back, my fingers stinging with the heat. He took it in his old tough hands as if they were asbestos and sucked a long last drag.

'Thanks. Put it out please.' Then he said, like it was the most natural follow-on: 'What about that girl whose friend accosted us at Felix's villa?'

I think I mentioned how when we went to get his stuff from his villa we had to deal with yet another mess made by Felix. It wasn't the washing-up. It was Benny Wu. He'd arrived in his Porsche as we were about to leave. He blocked us in. Me and Charlie were in the door with Felix's bag of clothes and swimming trunks.

Benny stormed up to us but he didn't know what to say. He'd been expecting Felix.

'Hi, it's Benny, isn't it?' I said.

'Is Felix here?' he said. 'Who are you?'

'We've met actually. I'm Johnny, and this is Charlie, Felix's godfather. And no, Felix is not here.'

Benny turned to Charlie. 'I need to find Felix,' he said, less agitated, the respect for the older generation kicking in. 'There is a serious matter I must discuss with him.'

Charlie had motioned to me to put the bag down. He wanted to go back inside and sit down, but Benny didn't respond. He was happy to have it out on the street.

'Which is?' Charlie said.

'It is personal.' Benny glanced at me.

'That's okay,' Charlie said, 'Johnny and I are trying to help Felix. There are no secrets.'

'Where is he?' Benny asked.

'Ah, yes, well,' Charlie said. 'That is rather delicate. What's this "personal" thing you want to find him for?'

Benny was impatient and Charlie, as 'Godfather', was actually better than speaking to Felix. But he couldn't help sputtering with anger.

'Tell him Maggie Yu is pregnant, again, with his baby.'

'What? You mean this isn't the first time?' Charlie said.

'No, it is not.' Benny didn't realize he'd created a misunderstanding. 'What are you going to do about it?'

'Jesus Christ, is there no end to the trouble this boy creates?' Charlie ignored Benny's demand. 'How the hell... sorry, that's a stupid question. Johnny,' he turned to me, 'you know this girl?'

'Yes. And I'm not surprised. My guess is she did it deliberately. She struck me as the type. Bit of a nutcase. Bunny boiler.'

Benny misheard me. 'Benny boil her? Benny boy her? What do you mean? That I am involved?'

I stared at him for a second before I heard him right. 'Sorry, Benny, no, nothing to do with you.'

'But it is!' He got excited. 'Xiao Yu is my sister.'

'But not your real one right?'

'Yes, she is.'

'I mean not actual blood relation.'

'No, but she is my sister. I have a duty to protect her, as you,' he spoke to Charlie, 'have a duty to be responsible for your Godson.'

'Look here, young man,' Charlie took hold of Benny's arm, 'We *are* taking responsibility.' He started walking Benny towards his car. 'So you leave us to it and once we've sorted out Felix to our satisfaction we'll make sure he takes care of your sister in the appropriate fashion, you happy with that?'

'But what will he do? What do you mean?'

'I mean you do not need to worry.' Charlie pushed Benny towards his car. Benny was used to being the leader of his pack and here he was being bossed around by a grumpy old Brit. The tradition of respect, however, made him submit. 'We'll be in touch. Please excuse us. Johnny, get the bag. We're going.'

Once Benny had gone I turned the car round – it was Ivy's Santana – and Charlie got in beside me.

'Whatever next?' he said.

'I'd rather not think. This girl Maggie by the way; her dad's a general. Felix told me about her. I guess he did the deed the night of that party in the hotel. I reckon she's one of those girls who wants a baby, and a half-English one is even better. I've seen it, had it happen to me once.' Charlie grunted. 'No, I don't mean I put one in the oven, Charlie. Relax. I mean there was a girl I used to hang out with, party-set, fancied herself as this cool writer though all she wanted was to live the life. She was desperate to have a baby. She thought it would make her cool, hip, especially if she wasn't married to the father.'

'Don't worry, Johnny. Nothing new in that. Maybe Felix can marry her if he does decide to stick around in China. He could use the protection of a military family.' He laughed to himself. 'And wouldn't that put his dad on the spot, if Felix married the daughter of someone who outranked him.'

We'd put the Maggie problem to one side while we dealt with getting Felix out of that guesthouse in Wankou. I'd forgotten about it.

At Charlie's bedside in the hospital I told him I'd try to find the girl, or at least Benny Wu, and get her side of the story as in: would she be having the baby. Felix could take it from there. Not that I was sure I'd be in touch with him again.

The next day I forgot about Maggie and Benny. I also forgot about Felix, Anita, going home to the UK, and everything else in my life.

Charlie Thurrold died.

I couldn't believe it. I also can't believe I was the last foreigner, his last friend or acquaintance, to see him alive. It was so sudden. I suppose death is. One minute you're alive, the next you're dead. But it was wrong, in the first place that he died when he'd been sitting up, okay, propped up, and chatting ten to the dozen, hours before, and in the second place that it was me with him. Surely there was someone more worthy. Of course there was. I never knew that Charlie had a daughter, for example, which means he had an ex-wife. His parents were long gone. Or shouldn't it have been a colleague from the Consulate? Or one of the older guys he drank with in the Backstreet. Why me, the 'Young pup'?

I find myself wondering if our conversation was his last gasp, his final wind. I've heard that people have a sudden spurt of energy right before they give up on life. I also wonder if it made him happy, to go out like that, with his last rant on his lips. He'd been so negative, more frank than usual even for Charlie, and so honest I suppose because he wasn't playing to the crowd in the Backstreet but only me. I was honoured. Or is that what killed him, the final acceptance, conclusion, that he'd been wrong. He'd lost hope, lost the will to live. Should I have bucked him up? What could I have said?

He'd been happy when he talked about Felix's mum though. Judy. Her name had been on his lips at the end, or near enough.

The hospital's official statement was confusing. Charlie had died from two separate causes. One was a blood clot that gave him a fatal heart attack and the other was a sudden, traumatic worsening in the internal bleeding. I'm no medical whiz but I know that if you're having trouble bleeding, that means it's not clotting, and vice versa, so the doctor was hedging his bets. And no mention of the poisoning from his liver or whatever it was.

There was no autopsy. The Consulate didn't demand an inquiry. Charlie hadn't been on official business when he went to Wankou with Chen Daming. That he was being chased by a bunch of police when he took his tumble was ignored. His death was put down, officially and amongst the community, to him slipping up on the street. Most people assumed he was drunk, on his way back to his bachelor pad from the Backstreet.

We weren't un-used to people dying at short notice or no notice. Back home, or in the big wide world, you hear or read about people dying every day, but like I keep going on about, sorry, in Shanghai we lived in a world where you were more than likely to know the person or the location or his good friend. And you didn't read about it in the paper either. Someone told you in the bar, face to face.

In Charlie's case I was the one in the bar, in your face, like I'd been a week ago with Felix's newspaper. I didn't enjoy the attention, not one little bit. The night I told them about my last time with him in the hospital was the last night I ever went to Backstreet.

Charlie's funeral was in the UK. The consulate repatriated his body. We held our own memorial in the Backstreet. It was the obvious venue. We put a bag of tobacco, papers, a lighter and a full pint of beer on the bar where he used to sit, under the overhead light that made his bald patch shine like a beacon. There were old hands who used to pass the evening with Charlie and a few of his young pups, other young Brits like me who Charlie used to keep an eye on. I only ever met them in passing. They had proper jobs with trading companies, consultants and banks, lived different lives to grubby entrepreneurs like me or Bill Connor or Joe Karstein. (Joe was the only American there.) They wore suits like Felix used to and talked about Party politics and who'd been to drinks with the ambassador in Beijing. Our paths didn't cross much, but we'd been pushed along them by Charlie. He united us, brought us together, for one last time.

I was sure of my decision. I'd leave Shanghai any day now. I kept it to myself. It would have been disrespectful to announce, when we were there to remember him, that I was off, abandoning the China Dream that Charlie had lived all his life. I wasn't going to share that last conversation I'd had with him with these people. I looked around at the youngish faces, taking turns to tell a funny story, what Charlie had said or done to us. No. It wasn't the time and place to declare as he had: that it was as fucked up as your parents, and so are you.

One of the smart suit boys whose name was Rupert and worked for an old Hong Kong-based British trading firms asked me what news I'd had of Felix.

I think Rupert and Felix were connected through school, or been in Oxford at the same time.

'No idea,' I said.

'Terrible, the situation he'd found himself in. Awful. Real shame he picked the wrong horse, so to speak. Wonder what'll happen to them. Off to the gulag I wouldn't be surprised.'

'If you're talking about Zhou Jianguo, the latest is that he's fled the country. Gone to Canada or the States.'

It would be out soon, but not in the Chinese press.

Two days after I'd seen him, precisely the time he said it would take his eavesdroppers to translate and report our conversation, the powers-that-be decided to move him to a proper detention centre. They had sufficient evidence, from their tapes, that he was a traitor to the Party.

I knew, in my gut, that he'd deliberately led our conversation that way. I got it, the shouting at the ceiling. And his insisting on calling me James was to keep me out of it.

He'd wound them up because his best chance was during a transfer. House arrest is supposed to be low key. They don't come round with a prison van and a police escort. It can only be a black sedan, which has room for a couple of people, who were his people on the inside. Or should that be outside? There'd have been a pair of unmarked police cars in front and behind, but without making a fuss they couldn't stick right next to Zhou all the way. And there's the Shanghai traffic, drivers who cut you up and jump lights. I'm sure it hadn't been difficult for Zhou's car to slip down a side street.

And Zhou had got away.

I condensed that for Rupert. He was surprised. I didn't let on it was a guess. 'Still,' he said. 'Best thing for Felix to be out of that, wouldn't you say?'

'What I'd say,' I said, mimicking him, 'is that if he'd listened to Charlie,' I nodded down the bar to the pint and the tobacco, 'he wouldn't have got himself into it in the first place, and if he hadn't gone and done that, and it hadn't been for Charlie trying to help, despite the thanks he *didn't* get, we wouldn't be here today, or if we were, we wouldn't be staring at an empty bar stool. Charlie Thurrold would be sat on it.'

Rupert was mystified.

I was bitter. I'd had enough of Felix Fawcett-Smith. I didn't want to talk about him. These were the days when the 'I knew Fawcett-Smith when he first arrived in Shanghai and I could see he was going to come to a sticky end' stories started. You couldn't go anywhere, meet anyone, without him raising his chubby ghost on you. Not that he was dead. Charlie was.

I looked at this Rupert, head to toe. He was another one, like Felix only cleverer. He'd be an ambassador himself one day, or an MP. I'm sure he was a good bloke, but he was one of 'them' and I was me, for all my idea that I could mix with his type, cross the tracks in this weird and wonderful egalitarian expat world.

Fuck it.

# 23

## PLEASE

Anita wasn't answering her mobile. She didn't reply to messages or emails. I went to her flat but she wasn't in. I called Joe.

'Don't sweat it,' he said. 'She'll reappear.'

'I won't,' I said, 'be "appearing" myself for much longer.'

'So why so desperate to see Anita?' he said.

'Because, and I appreciate this sounds mad, I want her to come with me.'

'You are mad, and sad. Anita would never date a guy like you, or any of us.'

'Just wait,' I said.

I began to suspect that Anita wasn't hiding from everyone, only me. I wondered if she'd gone off with Felix. It was torment. But I couldn't help it. They'd both disappeared.

I went all the way out to Paradise Island. Someone must be close enough with Anita to know where she was, a colleague or friend, or in an official work capacity.

I asked at reception, the duty manager and Mr. Wang the boss's other personal assistant. None of them could help.

While I drank a warm beer at the bar and smoked a couple of cigs before I left, I had an idea. It was prompted by Felix's trick for tracking James Li.

I slugged the beer and went to find the finance department. I had a vague impression where it was from when I'd wandered the back corridors at the Buckingham launch party. I found it and sauntered up to a counter.

'Hi,' I said to a young man sitting at the nearest desk behind it. 'I'm with a Shanghai English language magazine, on my way back to the city from a travel story and thought I'd drop in. Sorry. No appointment. My boss says you owe us for advertising. He wanted me to have a quick word with your finance manager. You mind?'

The man did not seem surprised. He asked me to wait and walked to a glassed-in cubicle on the far side of the open plan office. He tapped on the glass, stuck his head in and had a word. An older man came to the door. I lifted the countertop and strode over. A sign said 'Senior Accountant' in English.

Face-giving politeness kicked in automatically. 'Come in,' he said. 'Have a seat.' No need for names.

I repeated my story, with apologies for interrupting his day. He asked me which magazine I worked for. I said *Shanghai Scene.*

'I don't think I know it,' Senior Accountant said. 'Can you tell me more? Which month? Your invoice number?'

I gave it the old 'Silly me, like I said, I'm in editorial and was on my way past,' and, 'Let me call the office. Do you mind if I borrow your phone? My mobile's out of battery. I was on a boat trip on the lake.' I gave him a shrug.

He pushed his desk phone towards me and sat back.

I dialled Anita's mobile. It rang. She picked up before the second one.

'Lao Ma,' she said. She spoke in a familiar yet respectful voice. She didn't sound like she was sick. 'Thank you for calling. I've been waiting. Is it ready? I'll come to your office to save time. Is this afternoon okay?'

So she was in Shanghai. I hadn't thought of what to say.

'Lao Ma?' she repeated. It was so good to hear her voice. 'Can you hear me?'

'Hi Anita,' I turned away from Mr. Ma. I doubt he spoke English. 'It's me, Johnny. I'm out at Paradise Island.' I paused. 'Please don't hang up.'

Silence on the other end. I really did expect her to hang up. A sigh. More silence. 'What do you want? What are you doing in Mr. Ma's office?'

I guess she didn't hang up because she was worried I might have come to an arrangement with Mr. Ma. It was obvious he owed her money. She had no idea what me and him might be up to.

'I have something for you.' I made that up on the spur of the moment.

'Something to give me? From Mr. Ma?' She sounded surprised; not that she'd be getting something, but that it was me who'd be giving it.

'Yes, from Mr. Ma.' I turned back to him and nodded and smiled when I said his name. He smiled back. He thought I was talking to my 'office'. 'Where can we meet? I'll come straight over. Hey, how about the bar off Hengshan Lu?'

'When? And what do you have for me? The cheque?'

This was too easy. 'Yes, the cheque. Soon as I can get there, say two hours. See you.'

'See you.'

I was amazed. Anita and Mr. Ma had played right into my hands. Weird. Too good. Massive hits of the two chemicals, one that says, 'You've scored,' and the other one that goes, 'Don't believe it yet, wait for the ref,' were coursing round my brain. To put it the normal way: my head was spinning. But at the same time it was on fire, working like it never did. I was thinking faster and clearer, smarter. I was supercharged.

'I'm sorry Mr. Ma,' I said. 'It seems your cashier paid the other day. My office didn't tell me. I was away.' I was prattling, grinning and wincing, getting him to focus on my face. I pushed the phone back across the desk, with both hands, gently. He was looking at me and smiling.

'No problem,' he said. 'These things happen.'

I pulled the phone cable a millimetre out of the socket, enough so that it clicked but stayed in the phone. All I needed was Anita not to call him back for a couple of hours. Mr. Ma saw me to the door, picking up his mobile and man-bag on the way.

The traffic was light, another sign I was on a lucky streak. I had time to go back to my place and pack a bag. I didn't need much. The place I had in mind was warm year round. I threw in the new Clancy novel, a carton of real Marlboros, aftershave, passport, ten thousand in cash.

I picked up a gift. Nothing too special. Only a token, a sign of sincerity. It was a pair of pearl earrings I'd bought for a girl but never given her because we'd split up so quick. They were expensive. I can't remember how much. They were in a nice red box. I headed out the door.

The bar was empty because it was early evening. I went to sit in the window like I had with Anita the last time we met there, and got out my cigarettes and lighter. I thought about smoking while I waited, couldn't make my mind up if I needed one to calm my nerves or if not smoking would get me approval from Anita, proof I'd turned a corner.

I lit one and sat back. I could give up later. There are only so many big decisions you can make in a single day.

I was on my third puff, barely sipped a beer, when Ivy appeared in the door. It was an effort not to show my annoyance. I kicked my bag under the table.

Ivy was in a long, dark red skirt and a cream silk blouse. She had a black jacket over her arm. In the same hand was a laptop case, the slim envelope type. She looked the business. I glanced at my watch. Anita would arrive any minute. Ivy walked over. Her heels stabbed the wooden floor with a sharp clack.

'Hello, Johnny,' she said. She hung her jacket on the back of the chair facing me. 'Anita told me you'd be here.' She sat down.

'Did she? Oh.' I looked at my watch. 'She'll be here in a moment. I wanted to see her because...' I spoke slowly. I didn't really want to tell Ivy.

She pulled a face as I stubbed out my cigarette. She hated smoking.

'Anita isn't coming.'

'What?'

'She isn't coming.'

I picked up my cigs, pulled another one out, looked Ivy in the eye, and lit it.

'Why not? What's up?'

Ivy ignored my small act of defiance. She asked the waitress for a glass of wine.

'She wants me to come in her place,' she said. 'You can give Mr. Ma's cheque to me. And she wants me to give you a message.'

I took a deep drag and blew it to one side. Ivy flinched. The smoke hit the window and spread across and up the glass. Ivy's wine arrived. She sipped it and put it down.

I exhaled, blew it over the table.

'What message?'

'Johnny, she knows you're leaving and she doesn't want to see you before you do.'

'Why not?' I only asked for form's sake. I knew it would be because Anita had realized what I had, about us, and she was nervous.

'Because of what she has been through.'

'What do you mean? Been through?'

'With you.'

'We haven't "been through" anything together,' I said.

'Yes, you have. You know she liked you very much, that she actually wanted you to be her boyfriend, but you pushed her away, pushed her onto Felix.'

'What?' My voice squeaked.

'You hurt her, Johnny. I'm her friend. I can tell. She told me.'

'You could have told me too,' I said.

Ivy sipped her wine. I finished my beer and wanted a glass of whisky.

'Shit. Sorry. I mean damn.' Ivy was sensitive to swear words as well as cigarette smoke. 'Fuck. That's what I really mean. I'm going to get another drink.' I called the waitress and asked for a whisky. She said she'd get the list and I said don't bother, Red Label.

'And there is the trouble with Felix, how she helped. She did that for you, but do you know what happened?'

'Yes, I do. Charlie Thurrold died, Felix fucked off, we got him off the hook, and all that's left is me and Anita, but she's been avoiding me and it's taken me ages to track her down and yes, I realize that Anita had feelings for me, and the fact is I've always had feelings for her too, but I haven't shown it very well...'

'Or at all.' Ivy was unfazed.

'... if you insist. Yes, you're right. I didn't show it, but I had them. I didn't think she'd want someone like me. I'm hardy rolling in cash or a big shot businessman or have a proper job. I know what you Shanghainese girls like.'

'I like Joe.'

'Yes,' I said. 'But you're different.'

She left a short silence, straightened up a fraction, looked at her wine like she was wondering whether to have another sip. I sensed her discomfort. 'It is terrible what happened to your old English friend, but something terrible also happened to Anita.'

'What?'

She picked up the wine and drained it. I had never seen Ivy do that before. She was definitely stepping outside her comfort zone. Her hand was heavy when she put the glass down.

'She was beaten up by Zhang and his men that night you went to see Zhou Jianguo.'

She gave me the basic story and a couple of details. They'd given Anita a black eye, for example. Then Ivy added the sexual assault. She kept it vague, like I just did.

I had to ask. It was hard to get the words out.

'Ivy, did they rape her?'

'No, they didn't.'

I felt a surge of elation.

'Someone else did.'

'What? Who? When?'

'You can guess.'

'What do you mean? Ivy, tell me. What the hell are you talking about?'

'Felix. I think in English you have the expression "take advantage of someone", correct? Maybe it was more like that. Anita told me she thinks he used a drug on her.'

'Where?'

'It was in England, when they were at his brother's wedding.'

The bastard. The utter, evil, dirty scumbag bastard. I hated him. I wanted him to suffer. I wished he was back in that black jail, that we had left him there to rot. I couldn't believe that barely hours beforehand I had been helping him. I suddenly made sense of that comment in the pub in London, how well things had 'worked out' at the wedding. It struck me like a brick between the eyes.

I can't remember what I said to Ivy. I might have said nothing. I went mad, at everyone, the whole world. I could have smashed the bar to smithereens. I didn't go nuts in there because the owner was a friend. And I didn't want Ivy to see it.

I think I was pulling my hair out, really pulling at it. I can't clearly remember. My whisky glass was empty. I remember that. I asked for a second one and lit another cigarette.

'She's got to let me see her.' I was on the point of tears.

Ivy explained the reason Anita had hidden away, from everyone, to start with, had been because of the black eye. She'd done a lot of thinking.

I interrupted to ask if Anita had been alone and Ivy's answer was yes, she'd wanted to be, but Ivy had been with her lots too. Anita had been in her apartment. She looked embarrassed when she owned up to that. They'd spent a lot of time talking.

Anita had declared she was going to marry her high school sweetheart. He'd been waiting like a faithful puppy out in the garden while she partied with us foreigners. Now Ivy mentioned it, I remembered a guy I'd met at a dinner when we were mixing it up.

His job was in a tax bureau or state trading company. Maybe he was in a bank. He hadn't made much of an impression. Anita had introduced him as her older cousin, like they do, and I'd thought he really was. It was before I learnt the name game.

'Anita wants a simple life,' Ivy said.

'I can give her that.'

'No, you can't. Not the way she wants it.'

'It would be better than the way she wants it.'

'Johnny, listen,' she sighed. 'Anita is not going to see you. She wants you to leave her alone, to leave.'

'It's not right. Those awful things happening to her, because of me, and I don't get the chance to put it right.' My voice was squeaking.

'So she is doing the Chinese way: she is moving on and forgetting about it.'

'Your Chinese way is to ignore it, not forget it.'

'You leave that to us,' Ivy found her icy aloofness. I wasn't going to submit to it now, not with my mood.

'Yes,' I said.

And I let rip. 'You do that. And you'll always be as fucked up as you've ever been. It's amnesia you people have got, deliberate amnesia. You can't face it, the awkward past, you Chinese with your obsession about face too. You'd prefer to pretend it didn't happen, like the Cultural Revolution or the famine in the Great Leap Forward, or,' and I thought what the hell, 'your heroes like Zhou Jianguo's dad. He's actually a nice bloke by the way. I met him the other day. And how about Tian'anmen. You can't face that either can you? Well, I can. We can. Us foreigners. I can face it for Anita too.'

My third whisky came. It didn't occur to me that I was demonstrating how foreigners face tough times: through a haze of alcohol and cigarettes.

'Johnny,' she said, 'It's time you went home.' She said it without irony, no second glance at my whisky to make her point.

'I am going home, to the UK.'

'I know. That's what I mean.'

'Oh, shit. Sorry.' I was. She didn't deserve the abuse.

'It's okay.' She was composed. She never really lost it.

I put my hand in my pocket. 'Will you give something to Anita for me?'

'Yes, of course.'

I pulled out the earring box. Ivy got the wrong idea. It could be mistaken for that kind of box.

'Oh,' she put her hand up to her mouth. 'You weren't? You were? Oh. I am sorry.' So she did have a heart.

'It's earrings.'

'Oh, that's better.' That I call callous, but she didn't mean to be. She took the box. 'May I see?'

'Sure. Open it.' It was the waitress's turn to get the wrong idea. She gave us both a warm smile and clapped her hands together under her chin.

'Pretty,' Ivy said. 'But you do know that Anita's ears aren't pierced? She has an allergy.'

'Oh dear.' I was talking like her.

'But don't worry. I will get them changed to the clip-on type.'

'Thanks.' Did I care? Probably not. 'Will you tell her something for me?' I asked.

'Of course.'

'Tell her I'm sorry, so sorry.'

'About what?'

'Everything.'

'I will.' She stood up and picked up her jacket. She looked down at me and opened her mouth to say something but I had to ask first. I avoided her gaze, stared straight ahead.

'Where is Felix?'

I was surprised how self-controlled I sounded. There was a crystal-clear picture in my mind of my fists beating his face to pulp.

'You do not need to know where he is,' Ivy said. She was calm too. 'But I can tell you it is not in China and I can tell you who he is with.'

'Who?'

'Maggie Wang. And her father.'

I must have twitched. I turned my face up to hers.

'Do not worry, Johnny. I know what you are thinking. I can also tell you that Felix will pay. He will pay in a way he does not realize.' She stood stock still and looked me in the eye. There was something really strong there but I couldn't read it. 'Trust me,' she said.

She let her shoulders drop a fraction. That body language I could read. I got the message. I trusted her. Felix would be served his just deserts. One day, if we stayed in touch, which somehow I doubted, Ivy would let me know.

She turned to leave. 'There's one more thing, the other reason I came.'

'Which is?'

'The cheque, from Mr. Ma, remember?'

'Oh,' I fumbled. This was embarrassing. It wouldn't have been in front of Anita, because I had been going to explain I'd take care of everything, including money worries, so she didn't need her back pay. Admitting to Ivy that I'd lied about the money was going to be awkward. I stared at her, open-mouthed. She stood and waited.

I reached for my bag and pulled it up onto my lap.

'Mr. Ma gave me cash,' I said.

'Eight thousand?'

'Yup,' I said straight back, as if it was the most natural thing in the world and I knew how much the cheque was for. My hand had found the tight-wrapped bundle in its envelope. I slipped a finger in between the notes and ruffled them. What was I going to need it for now? I smiled up at Ivy. 'And he threw in a bonus as well. Another two.' I pulled the envelope out and held it up to her. 'You'll see she gets it?'

'Of course.' Ivy half turned away as she put the envelope into the laptop case. It made it bulge. 'Goodbye, Johnny. And good luck.'

I didn't get up, like a gentleman would.

I stared at her.

'Bye. Give Anita my love.'

She walked away, those bloody heels clacking like wooden clogs.

I sat at the table for half an hour, smoking and trying not to drink. I switched back to beer. I didn't want to get stupid drunk so early. I could buy a bottle of vodka and knock myself out back home. I checked my wallet to see how much cash I had, not what I'd expected to be doing. I was contemplating going to Ivy's apartment in case Anita was there. But something held me back, made me think this was it, final. I knew Anita well enough. There'd be no changing her mind. And did I really want to fight? Because it wouldn't be fighting 'for' her, it would be fighting against her.

So I sat there and beat myself up. There was a simple process of damage reporting going on in my head, like my relationship with Anita was a ship that had been torpedoed.

I'd rejected her obvious attention and affection. First hit.

I'd pushed her into the arms, or at least the orbit, the sway, of a two-faced, gutless, self-seeking upper-class bastard. Hit two.

Oh, and he date-raped her. Torpedo number three.

And, more than likely for my sake, not Felix's, she put herself in harm's way, and suffered, to help him. Hit number four.

Ship sinks.

If it hadn't been for me...

'Well, Johnny Trent,' I said to myself as I got up from the table. I grabbed my bag. 'You've paid. That's nothing to be proud of, and let's not call the ten thousand "spring money" like the rich Shanghai give their mistresses. But you paid. You can go now.'

I didn't even get to kiss her.

# About the Author

MARK Kitto lived in China for eighteen years, having studied the language at SOAS, University of London. In China he founded and built a successful English-language magazine business known as *that's* magazines. The Chinese government seized the business in 2004 and is still running it profitably. Mark told the story and its aftermath in two popular memoirs: *That's China: a British entrepreneur versus the China propaganda machine* and *China Cuckoo: how I lost a fortune and found a life in China.* From his mountain retreat near Shanghai, the subject of *China Cuckoo*, he wrote a popular monthly column for *Prospect* (UK) magazine. He also wrote the magazine's most widely read – to date – feature article about China: 'You'll Never be Chinese'. He returned to the UK in 2013 and is a professional actor, writer and editor. His self-penned one-man show, 'Chinese Boxing', set during the Boxer Uprising in 1900, is staged on a regular basis. Mark has had short fiction published in the Asia Literary Review. *China Running Dog* is his first novel. He now lives in Norfolk and London. Mark spends his spare time sailing and trying to remember how to cook Chinese food.